Praise For

THE WHITCOMB DISCOVERIES

Adventurous and historical, this delightful story is a page turner and engaging, providing a vivid reminder of the challenges of the California Gold Rush era as the miners and settlers clashed with the Native Americans over resources. Daniel's character was particularly enjoyable. He is human, kindhearted, and imperfect in a wonderful way. He is introspective as he works through an internal struggle with past misdeeds and life decisions.

~Kim Hamm
Middle School Teacher
California

Yosemite Trail Discovered reveals much about the California Gold Rush era, Westward expansion, slavery, U.S. treatment of Native Americans, growth of California towns, and more. Best of all, it provides a gripping story. This YA historical novel will be an entertaining goldmine for young people, especially those learning about the origins of California as a state. Teachers will find it a useful tool.

~Colleen Peterson, PhD
author of *Lucia's Renaissance*

Marie breathes new life, intrigue, and hope into the familiar story of the Donner Party and the Western Movement. As Daniel's story is masterfully intertwined with history, he becomes a character I quickly began rooting for. This story is a wonderful addition to the classroom collection of historical fiction. Teachers will love the STEM activities and recommended extensions. *California Trail Discovered* has universal appeal!

~Mary Pat Vargas
Elementary STEAM Teacher
California

This book [*California Trail Discovered*] contains History, Literature, Geography, and STEAM all in one! As a homeschool teacher, I appreciated how all of these subjects were woven together in one place, and as an avid reader, I loved that the lessons did not make the storyline feel awkward or forced. Pacing in this story was excellent, and character development was not sacrificed on behalf of action, as there was an abundance of both. I loved reading Daniel's story; I highly recommend it!

~Rachel Summey
Homeschooling Mom
Richardson, Texas

Marie Sontag once again displays her brilliant talent for storytelling in this book. The hardships, the endurance, the conflicts, plus the emotional depth of the characters all come to life in this wonderful tale of resilience and tenacity! [*California Trail Discovered*] is historical fiction that is filled with rich detail and perfectly tuned for the middle grade reader. It left me craving for more!

~Roberta Hendricks,
Reading Intervention Specialist
Pampa, Texas

While reading *Yosemite Trail Discovered*, I felt like I was really in California being a part of the gold rush with these characters. In the story, there was a moment when Virginia's character surprised me. It's worth reading to find out. The story made me want to read another one written by Dr. Sontag.

~Joy T.
Age 13

YOSEMITE TRAIL DISCOVERED

ALSO BY MARIE SONTAG

The Bronze Dagger
The Alabaster Jar
The Silver Coin
Rising Hope

THE WHITCOMB DISCOVERIES
California Trail Discovered

Yosemite Trail Discovered
Copyright © 2022
Marie Sontag, PhD

ISBN: 978-1-957344-04-1

Cover design by Farhan Harits.
Map designs by Marie Sontag

Published by WordCrafts Press
Cody, Wyoming 82414
www.wordcrafts.net

YOSEMITE
TRAIL DISCOVERED

Book 2 of the Whitcomb Discoveries

MARIE SONTAG

WordCrafts

OREGON COUNTRY TERRITORY
UNORGANIZED TERRITORY
SIERRA NEVADA MOUNTAINS
FORT HALL
INDE
SUTTER'S FORT
FORT BRIDGER
PL
P
YERBA BUENA (SAN FRANCISCO)
N
MEXICO

WISCONSIN TERRITORY
DA RITORY
Rock
ARAMIE
CHIMNEY ROCK
INDEPENDENCE MO
PRINCETON TOWNSHIP IL
KEY
Oregon Trail
CA Trail
Greenwood Cutoff
Hastings Cutoff

1
YOSEMITES ATTACK

April 10, 1849
Big Oak Flat, California Gold Country

Daniel's face heated. The half-naked Yosemite crouched behind the pine looked only a year younger than him—maybe fourteen or fifteen? Both he and his guardian, Jim, kept their rifles trained on her.

"Come outta there. Now!" Jim yelled.

The young Indian girl peered out but stayed behind the tree.

Jim repeated his order in Miwok.

Harsh-sounding words spewed from the girl, but she didn't budge.

"What'd she say?" Jim wiped sweat from his forehead with his shirtsleeve.

Daniel shrugged. "You don't know? I thought you spoke all the Injun languages 'round here."

"Never learned Yosemite."

After pulling in a lungful of air, Daniel relaxed his rifle grip. At dawn, Yosemites tried to burn down their trading post. Braves tossed burning branches inside the tarp-covered structure and fired arrows when the men scrambled from the bunkhouse to douse the flames. By mid-morning, Daniel, Jim, and the clerks had chased the Indians back into the woods and secured a perimeter around the post. Now that things had calmed, the girl seemed the only Yosemite left.

"I do not think she understand Miwok or Yokuts language." A girl's soft voice came from behind Daniel.

He turned. Limik stood a few feet away. Their teenage Miwok

helper must have followed them into the woods. Daniel raised a brow. "You speak her language?"

Limik nodded. "She speak Yosemite. She say her name Totuya."

The Yosemite shouted more unintelligible words.

Limik eyed the girl and clutched her gray blanket closer to her shoulders. "She say her grandfather Yosemite leader, Chief Tenaya."

Like a hawk eyeing its prey, Jim glared at the young Yosemite and stepped closer. With a sideways glance at Limik, Jim brushed back a strand of his blond, sweat-soaked hair. "Tell her I'll shoot her in the leg if she doesn't come out right now."

Limik translated the trader's demand.

When the Yosemite spat out more harsh words, a corner of Limik's mouth drew up. "She say she Yosemite chief granddaughter and will not obey white man."

Loud shrieks rose from deeper in the woods.

"I don't have time for this." Jim's gray-blue eyes flashed with anger. "Daniel. Keep an eye on the girl. Shoot her if she tries to run."

A chill washed over Daniel despite the late morning sun that beat down on him through the pines. On the wagon train from Illinois, his guardian had taught him how to shoot buffalo and deer. But that was for food. Daniel had never shot a human.

As if reading Daniel's mind, Jim narrowed his gaze. "This is war, boy. If she's Chief Tenaya's granddaughter, we can use her. Maybe wrangle a promise from the old man to stay out of Big Oak Flat. I'll see if our clerks spotted other renegades." He turned to leave.

When the Yosemite shouted again, Jim paused and shot Limik a raised brow.

"She say she come out now to show she not fear white man."

More cries rang out. Jim peered into the forest. A second later, swift as a mountain lion, Jim sprang off.

Totuya stepped out from behind the tree.

"It's okay." Daniel lowered his rifle barrel. "I won't hurt you. Sit."

Limik translated.

Totuya's gaze bore into Daniel as she placed her hands on her hips and remained standing. Keen to follow Jim's instructions, Daniel returned her glare, lunged forward, and raised his rifle.

Totuya sat beneath the pine and massaged her left ankle.

Daniel stepped closer. Her ankle had turned purple and appeared swollen. Maybe she'd twisted it when she ran off.

With his rifle still pointed at Totuya, Daniel moved to a nearby rock and sat. He motioned for Limik to join him.

Lifting her small form onto the boulder, Limik sat near the edge. "I think it wise *El Rey* keep the Yosemite girl." Limik shifted her gaze from Totuya to Daniel. "Yosemite not call self this name. Only other tribes call them Yosemite."

"What do you mean?" Daniel scratched his full head of dark brown hair. "If the Yosemites don't call themselves Yosemites, what name do they go by?"

"They call self Ahwahneechee."

Totuya raised her head.

Continuing to eye the girl, Limik narrowed her gaze. "Ah-wah-nee´-chee mean, *people who live in gaping mouth*. No one can say where most Ahwahneechee live."

"You've never been to their tribal grounds?" Daniel rested his rifle barrel across his knees.

Limik shook her head. "No. But it said Ahwahneechee call self *people who live in gaping mouth* because they live in beautiful, wide valley. Only Ahwahneechee know where gaping mouth is."

Daniel shifted his position on the cold boulder. "If their name is Ahwahneechee, why do other tribes call them the Yosemites?"

"To Miwok and Yokuts, name Yosemite mean *those who kill*. Yosemites most feared of all tribes. Yosemites sooner kill than talk."

Once again, Daniel shivered, and not because his trousers pressed against granite. "Well, if they'd sooner kill than talk, maybe we should let her go."

As if to ward off an evil spirit, Limik raised her hands. "And disobey *El Rey Güero*? No. I think this not good."

Daniel kicked twigs beneath his feet. "Jim's not a white king. He's just a man with a pale face and blond hair." To his Indian friends, Jim might seem like a protective, *blond king,* but his guardian certainly wasn't royalty to *him.*

Jim made a handsome profit selling goods to miners at inflated prices. At the same time, he protected local tribes from prospectors who tried to kidnap Indian women or overrun unprotected villages. A shrewd study of human nature, Jim took advantage of the natives' superstitious tendencies and gained their favor by telling lies.

On several occasions, his guardian boasted that the Yokuts and Miwoks' Great Spirit had sent him to them on a moonbeam. Winning the local tribes' admiration, Jim also married into their families when chiefs offered him their daughters as wives. Having won their respect, Jim convinced many natives to help him.

All except the Yosemites.

Twigs snapped from the girl's direction.

Daniel glanced up just as Totuya stood and whipped out a knife.

Gulping in a panicked breath, Daniel lunged forward, his rifle pointed at her chest. "Tell her to drop it," he told Limik.

Limik translated.

Totuya dropped the knife and sat.

Limik ran forward and snatched up the blade. "See!" She held up the knife. "I say Yosemite rather kill than talk."

Keeping his rifle aimed at Totuya, Daniel willed his pulse to slow.

The girl stared at her ankle and massaged it.

When the thumping in his ears lessened, Daniel stepped back. "If she really wanted to kill me, I'd already be dead. I think she's just scared." He lowered his rifle. "Go."

Totuya lifted her gaze. Her fierce dark gaze met his.

When she didn't move, Daniel glanced at Limik. "Tell her she's free to go. I won't stop her."

Limik clutched his arm. "No. This you must not do. *El Rey* tell us keep her here. We must obey."

Daniel nodded his head toward Totuya. "Remember how you felt when white gold diggers kidnapped you last year? That's probably how she feels. Tell her she can leave. That'll earn us more goodwill with the Yosemites than kidnapping her."

Turning the knife over in her hand, Limik studied it for a moment. Then, in one swift movement, she slashed Daniel's arm.

Howling, he grasped the bleeding gash. His rifle clattered to the ground. "What'd you do that for?"

Cutting off a strip of cloth from the bottom of her tunic, Limik shouted something at Totuya.

The Yosemite stood and limped off into the woods.

"I sorry, Dan'l." Limik wound the piece of material around his arm, cinched it, and secured it with a knot. "I put herbs on your cut when we back at post."

Wide-eyed, Daniel started at their Miwok helper. "Why in the world did you cut me?"

Limik retrieved Daniel's rifle and handed it to him. Before she could explain, Jim and two of his store clerks appeared.

After scanning the area, his guardian stared at Daniel with wide eyes. "Where's the girl?"

"I told her to go," Daniel said.

"You did what?"

As if merely an innocent bystander, Limik adjusted the cloth around Daniel's wound. "The girl have knife hidden behind back. She stab Dan'l and run off. It good I here to help. I stop his bleeding."

A warmth ran through Daniel. Their Miwok helper lied to Jim rather than let his guardian know Daniel had disobeyed him. Limik was related to one of Jim's Miwok wives. The teen helped cook for the men and laundered their clothes. Until now, Daniel hadn't paid her much attention.

Twigs and dead leaves crackled as Jim stepped toward Daniel. "I told you to keep an eye on her, boy." He grabbed Daniel's chin and forced him to meet his gaze. "I can't believe she got the drop on you. Like I've said before, your own survival comes first in this wild, god-for-saken country." Jim's pitch raised. "I'm your legal guardian until you're eighteen, but I can't keep you safe if you don't do as I say. Ya got that?"

"Yes, sir." Daniel stepped back. His throat burned. He shouldn't have let the girl go. Ashamed he'd disobeyed Jim, he felt as though a grizzly had stomped on his chest and punctured his lungs with rib-splintered bones.

For all his faults, Jim was a survivor. Pa hadn't really taught him anything about survival, and Pa was dead. Out here, their own survival had to come first. On that point, Jim was right. But that didn't mean he liked it.

2
VIRGINIA REED

May 24, 1849
Big Oak Flat, California Gold Country

A month after the Yosemites attacked Jim's trading post, business returned to normal. Since his guardian couldn't read or write, Daniel agreed to work as Jim's accountant one more year until he turned eighteen. One more year. After that, he'd return to Illinois to investigate his parents' mysterious deaths.

Daniel rubbed his eyes as he stared at the accounting book he'd set on top of a barrel. He recalculated the figures once more. They didn't balance. His head throbbed. He hadn't made any errors. Was someone taking money from the till?

The thunk of boots tromping into the trading post brought his nose out of the ledger.

"Savage around?" A bearded young man dressed in buckskins pulled out his knife and scraped mud from the bottom of his boots.

Recognizing the customer as John Murphy from Dry Diggins, the site of the first trading post he'd worked at with Jim, Daniel stood and stretched. "Probably eating supper out back in his tent."

"Ha." Murphy snickered. "Wonder which one of his five Indian wives fixed it for him."

Heat gathered under Daniel's skin. Some miners looked down on Jim for taking native wives. Murphy had also married an Indian, a Miwok, but Murphy only had one wife.

Daniel squinted at Murphy. "Can I help you with something?"

"Lookin' to buy four barrels of flour, three sacks of beans, and seven cans of coffee. Can pay a handsome price."

Jim had restocked their supplies in San José before last month's hard rains. Daniel slid his jaw left. They had enough on hand, but if he sold Murphy everything he wanted, they'd have to restock sooner than planned.

"Know it's a lot." Murphy placed a hand behind his neck to massage it. "But easy gold's been found about forty miles north, up Coyote Creek. Been flooded with new prospectors ever since. They're paying top dollar for grub. After the gold at Dry Diggins played out, my brother and I set up our own post near the creek. Don't have time to get more supplies. Hoped you could tide us over till we make a trip to Stockton."

The inflated prices they could charge the Murphy brothers for their flour, beans, and coffee would cover most of Jim's debts. Maybe even balance the books. And to boot, a trip to San José to restock meant he could follow up on a clue Jim recently gave him about his parents' deaths.

Daniel folded his arms across his chest. "Give me some figures you're willing to pay. I'll see what Jim says."

After haggling over prices, Murphy agreed to his terms, and Daniel took the quote to his guardian.

Jim clapped Daniel on the back. "You're becoming quite the businessman, son. Good job. We'll have to restock soon, but that profit'll help us buy twice as much. I'll have you and Brown ride out next week to San José."

Quite the businessman? Daniel bit the inside of his cheek to keep from smiling. These days, words of praise rarely passed his guardian's lips. Things weren't like they used to be when they traveled the Oregon and California trails back in '46. Daniel shook his head. They'd both changed a lot in the past three years.

The morning before his trek to San José, Daniel received a leather pouch from Jim. "This gold should be more than enough to pay for what's needed." Jim's gaze narrowed. "Make sure you get receipts." He handed him a second, smaller pouch. "And here's a bonus for you. You struck a good bargain with Murphy for those supplies last week. There's about twenty ounces of gold in this bag. Buy whatever you'd like."

A $400 bonus? Back in Illinois, that would have been a fortune. Here in California, however, with inflated gold rush prices, he figured he'd use the money to buy a few shirts, pants, maybe even new shoes. He'd store the rest of the money in the toe of his father's old boots. That, along with the monthly salary Jim gave him, would eventually pay his way back to Illinois. Daniel gritted his teeth. Someday he'd get back there and solve the mystery of his parents' murders.

Jim interrupted his thoughts. "Once you get to San José, look up our friend James Reed. I saw him at the old mission in San José back in the summer of '47. That was before I found you with the Arnolds in San Francisco. Remember?"

How could he forget? A twinge of pain shot through his chest. Without saying goodbye, he'd left the Arnolds to join Jim in the gold fields. Dr. and Mrs. Arnold had been his only friends in California after Jim abandoned him on the wagon train.

"When I saw Reed at the old mission," Jim continued, "he told me he planned to purchase property in Pueblo San José. He said to stop in for a visit the next time I passed through. If you find him, he might let you and Long-Haired Brown camp on his land while you buy supplies. I doubt there are any hotels in town yet." Jim flashed him a teasing smile. "And I'm sure you won't mind catching up with his daughter. What was her name? Virginia?"

Daniel's stomach clenched. He flashed back to their days on the wagon train. Had it only been three years? He pictured his little stepsister, Hannah, walking alongside thirteen-year-old Virginia as they collected buffalo chips and wildflowers. That was before Hannah was killed by Indians on their trek to California. And before Jim abandoned him to finish the trail alone.

Pueblo de San José, June 12, 1849

Seven days later, with little small talk, Daniel and Long-Haired Brown reached San José. Daniel obtained directions to the Reed's ranch from a plaza merchant, then guided the wagon's horses north to the family's home.

While Brown tended the animals, Daniel tromped up the wooden steps to the Reed's front door. Would his friends remember him? Sweat gathered under his armpits as he knocked.

Moments later, the door creaked open, and Mrs. Reed appeared. Lines formed across her forehead as she studied his face. Clamping a hand over her mouth, she let out a small cry. "Daniel. Daniel Whitcomb. Oh, my Lord. Come in, come in!"

Mr. Reed joined his wife in the entryway. "Well, I'll be." Mr. Reed greeted Daniel with a two-handed shake. "So good to see you, son. Please, come in."

Mrs. Reed ushered everyone into the parlor and invited Daniel to sit in a gold-tufted armchair. Mr. Reed sat on the gold brocade couch.

It appeared the Reeds had done well since their near-death experience in the Sierras with the Donners and the Breens. He only knew what he'd read in the newspapers. He hoped to get a first-hand account while staying with them.

As Daniel and Mr. Reed exchanged pleasantries, Mrs. Reed scurried to the kitchen to brew a pot of tea.

"Of course you can pitch your tent on our property," Mr. Reed said after Daniel explained his business. "There's a water pump near the corral. That would be a good spot." The middle-aged man spread his hands out in front of him. "As is apparent from our half-papered parlor, our house isn't quite finished yet. We've only lived here about six months, but finished or unfinished, you are welcome anytime."

Daniel eyed the man's high-collared white shirt, black waistcoat, and dark trousers. Quite an improvement over the ragged clothes they'd worn on the trail. Much had changed in the last three years. He tugged on the sleeves of his red flannel shirt that didn't quite reach his wrists.

Mrs. Reed returned with a ceramic tea service, set it on the mahogany table, and poured a cup for everyone. When she took a seat next to her husband on the ornately carved couch, Daniel noted the colorfully stitched trim on her blue flounced skirt. His seamstress stepmother certainly would have noticed it. The fashionable skirt was certainly a contrast to the simple plaid cotton dresses the women had worn when they crossed the prairie.

Balancing her blue-flowered teacup and saucer in one hand, Mrs.

Reed turned to her husband. "I heard you tell Daniel he could camp out on our property."

Mr. Reed nodded as he sipped his tea.

"Well certainly, James, we can do better than that. He can sleep in the boys' room. I am sure either one of them would be willing to give up his bed for a few nights."

Daniel gazed at the parlor's walls, only half-covered by white and gold diamond-shaped wallpaper. "Thank you, Mrs. Reed, but I couldn't impose. Besides, Long-Haired Brown might get lonesome out there in his tent."

Mrs. Reed set her saucer and cup on the table. "Daniel, the boys won't mind sharing their room with both you and Mr. Brown. They grew quite attached to you and your stepsister during our long months on the wagon train. They looked up to you like an older brother. And they treated little Hannah like one of their own sisters, as did Virginia and Patty."

Daniel shifted uncomfortably in the padded parlor chair. Grief stabbed at his heart. *Why did she have to mention Hannah?*

From somewhere behind him came the soft patter of shoes across the rough-planked flooring. "Patty told me you were here."

Daniel turned to see who had spoken.

Virginia.

She returned his wide-eyed gaze.

Could it be true? He barely recognized the young woman. Yes, much had changed in the last three years. Virginia looked a far cry from that calico-dressed girl he knew on the wagon train. His throat went dry. Recalling his manners, he stood. "It's good to see you again, Virginia," he squeaked out.

"And you." She nodded.

When she slid past him, he caught a scent of lavender as she moved to sit on a parlor chair next to her parents.

He clasped his hands in front of him and studied her well-fitted yellow satin dress. He tried to think of something to say, but nothing came to mind. Finally, he sat.

"It's been a long time since we've seen each other." She let her gaze meet his and offered a smile. A smile that reached her eyes.

Mr. Reed cleared his throat. "I assume, Daniel, that you plan to buy your flour from Mr. Campbell out at his grist mill?"

Still unable to find his voice, Daniel nodded.

"Mr. Campbell has planted several acres of wheat out near his mill," Mr. Reed said. "I've planted a few acres of wheat myself, but William is the only one in the area with a mill to grind it. I will put in a good word for you, and I am sure he will give you a fair price." Mr. Reed sat back and crossed his legs at the knee. "The going rate for flour is $20 a barrel, but he might see his way to charge you less."

Daniel's spine stiffened. Murphy had paid them $325 a barrel at Big Oak Flat. They'd be able to sell local miners the flour he brought back from San José for $400 a barrel. Jim would be pleased with the profit.

Virginia's father continued. "I know Mr. Campbell from the Mexican War. He is an honest man and a friend. It may take him a day or so to fill your order, but you are welcome to stay here until you complete your business."

"I'd be much obliged, sir." Finally, he found his voice. "Also, Mr. Savage said Isaac Branham owns a lumber mill near here. I believe Mr. Branham was also part of our wagon party in '46. Can you give me directions to his mill?"

Mr. Reed nodded. "Yes. It' not far from here. And yes, Mr. Branham was part of our group. At least until we broke off to join the Donner Party." He dropped his gaze to the floor.

An uncomfortable silence filled the room.

Mrs. Reed finally broke in. "The lumber mill is about seventeen miles southwest of here, but Mr. Branham doesn't own it anymore. He sold it last year to Zachariah Jones."

Appearing to have regained his composure, Mr. Reed chuckled. "Son, why do you want to go the lumber mill? You don't plan to drag the logs back to the Sierra foothills, do you?"

Daniel studied his cup of dark tea. "No, sir. I hear that a Mr. Brody works at the lumber mill. It's Mr. Brody I'm anxious to see."

Virginia pressed one of her golden curls between her thumb and forefinger. "Mr. Brody?" She raised a brow. "He was on our wagon train, wasn't he? Weren't his boys always fighting with you?"

Daniel bristled at the memory. "Yes. Matthew and Josiah. They always had it in for me, even before we left Princeton Township."

Mr. Reed shook his head. "Mr. Brody was quite a drinker, but I hear he sobered up once he and his boys arrived in San José. Didn't his sons die in the Mexican War? I think it was at the Battle of Natividad."

Daniel set his saucer and teacup on the table. "Yes. Mr. Savage told me he was there when the Brody brothers were killed. Before they died, the older one, Matthew, told Mr. Savage something about my parents' deaths. I plan to ask Mr. Brody about it before I return to Big Oak Flat."

Mr. Reed also set his teacup on the table. "May their souls rest in peace."

Before Daniel left, Mr. Reed handed him a letter of introduction for Mr. Campbell.

"I'm mighty thankful, sir." Daniel took the letter and shook Mr. Reed's hand.

To his delight, Virginia walked him to the door.

Daniel hooked his thumbs beneath his suspenders. Willing the sweat to stop tickling his back, he squared his shoulders. "After I meet with Mr. Campbell this afternoon, may I come by the house for a visit? Perhaps after supper?"

Virginia offered him her hand. "Why, I would be flattered, Mr. Whitcomb." She gave him that dimpled half-smile he remembered from the early days of their friendship.

His insides trembled. Not sure what to do next, he grabbed her hand and shook it. "All right. I'll see you around half past seven. Um… good-day, Vir… ah, Miss Reed."

3
THE PORCH SWING

June 12, 1849
Pueblo de San José, California

Daniel and Long-Haired Brown completed their business with Mr. Campbell by six o'clock that evening. The man couldn't fill their order immediately but promised to have their barrels of flour ready by noon the next day—not that Daniel minded spending an extra day in San José.

While Long-Haired Brown led the horses to Mr. Reed's corral, Daniel prepared a quick meal of beans and bacon outside his tent.

He checked the pocket watch Dr. Arnold had given him. Half-past seven. Daniel spit on his hand, slicked back his hair, and walked the short distance to the Reed's house.

When he arrived, Mrs. Reed directed him and Virginia to sit on the wide porch swing. She went inside, and after a few minutes, returned with a tray of lemonade and fig cookies. Mrs. Reed set the tray on a nearby table. "I'll be right inside if you need me."

Daniel smiled. *I guess that's a hint she'll be watching us through the front parlor window.*

He gazed at the shadowed outline of the Diablo Mountains in front of them. If he stared long enough, maybe he'd get an idea of how to start a conversation. Time moved slowly as he sat with Virginia on the swing.

Neither spoke.

Glancing sideways at Virginia, he took in her white, high-necked blouse and slender figure. Gazing down, he noted the pink, black, and white chain stitches embroidered at the bottom of her long, pleated skirt. It was as fine as the embroidery work his stepmother used to sew onto the clothing she made for the wealthier people of Princeton Township. A tug pulled at his heart. Would he ever have his own family?

The silence was deafening. Sweat gathered on his palms. He rubbed them on his gray woolen trousers. He finally broke the silence. "So. Do you miss your old life back in Illinois?"

Virginia tucked the folds of her blue skirt more firmly beneath her legs. "I miss my cousins and my aunts and uncles, but I love it here."

Picking up her glass of lemonade, Virginia sipped, then returned the glass to the tray. "Mother no longer has her crippling headaches, and Father has done well in his business dealings."

Beyond the ranch house, Daniel gazed at the fields of wheat swaying in the evening breeze. "I can see that. Earlier today, your father said he plans to subdivide the land he's not farming. With all the new settlers coming to California, he'll be able to sell off the lots at a handsome profit." Reaching for a cookie, he bit, then talked around the morsel. "He said he's already advertised the lots in a San Francisco paper."

Virginia leaned back and forth several times. The swing propelled into motion.

Catching the swing in one of the forward sways, he retrieved his lemonade from the tray. Taking another bite of his moist cookie, he leaned back. The cookie was sweet, but the company sweeter.

She continued to rock. "Father has always been an ambitious man. He hopes to see San José become California's capital once we're admitted into the Union."

Sipping his drink, he was careful not to swallow the mint leaf floating on top. "And I suppose having San José as the state's capital won't hurt his business dealings here at all, will it?"

She stopped the swing and punched him in the arm, just as she had done whenever he teased her during their long trek from Illinois to California.

He cried out in mock pain, set down his glass, and rubbed his upper arm. "And I suppose he will want his daughters to marry ambitious men as well?"

She turned and massaged the area where her playful punch had landed. "Well, you certainly seem ambitious—giving up your blacksmith apprenticeship in San Francisco to follow Jim Savage into the gold fields."

Her tender touch against his rough woolen shirt made his mouth go dry. He licked his lips and eyed his glass of lemonade. No. It could stay on the tray. He wanted this moment to last as long as possible.

"I see you still have the muscles of a blacksmith." She patted his upper arm. "What are your plans after you strike it rich in the gold fields? Will you return to Illinois?"

He tilted his head and gave her a don't-get-ahead-of-yourself smile. "I don't know if I'll strike it rich, Virginia. Working as Jim's bookkeeper keeps me pretty busy. There's no time to do my own prospecting. But Jim says he'll give me five percent of his stake when I turn eighteen." He didn't want to make any promises. But he also didn't want to discourage her.

"After just a few months in the gold fields, Pa came home with bulging bags of gold. And remember John Breen? He and his family now live south of here at the old San Juan Bautista Mission. John went to the gold fields and came back with $12,000 worth of gold dust. He bought a large piece of land near the mission. Now their family farms and raises cattle there."

Daniel reached again for his glass. "John was a good friend to me on the wagon train. He saved my bacon several times from those Brody boys."

She laughed. "I remember."

"I'm glad John's doing well. Wasn't he also trapped with you and the Donners in the Sierra snows?"

Virginia planted her feet on the ground, abruptly bringing the swing to a halt.

A lump formed in his throat that he couldn't wash down with lemonade. He wanted to know more about what happened in the Sierra snows, but not if the memories upset her. Maybe he shouldn't have brought it up.

Virginia drew in a breath. Her chest rose, then fell as she slowly exhaled. "We and the Breens were the only ones who didn't lose a family member that winter. So many died. The Donner family—"

Daniel touched her shoulder, the fringed shawl soft beneath his fingers. "I'm sorry. You don't have to talk about it if you don't want to."

Her dark brown eyes filled with tears.

What'll I do if she starts to bawl? His insides quivered.

"Daniel, if it hadn't been for the Breens, I don't think I would have survived." She turned her head and appeared to study the darkening sky.

He followed her gaze, waiting to see if she'd speak again.

She didn't.

I should say something. He pressed his thumbs into his forefingers.

A cloud slowly slipped across the early moon.

"The Breen family prayed together day and night." Her voice came soft and breathy. "Often our only light came from the little pine needles we kept burning in the hearth. Sometimes I'd kneel next to Mr. Breen and hold up one of those little torches so he could see enough to read from his prayer book." She brushed a hand across her cheek. "I'm thankful Pa wasn't there to see that." She chuckled. "You know, with him being a Freemason and all, he really doesn't like Catholics."

Turning toward her, he wiped a single tear from her cheek with his forefinger. "I heard the Catholic popes condemned the Freemasons." He'd finally thought of something to say. "But that's about all I know about them."

"Anyway..." She continued to stare at the moon as a cloud dimmed its view. "One night after we'd all gone to bed, I found I just couldn't nod off. As starved as we were, I figured it wouldn't be so bad if I just went to sleep and never woke up. The next moment, I found myself on my knees with my hands clasped, looking up through the darkness. I vowed I'd become a Catholic like the Breens and spend the rest of my life serving God and others if He would just save us."

Daniel's muscles tensed. He hadn't thought about God or prayer since Hannah died.

Virginia went quiet.

He studied the stars in silence.

Again, she touched her cheek. "Shortly after I prayed, Pa arrived with a relief party."

At the mention of prayer, Daniel's heart went cold. He rose and strode over to the Reed's half-finished railing. "Back home, Ma and Pa used to read to us every night from the Bible." He turned and stared at the darkened fields, as if addressing the stalks of wheat. "It always made me feel peaceful." He swallowed hard. *Will I ever feel that way again?*

He turned back toward Virginia, hypnotized by her golden hair shimmering in the glow of the oil lamp. "I'm glad praying helped you get through that awful time. To be honest, between my parents' deaths and Hannah getting killed by Indians, I've had a hard time praying. When I do, I feel like God doesn't really hear."

He reached back and rested his hands on the railing. "Now all I want to do is get back to Illinois and find out what happened to my parents. I'm positive our housefire was no accident." Clenching his jaw, he dug his fingernails into the wooden rail's fibers. "I won't rest until I find justice for my parents."

She joined him at the balustrade.

His pulse quickened.

"What makes you so sure it wasn't an accident?" Her warm fingers touched his forehead. She brushed aside strands of his dark brown hair. "Have you ever thought—" She hesitated.

"Thought what?" The scent of mint floated between them. Close. So close. Those soft lips.

"Well, perhaps having someone to blame—"

He leaned closer.

"Maybe having someone to blame—" her voice came as a whisper. "Maybe that makes it easier to deal with losing them?"

Like wind whipping up bits of dust, her words swirled around in his head. Pulling back, he held up a hand. "No. I'm not trying to find someone to blame." He scrunched his brows together. "You don't understand."

She strolled back to the swing and sat. "You know, my real father died when I was two. When I got a little older, I told my mother it was her fault."

Her soft, gentle voice tugged him to face her. He couldn't resist.

Locking onto his gaze, she continued. "I told my mother if she had been a stronger woman my father wouldn't have died. When I got older, she explained he died of cholera. I realized then she couldn't have prevented it. Lucky for me, a few years later, Mother married James Reed."

Daniel planted his arms across his chest. "Well, it's not like that for me. Someone purposely set fire to our house. It was a miracle Hannah and I weren't there that night."

"But how do you know for sure it wasn't an accident?"

A fire burned in his chest as hot as the first day he learned the truth about his parents' deaths. "Remember how I told you at tea this afternoon that Jim fought alongside the Brody brothers during the Mexican War?"

She nodded.

"Well, Jim told me he was there when the Brody brothers were killed at the battle of Natividad. Before they died, the older one, Matthew, apologized for what he and his brother did to my parents. Jim asked what they had done, but Matthew died before he could explain." He clenched his jaw. "I plan to ask their pa about it before I return to Big Oak Flat."

She studied her hands resting in her lap. "I'm so sorry, Daniel. If it were my parents, I guess I'd want to find out the truth too." Her lips rolled inward. "So, after you turn eighteen, you'll pack up all your inherited riches and go back to Illinois in order to find justice?"

He shoved his hands into his pockets and returned to the swing. "I'll find out what Matthew's father knows and see where that trail leads. But, yes. I plan to go back to Illinois."

She offered him a teasing half-smile. "Well, Mr. Whitcomb, I'd rather you spent your riches around here, but, if you're bent on solving this mystery, I won't stop you."

He brushed his fingers across her hand. "Well, if you did try to stop me, I suppose that wouldn't be such a bad thing. Besides, if Mr. Brody doesn't know anything about my parents' deaths, perhaps I *will* end up spending my riches here in San José."

4

THE DINNER

June 13, 1849
Pueblo de San José

Early the next morning, Daniel and Long-Haired Brown visited several San José merchants. They purchased cans of sardines, coffee, brown sugar, wash bowls, gold mining cradles, picks, and shovels. After checking the items off their list, Daniel spent some of his bonus money on two new shirts, a vest, trousers, and leather shoes. In another shop, his eyes fixated on a turquoise- and diamond-studded gold cross.

"She's a beauty, ain't she?" The shop owner wiped his hands on his dirty white apron and gently lifted the small cross from its black velvet box. "A Russian captain pawned this necklace in exchange for mining tools. Said he wouldn't need it after he made his fortune in the gold fields. I'll sell it for $100."

Daniel weighed out five ounces of gold on the merchant's scale. He estimated he still had about $120 left. As the merchant wrapped the velvet box in newsprint, Daniel spotted a silver pocket watch. A gift for Mr. Reed. That would surely impress the man. "How much for that key-winding watch?"

The merchant scratched his stubbled chin. "I just bought it yesterday from a Swiss fella going to the gold fields. Since you're also buying the cross and necklace, I'll let you have it for an ounce of gold."

"Deal." Daniel poured out more gold dust onto the merchant's scale.

Just before noon, Daniel and Long-Haired Brown picked up their barrels of flour from Campbell's mill. Daniel unhitched his horse from the back of their wagon once the barrels were loaded. Brown drove the merchandise back to the Reed's ranch while Daniel rode out to find Brody at Jones' lumber mill.

Once Daniel arrived at the lumber mill, he asked about Brody. A worker showed him a dirt-packed trail leading into the mountains. "Brody and his crew'll be haulin' back a load of logs any time now. You can wait for 'em here at the end of the path."

Thirty minutes later, Daniel saw Brody's crew, their wagon, and team of oxen emerge from the tree line of the redwoods. Chains and harnesses clanged as the wagon lumbered forward. For a moment, the rig disappeared in a cloud of dust. It reappeared when the log-filled wagon met him at the end of the trail.

After Brody brought the wagon to a halt, the lumberjacks jumped down and brushed off their flannel shirts and leather vests. The air filled with another cloud of dust.

Daniel coughed, then introduced himself to Brody and stated his business.

"Yeah, I remember you," Brody said from his wagon seat. "My two boys and me weren't that close when they went off to war. Some people say it's 'cause I drank too much." The man's eyes moistened. "But, since they died, I've stopped drinkin'." He pursed his lips. "Other than that, I'm afraid there ain't much to tell."

Sour milk. That's what the man smelled like. Daniel rubbed his nose and followed alongside the wagon as Brody steered it toward the barn then unhitched the oxen.

"Before your sons went off to war," Daniel asked above the clank of chains, "did they ever talk about Princeton Township? Or the fire at my parents' house?"

Brody removed the animals' yoke, then ran a hand across his rough, day-old beard. "You say you're a-workin' with that Jim Savage feller up in the gold country?" A slow smile crept across the man's face. "I bet Savage has made a king's ransom in them gold fields by now."

What does that have to do with anything? Daniel stretched his neck to loosen his tight muscles. "He's doing all right, sir. As I was saying, Mr. Savage said your boys seemed to have some information about my parents' deaths. He thought you might know something about that."

The grizzle-haired lumberjack shrugged, opened the paddock, and slapped the oxen on their hind quarters to urge them inside. "I've still got more work to do. Grab that feed bucket. After we take care of the animals we'll talk more at my cabin."

Daniel pumped water into the troughs while Brody shoveled fodder into the animals' food rack. Brody then led Daniel over a rickety bridge that spanned the swift-moving creek powering the mill's waterwheel. A short path through a grove of live oak brought them to a small, one-room adobe.

"Branham's foreman built this shack," his host explained as they entered, "but he took off for the gold fields four months ago. Jones, my new boss, rents it to me now."

On the far side of the dim room stood a crude wooden table with two rough-hewn chairs. The smell of stale urine emanated from a wood-framed straw mattress that butted up against the left wall. Various tools suspended by leather hooks hung on the wall to the right.

The man motioned for him to sit. Mr. Brody removed crusty brown bread and a hunk of cheese from a tin and placed them on the table. He also brought over a jug of water from a shelf near the door. Carrying over two tin plates and cups, he sat across from Daniel on the other wooden chair. "Before my boys left to fight in the Mexican War, they charged me to safeguard four bottles of whiskey for their homecoming," he began.

Brody tore off bits of bread and cheese, stuffed them into his mouth, and talked as he chewed. "See, when we left Princeton Township, Sean Flannery, the saloon keeper, owed me money for odd jobs. Along with my wages, he threw in a case of his fine Overholt whiskey, brought in from Pennsylvania. Flannery said half the case was for the boys when they got older, 'cause they'd worked for him too. The other half was for me."

Daniel clenched his teeth. He'd had enough of this man's blabbering. The musty rank odors trapped in the small room threatened to bring up his breakfast of biscuits and bacon. "Mr. Brody—"

The man held up a hand. "Turn your back now, so you don't see." Brody shuffled over to a corner of the room near the tools.

Daniel sighed, turned, and jiggled his leg while he waited.

"Here's one of them bottles," Brody said.

A clunk on the table signaled Daniel could now turn back around. He glanced at the bottle and read the label. "Old Overholt dry whiskey." He reached for it.

The scruffy man snatched it away before Daniel could examine it.

"Mr. Brody." Daniel's voice caught in his throat. The stench of the man's sweat, mixed with the smell of urine, had grown to gagging proportions.

Brody hugged the unopened bottle to his chest. "When the boys left, I promised I'd stop drinking till they got back. That way, I'd be sure not to drink any of the whiskey that belonged to them. I'd already finished off my half of the case before we reached California. And, though I told them not to, they had drunk most of theirs too. Guess I wasn't much of an example."

Creating a little more distance between himself and the foul-smelling man, Daniel inched back his chair along the hard-packed dirt floor. "What's any of this got to do with my parents' deaths?"

Brody lifted his chin. "Now boy, I'm a-comin' to that." The man placed the whiskey bottle close to his plate and pulled off another chunk of bread. "My boys made me swear not to touch their last four bottles. I promised, but they feared my penchant for drinkin'. They made me swear that, even if I did drink the whiskey, I'd at least save the empty bottles." He leaned closer. "Said they hid somethin' beneath those Overholt labels. Somethin' about a job they did for Flannery. Said the information was some sort of insurance in case trouble followed us from Illinois."

Daniel raised his eyebrows. *A secret's hidden beneath one or more of those whiskey bottle labels? Perhaps a clue about Ma and Pa's deaths?*

Brody smiled, revealing yellowed teeth. "Ah, I see you're trying to make a connection. To answer your question, I never did peek under them labels. I also kept my promise. I never drunk their whiskey neither."

Daniel's hand shook as he poured himself a drink of water. "Mr. Brody, can I see those bottles?"

"Not so fast, son. See, I figure whatever's under those labels might be worth a sizeable sum. And, with you workin' in the gold fields all this time with Jim Savage, you might be willin' to pay, say, $800 for the lot?"

The trembling he'd seen in his hand now snaked its way throughout his body. *How could this greedy man justify such an enormous price?* Daniel folded his arms across his chest in an effort to rein in his rage. "Mr. Brody, $200 for each bottle of whiskey is a high price to pay for liquor. Besides, I don't have that kind of money on me."

A shadow crept over the man's face. "You know darn well you ain't payin' for the whiskey, boy. It's the secret under one of them labels you want. I'm sure $800 ain't nothin' for a rich man like Savage."

Daniel worked his jaw to keep it from quivering. He estimated how much money he had left. *Why did I buy that cross and watch?*

"How about I just buy the bottle that has the note," he finally said. "I'll pay you $100 for it. That's all I have right now."

"No deal, Whitcomb. See, if I just sell the bottle with the note, I fear I'll end up drinkin' the whiskey in the other bottles. I don't need that temptation. I got a good job here, and I don't plan on losing it. My work slows down during the rainy season, and I need a cushion of cash I can count on. It's $800 for the lot, or nothin'."

Daniel crossed his arms. "That's a steep price, Mr. Brody. There's no way I can get that kind of money before I leave tomorrow." He inhaled a shaky breath. "When I get back to the gold fields, I'll see if Mr. Savage will give me a loan on my wages. If he agrees, I won't be able to pay you until I come back for more supplies. And I have no idea when that'll be."

Brody leaned back. "Well, I ain't goin' nowhere. I kin wait."

When Daniel returned to the Reed's ranch, he found Virginia waiting for him outside his tent.

"Oh, I'm so glad you're back." Virginia pulled at the pleats of her skirt. "Pa's having some men join us for supper, and he asked me to invite you and Long-Haired Brown to join us."

Even in her purple-and-white plaid walking dress, she took his breath away. Daniel removed his broad-brimmed felt hat and twisted it between his hands. Suddenly, her words sank in. *Dinner with Mr. Reed and his friends?* He gulped.

Long-Haired Brown glanced up from the campfire. "If it's all the same to you, Miss, I'd rather stay out here and keep an eye on the merchandise we purchased today."

Virginia's eyes widened, and she pinched her lips together. "Very well, Mr. Brown, I understand."

Turning to Daniel, she lifted her chin. "And what about you, Mr. Whitcomb?"

His palms grew sweaty. He rolled in his foot to the side and studied the dusty sole that pulled away from his shoe. "I don't think I can. I don't have anything decent to wear."

Brown laughed. "What about those new shoes and clothes you bought in town today?"

He'd almost forgotten. They might not be fancy, but at least his new shoes and clothes were clean and in good condition.

"Well, that settles it." Virginia bounced on her toes. "See you at the house around six o'clock. Ma will ring the triangle to let you know it's time."

When Daniel responded to Mrs. Reed's call for supper, Virginia ushered him into a corner of the parlor. Well-dressed gentlemen locked in animated conversations filled the room.

Pushing back a renegade strand of his dark brown hair, Daniel berated himself. *Should've gotten a haircut while in town.*

Virginia tugged the sleeve of his new white shirt. "Daniel, I won't be able to join—"

In the bustling room, Daniel couldn't make sense of her soft words. Eager to share his own news, he cut her short. "I might not have to go back to Illinois to find out what happened to my parents." He leaned closer to her ear and raised his voice. "Mr. Brody said his boys wrote something beneath the label of an old whiskey bottle, then pasted it back on the bottle to hide what they wrote. He says I have to buy all four of his whiskey bottles to find the message. The next time I'm in town, I'll bring enough money to satisfy the greedy man. Then, I'll finally be able to get to the bottom of this mystery."

Virginia leaned closer and said something else, but he couldn't hear her well enough to understand.

Her father's voice rang out above the clamor. "Would everyone please join me in the dining room?"

Once the guests moved to the next room, Mr. Reed invited them to take a seat around the mahogany dining table. Mr. Reed, however, continued to stand as he gathered his children and wife behind him.

"My family won't be joining us for dinner," the man explained, "but I'd like you all to meet them."

Daniel squirmed in his dining room chair as Mr. Reed presented his family. *So that's what she wanted to tell me. She's not staying for dinner.* He shifted again, hoping to find a more comfortable position.

Virginia slipped past him on her way out. "I do hope you have time to join me on the front porch again after supper," she whispered. Her soft breath tickled the hairs on the back of his neck.

A thin layer of sweat gathered on his forehead. He reached into his trousers' pocket for a handkerchief but came up empty. He'd neglected to buy one. He watched her leave, desperately wishing she could stay.

Pulling himself up straight, he studied the six men seated around the table. They were all dressed in the latest fashions. Daniel's seamstress stepmother had sewn outfits like theirs. He'd always fancied himself wearing gentlemen's clothing someday. But, fated to the life of a blacksmith, he had considered that a far-fetched fantasy. He especially admired Mr. Reed's double-breasted gray tailcoat, burgundy brocade vest, and fancy silk ascot.

And me without coat, vest, or neckwear. He tugged at the high collar of his white button-bibbed shirt, hoping to alleviate his constricted throat. The warmth of the room pressed in on him. He diverted his attention to the table's lace covering, the shiny silverware, and the fine-ribbed wine glasses. He finally fixed his eyes on the blue, gold-rimmed plates. *I wonder what we'll eat tonight. I hope it's beef.*

Mr. Reed, still standing, glanced at each guest. "Gentlemen, I have invited you all here so we can get better acquainted. I believe each of us is destined to play an important role in California's future."

Then what am I doing here? He sipped from his water glass.

Mr. Reed turned to the man on his left. "First, I'd like to introduce Mr. Benjamin Lippincott."

Daniel gazed in Lippincott's direction. Black frock coat, knotted neckstock, blue vest.

Lippincott nodded to the guests.

Mr. Reed reached an upturned hand toward Daniel. "And this is Daniel Whitcomb. I came to California with Mr. Lippincott and Mr. Whitcomb on the Russell-Boggs wagon train in '46."

Mr. Whitcomb? He felt as out of place as a piece of wood in a savory stew. A stew of his own making. And he was a terrible cook. He wished the floor would just open up and swallow him.

Virginia's father gestured to the man seated on Mr. Lippincott's left. "And this is John Tyndale. He recently came out West from Missouri where he owns a large plantation. He is one of the two southern gentlemen I have invited to this dinner."

Daniel studied Tyndale. Something about him seemed familiar. A short, stocky man with black hair graying at the temples, he wore a black double-breasted, gold-buttoned tailcoat, and a white ruffled shirt with a tan cravat.

"Mr. Tyndale still has business interests in Missouri," the host continued, "but he plans to develop land in San Francisco and make California his home. Most important, he supports our bid for California as a state. And like most of us, he hopes to see San José become our new state's capital—"

"And, James, don't forget," Lippincott interrupted. "Mr. Tyndale is willing to back those interests with hard-earned cash."

The men chuckled and nodded.

"Hear, hear," added one.

Daniel continued to study Tyndale. The man stared back. Tyndale's bushy brown eyebrows and dark hooded eyes reminded him of his own. It never occurred to him that partially hidden eyelids could cast such a crafty demeanor. He squirmed under the man's scrutiny.

Mr. Reed continued. "Seated next to Mr. Tyndale is William

Gwin, originally from Tennessee. He served as personal secretary to President Jackson, and later as a congressman from Mississippi."

Daniel shifted right to get a better look. Gwin reeked of tobacco. His white, upturned collar and black silk neckstock framed a resolute jawline. His high forehead, dark swept-back hair, and long, straight nose spoke of a man who usually got what he wanted.

Gwin grabbed the black velvet lapels of his tan waistcoat and tucked his thumbs beneath them. "I did once serve as a congressman from Mississippi," he drawled, "but I plan to return to Washington as a senator from California."

"You've got my vote, sir." Tyndale raised a hand in Mr. Gwin's direction.

Mr. Reed cleared his throat and turned to the gentleman on his right. "Most of you are acquainted with Edward Gilbert, editor of the *Weekly Alta California*. He originally hails from New York, but now resides in San Francisco."

Heads nodded in Gilbert's direction.

Simply dressed in a black frock and vest, white shirt, and black neckstock, Daniel took an instant liking to the man. Gilbert's dark, horseshoe mustache and pointed beard that traced his jawline reminded him of some of the miners back at Big Oak Flat.

"That now brings us to *Alcalde* Walter Colton." Mr. Reed nodded to the man on Daniel's left. "Before the war with Mexico broke out, he served as chaplain aboard the USS Congress."

Again, Daniel wondered why he had been invited to Mr. Reed's dinner. He pulled on the cuffs of his sleeves. Could he make up an excuse to leave? No. He wanted to impress Virginia's father. He'd stay.

Mr. Reed raised his chin. "Once the California territory was claimed for the United States, Commodore Stockton appointed Chaplain Colton as the first American Alcalde of Monterey. Now, Alcalde Colton's authority holds sway as judge, sheriff, and governor over much of northern California."

Alcalde Colton slid two fingers across his chin. "A position that will hopefully end soon, once California enters the Union. I am anxious to get back to my family in Philadelphia."

Daniel searched the alcalde's face. Something about the

man—his noble nose, deep-set eyes, and gentle voice brought to mind his father.

The meal of savory steak, roasted potatoes, biscuits and gravy, and green beans with bacon did more than tantalize his tastebuds. The combined aromas and flavors brought back images of his family at mealtimes. Daniel pressed a hand over his heart, fearing it would burst.

Talk around the table focused on politics, a subject he knew little about.

"Is it true, Alcalde Colton," Mr. Tyndale asked, "that Territorial Governor Riley plans to call for a Constitutional Convention soon?"

The former chaplain suspended a forkful of green beans in mid-air and raised a brow. "Yes, that is what I have been told, Mr. Tyndale. But remember, California has not even been declared a territory of the United States. General Riley serves more as a military governor than a territorial governor."

"Well," Mr. Gwin drawled, "callin' for a Constitutional Convention might just force that issue, and I'm all for it. It's high time Congress stopped dilly-daddlin' over our future."

Mr. Tyndale leaned forward. "They let the Republic of Texas join as a slave state three months ago. Do you think Congress is afraid California will also join the Union as a slave state once they declare us a territory?"

Mr. Gwin raised a hand, fingers spread wide. "I, for one, would vote for that."

"As would I." Tyndale shot Gwin a toothy grin.

"Of course you would." Mr. Lippincott stabbed a piece of meat with a thud. "You and Mr. Gwin still have business interests in your home states. Slave states. Where you profit from the enslavement of human chattel." Lippincott carved into his steak. Red fluid flooded out.

Mr. Reed stared at Lippincott. "For the sake of civility, I suggest we defer any discussion regarding slavery. That is an issue for California's Constitutional Convention to decide."

Daniel stole a glance at Mr. Reed. Surely the man didn't agree with slavery, did he? He'd have to ask Virginia about that.

Alcalde Colton lifted a hand and coughed. "Either way, California's statehood would certainly make my job easier. Since we are neither a territory nor a state, I must continue to govern by the laws of Mexico. It complicates things greatly."

"Not an easy task, to be sure," Mr. Reed said. "And without a state government to back up the local authorities that do exist, lawlessness increases unabated, especially in the gold country." Mr. Reed locked eyes with Daniel. "Isn't that right, Mr. Whitcomb?"

It took a moment for Daniel to respond. Before this dinner, no one had ever called him Mr. Whitcomb. Now, Virginia's father had called him that twice. "Ah, yes, sir, Mr. Reed. Out there, it's only the lead in your gun that lays down the law. As Mr. Savage says, 'You can't possess what you can't protect.'"

Mr. Gwin rapped his knuckles on the table. "Well said, son."

Heat flamed through Daniel. He didn't like finding common ground with a slave owner. Like his parents, he hated slavery. He'd considered the possibility that his parents were killed because they helped runaway slaves find safe passage through Illinois on their way north to Canada. Those slaves were human beings. Not possessions.

The newspaper man, Mr. Gilbert, held his wine glass aloft. "My sources say General Riley will soon call for a Constitutional Convention, perhaps as early as next month. Once we've drawn county lines for our proposed state, he will order an election so the voters in each county can choose their delegates."

"Since I'm now a resident of San José," Mr. Tyndale said, "I would like to throw my hat into the ring as a delegate."

"I'm sure you would," Mr. Lippincott mumbled beneath his breath.

After the last guest left, Daniel hoped he still had time to visit with Virginia out on the porch. He curled his fingers around the gold cross in his pocket. His pulse quickened.

"May I visit with Virginia before she retires for the evening?" he asked her father.

Mr. Reed laid a hand on his shoulder. "Not tonight, son. I have some things I'd like to discuss with you.

5

THE CROSS

June 13, 1849
Pueblo de San José

Daniel shifted his feet as he stood near the parlor's open window. He hoped the cool bay breeze would dry his damp armpits. Too soon, Virginia's father entered the room, removed his gray tailcoat, and hung it on a wooden stand.

The lanky man walked to a corner table and poured himself a brandy. He then moved to the brocade couch and motioned Daniel to sit in the gold-tufted armchair.

His host, still clad in his buttoned-up burgundy vest and gray silk ascot, sat and crossed his legs at the ankle. He sipped his brandy and gazed at Daniel. "I've invited you here tonight because I believe you can play an important part in California's future."

Is someone else in the room? Daniel turned his head. Not seeing anyone else, he shifted his focus back to Mr. Reed. "Me, sir? No, I don't think so."

"And why not?"

Daniel shrugged. "I'm just a blacksmith-turned-accountant from Illinois, scratching out a living in the gold country until I turn eighteen."

With a light thud, Virginia's father set his glass on the low mahogany table in front of him. "Daniel, as immigrants to California, we all came from somewhere else. We all used to do something else. And most important, we are all risk-takers bent on making a better life for ourselves and our families." He quirked a brow and leaned forward. "I see that drive in you."

Daniel placed his clammy hands on his hips, arched back, and studied the ceiling. Mr. Reed saw more in him than he did in himself. When he focused again on his host, the man pinned him with a stare.

"Daniel, the men I invited here tonight all have something in common. Ambition. Ambition for themselves and for the future of California. I believe you have the potential to join their ranks. Have you ever thought of a career as a lawyer or a politician?"

This man has spent too much time in the sun. He flexed his toes inside his new leather shoes. Too tight. He squirmed under Mr. Reed's scrutiny. "Sir, I don't have the schooling or the money to pursue such ambitions."

Virginia's father inhaled. He loosened his silk ascot, retrieved his brandy from the table, and settled back into the couch. "Neither did my friend, Abe Lincoln. Remember him? On the trail when you and the Savages visited our evening campfires, I told stories about my time with him in the Black Hawk War."

Daniel nodded and glanced around the room. Anything to keep his eyes off his host. He studied a framed picture on the wall above the fireplace. The crystal decanter on the corner table.

Unbuttoning his vest with one hand, Mr. Reed continued. "Abe was only twenty-three at the time of the Black Hawk War. I was thirty-two. Even though he was younger than most of the men in our volunteer regiment, we recognized his leadership skills and elected him captain."

Mr. Reed draped an arm over the back of the couch and continued. "Like you, Abe lost his mother at an early age, and later, his sister. He once told me that, between farming with his father and taking on odd jobs, he only attended school for twelve months. But he had a thirst for knowledge and a keen sense of justice."

Daniel pulled at his shirt collar. Mr. Reed's foot, now bobbing, summoned his focus.

"Encouraged by his stepmother, Abe took an interest in reading. He borrowed books from neighbors, clergymen, traveling teachers— anyone who would loan them to him." The man paused for another sip. "I remember how you used to borrow books from the Arnolds and read them by the light of the evening's campfire."

At the mention of the dear Arnolds, Daniel's focus shifted back to Mr. Reed's face.

"At twenty-four," the man continued, "Abe won a seat in Illinois' General Assembly. Not bad for a man with twelve months of schooling. Wouldn't you agree?"

Daniel nodded and squirmed in his seat, uncomfortable with where Mr. Reed seemed to be steering the conversation.

Virginia's father drained his glass. "The major of our Illinois Battalion, John Stuart, was a lawyer. After the war, he encouraged Abe to study law. He loaned him the books he needed to study. After four years, Abe received his license to practice law. In '46, he was elected to the U.S. Congress."

Daniel placed his hands behind his neck, interlocked his fingers, and leaned back. *What did the man expect him to do with this information? Abandon Jim Savage, go back to the Arnolds, and borrow books from lawyers?*

"Son, I'm sure you've noticed my daughter has taken an interest in you." A corner of his mouth drew up. "What do you plan to do after you turn eighteen?"

Daniel's stomach twisted. He felt like a deer surrounded by hunters. *Was Mr. Reed saying he wasn't good enough for Virginia? That he needed to pursue a career as a lawyer or politician if he was interested in his daughter?* He dropped his hands to his sides and ventured an answer. "I—I plan to return to Illinois and find out what happened to my pa and stepmother. When I turn eighteen, Mr. Savage promised me five percent of all he's made through his prospecting and trading post ventures."

His inquisitor moved to the edge of the couch and took off his loosened neckstock. "Trying to find out what happened to your parents is a noble endeavor, son, but what is your passion? What are your future goals?"

The skin on the back of Daniel's neck prickled. *Is this a future son-in-law interrogation? I like Virginia. But marriage?* No, he hadn't thought that far ahead. He'd only bought the cross on a whim and the watch to thank Mr. Reed for introducing him to Mr. Campbell. "Honestly, sir, I don't know as I have future goals."

Daniel thought about Limik as a young girl, kidnapped and forced to work for white miners. He thought about the black runaway slaves his parents helped ferry through Illinois and on to Canada. Once again, he rubbed his sweaty hands on his gray woolen trousers. "If I had to name a passion, sir, I guess I'd say I care about justice. Doesn't seem there's much of that in this world."

Mr. Reed leaned forward. "Son, we need more lawyers and politicians with that kind of fervor. And I saw that in you on the wagon trail. I saw the rage in your eyes when Mr. Keseburg stole the buffalo hide from the Lakota Indians' burial grounds. And I admired the way you challenged that German when he excused his actions by claiming that Americans say, 'Da best Indyan ist a dead Indyan.'"

Daniel chuckled at his host's attempt to recreate a German accent. "And I admired the way you punched him in the jaw when he refused to return the buffalo skin."

"If Keseburg hadn't taken it back, we might not be sitting here today." Mr. Reed rubbed his hands together. "If you'd like, I can ask some of my lawyer friends to loan you a few books. You must have some leisure time when you're not working on Mr. Savage's accounting ledgers."

Daniel brushed his hands across his knees. No one had ever asked him such pointed questions. No one had ever expressed such confidence in his ability to rise above his circumstances. "I think I'd like that, sir."

Virginia's father slapped the couch's carved-wood framing. "I will have the books by your next visit." The man's eyebrows rose. "Can I be candid, Daniel?"

Candid? He chewed on the word for a moment. Thinking it meant *honest*, he slowly nodded.

"If you are truly interested in Virginia, her mother and I welcome it."

Stunned by the man's bluntness, he sat with his mouth open, unable to move.

"Last spring, our family attended a dinner party at Don Antonio Suñol's home. Virginia danced several times with a *Catholic*—a Mr.

John Murphy. I hear he is now a man of some means, having struck it rich in the gold fields."

John Murphy? Recalling Virginia's mention of her father's Masonic views, he understood Mr. Reed's tone when he said the word Catholic. Daniel frowned. *How can Murphy have an interest in Virginia? He married an Indian in Dry Diggins.*

Virginia's father continued. "Murphy's parents and siblings came out to California with the Stephens party in '44. They've acquired a substantial amount of land in this valley. Although twelve years Virginia's senior, John Murphy appears quite fond of my daughter. I shudder to think of *that* alliance. I just wanted to get that out in the open." Virginia's father stood, signaling the end of their visit. "I know you'll need to leave early tomorrow, so I won't keep you any longer."

Mr. Reed walked him to the door and shook his hand.

Daniel returned the handshake, then pulled the watch from his pocket. "This is for you, sir. I wanted to thank you for introducing me to Mr. Campbell. He gave me a fine price for his wheat."

Mr. Reed's eyes widened as he accepted the gift. "Thank you, son. I will treasure this."

Daniel fingered the turquoise- and diamond-studded cross in his pocket. He hoped he could give it to Virginia before they left the next morning.

After an early breakfast, Daniel and Long-Haired Brown harnessed their horses and hefted the last of their gear into the freight wagon. Brown, with rifle in hand, swung himself into the seat next to the brake.

Daniel clambered up behind the left wheelhorse. Even though he had slept little last night, his body vibrated with energy. He tried to imagine the expression on Virginia's face when he gave her the cross. With a flick of the reins and a "Haw," he guided the wagon forward. Pulling left at the large oak, he brought the team to a halt in front of the Reed's home.

He handed Brown the leather leads and jumped to the ground. "I'll just be a minute."

Taking the porch steps two at a time, he drew himself up at the front door and knocked.

Mrs. Reed, her dark brown hair wound atop her head, greeted him.

"Good morning, Mrs. Reed." He removed his wide-brimmed hat. "I'm about to head back to Big Oak Flat. May I speak with Virginia before I go?"

Mrs. Reed dried her hands on her muslin apron. "I'm sorry, Daniel. She's out riding with Patty. She thought she'd be back before you left. Can I give her a message?"

He fingered the gem-studded cross in his pocket and glanced at Long-Haired Brown on the wagon seat. "No, ma'am. I just wanted to say good-bye. I'll stop in again the next time I'm in town."

6

INDIAN OUTRAGES

June 25, 1849
Big Oak Flat, California Gold Country

With their wagon full of supplies, the return trip to Big Oak Flat took twelve bone-numbing days. In a cloud of dust, they pulled up in front of the trading post late in the afternoon. Daniel dropped from the wagon and held on to its rough wooden side until his legs regained their strength. After a few moments, he stumbled inside since Brown volunteered to take care of the horses.

Spotting Jim at a table in the back, he ambled over, pulled out a chair, and flopped into it. Limik carried over two cups of coffee. A moment later she brought two plates of hot beans and biscuits.

Jim grunted from behind a newspaper. "Glad you're back. Hope ya got a good price for all the merchandise." With the paper still in front of his face, he called out. "Banyon. Greeley. Unload the merchandise the boys just hauled in."

Ouch. Jim's gruff exterior still pricked his heart. What happened to the man he'd known on the trail? The man who taught him how to shoot? Who clapped him on the back when he brought down his first buffalo? The Jim he knew before he'd lost his wife and child?

Shaking his head, Daniel sipped his warm coffee, scooped up beans with a biscuit, and in two bites downed his little feast.

Jim laid the paper on the table and continued to pore over it.

What had captured the man's interest? Jim rarely picked up the newspaper. Sometimes he'd glance at it, pretending he could read, but Daniel knew better. That's why he'd brought Daniel to the gold country—to protect his secret, and to make sure no one took advantage of him as he grew his trading business.

With the paper now on the table, Daniel cocked his head to the side and strained to decipher the upside-down newsprint. He made out its masthead, *The Placer Times*.

Savage pounded the paper with his fist. "According to this, Injuns killed Benjamin Wood last month while he was prospectin' on the American River."

Daniel raised a brow.

"You remember Wood." Jim return his gaze. "I teamed up with him and his partners after I rescued you from the Arnolds in San Francisco."

The Arnolds. Daniel's stomach pulled at the mention of their name. He bit into another biscuit and washed it down with the rest of his coffee. After Jim abandoned him on the trail in '46, the elderly couple watched out for him. Once they reached California, he lived with them in San Francisco. For two years, he did odd jobs for room and board. Two months after their arrival, Dr. Arnold secured him an apprenticeship with a local blacksmith.

And how did he repay them? Against their advice, he ran off with Jim to the gold fields, hoping to strike it rich. *Fat chance of that. I wish I had never left.*

Savage shoved the newspaper under Daniel's nose, pulling him back to the present.

"A prospector brought this in today." Jim reached for a biscuit. "Says the feature story is about Miwoks killing Wood and his partners. Happened almost two months ago. News like this should've reached us long before now."

Daniel righted the paper and scanned the date. May 5. The headline screamed: *Indian Outrages—Seven White Men Murdered.* Flashing back to the Yosemite's attack on their outpost in April, a volcano of emotion erupted beneath his breastbone. Would the next headline list *their* names as victims? Tensions between the Indians and the whites escalated daily. As more gold-seekers swarmed the hills, more miners killed Indians. As more miners killed Indians, more Indians killed miners. As Jim constantly reminded him, *You can't possess what you can't protect.* That was true for both the whites and the Indians.

Daniel continued to browse the article. For Jim's benefit, he read a few lines out loud. "In April, Indians killed four men near a stream three miles below deposits known as the Spanish Bar: James Johnson, Nathan English, Benjamin Wood, and a Mr. Thompson."

As he continued to skim the article, Daniel read about the murders of three other whites a few days after Wood's death. *Two men killed by arrows. The third had his skull bashed in. Both events reported by the few who survived.* Despite the June heat, Daniel shook with a sudden chill.

"Good man, Wood." Jim rubbed a hand across his clean-shaven face. "Remember how he and I worked that creek in Dry Diggins back in July of '48? With just a pick and a knife, we scraped out $200–$300 a day."

Of course, he remembered. It had only been a year since Jim had convinced him to leave the Arnolds to help with his trading post at Dry Diggins.

Back then, he thought it was a good idea.

Back then, he'd hoped to earn enough money to return to Illinois.

Back then, the gold fields hadn't been so dangerous.

Jim stood and stretched. "Yes sir, we pulled a lot of gold outta those creeks at Dry Diggins. But when the new prospectors came in and overran the place, it was time to move on."

He'd only been with Jim two months before Wood and his guardian pulled up stakes and established a new trading post thirty miles south of Dry Diggins. Jim always claimed it was due to the flood of newcomers. He also knew it was because of the rival trading post set up by Weber and his helpers, John and Daniel Murphy. When those traders moved in, Jim moved out. The man did not like competition.

Daniel flinched at the memory of transporting their goods over mountainous terrain and setting up a new post on the Tuolumne River. But, their back-breaking work paid off. The new area proved just as profitable. For the next eight months, Wood and his partners, along with Jim, Chief Pasquale, and his 500 Yokuts Indians, prospected an area they later named Wood's Creek.

Daniel scooped up the rest of his beans. Jim must have taken the news of Wood's death to heart. He never reminisced.

Still standing, Jim lifted his tin coffee cup and drained it. "Yes sir, we worked that creek for eight months. Remember? And then more greenhorn prospectors arrived. Only this time, they brought in Miwok helpers. Those Miwoks and my Yokuts never got along. I hated to leave Wood and the easy gold we found at Wood's Creek, but there was no makin' peace between those enemy tribes. Wasn't till we moved here that I could get a few Miwoks to work alongside my Yokuts."

The thump of men rolling barrels of flour into the trading post didn't faze the faraway look in Jim's eyes. Maybe Jim was reliving scenes of those new Miwok workers attacking his Yokuts Indians. When fighting broke out between the two tribes, Wood and Jim had parted ways. Jim moved his Yokuts Indians and trading post farther south, this time into the hills of Big Oak Flat. Wood and his company went farther north. Now, Wood and his men were dead.

The biscuits in Daniel's stomach turned to rock.

Jim sat and picked up the last biscuit from the plate. The man chewed as if his jaw were partially frozen.

Daniel studied the article again and read another section out loud. *"The murders on the American River—the barbarities related above—to what prime cause can these be traced? Will it ever be effectually revealed? Will it ever be said with truth?"*

He shook his head and pushed the paper away. In his limited experience, the paths of murder and truth seldom crossed.

7
THE THEFT

September 1849
Big Oak Flat, California Gold Country

The fall of '49 brought changes into Big Oak Flat—more than just a chill in the air, the scent of decaying foliage, and yellow-leafed oaks. A melancholy spirit settled over the miners, palpable to anyone aware enough to notice. Daniel sensed it in the way Jim's clerks grumbled over their low pay, the almost daily news of brawls between miners, and the swelling reports of skirmishes between prospectors and Indians. He wrestled against the overarching depression but eventually succumbed.

One morning in late September, Daniel, as usual, walked into the canvas-covered trading post and greeted Greeley as the man inventoried items behind the counter. He retrieved his bookkeeping journal from a shelf he'd created out of stacked crates and carried it to the rough-hewn oak table in the back.

A few minutes later, Limik arrived with hot coffee, dried pork, and cornmeal mush.

His insides groaned as he wrinkled his nose. He hated mush. "No, please. Not again." He shoved the bowl away. "You've made the same breakfast for weeks." Heat flamed his face. "Even tortillas would be a welcome change. Is that too hard for you?" He glared at her with pinched eyes.

Her face went limp. Her mouth opened, then closed.

Was that frustration, fear, or fury he saw in her trembling lip?

Whatever it was, he ached to pull back his words. He reached out a hand, but she left before he could apologize.

Slumping in his chair, he tore off small pieces of dried pork and added them to the mush, eventually spooning it all it down.

"Got another copy of the *Alta California*, if you wanna see it," Greeley called over to him. Greeley slapped the paper that lay on a makeshift counter the clerks had created from a wooden plank suspended between two barrels.

Whenever someone brought in copies of the *Alta California* or the *Placer Times*, Daniel eagerly snatched them up. *Maybe reading the paper will lift my spirits.* He retrieved the newsprint from Greeley, returned to the table, and laid it out before him.

Was it the daily doldrums of deciphering figures that made him crave news from the outside? No, it was more than that. His dinner with the prominent men of California, his discussion with Virginia's father—it had altered his focus. He pulled himself up.

I'm not just a blacksmith-turned-accountant from Illinois, trying to scratch out a living. I'm a young man with a future. A future linked to the emerging state of California. A future that, before long, might include a bride.

He pressed his hands on the table and leaned back. *A bride?* His breath hitched. *Where did that thought come from?*

Leaning over the newspaper, he scanned the first page. It gave statistics for California's new arrivals. During the month of April, 3,806 people had entered the port of San Francisco. Five hundred arrived from outside the United States—immigrants from Manila, Hong Kong, Panama, and the Sandwich Islands. Only 87 of the nearly 4,000 were women.

Rubbing his forehead, he ciphered the difference. With an influx of only 87 women, that left 3,719 newly arrived men. And what about the number of prospectors who'd recently made the overland trek? In his experience, married men rarely brought their wives, and many of the new gold miners would be single. If those unmarried men remained in California, competition for a new bride would be fierce.

A pain shot through his ribs. *How long before I can return to San José?*

Daniel downed his coffee and scoured the paper for news about the Constitutional Convention he knew was underway in Monterey. One article listed the names of delegates voted in by people from the various counties. Three of the names were men who had attended the Reeds' dinner party—Benjamin Lippincott, a former wagon-train companion, Edward Gilbert, the *Alta California* editor, and William Gwin, the former U.S. Congressman from Mississippi. His jaw clenched as he recalled meeting that arrogant man at the Reeds' home. *Gwin. Well, I guess there's no accounting for taste.*

The paper printed several resolutions set forth by convention delegates. One urged Congress to allow California to enter the Union as a state instead of it first joining the Union as a territory. He was all for that. It would speed up California's development.

Next he read some of the delegates' proposed resolutions that were still under debate. The mush in his stomach moaned in protest. Southern-born delegates had suggested they exclude free blacks from entering California. No doubt Gwin and Tyndale were behind that. *How dare these southerners infect my budding state with their poison.*

He shook his head. *My state?*

The next paragraph made him realize he wasn't the only one disturbed by the southerners' proposal. Edward Gilbert, editor of the *Alta California*, one of the few dinner guests to whom he'd taken a liking, had spoken out against it.

> *Exclude free blacks from entering California? Sirs, if you insert such a provision into the state Constitution, you will be guilty of a great injustice. Are we to attempt here to turn back the tide of human freedom which has rolled across from continent to continent? Are we to say that a free negro or Indian, or any other freeman shall not enter the boundaries of California? I trust not.*

The sound of angry voices pulled Daniel's attention from the paper. Greeley and Banyon stood behind the counter, their arms flailing as their voices rose. Daniel strained to make sense of their argument.

The shouts grew louder.

Greeley's face reddened. "Savage can afford to give us a raise. Especially at the inflated prices he charges for supplies." As if to make his point, Greeley jabbed a finger in Banyon's chest.

Banyon batted Greeley's beefy hand away. "And I say you and I should just keep skimmin' off the top. Savage'll never be the wiser."

Daniel's pulse raced. The clerks were stealing from Jim. *No wonder I can never get the books to balance.*

Greeley glanced over at Daniel. Like a child caught with his hand in the cookie jar, Greeley's eyes went wide, and his mouth fell open. He quickly shoved the other clerk's shoulder. "I've no idea what you're talkin' about, Banyon. Get back to work. Bring out the last two barrels of flour. We've only got half a barrel left up here."

Daniel glared at Greeley. The man's attempt to cover his complicity fell on deaf ears. Not that he didn't sympathize with the men. The clerks asked Jim for a raise at least once a week. Always the negotiator, Jim would say they'd get one as soon as he paid off his debts. Since Daniel kept the books, he knew all about the money Jim owed his business partners. He also knew his guardian didn't always accurately record his daily income. In fact, two nights ago, the man had secreted away some of the day's profit before Daniel had a chance to count and record it.

Under the cover of darkness, Daniel had followed Jim to a spot about a hundred yards from the trading post. There, beneath a tall pine, he watched the man bury a bag of gold. How many other bags of unreported gold had Jim buried?

As Banyon shuffled to the rear to roll out a barrel of flour, Greeley, his head hung low, approached Daniel's table. As if they were old drinking buddies, the burly man clapped Daniel's shoulder. "Well, Cipher, guess you heard Banyon mouth off about skimmin' from the top."

Cipher. He hated the nickname. When Greeley first came to work for Jim, he asked Daniel what he did. When he said he kept Jim's books, Greeley asked, "Like cipherin'?" Since then, the name had stuck.

Greeley leaned down, his stale breath too close for comfort. "Fact is, we were about to cut you in on our little scheme. We know Savage hasn't been fair with you neither. Won't even give you money to pay for information 'bout your parents' deaths. All the while, he's makin' hand over fist with those Injuns who dig for him. Why, them Yokuts practically worship the ground he walks on. But he only gives 'em pennies on the dollar in trade for blankets and trinkets."

Banyon reappeared with the flour barrel.

Greeley pulled Daniel even closer. "Just think about it, Cipher. That's all I ask."

Shaken, Daniel stepped outside, inhaled the crisp autumn air, and considered Greeley's offer. Like the clerks, he also argued with Jim about money. After he and Long-Haired Brown returned from San José, he'd told Jim about Brody's demand of $800 in exchange for information about his parents' deaths. When he asked for an advance on the money Jim had promised him when he turned eighteen, his guardian just laughed.

"If I give you $800 to pay Brody, that ol' weasel will simply up his price. Can't you see? He's just an old drunk, lookin' to make money off another man's sorrow."

Were Greeley and Banyon really stealing from Jim? Didn't the greedy man owe his employees more than he paid them? Didn't *he* deserve more than Jim paid him?

No. That's not how he was raised. Like he'd heard his pastor in Illinois preach, *two wrongs do not make a right.*

Five days passed. Daniel kept quiet about Banyon and Greeley stealing money from Jim. But he also didn't give Greeley an answer about joining up with them.

Later that week, Jim reviewed the store's inventory with Daniel and his two clerks. It had been three months since Daniel's trek to San José, and it was time to restock.

After Daniel jotted down the next item Jim called out, he paused and tapped his pencil on the paper. His insides twisted as his guilty conscience got the best of him. After they finished the inventory, he'd tell Jim the truth about his workers.

"And don't forget to pick up about twenty bars of soap," Jim called out as he inspected an empty upper shelf. "I don't condone it, but with all the brothels springing up 'round here, more men are goin' down the line." Turning to Greeley and Banyon, Jim pursed his lips and gave them a you-know-what-I-mean smile. "I hear the fancy girls give preference to the better smellin' miners."

Heat flamed Daniel's cheeks. He glanced away as he added twenty bars of soap to the supply list.

As if he could read, Jim snatched the sheet from Daniel and gave it a once-over. Appearing satisfied, he handed it back. "You and Long-Haired Brown'll leave tomorrow for San José. And don't bother askin' me again for that advance, son. I've got no money to spare. Like I said, that Brody is just out to swindle ya."

Daniel glanced at Greeley.

The man nodded his huge head, as if to say, *I told you so.*

Daniel's insides boiled. Jim *did* have money to spare. He'd seen him bury it. If he never got the $800 to pay Brody, would he ever find out the truth about his parents' deaths? Maybe two wrongs *did* make a right. Jim was the thief, not them. Yes, he and the clerks deserved their fair share.

Once Jim left, Daniel turned to Greeley and Banyon. "Okay. From now on, I want fifty percent of everything you two skim off the top."

Greeley opened his mouth as if to protest.

Daniel raised a hand to end further discussion. "Fifty percent. Take it or leave it. Since I do the books, I'll know if you cheat me. If you don't like my terms, I'll tell Jim I discovered you've been stealing from him for the past two months."

He had them over a barrel. A barrel he could easily roll over both of them. The pinched lines that appeared around the clerks' eyes and mouths showed they knew it too.

"And," he added, "I expect $200 from each of you before I leave tomorrow. I'll accept that as payment for the monies you stole before I found out about your scheme."

Later that night, after Jim retired to his tent, Daniel carried a lantern and a shovel to a pine tree near the edge of camp. He dug up Jim's hidden stash and removed about twenty ounces of gold. The greedy man would never miss it.

8
HIDDEN MESSAGES

September 28, 1849
Pueblo de San José

On the trip to San José, Daniel struggled to silence his conscience. *Why do I feel like I've done something wrong?*

No, he reasoned. Jim Savage's arrogance, greed, dishonesty—those were the guilty parties. Jim's workers deserved better pay. His Indians deserved better treatment. And with the profits his guardian raked in, *he* certainly deserved an advance on the monies coming to him when he turned eighteen. Thanks to the $400 in gold he gleaned from the clerks and the twenty ounces of gold he'd taken from Jim's stash, he now had enough money to pay Brody for the clues about his parents' deaths.

"It's a pleasure to see you again, Daniel," Mr. Reed greeted him at the doorway once they arrived in San José. "Won't you come in?"

Daniel removed his felt hat and twisted it between his hands. "If it's all the same, sir, we've had a long ride. I'd like to clean up first. May we camp out on your property again?"

"Of course. You are always welcome here. And please, we would love to have you and Long-Haired Brown join us for supper."

As before, Brown declined the dinner invitation when Daniel relayed the message.

"If it's all the same to you, I'll just fix me a quick bite out here and turn in early."

"Suit yourself," Daniel said. "But I'm never one to turn down a home-cooked meal."

Brown laughed. "Is it the meal or the company ya don't wanna turn down?"

Daniel grinned. Brown wasn't much for talking, but on their previous visit, he'd whistled when Daniel showed him the cross he'd purchased for Virginia.

Daniel washed, shaved, and put on his best clean clothes. He made sure to slip the diamond-studded necklace into his pocket. The necklace. He'd first bought it on a whim as a sign of friendship. Now, he wanted it to convey much more. Unsure of how to put his growing feelings into words, he hoped they'd come once she accepted his gift.

Daniel salivated at the meal set before him—ham, potatoes, carrots, homemade jam, and bread. The only thing missing was Virginia.

Mrs. Reed passed him a basket of bread. "I'm sorry Virginia couldn't join us for supper." She glanced at the empty chair. "She's had the flu for three days. I didn't want to risk exposing you and Long-Haired Brown to it."

The flu. Hadn't Virginia's real father died from cholera? What if she had more than just the flu? He'd already lost so much. He couldn't lose her too. He wasn't hungry anymore. Without taking a slice, he passed the bread to Virginia's younger sister.

"Daniel, aren't you feeling well?" Patty took the basket from him and added a piece of bread to her dinner plate. "You never pass up Ma's homemade bread."

"I think he looks sick," six-year-old Thomas said.

Mrs. Reed leaned forward. "Thomas, that's not polite. You should apologize to Daniel."

Thomas widened his eyes. "I'm sorry you look sick, Daniel."

Eight-year-old James Jr. giggled. "I think he looks sick too. Love sick."

"Now boys," Mr. Reed broke in. "Daniel is just concerned about Virginia." He glanced at Daniel, a slight tug pulling at the corners of his mouth behind his beard and mustache. "It's just a mild flu, son. Nothing to worry about. Actually, she's much better today. Mother just likes to be careful."

Mmm. The savory sweet flavor of freshly cooked carrots. Daniel chewed slowly, their earthy taste tantalizing his tongue. In between forkfuls of potatoes, he stole discreet glances at Mr. and Mrs. Reed. The way they leaned in to listen to a child's comment. The way Mr. Reed narrowed his eyes, but slightly grinned at little James when the boy poked Patty's arm, then feigned innocence. A tender ache squeezed Daniel's heart. Memories of dinner around his own family's table now formed only ragged fragments in his mind.

After supper, Virginia's father ushered Daniel into the parlor and pointed to a stack of books on the low mahogany table. "As promised on your last visit, I spoke with my lawyer friends about the possibility of you pursuing a law career. They were more than happy to loan you these materials to get you started. They suggest you take copious notes of anything you might not understand. They've agreed to meet with you on your next visit to discuss any questions you might have."

Unable to speak his thanks, Daniel nodded. A warmth flooded him. Perhaps this career path could become a reality. "I don't know how to thank you, Mr. Reed." His throat constricted as he tried to swallow a lump that had suddenly formed.

Blinking hard, Daniel gathered his books and turned to leave, then stopped short. He returned the books to the table, thrust a hand into his trousers pocket, and clutched the necklace.

A bead a sweat ticked the back of his neck. *It's now or never.*

"I do have a question now, sir," Daniel blurted out.

"Of course, by all means." Mr. Reed motioned for Daniel to take a seat in the gold-tufted armchair as he positioned himself on the matching brocade couch.

Daniel glanced at the chair, shook his head, and withdrew the necklace. In two quick steps, he strode to the couch and placed the jewelry in Mr. Reed's hands. "Sir, I'd like to give this to Virginia when I see her. I thought about what you said the last time I visited. About you and Mrs. Reed welcoming my interest in your daughter. I want to tell you that, well—" He stumbled, searching for the right words. "That I'm very interested."

Virginia's father turned the necklace and cross over in his hands.

"Turquoise and diamonds." His brows lifted, and he slowly nodded. "Yes, I'd say you are very interested."

Daniel squeezed his toes inside his leather shoes and forced his rambling thoughts to formulate words. "I–I guess I'm asking your permission to—to ask her to marry me."

Mr. Reed pulled in a deep breath, rose from the couch and handed the necklace back to Daniel. "Yes, son." He shook Daniel's hand. "You have my permission."

The following morning, Daniel rode out alone to Mr. Campbell's mill and placed his order for flour. Thoughts of Virginia filled his mind. His pulse raced and his insides quivered as he imagined how he might propose.

Later that afternoon, he and Long-Haired Brown drove the wagon into town and bought the items on Jim's supply list. Returning to the Reeds after sunset, he found a note inside his tent. He rummaged through his gear and grabbed the oil lamp. Struggling to control his shaking hand, he struck a match and lit the wick.

Dearest Daniel,

I am so sorry I couldn't join you for supper last night. I was quite fine, but Mother feared I might still be contagious. You know how overcautious she is. If you have time tomorrow, Mother says I can join you for a Sunday afternoon ride. I look forward to seeing you soon.

Your Friend,

Virginia

Daniel brushed his calloused thumb across the word, *Friend.*

Friends, yes. And after tomorrow, he hoped, much more than friends.

The next morning, to his delight, Virginia's parents gave him permission to spend the day with her as long as they returned by suppertime. Daniel explained his plans for them to ride out to the lumber mill where he would purchase the bottles from Mr. Brody. She told of her plans to picnic with him on the banks of the Guadalupe River. Agreeing they could do both, Mr. and Mrs. Reed walked them to the front door.

Before stepping outside, Virginia handed Daniel a bulging satchel.

"What's this?" he asked, hefting the heavy load.

"Our picnic lunch."

The early morning sun warmed Daniel's back as they headed toward the barn. "Feels like you've brought enough to feed an army." He paused and pumped his arm to sense the bag's weight. A muffled metal clank sounded from somewhere deep within the bag's folds. Raising a brow, Daniel shot her a quizzical look.

She flashed back a dimpled grin—the one that had always melted his heart.

"I like to come prepared."

The smell of manure, leather, and fermented feed tickled his nose as they entered the barn's shadowed space.

Virginia fastened her bonnet more securely on her head, picked up a brush, and groomed loose hairs from her mare's back. "So you really plan to pay that man whatever he asks for those whiskey bottles?"

Helping Virginia saddle her horse, Daniel secured the bulky lunch satchel to the back of it. "We settled on an amount the last time I visited. It's an outrageous price, but it'll be worth it to find out who murdered Ma and Pa." He cinched the satchel's leather ties tighter than necessary.

"I figured as much," she said, adjusting her stirrups. "That's why I came prepared."

Pulling his brows together, he studied the Cheshire grin that played on her lips. "Care to elaborate?"

With the corner of her lips still upturned, she glanced at her picnic bag and shrugged. "No."

Back in the gold fields, fall had hit with full force. Here in the valley of Pueblo de San José, however, the warm September sun shone as if it were still mid-spring.

Riding western style, Virginia rode in rhythm with her horse. The way she cantered alongside him in her blue and white cotton plaid dress and blue shawl reminded him of their free-spirited days on the wagon train.

Travelling across the Oregon Trail, he recalled how, in the early morning hours Virginia often rode with her father ahead of the wagon train. It was Mr. Reed's job to scout out a safe place for the group to camp at night. Returning by late afternoon, Virginia and his stepsister Hannah would walk alongside the wagons, picking flowers or wild berries. That was before the Reeds left the wagon train to join the Donners on a supposed shortcut trail.

Those days seemed a lifetime ago.

Reaching Jones' lumber mill by late morning, they found it quiet. No steam-powered saws buzzed in the background. No harnesses jangled near the corral. No drivers shouted to their oxen.

Dismounting, Daniel helped Virginia from her mare. He then grasped the horses' reins, led them over a worn wooden bridge, and down an oak-lined path to Brody's mud-brick house. As they approached, Daniel spotted the lumberjack behind his adobe. The muscled man leaned over a wooden washtub scrubbing a red shirt on a grooved washboard. Apparently, Sunday was wash day.

Dressed in sweat-stained long underwear that had obviously yet to be washed, Brody greeted them with a wide, yellow-toothed smile. "Mighty glad to see ya, Whitcomb."

Daniel tied the horses' leads to a nearby branch, removed one of his saddlebags, and flung it over his shoulder. "I'm ready to pay your price."

"Thought you'd come to see things my way. Why don't we step inside?"

As the trio tromped to the doorway, Brody shot Virginia a sideways glance. "And who's this fetchin' girl?"

Virginia nodded curtly. "Miss Virginia Reed. You might remember me from our overland trek from Illinois. I was with the Donner-Reed party."

Brody stopped in his tracks and surveyed her from head to foot. "Then you was one of the lucky ones. I heered most of them folks died in the Nevada mountains. Been told some survived, 'cause they ate the weak ones. That how you made it through?"

"Brody," Daniel roared as he stepped between Virginia and the lumberjack. "How dare you speak to a lady like that." The veins in his neck pulsed. "I've a good mind to—"

Just as Daniel pulled back his arm to sock the man, Virginia gripped his shoulder.

He wished she hadn't. He really wanted to punch the brute in the face.

"No, Mr. Brody." Her voice came soft and even. "That's not how I survived. It's only by the grace of God that I'm alive. If it weren't for prayer, I would've perished with the others." She lifted her chin.

Daniel's tense muscles quivered, but he lowered his arm.

"Now, if you gentlemen don't mind," Virginia added, "I think I will stay outside and enjoy the sun while you two conduct your business." She turned and strode back toward the horses.

Growling beneath his breath, Daniel dug his fingers into the leather pouch draped over his shoulder and followed Brody inside. He still wanted to clobber the man.

"So, you've got the $900?" Brody asked once they sat.

Daniel dropped his bag onto the table with a thud and gritted his teeth. "You demanded $800, and that's exactly what you'll get. Take it or leave it."

A stony silence surrounded their visual showdown.

"Well, I reckon it's done to a turn." The broad-shouldered lumberjack slapped the table. "Eight hundred dollars. Them bottles is all I got to remember my boys by, but whiskey bottles don't pay the bills. I'll take it."

Opening his saddlebag, Daniel withdrew a small leather pouch.

Brody's eyes pinched. "How do I know you ain't cheatin' me?"

Still resisting the urge to wallop the man, Daniel withdrew a small scale from his bag. "I figured you'd say that. Weigh it yourself. Gold is worth $20 an ounce. That means I owe you 40 ounces."

Brody scratched his stubble. "Guess I'll take your word for it." He reached for the gold.

"Not so fast." Daniel yanked back the pouch. "Let's see the bottles."

The lumberjack scowled and moved to a wooden chest in the corner. After pulling out four bottles, he returned to the table. "Nice doin' business with ya." With a clink, he set the glass bottles on the table.

Virginia poked her head inside. "Have you gentlemen finished?"

Turning his head, Brody nodded. "That we have, missy."

She entered the dimly lit room and placed a folded woolen blanket on the table. "I thought we might wrap the bottles in this for safekeeping."

Daniel shot her an I'm-so-glad-you're-here smile. As he'd experienced on the trail, Virginia always thought ahead.

After completing their business with Brody, they steered their horses away from the lumber mill and trotted toward the banks of the Guadalupe River. Along the way they laughed over memories almost forgotten and discussed dreams yet unborn. They spoke of California soon becoming a state and marveled over the explosive growth of their young nation.

During quiet moments, Daniel pondered what he'd do when they reached the river. Should he give Virginia the necklace and propose while they ate lunch? Should he wait until after the meal? What if she said no?

His brain whirred faster as he thought about the whiskey bottles. What clue might be hidden under one of those labels? What if Brody had swindled him? What if there was no message? That thought made his blood boil. Lifting his hands forward to provide a little slack on the reins, he squeezed the calf of his outside leg, prompting his horse into a lope.

"In a hurry for lunch, Mr. Whitcomb?" Virginia gave her horse a cluck and a command to canter to match Daniel's stride.

By the time they reached the river, Daniel's attention had shifted from his shredded emotions to his rumbling stomach. "I'm glad you packed a large lunch." He fastened the horses' reins to a low hanging willow branch. "I'm starved."

As soon as the words tumbled from his mouth, Daniel's stomach clenched. What did he know about starvation? He stole a glance at Virginia.

If she had taken offense at his insensitive choice of words, her expression didn't show it. Dismounting, she stood on tiptoes and loosened the picnic satchel from the back of her horse.

Reaching over her from behind, he untied the last of the bag's leather-corded strands. Before he lifted the bag from the horse, she laid a hand on his arm.

"Wait." She opened the pack. Pulling out a copper pot and several dish towels, she handed him the items.

Grasping the pot in one hand and the towels in the other, he cocked his head to the side. "Do you plan to cook and wash dishes out here?"

She raised her head and laughed. "No. Don't worry. Lunch is all prepared." She paused and stared into his eyes.

He leaned closer. How he ached to brush her lips with his.

Pressing a hand to his chest, she giggled.

Did she feel as nervous as he did?

"Ahh, to answer your question, no, I don't plan to cook out here." She hesitated. "And I don't plan to wash dishes." Her voice came soft. "But I do need some hot water. While I assemble our lunch, would you please fetch wood and build a fire?"

He raised an eyebrow. "We don't need a fire. It's a warm day, and we'll be back before sundown."

I certainly feel hot enough, he mused. He studied her lips again, then glanced at her hand pressed against his chest. A hand that kept him at arm's length. "Besides," he shrugged. "I didn't bring any matches."

"Lucky for you, I did." She turned toward her horse. Hoisting the lunch satchel from the horse's back, she made a beeline to a grassy area near the riverbank.

"I can carry that," he offered.

She seemed in too much of a hurry to respond.

He followed along behind, toting the pot and dish towels.

Kneeling next to the bag, she rummaged through it, handed him a small tin matchbox, then withdrew a white apron.

As she prepared lunch, he gathered kindling and built a fire near the water's edge. When her back was turned, he moved to the horses and pulled out the black velvet box from his saddlebag. Yes. He'd give her the turquoise- and diamond-studded cross after lunch. His heart raced as he slipped the box into his pocket. *And then I'll—*

"Daniel," she disrupted his thoughts. "Would you please fill the pot with water and set it on to boil?"

He turned and gazed at her, allowing his eyes to roam her golden curls. The perfection of her petite figure. Her fluid movements as she spread a white tablecloth atop a blanket she'd spread out on the grass.

A white tablecloth for lunch. Just as Virginia's mother had done during their midday stops on the prairie. He shook his head and fetched the pot. Filling it with water from the river, he pulled in a full breath of the crisp fall air. Someday he'd have a wife and family of his own.

After setting the pot on stones he had arranged in the fire, he returned to Virginia. She had set out slices of ham, cheese, bread, fruit, and canning jars filled with milk. He fingered the velvet box in his pocket.

The meal satisfied his hunger but heightened his senses. He leaned on an elbow and watched as she chewed the last of her apple. He ached to take her in his arms. Kiss those full lips. Hold her and never let go.

She tossed her apple core aside and dabbed her moist mouth with a cloth napkin. "And now, Daniel, aren't you curious about the secret hidden beneath one of those labels?"

As if she'd doused him with a bucket of cold water, he bolted upright. "Of course, I'm curious." His thoughts raced like two squirrels chasing each other up a tree. He didn't want to tear himself from visions of her embrace—of grasping her hand and proposing marriage. But he *did* want to know what secrets the bottles might reveal.

"We should wait until we get back to the house," he finally said. "We have to remove the labels carefully so we don't destroy whatever's underneath."

"That's why I brought the pot." Her half-smile reached her eyes. "I figured you'd want to uncover the message as soon as possible. Why don't you get the bottles and take them over to the fire? The water should be hot enough by now."

Shrugging, he stood. "What do you have in mind?"

Still sitting, she reached out and picked up a tin funnel, then grasped their now empty milk jars. "You'll see."

He couldn't resist. Her lavender fragrance drew him even closer. Perhaps it wasn't proper, but he couldn't help himself. He leaned down and kissed those delicious lips. To his delight, she didn't pull away.

She emptied her hands and wrapped her arms around him as he sunk to his knees.

His eyes closed. Time stopped. All heaviness lifted. He drew her in, fully embracing her and the moment.

She finally pulled away and took in a few short gasps of air. Her chest rose as she inhaled deeply. Her mouth curved up.

He moved in for another kiss. Another embrace.

As before, she pressed a hand to his chest. "I think," she whispered, "we should check the water."

He pursed his lips into a pout. "Yes. I suppose it's hot enough by now."

She giggled. "Yes, I suppose it is."

He stood and extended his hand to help her up.

Instead of taking his hand, she passed him the glass jars.

"What do we need these for?"

"You'll see." She picked up the funnel and towels, then stood.

After they reached the campfire, she asked him to fetch the whiskey bottles from his saddlebag.

When he returned, she withdrew a corkscrew from her apron pocket.

He arched a brow. "What's the plan?"

"I figured it might damage the hidden message if we tried to pull the labels off with a knife. However, if we empty the bottles and fill them with hot water, it might loosen up whatever sticky substance the boys used to reattach their secret note."

He refocused his thoughts from her kisses to his main mission. The box in his pocket would have to wait. With a quickening pulse, he dared to believe he might finally discover the truth about his parents' deaths. He set the bottles on the ground.

She handed him the corkscrew and placed her hands on her hips. "You didn't tell me how much you paid for the bottles, but having met Brody, I'm sure they came at a high price. Perhaps you might want to save some of the whiskey from these bottles for future use. After you're eighteen, of course. That's what the empty jars are for."

He wagged his eyebrows and smiled. "Eighteen? Haven't you heard? In the gold fields, the legal drinking age is sixteen, and I turned seventeen two months ago."

Her mouth fell open. "Daniel Whitcomb, don't you dare. If Pa smells alcohol on your breath when we get home, he may never let me see you again."

"I'm just teasing." He held up a hand. "I can't even stand the smell of that poison. But you're right. We shouldn't let it go to waste. If we empty the whiskey into the jars, we can pour it back into the bottles when we're done and recork them. Maybe I could sell them to some poor prospector who needs to dull his senses."

He twisted the corkscrew into one of the corked bottles and wriggled out the stopper.

Virginia rinsed out the milk jars and held the funnel over one of them.

He slowly filled the glass container with the amber fluid.

She handed him the funnel and two cloths, then used another towel to retrieve the pot from the fire. "Wrap one cloth around the funnel, and another around the empty bottle," she instructed. "Hold the bottle with the cloth and place the wrapped funnel on top of it. I'll pour hot water into the funnel, and we'll see if my plan works."

They both squatted on the ground. He held the bottle and funnel while she poured. After she filled the bottle with hot water, she took a butter knife from her apron pocket and handed it to him. "Let's give the adhesive a minute to soften. Then see if you can pull back a corner of the label with the knife."

He waited, then gently slipped the knife between the bottle and the Overholt label. The paper remained firmly attached.

Picking up the warm pot, she pressed it against the label.

He met her hopeful gaze.

They waited several more seconds.

He tried again. The paper began to peel.

She laid one of the towels on the ground.

The paper came off in one sheet. With slow movements, he spread the curved label onto the dishcloth. A childish scrawl appeared on the back.

We were hired to scare em, not kill em. Not our fault. Dropped burnin branches down chimney. Closed it off. Just smoke em out. Make em stop helpen slaves.

He struggled to inhale but felt as if he'd swallowed a stone. *That's it?* Too many unanswered questions. If the Brody brothers played a part in his parents' deaths, who hired them? Their names weren't even on the note. Nothing here to incriminate anyone. Like a bubbling pot of water, his frustration churned and boiled over. He stood and screamed. He gritted his teeth and flung the water-filled whiskey bottle into the river.

Virginia stood and grabbed his shaking hand. "Daniel."

Her quiet voice did little to quell his rage.

She held him with a stare. "Who said there's just one message? See how this handwriting fills up the entire space? Perhaps it's only part of a bigger message. What if there is more written under the other labels? We should check all the bottles."

He wanted to believe her, but his hopes felt as smashed as a prairie dog squashed by wagon wheels.

She lifted her head and kissed his lips. "It won't hurt to try."

Her bold display of affection buoyed his flagging faith. He nodded and reached for the second bottle.

They squatted once again and repeated the process with the remaining three containers. All revealed hidden messages. They carried the loosened papers to the tablecloth and spread them out, arranging and rearranging them until they appeared to make sense.

Pa and us worked for Sean Flannery doin odd jobs. Pa always drunk. Flannery offered big money. $300 each. Said pay way to California too. New life. Took us to Whitcomb home. Brought bottles of whiskey. We drank some.

We were hired to scare em, not kill em. Not our fault. Dropped burnin branches down chimney. Closed it off. Just smoke em out. Make em stop helpen slaves.

Burned twigs and branches under windows. Flannery opened front door. Poured whiskey on chairs. We lit em up and tried to run. He threatened to lay blame on Pa. Forced us to stay.

Flannery poured out more whiskey. Heard Whitcombs coughing upstairs. Flannery lit more matches. Tossed em on spilled whiskey. We ran. Never meant to kill. Why they help slaves? Why Flannery care? So sorry. But sorry won't bring em back.
Josiah Brody
Matthew Brody
October 25, 1846

Daniel's knees buckled. He thought learning the truth about his parents' deaths would relieve his grief. It didn't. The harder he tried to restrain his tears, the more they flowed until they swelled into a stream. His nose ran. He gasped to suck in air that refused to reach his lungs. Letting his head drop to his knees, he covered his damp face with his hands. His shaking sobs grew into groans.

Virginia rubbed his back, but he couldn't stop the flood. He had no idea how long he knelt there, but he didn't care. Exhausted, the deluge slowly ebbed. Finally, it stopped. Still kneeling, he glanced up at her.

She handed him a towel.

As he wiped his face and blew his nose, he heard her do the same.

Like a wrung-out dishrag, he felt totally spent. But a sense of relief also washed over him. While travelling the Oregon and California trails, he'd bottled up his grief over his parents' deaths for Hannah's sake. After Hannah died, he allowed his raw emotions to callous over. Now, although sadness raked his soul as he released the grief, it also ushered in a sense that he was finally free to love again.

As he and Virginia rode back in silence to the Reed's home, he mulled over the day's events. Together, they had discovered the meaning of the hidden messages. She had seen him in one of his weakest moments and yet remained by his side. But he hadn't proposed. He couldn't. Not yet.

For the first time, justice for his parents seemed within reach. The tavern keeper, Flannery, had paid the Brody brothers to start the fire, and then escalated the tragedy until it resulted in his parents' deaths. To prevent the truth from coming out, Flannery paid the Brodys' way to California. But why? What did Flannery gain from murdering his parents? Was he trying to stop them from helping runaway slaves? He needed more answers.

He resolved that, before returning to the gold fields, he'd post a letter to Paster Lovejoy back in Princeton Township.

Pastor Lovejoy knew he believed his parents' deaths were not an accident. Now he had proof. Maybe the good pastor could help him make sense of things. He would ask him to inform the sheriff about Josiah and Matthew's written confession, and Flannery's part in it all. Hopefully, then, the sheriff would continue the investigation. In the meantime, he'd hang on to the bottles' labels for safekeeping.

And before he went back to Big Oak Flat, he'd ask Virginia to marry him.

9

THE PROPOSAL

September 28, 1849
Pueblo de San José

During their thirty-minute ride from the Guadalupe River to the Reeds' home, Daniel tried to process the Brody brothers' confession. Once back at the ranch, however, his thoughts returned to Virginia.

After they entered the barn and unbridled their horses, Daniel removed the horses' saddles while Virginia watered and fed them. With supper still two hours away, they brushed down the animals and picked pebbles from their hooves.

Daniel enjoyed the comfortable silence that fell between them. Every few minutes he'd steal a look at Virginia, then slide his hand into the pocket that held the box.

As he worked on his gelding's last hoof, he recalled those tender moments by the river. The kiss. The embrace. The desire to never let go. If he didn't propose now, he might never get another chance.

But he wouldn't receive his inheritance from Jim for another year. Would she wait for him? Did he have what it took to become a lawyer? Would he fail at that like he'd failed to become a blacksmith?

"Daniel?" He glanced up at the sound of her sweet voice. She had completed her mare's grooming and now stepped to stand next to him. He released his horse's leg.

"Are you almost finished?" she asked.

Her doe-like eyes silenced his unanswered questions. He'd find a way to do it all. To be all she needed him to be. Glancing around the barn to make sure they were alone, he reached out and framed her face with his hands. "No. To answer your question, I don't think I'll ever be finished." He pressed his lips to hers and wrapped his arms around her.

She relaxed in his embrace and tugged him even closer as they continued to kiss.

Sweet honey. He closed his eyes. *Sheer bliss.* Finally, in need of air, he paused and brushed his lips from the tip of her nose to the top of her head, stopping to inhale the lavender fragrance of her hair.

Taking a step back, he reached into his pocket and pulled out the velvet-covered box. "I bought this for you on my last trip to San José, but I didn't get a chance to give it to you then." He placed it in her hand. "Now, more than ever, and with all my heart, I want you to have it."

With raised brows, she opened the gift. "Oh, Daniel!" She lifted the turquoise- and diamond-studded cross from the box, pressed its chain around her neck, and turned to let him fasten it.

His hands trembled, but he managed to secure the lock. He wrapped his arms around her waist, and drawing her close, let his head fall against hers. "Virginia Reed, will you marry me?"

She whirled to face him, fingering the cross that adorned her neck, her eyes wide, her lips parted.

Daniel held up a hand. "Wait. We're in a barn, of all places. I can't believe I just proposed to you in a barn."

The corner of her mouth turned up as she gave him a teasing grin. "Well, it's not the worst proposal I've ever received."

"What? Someone's already proposed to you?"

"Didn't I tell you?" Her eyes twinkled. "When a group of men rescued us from the Sierra snows, one of them, Edward Pyle, proposed to me on our way down the mountain. He was twenty-two. I was only thirteen, and literally starving to death. I'm sure I looked frightful, but I guess he was desperate. Of course, I said no."

Daniel stepped back and scratched his head. "You're right. That proposal is worse than mine. But still—a barn? What was I thinking?"

She circled her arms around his waist. "You were thinking that you loved me." She kissed his earlobe. "And you were thinking that I love you. And you are correct in thinking that, Mr. Whitcomb."

Leaning her head back, she trapped him with a stare. "Yes. I will marry you."

He let his forehead rest on hers for a quiet moment. As if the world had stopped spinning, everything stilled. He wanted this moment to last forever.

She slowly lifted her head and pressed her lips against his.

Taking her into his arms, he embraced her, softly at first. *She said yes.* If this was a dream, he didn't want to wake up. *She said yes!* He drew her closer, pressed his lips more firmly against her.

She finally pulled back, drew in a deep breath, and held him at arm's length. "I suppose," she almost whispered, "we should get ready for supper."

He frowned, then grinned. "I suppose."

Lightheaded, Daniel floated to his tent. Filling a basin with water from the nearby water pump, he washed up and changed. *Is this what it's like to be drunk? Then I guess I'm drunk with love.*

After taking his place at the supper table between Virginia's two younger brothers and sister, his breath caught at the sight of Virginia. She had changed into the well-fitted satin yellow dress she'd worn when he first visited the Reeds. Above its petite lace collar lay the cross necklace.

Mr. and Mrs. Reed glanced at his gift, then grinned at each other.

Should he announce his proposal during dinner? Would Virginia say something first?

"Pa," Virginia said. "Daniel and I were able to remove the labels from those whiskey bottles he bought from Mr. Brody."

Daniel released a sigh of relief. He'd dodged the proposal-discussion bullet. At least, for the moment. He explained about the messages beneath the labels, and how they incriminated the Brody brothers and Sean Flannery.

"And I would be more than happy to leave the three refilled whiskey bottles with you, sir," Daniel concluded.

Virginia's father shook his head. "I'm more of a brandy man, myself. But those confessions are quite a find, aren't they, son?

What will you do next? Do you think Mr. Flannery is still in Princeton Township?"

"I plan to get a letter off to my pastor back home, Reverend Lovejoy. I'll tell him about the Brody brothers' notes and have him contact the sheriff. I'll wait to see what they say."

Mr. Reed rubbed his bearded chin. "You might want to leave the evidence, those labels, with me. I can store them in my safe."

Daniel nodded. "Thank you, sir. That's a good idea."

Mr. Reed's attention shifted to his daughter. "My dear, is that a new piece of jewelry I see around your neck?"

Heat flamed Daniel's neck and face. He should've said something before now.

"Why yes, Father. It's a present from Daniel."

Although his insides quivered, Daniel filled his lungs with air, held his breath for a second, then stood. "Mr. and Mrs. Reed, I am pleased to announce that I have asked your daughter to marry me."

Virginia's two little brothers clapped their hands.

Thirteen-year-old Patty chuckled. "It's about time."

With his insides still trembling, he shot a glance at Mr. and Mrs. Reed. Their affirming grins uncoiled his knotted stomach.

James Jr. turned to Virginia. "Well, did you say yes?"

Virginia blushed. "I said yes."

After supper, Virginia's parents suggested she and Daniel retire to the parlor to share a last visit before he returned to Big Oak Flat the next morning. Aware that Mrs. Reed had taken her embroidery to the nearby sitting room, and Mr. Reed had retired to his study in the adjoining chamber, Daniel made sure he was on his best behavior. No more kissing tonight.

A warm fire flickered in the fireplace. A sweep of wind rattled the window and swirled leaves onto the porch, but seated next to Virginia on the gold brocade couch, a peace enveloped him.

She rested a hand on the couch in the space between them, fingering the outline of an embroidered flower. "I know it will be another year before you receive your inheritance from Mr. Savage." She shifted her gaze to study his eyes. "But after that, will you return to Illinois to find justice for your parents before coming back here to claim your bride?"

He turned to face her and ached to grace her upturned mouth with a kiss. Eyes so full of longing. So full of hope. He brushed her hand with his fingertips. "No. I don't plan to return to Illinois. By this time next year, I will make you Mrs. Daniel Whitcomb. And with the help of your father's friends, I will aspire to the title of Daniel Whitcomb, Esquire. Until I can practice law, I'll work in San José as a blacksmith to supplement Jim's inheritance." He squeezed her fingers. "I can hardly wait."

She placed her hand atop his. "So, your pastor friend, Pastor Lovejoy. You will have him convey the Brodys' confessions to officials back in your hometown?"

"Pastor Lovejoy's a trustworthy man. And he was a great friend to my family."

The fire crackled and sizzled. He turned at the sound. A portion of a log broke away and fell to the grate below.

He sighed as he continued to stare at the sparks. "We attended Pastor Lovejoy's Congregational church twice on Sunday and every Wednesday for prayer meetings. After my parents died, I had hoped he would adopt Hannah and me—even though he and his wife already had nine children. Pastor Lovejoy said he would have taken us in, but in Pa's will, Pa named Morgan Savage our legal guardian."

Blinking several times, he continued to stare at the fire. "Since we had no living relatives, I guess Pa figured I could still apprentice as a blacksmith with Morgan as our guardian—Morgan being Pa's business partner and all. I could finish my blacksmith apprenticeship and then earn a living for myself and Hannah. But Morgan decided to come West with his brother Jim and the rest of the Savage clan, so we had to leave Illinois."

"You mean Jim Savage isn't your legal guardian? His brother, Morgan, is?"

Daniel nodded. "Morgan was at first." Entranced by the flames, Daniel watched as another chunk of wood fell from a log. "Ma and Pa died in February of '46." He spoke in a monotone. "Two months later, the Savages all decided to emigrate to California. Morgan joined them, so Hannah and I had to go, too. We teamed up with Colonel Russell's group when we got to Missouri."

"That was before my family and the Donners joined your wagon train."

"Right." Daniel shifted his gaze to Virginia. "You linked up with us about a week later when we were camped on Indian Creek. Jim and his wife had their own wagon. Four of Jim's cousins and their families each had their own rigs, and Hannah and I rode in Morgan's schooner. Halfway across the prairie, Morgan took a fancy to Miss Frances Brisbin. Next thing we knew, he up and married her on the trail."

"I remember that. Ma and I baked pies for the party after the ceremony. But I didn't realize Morgan was your first guardian."

Daniel eyed the flames again, squinting as they suddenly brightened. "If you ask me, Morgan was never much of a guardian. On the trail, when I wasn't driving our oxen, I spent most of my time with Jim. He taught me how to hunt, skin buffalo, and make rope from sinew. I learned more survival skills from Jim than from both Pa and Morgan combined." His throat tightened at the memory. Morgan's abandonment of him and Hannah must have cut deeper than he thought. He found it hard to continue.

Virginia squeezed his hand.

He let his gaze meet hers and swallowed hard. He'd never been so vulnerable with anyone. Encouraged, he pressed on. "After Morgan and Miss Brisbin married, he told us he would travel with her, her pa, and all the Brisbin relatives to Oregon. Without even asking what we thought, he said Jim would take over as our custodian. I guess the new Mrs. Morgan Savage hadn't bargained for a marriage that included two children who weren't her own. So, Morgan moved all his stuff to the Brisbin's wagons and gave us full ownership of the schooner. Instead of going to Oregon with Morgan, we followed Jim and the rest of the Russell party to California."

"Just like us," she added, "that is, until we decided to take that supposed shortcut."

An awkward silence filled the room.

She pulled in a ragged breath. "I guess that's why I always thought Jim was your guardian." She shifted in her seat. "So, having attended a Congregational Church in Illinois, do you think you'll have any problem becoming a Catholic?"

He blinked and stared at her wide-eyed. "A Catholic?"

"Why, yes. Certainly, you remember." Furrows formed between her brows. "We spoke about it on the porch the first time you visited. I told you how I asked God to save me when we were trapped in the Sierra snows. I was near death but promised God I'd live to serve Him and become a Catholic if He saved us. The next day, a rescue party appeared."

Daniel shook his head. He remembered the night on the porch—the cookies, the lemonade, the temptation to kiss her. But he didn't recall her saying she promised God she'd become Catholic.

Offering him a confused gaze, she frowned. "Do you mean, no, you don't remember me telling you I planned to become a Catholic, or, no, you don't want to become a Catholic so we can marry?"

10
INDIAN WARS BEGIN

October 1849–February 1850
Big Oak Flat, California Gold Country

Yes, he'd become a Catholic if it meant holding Virginia in his arms forever. The thought of leaving her to go back to the gold fields tore him apart, but he was obliged to Jim. Only one more year. Once he turned eighteen, he'd receive five percent of his guardian's profits—more than enough to start a life with Virginia. He pictured the house he'd build her. Small, at first, then a larger one after his law practice started. He'd buy her fine clothes, attend balls, and discuss business and politics with the town's leaders.

Daniel's daydreaming ended abruptly, however, once he and Brown returned to the post. Big Oak Flat was on the verge of war.

"The man's body had arrows sticking out every which way," Banyon told Daniel and Brown as they unloaded their supplies. "Looked like every brave in the tribe had a go at him." Banyon dragged a barrel from the front of the wagon bed to a notched ramp at the back, then rolled it down to Daniel.

As they unloaded the supplies, Banyon explained what happened while they were gone. "This large Texan, name was Rose, started prospectin' an area close to this chief named Latario. The chief tried to ignore the man's invasion into his territory, but Rose killed more game than he could eat. Stirred up the chief and the braves worse than shakin' a hornet's nest. The tribe already didn't have enough to eat as it was."

Banyon paused to roll another barrel down the ramp. "Seems Rose would even taunt the braves, pretend he was gonna shoot them too, along with the deer or elk he'd hunt. Finally, it came to blows between Rose and the chief, and Rose ended up stabbin' Latario to death. Got them braves so riled up, they filled Rose's body with arrows."

As they lugged in the last of the supplies, Banyon finished his story. "Miners 'round those parts didn't bother to ask if Rose deserved what he got. Just took their own revenge. Stormed Latario's village and murdered as many braves and squaws as they could. After that, other tribes up and attacked our miners' camps. Fortunately, Jim intervened and made peace with the natives. Otherwise, we would've had an all-out Indian war."

Even though war had been averted, some vengeful miners still continued to shoot any Indian in sight. Two weeks after Daniel returned, Jim pulled up stakes and prepared to move fifty miles southwest.

"A deep gash in the mountains separates this new area from Big Oak Flat," Jim explained as he and Daniel loaded mining tools and canned goods onto pack mules. "Gold deposits have been found farther south along the Merced River. As soon as new prospectors hear 'bout it, they'll flood that new region. Like always, they'll need equipment and supplies. There's no trading post there, so we'll be able to charge premium prices for goods."

Once they reached the Merced River, Jim set up two trading posts. He hired an old friend, a Californio named Don Antonio Lugo, to run a post on the Merced River at Horseshoe Bend. Californios, descendants of early Spanish settlers, knew the Spanish language. As Jim explained it, many of the Indians learned Spanish from decades of trading with them. Others learned it while living with the padres at the missions. However they learned the language, it was good business to hire a Spanish-speaking clerk.

Jim also established a post fifty miles east of Horseshoe Bend on the south fork of the Merced River—the first they'd ever built with logs.

Chopping down trees, sawing off branches, and notching trunks into place made for long, backbreaking days, but Daniel enjoyed the physical labor. He'd forgotten how much he liked working with his hands. Before long, he'd helped them build not only a trading post, but also a crude cabin to house the men, another for the female Indian cooks, and one for Jim and his wives—all before the heavy November rains.

One wet evening, Daniel, along with several of Jim's workers, huddled near the wood stove Jim had recently purchased for the trading post. Many wore hats and woolen coats as they played cards, read newspapers, or wrote letters home to loved ones.

Daniel hunched over one of the law books he'd spread on a back table and tugged the corners of his buffalo blanket more firmly around his shoulders.

"May you and I speak?" A soft voice interrupted his thoughts.

Limik, cocooned in a gray woolen blanket, stood beside him.

"Of course." Daniel huffed on his chilled fingers. "I've been at this too long and could use a break. What can I help you with?"

Rolling her lips inward, Limik glanced at his open book and pages of scrawled notes. "Why you bend your head over these writings when many others go to sleep?"

"I'm reading these books and taking notes because I hope to become a lawyer someday."

Limik squeezed her dark brows together. "What this mean, lawyer?"

Not quite sure how to answer, he drew a hand across his face. "A lawyer is someone who helps people get justice."

She knit her brows again. "Justice?"

Daniel jut his jaw forward and searched his mind for an explanation. "Justice means fair. Helping people get what they deserve, what's fair and right."

Limik shifted her gaze to the floor and clasped her hands in front of her. "You learn how do this in book. You teach me read?"

Limik, like Jim's wives Homut and Eekino, cooked and did laundry for the men who lived and worked at Jim's Merced River Post. Daniel never considered the fact that these women couldn't read. What had prompted Limik's sudden interest?

With Limik standing in front of him, eyes to the floor, a thought came to him. Limik and the other Indians who worked for Jim would never rise above their servant status if they couldn't read or write. If he really wanted justice for all people, maybe helping Limik learn to read would be a start.

For the next several weeks as Daniel pored over his books or created reading lessons for Limik, he mulled over Jim's treatment of the Indians. In addition to Jim's five Indian wives, only two of which lived with the man on a daily basis, his guardian had over three hundred native helpers who dug gold for him. The prospecting Indians set up their own shelters near the post—usually cone-shaped frameworks made of branches covered with pieces of bark. They gladly brought *El Rey* Güero shiny yellow nuggets in return for goods they purchased at the post, and never questioned Jim's exchange rate.

Jim supplied his workers with a daily ration of food. He also told his clerks that, for an ounce of gold, the Indians could purchase either a can of oysters, five pounds of flour, or a pound of bacon. They could buy a shirt or a dress for five ounces of gold. A handful of dried apples or peaches could be had for an equal weight in gold dust.

Daniel knew, however, that those items were well below the value of the gold the natives recovered. Compared to most miners and traders, Jim was more than fair. And yet Jim also made an ungodly profit. He never gave his employees a raise, and he never offered Daniel another bonus.

The more Daniel turned things over in his mind, the more his conscience bothered him.

How is Jim's treatment of the Indians any different than the money Banyon and Greeley pay me to keep quiet about their scheme to steal from Jim? How can I claim I want justice for others, and yet extort money from the clerks and deceive Jim by reporting false balances in his bookkeeping?

On the other hand, without the gold he'd taken from Jim's secret stash and the money he'd gotten from Greeley and Banyon, he never would have uncovered the Brodys' confessions and clues about his parents' deaths. None of his arguments, however, righted his moral compass.

Since he now had to keep account ledgers for two trading posts, Jim refused to let Daniel make any more supply runs to San José.

"You're too valuable here," his guardian reasoned. "I'll send Banyon and Long-Haired Brown instead."

One afternoon, while reading *The Works of Daniel Webster*, he re-read a paragraph he'd already read three times, then jotted down a few notes.

*…*our *ancestors established their system of government on morality and religious sentiment. Moral habits, they believed, cannot safely be trusted on any other foundation than religious principle, nor any government be secure which is not supported by moral habits.*

Picking up his quill pen, he added a sentence to his notes. *If our country's system of government rests on morality, then it stands to reason that our citizens also need to base their lives on a system of morality.* His stomach churned. He didn't want to lose the extra income he'd been saving for the future. But if a government was not secure unless supported by moral habits, how could his future be secure if he financed it by blackmailing Greeley and Banyon, and deceiving Jim?

He pushed the book aside and sketched Virginia's image in the margin of his notes. Thoughts of her filled every waking moment. He had to find a way to get back to see her. But how could he do that if Jim didn't send him on any more supply runs?

Withdrawing one of Virginia's letters from his leather satchel, he opened it, probably for the 100th time. He pressed the parchment to his face and inhaled. Did it still hold any fragrance of her lavender scent? Not a trace. Unfolding its creased page, the worn top half tore away from the rest. Pressing the fragments together in his large hands, he skimmed it.

Virginia spoke of her recent trip to San Francisco, how she had purchased a fancy dress for an upcoming ball she would attend with her parents. Daniel's heart squeezed. *A ball she will attend without me.*

She spoke of her father's growing prominence in San José, and how he had influenced other citizens to secure a $34,000 note in order to lure California's first state legislature to meet in San José. If they held their first meeting there, it would strengthen the pueblo's bid for becoming the state's capital.

He put the letter aside and pulled out a sheet of blank paper to write her a return letter. He didn't know when Long-Haired Brown would make another trip to San José, but when he did, the letter would be ready for the man to deliver.

During the second week of December, a light snow covered the ground. With supplies running low, Jim sent Brown and Banyon on another supply run.

"The snow's only gonna get deeper if we wait any longer," Jim told the men. "Take the pack mules instead of the wagon to make sure you get through."

Daniel rushed to re-read all he'd written to Virginia before giving it to Brown.

Dearest Virginia,

I miss you. I don't know how I'll get through the next seven months without you, but, come July I'll turn eighteen, get my inheritance from Jim, and leave the gold fields to marry you.

The colder months here are slow, but that gives me more time to study the law books your father's friends loaned me. Long-Haired Brown is returning the ones I've finished. I'm also sending questions I have for your father's lawyer friends.

I must tell you, the prospectors' treatment of the Indians here gets worse every day. They think the natives are just ignorant savages. I suppose they figure this gives them the right to mistreat young girls and murder innocent braves any time they want. As more whites come in, the Indians retreat farther into the mountains.

But, as Jim always says, "You can't possess what you can't protect." It's a fact of life, especially in a lawless place like this. The natives are easily overpowered by the miners. Some Indians fight back, but they usually lose. I understand both sides, and it breaks my heart that I can't make it better.

I must admit, Jim works peacefully with the Indians, learns their languages, and marries into some of the tribes with the blessings of their chiefs. As far as I can tell, he doesn't take advantage of the women he marries. They are happy to live with him and serve him. His workers gladly dig up gold in exchange for supplies they need. Jim really seems to care for them and stands up to anyone who hurts them. They continue to call him their Blond King, El Rey Güero.

Although teaching Limik to read doesn't make up for the things the Indians have gone through, I figure at least I'm doing something. Waiting as patiently as I can until the day we can be together. Lovingly yours,
Daniel

Christmas and New Year's came and went without much notice. Most of the prospectors found lodging in nearby mining camp hotels, or waited out the cold months in Stockton, San José, or San Francisco. Jim closed the Horseshoe Bend store and housed those clerks at the Merced River trading post until more miners returned to the gold fields. Some of the trading post workers spent Christmas and New Year's in the saloons that had sprung up in Big Oak Flat. Others stayed at the Merced River Post and played lonesome songs on their harmonicas or penny whistles.

With extra time on his hands, Daniel threw himself into teaching Limik how to read and write. On Brown's last trip to San José, the man had returned with a generous gift from Mr. Reed—more paper and writing utensils so Daniel could write down his questions and make notes as he studied the lawyers' books. Having a bounty of writing materials, Daniel shared some with Limik.

"No. These I not take." Limik slid the sheaf of paper, ink bottle, and nib-tipped pen back across the table.

"Yes, you can." Daniel pushed them back. "You are my student, and you must practice writing all the words I've taught you. I have more paper and pens than I need. Besides, today, I'm going to have you make up your own sentences from the new words you've learned."

Limik's large brown eyes brightened. A smile tugged at her lips. "Sentences? That I can read and write by myself?"

"Yes." A shiver ran through him, and it wasn't from the cold. He was about to open up a whole new world for her.

"*¿Qué haces?*"

Daniel glanced up.

Don Antonio Lugo stood beside him—the Californio Jim had put in charge of the Horseshoe Bend trading post. Lugo's head poked through the opening of his colorful, fringed sarape as he gazed down at Daniel.

In the short time Lugo had stayed with them at the Merced River Post, Daniel had grown to dislike the man. He was rude and insensitive. He shot Lugo a cold stare as he picked up the scent of whiskey on the man's breath.

Having learned a few Spanish phrases during his time in the gold fields, Daniel understood Lugo's question, *What are you doing*, but figured it wasn't any of the man's business. Even so, he shot back a curt reply. "I'm teaching Limik to read."

Lugo leaned closer. "*¿Por qué?*"

Daniel clenched his jaw. He also understood that question. "Why am I teaching her how to read? Because I want to."

"*Sí*, but I think it is a waste of time." The man finally slipped into his heavily accented English. "What will she do with it? It is not like she needs to read directions on how to cook, clean clothes, or to please a man, if you know what I mean." Lugo wriggled his eyebrows.

Daniel sprang from his chair, his pulse racing, and grabbed Lugo's sarape near his throat. After shaking the man, he released him with a shove. The Californio's gaucho hat tumbled to the floor.

Daniel narrowed his eyes and held the man with a stare. "I know exactly what you mean, Lugo, and I'll make myself just as clear. We treat everyone around here with respect. If you can't do that, you'll find my fist in your face."

Lugo picked up his hat, pausing to dust it off on his pantleg. "*Lo siento*," he said, turning to Limik. He pressed his hat onto his head. "I am sorry. I will not make that mistake again."

Lugo flashed dark eyes at Daniel, then turned and left.

Blowing out a breath, Daniel pulled out his chair and sat. His heart thumped against his ribs. Although taller and more muscular than Lugo, he wasn't sure he could beat the Californio in a fair fight. If the man even offered a fair fight.

"That man I do not like," Limik whispered.

"Neither do I."

"Why El Rey let him work for him?"

"Lugo and Jim were mining partners at Wood Creek, but the Californio didn't like digging for gold, so he asked Jim to give him a job at the trading post. When Jim opened the Horseshoe Bend store, he put Lugo in charge."

Fingering the paper Daniel had passed to her, Limik raised her eyes to Daniel. "Then why he not there? Now?"

Daniel winced. "He will once the weather warms up. There's not much business there right now. Jim doesn't really like Lugo either, but since he speaks both Spanish and English, Jim keeps him around."

"It true, many Indians speak Spanish. Some learn at padres' missions. Some learn from years of trading with Spanish and, how you say? Mek-hee-co's?"

"Mex-i-cans." Daniel sounded out the word for her.

Limik shook her head. "Too hard for me to say." She gathered the writing tools he'd given her. "Thank you, Dan'l."

He offered her a warm grin. Like the letter *x*, some Indians also found it hard to pronounce the *yell* sound in his name. Some Indians called him *Hijo del Rey*. He'd been told it meant *king's son*. He didn't like it, but it made sense. He much preferred Limik's *Dan'l*. It warmed his insides. Hannah had called him Dan'l.

"Thank you," Limik uttered again as she stood to leave. "It now late." She hesitated and glanced at the oil lamp on the table. "You walk me to cabin for women, yes? Tonight the moon, it give no light."

He picked up the lantern and nodded. "Yes, of course."

He walked her to her cabin, then held the lantern high enough to light the path to his own sleeping quarters. He thought about his encounter with Lugo. Tonight, he'd be sure to sleep with his pistol beneath his pillow.

When Brown returned from his supply run to San José, he gave Daniel several more law books from Mr. Reed, and a letter. To Daniel's disappointment, however, the letter wasn't from Virginia. It was from Pastor Lovejoy in Illinois. He settled into a chair near the post's potbellied stove to read it.

Dear Daniel,

I was delighted to receive your letter and learn the truth about your parents' deaths. I have passed the information on to the sheriff.

Unfortunately, Mr. Flannery is no longer residing in Princeton Township. Rumor has it that he now manages a hotel and saloon in San Francisco.

Even if Sean Flannery still lived in town, the sheriff said he couldn't take any action against him without the Brody brothers' written confession. He also said to let you know that, in addition to the written confession, he still needs some other form of corroborating evidence to make a strong case against the man.

This may not be the news you wanted to hear but take comfort in what the Lord tells us in St. Paul's letter to the Romans. "Dearly beloved, avenge not yourselves, but rather give place unto wrath: for it is written, 'Vengeance is mine; I will repay, saith the Lord.'"

That means, in the end, our God of justice will see to it that evil people are repaid for their evil deeds. I hope and pray you continue to find solace in God's Word, just as your parents taught you to do. It is a rich place of comfort, both in joyous as well as in perilous times.

As you will recall, my abolitionist brother was murdered by a pro-slavery mob when they burned down the building that housed his abolitionist press. I miss him every day, but I trust the Lord will ultimately work this out for His good.

I applaud your efforts to work toward a more just world as you study to become a lawyer. As you may recall, I also have a law degree. However, for the moment, the Lord has chosen to call me in a different direction.

I am also delighted to hear of your engagement to Miss Virginia Reed. I wish you all the best.

Your friend,

Pastor Lovejoy

After reading the pastor's letter, Daniel dragged his chair closer to the stove, hoping to warm his chilled hands as well as his cold heart. How could any good come from evil men murdering virtuous people? Evil men like Flannery who murdered his parents? White prospectors who massacred innocent Indians? Pro-slavery men who killed Pastor Lovejoy's brother? If God was a God of justice, He wasn't doing a very good job of dishing it out.

He glanced at the new law volumes on the table that waited to be opened. *If I want to see more justice, I need to keep my nose in those books, not the Bible.*

He pulled his chair back to the table and opened the next leather-bound book. He read two pages and tried to jot down a few notes, but after a few minutes, he couldn't remember a thing he'd read. His thoughts turned to Virginia as he chewed the tip of his pen. Why hadn't Brown brought back a letter from her?

Without summoning it, a tune entered his mind. He remembered his stepmother humming it while she worked around the house. As the uninvited melody tickled his memory, his stepmother's voice broke in, putting words to the tune. *What would I not give to wander where my old companions dwell? Absence makes the heart grow fonder…*

Those were the only lyrics he could recall. He hummed the melody and, over and over, the last six words. *Absence makes the heart grow fonder…* Surely, his absence from Virginia would only make the love they shared grow stronger. Wouldn't it?

The cold winter continued to keep miners away from the gold fields, and Jim continued to keep the Horseshoe Bend post closed. To Daniel's delight, Lugo spent the month of January in Stockton. By February 5, however, the Californio returned.

As Daniel finished his supper of beans and tortillas, he opened one of the law books he had placed on the table. Just as he began to read, Lugo strode in.

"Brought you the latest news." Lugo pushed a copy of the *Alta California* between Daniel and his book.

"Not interested." Without looking at either Lugo or the newspaper, Daniel shoved the man's hand aside.

"Ah, *amigo,* I think you will be very interested in this article." The Californio folded the paper in half, thrust it in front of Daniel, and tapped the headline with his forefinger.

Daniel's jaw clenched. He grabbed Lugo's wrist. "I'm not your friend."

"*Sí,* but just look." He continued to tap the article's title.

Daniel glanced at it. It read:

Virginia Reed Elopes!

11
YOSEMITES ATTACK

February 5–7, 1850
South Fork, Merced River Post, California Gold Country

Daniel's head spun. Maybe the chill inside the post had numbed his mind. No. It was right there in front of his face.

Virginia Reed Elopes!

Like the crack of a whip, those three words leapt off the page, lunged down his throat, and lacerated his heart. With a trembling hand, Daniel ripped the paper from Lugo's hand.

The man patted him on the back and laughed. "They say misery loves company, but, as you say, I am not your *amigo*, so I will bid you *adiós*."

With shaking hands, Daniel read the article.

Virginia Reed Elopes!

On Saturday, January 26, Virginia Reed, belle of San José and daughter of business entrepreneur James Reed, eloped with gold rush millionaire, John M. Murphy. A visiting clergyman, Chester S. Lyman, was asked to marry them, but refused, being informed that Miss Reed's parents violently opposed the union. Instead, they invoked the services of Lieutenant Governor John McDougal, who agreed to perform the ceremony.

The paper fell to the table as he grabbed his hair above his ears and tugged. As if submerged beneath swirling rapids, he couldn't suck in a breath. He couldn't tell if he was upside-down or right-side up. Then, shock gave way to reality. He didn't care if he breathed or not. He'd lost her. But how? Why?

He hauled in a gulp of air and slapped his hands on the table. She'd promised to wait for him. How could she do this?

A thought tickled his mind. Virginia wanted to marry a Catholic. John Murphy was Catholic. Maybe that's why she married Murphy. But that night in the parlor he had promised Virginia he'd convert. Did she doubt his sincerity?

Obviously, Murphy wasn't a very good Catholic. He was already married. Daniel had told her so on his first visit. Murphy was married to the daughter of a Miwok chief. Daniel pulled his thoughts back to that night. Were they on the porch when he told her that? No. Wait. He hadn't told her.

He beat his forehead with his fists. Why hadn't he told her? She once mentioned dancing with Murphy at a ball. He thought of telling her then about Murphy's alliance with the Miwok, but he'd held his tongue. He was afraid she'd think he was jealous, or worse, a liar. And now, he had lost her forever. He picked up the *Alta California* and continued to read.

> *The evening before the wedding, Miss Reed's father met Murphy in the street, whereupon Murphy informed Reed of his determination to marry his daughter and requested her father's consent.*
>
> *Witnesses heard Reed respond, "I will not give my consent. Furthermore, I will shoot you, should you attempt to marry my daughter."*
>
> *Murphy replied, "Sir, you may shoot me, but I shall not shoot you, and I shall marry your daughter. I give you fair warning."*
>
> *Murphy's friends stood guard outside as Lieutenant Governor John McDougal conducted the ceremony. Murphy feared Reed might get wind of their elopement and intervene. After exchanging vows, the couple mounted their waiting horses and fled. Reed appeared three minutes later, and not finding the couple, raced off with friends to the Murphy ranch, eighteen miles away. Alas, Murphy had out-generaled Reed from beginning to end. Unbeknownst to Reed, the couple found refuge at the mission, just three miles away.*

Daniel stood. A guttural growl formed in his throat. Escaping his lips, it morphed into a scream. He grabbed one of the law books from the table and pitched it across the room. He'd never been shot before, but surely it had to hurt less than the pain that now pierced his chest and collapsed his lungs. He'd also never drunk whiskey before, but he'd seen men use it to drown their sorrows. The Overholt bottles. He still had them. He stomped out of the post and rushed to the men's cabin.

The next morning his head throbbed. Every heartbeat pulsed waves of pain through his temples. As he sat on the edge of his cot, the world spun. An empty whiskey bottle lay at his feet. When he stood, last night's dinner rose in his throat and forced its way to his mouth. He ran outside, bent over, and retched. Again. And again.

He steadied himself on the outside wall of the men's cabin and staggered toward the trading post. *Coffee.* He'd seen it help others who suffered from drinking too much. Hopefully, it would work for him.

He stumbled into the post. Nearby, loud voices shouted in Spanish, increasing the streaks of pain that pierced his skull. Searching for the grating source, he spotted Lugo near the counter standing nose to nose with a swarthy Indian. The native, dressed in a multicolored sarape, pantaloons that reached his knees, and knee-high boots waved his arms and pointed toward the post's entrance.

Daniel didn't understand a single word the Indian said.

The Californio shouted something back.

Seconds later, the Indian raced out.

Daniel grasped his head with both hands to keep it from exploding. "What was that all about?" Without waiting for an answer, he staggered toward the coffee pot atop the pot-bellied stove.

Lugo stepped in front of Daniel. "Hurry. Get Savage." With widened eyes, Lugo grabbed Daniel's shoulders. "Juárez says Yosemites attacked the Miwok and Yokuts. This morning. In the foothills above us."

"What?" Confused, Daniel shook Lugo off and staggered toward the coffee.

"They burned their villages," Lugo seized Daniel's arm and spun him back around. "They murdered everyone in sight. Juárez says now the Yosemites are coming here."

Lugo's words sobered Daniel faster than any cup of coffee. No time to nurse his pain. He passed the news on to Jim, who immediately shouted orders.

Forming the men into teams, Jim ordered them to tote logs, shove boulders, and roll barrels of flour around the post's exposed perimeter to form a barricade. Jim then stationed his best shooters behind the hastily constructed fortresses. The rest he positioned inside the post. A score of Jim's Yokuts Indian workers, equipped with bows and arrows, volunteered to lay in wait in the forest surrounding the post.

Rushing to carry out his assigned task, Daniel gathered up sacks of ammo. With his M1819 Hall rifle slung over his shoulder, and his Colt Paterson shoved into his waistband, he delivered ammunition to those behind the barricades. He then slunk down next to Banyon, Greeley, and Taylor, a cousin of Long-Haired Brown, and worked to slow his ragged breathing. *How many of us will be left when this is over?*

The Yosemites' chilling war cries rang out, followed by a volley of arrows. Daniel loaded his rifle while the others poked their weapons through gaps between the logs, shooting at anything that moved. Rounds of gunfire popped. Acrid smoke filled the air. Natives within fifty feet of the fortresses fell in their tracks.

A whiz of air rushed past Daniel's ear.

A shriek rang out.

"I'm hit!" Greeley screamed.

Glancing behind him, Daniel gaped at the sight. An arrow had pierced Greeley's shoulder. Banyon propped up his friend in a corner of the barricade and pressed a red bandana against the wound to slow the bleeding.

Daniel turned his attention back to the battlefield. Eight Yosemites fell, downed more by arrows than bullets. Jim's Yokuts had joined the fray. The advancing Yosemites retreated behind trees and rocks.

Soon, a tall, feathered Yosemite about a hundred yards away emerged from between the rocks. He raised his bow and appeared to shout orders. Brown's cousin took aim with his Walker Revolver and fired. The Indian continued to shout and wave his arms.

With his world still spinning, Daniel forced his mind to focus.

The Yosemites crept closer. They were still out of range for the men's revolvers, but a bullet from his carbine caplock rifle would reach them.

The feathered brave and his followers slunk closer. The Indian paused to notch an arrow in his bow, then stood tall and pulled his arm back.

Daniel aimed his rifle over the top of the barricade and fired.

He missed.

The Yosemites charged.

Brown's cousin screamed. Daniel turned just as Taylor collapsed. Blood flowed from the young man's chest as he clawed at the arrow that now impaled him. With eyes still open, he stopped moving. He didn't move again.

Daniel's heart raced as he stared at the sight. It was his fault. How could he have missed? Another arrow whizzed by, grazing the top of Brown's hand.

With clenched teeth, Daniel reloaded his rifle and popped his head above their tiny enclosure. The tall brave motioned for more Yosemites to follow.

With his finger resting on the rifle's trigger, Daniel held his breath, drew a bead on the Indian, and fired.

Blam.

The native fell.

Several Indians raised their arms and yelled. The Yosemites pulled back. An eerie quiet settled over the battle scene.

Daniel reloaded his rifle and filled his pockets with ammo. "Banyon. Cover me. I'll move up behind those rocks and pick off the Indians behind that ridge."

Banyon nodded. Daniel moved out. A few arrows rained down, but none reached him. He scrambled over loose stones and hid behind the safety of an expansive boulder. From here he watched the Yosemites gesture to one another. A medium-built, muscular brave did most of the talking. Probably another leader. He took careful aim and fired. The Indian stood still for a few seconds, eyes wide, then crashed to the ground.

Just as he predicted, several braves crept toward his position. Once they came within fifty yards, the barricaded men fired their rounds.

Several Yosemites clutched their chests where bullets found their mark. Others stopped in their tracks when Yokuts arrows pierced their bodies. After another thirty minutes, the renegades disappeared into the woods. Jim waited an hour, then gathered the men back into the post.

Limik and the other women scurried to patch up the wounded.

Banyon thumped Daniel on the back. "I'll have you in my barricade any time, Whitcomb. Good shootin' out there."

Four men staggered in, carrying Taylor's limp body between them. "No. Not good." Daniel stared at Taylor's corpse. "Not good enough."

Long-Haired Brown, bandaging his bleeding hand at the table in the back, glanced up. He spotted the men transporting Taylor and wailed. "No." He ran to his cousin's side and cradled the youth's head in his hands. "I promised his ma I'd keep him safe."

It's all my fault. Daniel's nose and eyes burned. *If I hadn't tried to bury my sorrow in a bottle, his cousin would still be alive.*

Jim and Lugo scuffled in with a Yosemite between them, blood oozing from the brave's foot. Tying the Indian to a wooden chair, Jim called for Limik. "Dress this Yosemite's foot to stop the bleeding." He then called two other clerks over. "When Limik's finished, move this brave to the back room. We'll question him to find out what other plans the Yosemites might have for us. Limik, I want you to join us to act as interpreter."

Lugo cracked his knuckles. "Let me at him, Savage. Bet I can make him talk."

Jim shook his head. "I want you and Smith to check the perimeter. Make sure no renegades are hiding nearby. Take some of my Yokuts with you."

After Limik dressed the renegade's injury, she joined Jim and his other clerks as they moved the brave to the back room.

After an hour, the interrogators took a break for supper. As the Indian women served the men, Daniel asked Limik if they'd learned anything from the prisoner.

She frowned. "They beat Yosemite until he—how do you say?" As if mimicking the brave, she closed her eyes and let her head fall to the side.

"Passed out?"

Limik nodded. "Pass out. He say Yosemites not stop until they kill El Rey Güero and all who help him."

Once again, Jim's words ran through his mind. *You can't possess what you can't protect.* They had to take a stand against the Yosemites to protect their post, didn't they? Why had the Yosemites attacked them? As far as he knew, they weren't in Yosemite territory. They were in Yokuts territory.

Friendly Yokuts populated the area around the Merced River's south fork, and they had welcomed Jim's arrival with a feast. The man's reputation of protecting Indians from lawless white miners preceded their arrival, and the local natives had received them with open arms.

Lugo entered the post, interrupting Daniel's thoughts. Behind him, bound in ropes, he led a young squaw wrapped in a bearskin. He pulled the rope attached to her as if leading a horse.

"Savage," Lugo called to Jim. "Look what I found while surveying the perimeter." He yanked the rope's lead until the girl stumbled to the floor.

Jim clenched his jaw and crossed his arms. "I sent you out hours ago. Everyone else already reported in. How far out did you go?"

Lugo leered at the girl. "A bit further than the others. But, when I found this fetchin' young squaw, I spent some time, ah, questioning her."

Daniel rubbed the heel of his hand in a circular motion above his right brow. His head still pounded. He gazed at Lugo, and then the girl. Why did she look familiar?

He shifted his gaze back to Lugo. "Since when did you learn the Yosemite language?"

"I spoke well enough to get what I wanted."

The man's wide grin told him more than he wanted to know. Daniel's cheeks flamed hot.

The girl glanced up at Daniel, her large, brown eyes housed beneath red, puffy eyelids.

Now he remembered where he'd seen her. Totuya. The Yosemite chief's granddaughter. The girl he'd let go last April when Yosemites attacked them at Big Oak Flat.

Jim kept the two captured Yosemites tied up in the trading post and stationed guards to watch them throughout the night. He also had the injured men bed down inside the log post so the Indian women could tend to their wounds.

Daniel and Brown's guard shift started at 2 a.m., but, since he couldn't sleep, Daniel arrived early. Brown hadn't come in yet. The wounded lay in cots near the wood stove, and the natives were tied to chairs near the back wall.

Limik worked at the counter with a pestle and mortar. Apparently, the women also worked in shifts. She was the only one attending the injured men.

He strode over.

"What's in there?" He pointed to the large hollowed-out stone where she ground up a dry substance.

She continued to grind without glancing up. "I clean and wrap Greeley's wound, but he not sleep. I now grind dried poppy seeds, roots, and leaves. Make tea to bring sleep."

"You mean those yellow and gold flowers that pop up around here in the spring?"

She gave him a tired smile. "Yes."

"Last night I could have used a few cups of tea like that instead of—"

"Yes. I smell on breath in morning. Why? You say you never touch firewater."

"Believe me. I never will again."

Brown shuffled into the post and approached Daniel. It looked like he hadn't slept either. "Don't know why we need to guard them Injuns." He ran a hand over his tired face. "I think they've said all they're gonna say. Should just take 'em out and shoot 'em."

Limik's eyes widened. "I make Greeley tea to warm him." she glanced at Brown. "I make also for you?"

With a grunt, Brown nodded to Limik and strode over to the prisoners.

Limik ground up more poppy leaves and roots, but Daniel grasped her hand that held the pestle.

"What are you thinking?" he whispered. "You're going to give Brown the same tea you're giving Greeley?"

She lowered her head. "You once save Totuya. I not think wise. But Lugo do bad things to Totuya before he bring her here." She pinched her full lips together. "I see El Rey beat Yosemite until brave pass out. Now, Brown say he shoot them. In tea, I put more calm medicine so everyone sleep tonight."

"And that's all you want to do? Just calm Brown down a bit?"

Limik crushed the leaves harder and faster. "You say you want justice, Dan'l. You see justice today? I think I only see—what you call it? Revenge?"

Glancing around the dimly lit room, he counted seven wounded men lying on cots. He'd helped bury three more outside in shallow graves, including Brown's cousin. A knot formed in the pit of his stomach. "That was a war out there today, Limik. You don't see much justice in war. You just see killing on both sides. Both sides protecting what they think is theirs."

She lifted her head, allowing her gaze to meet his. "I not want be part of it."

"What are you saying?"

Tears formed in her eyes. "Not know. I cannot run away. Nowhere to go. I think El Rey answer to problems, but when he beat Yosemite today to make him talk, I—" More tears flowed, choking off her words.

A ruckus at the back of the trading post drew Daniel's attention. He whipped his Colt from his waistband.

"And this is for my cousin," he heard Brown shout, followed by the sound of flesh striking flesh.

Daniel laid his gun on the counter and hurried to Brown's side. As the burly man readied to punch the brave's already swollen face, Daniel grabbed the man's arm. "That won't bring Taylor back."

"No, but it'll make me feel better." Brown shoved Daniel aside.

"I have something over at my bunk that might make you feel better." Daniel offered.

Brown quirked a brow.

"But promise you'll wait until I get back before you do anything else." The man shrugged.

A few minutes later, Daniel returned with one of his Overholt bottles and two glasses. "I know we're on guard duty, but these two aren't going anywhere." He nodded in the direction of the bound prisoners. "Why don't we warm up with some of this? No reason we can't make ourselves comfortable until the next shift arrives."

Brown gave him a disarming smile. "I never knew you to drink, Whitcomb."

"Neither did I, until yesterday."

"Well, maybe just one or two drinks. Then I'll have some of the squaw's tea to keep me awake the rest of the night."

They sat at the table. Daniel poured and pretended to sip, but the smell made him gag.

Brown downed his whiskey in two gulps.

He refilled the man's glass.

Brown finished off his second round, but refused a third.

Daniel carried his still-filled glass over to Limik where she sat next to Greeley's cot, helping the wounded clerk sip her poppyseed drink.

Daniel bent down and whispered in her ear. "Do you have Brown's tea ready yet?"

Nodding, she pointed to the counter. "I make special one for him. It ready now."

Moving to the counter, Daniel added his whiskey to the tea, and offered it to Brown. Within minutes, the man fell asleep in his chair.

Waiting until the man began to snore, Daniel finally retrieved his pistol from the counter and motioned for Limik to follow him. He stepped over to the prisoners and gently woke Totuya.

As soon as the girl's eyes blinked open, Daniel covered her mouth while Limik gestured for her to keep silent. After doing the same with the warrior, Daniel pointed his gun at them while Limik cut their bonds.

The flickering light from the stove and nearby oil lamp gave the brave's bruised face a haunted look.

Still training his pistol on the Yosemites, Daniel whispered instructions to Limik. "Tell them to gag and bind us to the chairs. We'll say Totuya had a knife hidden away somewhere, and, when we weren't looking, she cut their ropes. They took us by surprise, tied us up, and escaped."

Nodding, Limik explained the plan to the Yosemites.

Daniel kept his right arm free, pointing his Colt at the Indian as he let the brave tie them up. Once the Yosemites crept out of the post, Daniel hid his Colt beneath his waistband and pretended both hands were bound behind his back.

12

MORE THREATS

February 7–March 14, 1850
South Fork, Merced River Post, California Gold Country

Daniel stomped his boots to ward off the chill inside the men's bunkhouse. He then picked up his fur-lined leather gloves from the wooden crate next to his cot and dragged them over his rough, calloused hands.

Brown shrugged on his woolen coat. "Sorry I fell asleep on our watch last night." A faint smile poked through Brown's beard. "Surprised Savage is only making us cut a cord of wood. Thought he'd lay extra chores on us for the whole week."

Daniel tugged his red woolen cap down over his ears. "It's okay. I don't mind the extra work." A twinge of guilt pricked his chest, but he was glad he had secretly drugged Brown. What would they have gained if they kept the Indians as prisoners? If he and Limik hadn't helped them escape, the Yosemites would probably have died a very painful death.

After two hours of chopping wood in the brisk February air, Daniel carried his first armload of logs into the trading post and piled them in a bin near the back. He paused before retrieving the next load, taking time to inhale the woody warmth that crackled from the post's potbelly stove. The injured men lay in cots around it. Others sat at tables to play cards, read a newspaper, or sip coffee.

On the third trip back into the post, Daniel noticed Lugo and Banyon chatting with Greeley around his cot. The injured clerk, propped up on one elbow, leaned in close as Lugo spoke in hushed tones.

Both Greeley and Banyon nodded several times.

Daniel continued to glance at them as he added his wood to the pile, dropping each log with a loud thunk.

Lugo twisted in his chair and, meeting Daniel's gaze, shot him a cold stare. The Californio then raised an eyebrow and curled his lip into a sneer before turning back to the other two.

As though he'd swallowed a hot coal, Daniel's chest burned. His hands trembled, and not from the cold. *Are those three plotting something against me?* Each month, Daniel still demanded that Banyon and Greeley give him fifty percent of the monies they pilfered from the till. And Lugo had yet to make good on the threat he made when Daniel shoved him to the floor. He might stand a chance against one of them, but he'd never survive an attack from all three.

By the time Daniel and Brown finished cutting and lugging in all the wood, Lugo had left, but Banyon still sat with Greeley.

Determined to stop trouble before it started, Daniel clomped over to the clerks. Pulling off his leather gloves, he squeezed them under his left armpit and extended his chilled hands over the stove. He glanced at Greeley. "How's the shoulder?"

"It'll heal." The man's gruff voice signaled he wasn't interested in conversation.

Banyon, still sitting next to Greeley, raised his head, cleared his throat, then returned his gaze to Greeley.

Uninvited, Daniel pulled up a chair next to them and sat. "I've been thinkin'." He glanced at the two. "I know we haven't had much business at the post recently because of the cold weather—" He paused and lowered his voice to a whisper. "But I'm gonna stop taking my cut for keeping quiet about you skimmin' off the top of each day's profit. I know you're both loyal to Jim. If you weren't, you wouldn't have fought like you did to save the post yesterday. You deserve more than you're getting."

Greeley fingered his bandaged shoulder. "You got that right, Cipher."

Daniel winced at the nickname. "I'll keep balancing the books," he said, "and I'll keep quiet about it. If we're gonna survive out here, we gotta have each other's backs." He reached out a hand to Banyon. "What d'ya say?"

The grizzled clerk rubbed his beard. "You've got sand, Whitcomb, that's for sure. The way you set yourself up as a target to flush out those Injuns yesterday?" Banyon shrugged. "I reckon you're one to ride the river with." He shook Daniel's hand.

He wasn't quite familiar with Banyon's slang, but he took it to mean the man trusted him to keep his word. He turned to Greeley.

"Sure." Greeley pointed to Banyon. "What he said. Now let me get some shut-eye, will ya?"

As March's thaw weakened winter's sting, more miners returned to the gold fields. Daniel no longer demanded money from Banyon and Greeley in return for his silence, and Lugo went back to the Horseshoe Bend trading post. Daniel finally felt free to stop looking over his shoulder.

One issue still plagued him. Why had Virginia eloped with Murphy? Memories of her often filled his dreams. Until he awoke to the numbing cold of the cabin.

The numbing cold in his heart.

The numbing cold of her betrayal.

While struggling to awaken from last night's dream, he relived its sights and sounds. The sun-drenched ripples of the Guadalupe River, the sing-song whistles of the blue and rust-colored bluebirds, the creamy summer fragrance of the elderberry blossoms. Most of all, he relived the taste of Virginia's kisses.

Suddenly, like a mirror dashed to the floor, his dream shattered into a thousand pieces. Someone had yanked off his cozy woolen blanket.

"Whitcomb. Up. You're meetin' with Savage this morning. Remember?"

Long-Haired Brown. Of course. The human timepiece.

Daniel groaned and dragged his pocket watch from beneath his pillow. He studied its face in the dim light of the oil lamp. Six o'clock.

He sat on the edge of his cot and stretched, bringing his sore muscles to life. Brown seemed to have an internal clock that always woke him at 5:30 in the morning, no matter the season. He, on the other hand, preferred to stay up late and rise at least an hour after the sun found fit to do so.

After buttoning his red flannel shirt over his long underwear, he slipped on his trouser, thumbed up their suspenders, and tugged on a clean pair of socks. The cabin, cold from the night's chill, made him don his wool coat before grabbing his old leather boots from beneath his cot.

He examined the bottom of his left boot and poked a finger through a small hole. That wouldn't do. If he wore it that way, the muddied ground surrounding the post, still soupy from the last rain, would seep into his sock. Like a soothing sip of hot coffee, he remembered he still had his father's old boots—the ones he'd refurbished that night at their blacksmith shop. The night their house burned down. The night before his world changed forever.

He dug his father's boots out of his trunk and pulled them on. Still a little big. *Maybe if I just add another pair of socks.*

The extra pair of socks worked. The refurbished leather boots fit snug enough to walk. His insides smiled at the familiar clunk of his father's footwear as he traipsed over the wooden slats in front of the post. At the boots' familiar sound, he walked taller. He felt as though his father walked beside him.

Inside the post, Jim sat sipping coffee at the back table. Daniel's stomach wailed at the smell of breakfast. It might only be mush, but he hadn't eaten since yesterday afternoon before leaving the Horseshoe Bend post. He had spent the morning there making a list of the stock on hand, then immediately rode back to the Merced post. When he'd returned, he was too tired to eat, and went straight to bed.

As Daniel approached Jim's table, his guardian glanced up. "We're reviewin' the books this morning, right?"

Daniel nodded and sat. "Right."

Limik carried over a breakfast of cornmeal mush and dried pork. She also brought Daniel a cup of coffee.

He drew up a corner of his mouth. Although he still hated mush, he was now grateful for the hands that prepared it.

Daniel added bits of dried pork to his breakfast, shoveled in several bites, then slowly sipped his dark brown brew. The edge of his hunger abated, he ambled over to the iron safe where he kept his law books and Jim's ledgers. Setting the accounting journal on the table, he opened to the page that showed the posts' winter earnings.

As soon as Daniel began to explain the figures, Chief Juárez strode in. Still dressed in his colorful sarape, pantaloons that reached his knees, and knee-high boots, the Chowchilla chief had now added a Mexican sombrero and a purple sash to his flamboyant attire.

Juárez sauntered over to Jim, pulled out a chair, and sat. He splayed his palms out flat on the table. Tawny, wrinkled hands, Daniel noted, that had probably seen too much sun and too much physical labor. "I have more news of the Yosemites, old friend," the chief said. "This you must hear."

Daniel closed the leather-bound ledger with a thud and rose to return it to the iron safe. Maybe he'd read one of his law books while Jim talked with Juárez.

"No." Jim waved Daniel back down. "Stay. I'm sure this'll concern you as much as me."

Confused, but glad to be brought into the discussion, Daniel obeyed.

Juárez glanced at Daniel and let out a grunt, then turned to Jim. "Tribes loyal to me farther up the mountain say Yosemites plan more attacks. You and your Yokuts must prepare. They come soon. Maybe three days, maybe a week. Maybe two weeks. But they will come."

Daniel grasped the edge of the table and pressed back into his chair. Scenes of their recent battle with the secluded Yosemites raked across his mind.

The war cries of the natives.

Screams of the wounded.

Dead bodies laid out to bury.

Gripping the oak table even tighter, his fingers tingled. He didn't want to fight another battle like that.

Savage stood and shook the chief's hand. "Thanks for warning us, chief. I'll make sure we're prepared."

After Juárez left, Jim sat. He wrapped his hands around his coffee cup and stared across the room, his upper lip curled in a scowl.

Daniel scooped up another spoonful of mush. It didn't look like

Jim was ready to talk about the post's finances right now. He also didn't look ready to talk about Juárez' warning about the Yosemites. Maybe he could ask about the chief. Daniel was dying to find out if the man was really an Indian or a Mexican. After a moment of silence, he asked, "So, Jim. I have a question. Is the chief an Indian or a Mexican?"

Still staring across the room, Jim's glazed eyes finally focused on Daniel. "Sorry, boy. Was lost in thought. What'd cha say?"

"I asked about the chief." Daniel took a sip of coffee. "When Juárez warned us about the Yosemites last month, he spoke Spanish. Today, he spoke English."

Jim leaned back. "Juárez is a Chowchilla. He knows Spanish 'cause he grew up at Mission San José when it was run by Spanish padres."

Daniel downed another spoonful of mush. With the Americans having recently won the war against the Mexicans, and with all the whites pouring into California, it was hard to remember that only Spaniards, Mexicans, and Indians used to live here.

Jim rubbed the stubble he had yet to shave from his face. "Juárez is smart. He learned a lot while growing up at the mission. As an adult, he once served as an *alcalde* in Pueblo San José. Later, when Mexico gained their freedom from Spain, Juárez came back to the San Joaquin Valley. The Indians recognized his leadership abilities. Before long, he had a large following among the Miwok, Yokuts, and Chowchilla. He'd lead 'em on raids to steal the mission's horses and cattle."

"Is he one of the Indians you tricked with your galvanic battery?"

Jim's mouth twitched. "So, you've heard that story, eh?" His guardian bit off a piece of pork. "I met Juárez when I was part of Frémont's battalion during the Mexican War. My company, Company H, had twenty whites, two Californios, and forty Indians, including Juárez. I tricked all them Injuns with that battery. Before the war, I bought it off an Italian immigrant, thinkin' it might come in handy someday. It did."

Daniel shook his head. He had heard that story from some of Jim's clerks, but figured it was a tall tale.

"I'd hide that battery 'neath these grizzly cubs' skins." Jim continued.

"When I'd have an Injun touch the bear fur, he got a powerful shock that threw him to the ground. It made them Injuns think I had some kinda special power."

After he drained his cup of coffee, Jim wiped his mouth with his sleeve. "But we were mighty grateful to have them Injuns during the war. Those Chowchillas and Walla-Wallas were such great horse bandits, we nicknamed 'em the forty thieves."

Daniel widened his eyes. "Your company stole horses during the war?"

Jim shrugged. "Had to. Needed 'em for the war effort. Frémont told us to take horses from the Californios and give 'em a bill of sale. If they squawked, said to tell 'em they'd get paid after we won the war."

"Did they ever get paid?"

"Probably not." Jim shoveled a spoonful of mush into his mouth and paused to swallow. "After the war, Juárez introduced me to most of the tribes in the San Joaquin Valley. That battery trick's what started the rumor I came here on a moonbeam. Most every chief I met wanted me to marry into his tribe. Gave me the pick of my brides."

His guardian had married into at least five of the neighboring tribes. That much Daniel knew for certain. The thought of having more than one wife made him shiver. He sipped his coffee. Pastor Lovejoy taught that marriage was something special. He called it holy. Life lived together between one man and one woman. Trusting God together in bad times and thanking Him in the good. Like Ma and Pa.

Daniel took another sip to drown the pain that pinched his throat. "So that's how you eventually got 500 Indians to help you dig for gold?"

His guardian drew his lips into a thin line and nodded.

Eating the rest of his mush in silence, Daniel considered their conversation. He didn't like how Jim deceived the Indians. He took advantage of their superstitious nature. On the other hand, the man fed his workers, sold them supplies, and guarded them from attacks by white miners and renegade Yosemites.

Daniel opened the ledger to go over the figures, but Jim covered the page with his hand.

"You've been doing the books for me for over a year now, right?" Jim locked eyes with Daniel.

"It'll be two years come June. And I'll turn eighteen in four more months."

"Four months, eh?" Jim rubbed his stubbled chin. "Sorry I haven't been much of a guardian during that time." The man leaned back and sighed. "I was so focused on makin´ money and keeping peace 'tween the Injuns and miners, that I didn't pay you much mind. I put you in danger more 'n once. Just wanted to say—" He hesitated and blinked several times. "I'm proud of how you've come through for me."

Daniel squirmed under the man's scrutiny and his unusual frankness. *Is he afraid we might not survive another Yosemite attack?*

"Sorry too I never gave you money to get them clues about your parents' deaths." Jim slid his jaw right. "We're running low on supplies. I'll send you and Brown to San José tomorrow—along with an $800 bonus for all your hard work."

Daniel sucked in a gulp of air.

Jim pushed out his lips. "That's how much Brody wants for the information, right?"

The generous offer landed in Daniel's gut like a punch in the stomach. He'd never told Jim about stealing gold from his hidden stash in Big Oak Flat, or that he'd already retrieved the clues. Should he tell him now? He tried to breathe, but air refused to enter his lungs. No. He couldn't tell him. Not now.

His mind raced. He'd also never told Jim about his engagement to Virginia, or how'd she eloped with Murphy. He didn't feel close enough to the man for that. Would he ever?

And now, he wasn't so sure he wanted to go to San José. What if the Yosemites attacked their Merced River Post while he and Brown were gone?

Then again, maybe he should go. If he went to San José, he could try to see Virginia again. Find out why she broke their engagement.

Why she broke his heart.

13

A PAINFUL GOODBYE

March 25, 1850
San José, California

During Daniel's week-long trek with Brown to San José, he shared about his broken engagement with Virginia. It felt good to finally open up to someone. "Think the Reeds will still let us camp on their property?" Daniel asked as they neared the pueblo. "I mean, now that I'm not engaged to Virginia anymore?"

Brown scratched his bearded chin. "Best we can do is ask."

As they rode the last two miles to the Reed Ranch, the horses seemed comfortable finding their own way. Daniel doubted he'd ever feel comfortable finding his way here again.

When Mrs. Reed answered Daniel's knock, her lined face and sallow complexion revealed the toll of the last few months.

"Daniel, how nice to see you." Her smile didn't quite reach her eyes. "Are you in town for more provisions?"

Removing his broad-brimmed felt hat, Daniel twisted it between his hands. "Nice to see you too, ma'am. Yes, we're here to stock up on supplies. If it's not too much trouble, might we camp on your property again? Should only be about three days."

Mrs. Reed reached out a dry, wrinkled hand and squeezed his arm. "Of course, dear. You are always welcome here." Her eyes looked past him, as if fixed on something in the distance. "As you probably know"—her voice sounded far away—"Virginia no longer lives here."

He wrung his hat like a dishrag. "Yes, ma'am. I read about it in the newspapers."

A moment of awkward silence passed between them. *Do the Reeds blame me for Virginia's elopement?*

Daniel drew in a sharp breath. "Brown's waitin' in the wagon. Guess we'll set our tents up near the barn, same as usual, then head into town for supplies."

Her gaze returned to his face. "I'll send word to Mr. Reed that you're here. He's meeting with some men at Isaac Branham's home to discuss town council business."

"Thank you, ma'am."

Ma'am. The word soured on his tongue. He had once hoped to call her *Ma.* That was before Virginia had run off with Murphy. Yanking his felt hat onto his head, he turned and tromped down the porch steps.

After a long day of purchasing supplies, Daniel stood over his evening campfire, stirring a pot of beans to warm them. Brown had already retired to his tent. They'd driven back to the Reeds' at sunset, and now, glancing toward the east, Daniel could barely make out the outline of the Diablo Mountains.

"Mr. Whitcomb?"

Caught off guard, Daniel dropped his spoon into the bubbling mass of beans. A stranger emerged from the darkness that was slowly enveloping their camp.

"I'm Jacob. Met you last time you was in town."

As the middle-aged man approached the campfire, Daniel made out his familiar features. A carrot-topped head of hair and rust-colored beard. Hands too large for his body. A limp that slowed his gait to a snail's pace.

"Sure. I remember." Daniel picked up his Bowie knife from a nearby rock and rescued his spoon from the pot of beans. "Just fixin' dinner. Care to join me?"

Jacob raised a hand. "No thanks. Only came to bring a message. Mr. Reed wants to know if you can come up to the house for a chat this evening. He'd be much obliged. Wants me to bring back your answer. Says if it's too late, maybe tomorrow night."

He'd have to face Virginia's father eventually. Better sooner than later. "Sure. I can be there in an hour."

Jacob nodded. "I'll pass that along."

After his meager dinner, Daniel filled a basin of water from the water pump, washed, pulled on a clean pair of trousers, and tucked in the tail of his new blue and white striped shirt he'd bought in town.

As he knocked on the Reeds' door, he swallowed his growing ball of fear. Once again, the question rose in his mind. Did the family blame him for Virginia's decision to elope?

"Daniel." Mr. Reed opened the door wide, offered a soft smile, and waved him in. "Thank you for coming. After Virginia ran off with Murphy, we feared we'd never see you again. Come. Let's talk in the parlor."

Blowing out a sigh of relief, Daniel followed the man through the entryway to the parlor. This was where he'd sipped tea with the Reeds on his first day in San José. Where he'd told Mr. Reed he was interested in his daughter. Where he'd promised Virginia he'd return within a year to marry her.

What had gone wrong?

Mr. Reed sat on the gold brocade couch as Daniel took his usual spot on the gold-tufted armchair. As usual, Virginia's father wore a white shirt, vest, and tailcoat. Today, however, his burgundy cravat hung loosely around his neck. His shoulders slumped, and his dark brown beard showed flecks of gray.

"We are so sorry about what happened with Virginia." Mr. Reed paused. "And, frankly, Daniel, a little ashamed."

Daniel shifted his gaze from Virginia's father to the frayed threads on the sofa's armrest as Mr. Reed rubbed his fingers between them.

"I had so hoped that you and Virginia—"

"What's done is done, sir." Daniel sat up straighter.

"I tried to stop them but, well, you know how headstrong Virginia is." He pressed on the threads, as if trying to push them back beneath the armrest's mahogany-carved frame.

"Yes, sir. I do." Daniel curled his toes inside his father's boots and balled his fists. "She had promised to marry me. Do you know why she broke her promise? Did Murphy have some kind of hold over her?"

Mr. Reed sighed. "I wish I had an answer for you, son, but I don't."

Daniel clenched his jaw. *Did she marry Murphy for the money?* Newspapers had reported that, between Murphy's gold mining and trading post business, the man had returned to San José with over $1,500,000 in gold. He'd only returned to San José with $800.

Leaning forward, Virginia's father trapped Daniel with a stare. "Son, even though you are not my son-in-law, I would still like to support your pursuit of a law career. If you are still so inclined."

Daniel's breath caught in his throat. Had he heard the man correctly? Studying Mr. Reed's warm eyes, he found a fierce sincerity reflected there. But Virginia's betrayal had shaken his confidence. Did he really have what it took to become a lawyer?

He finally found his voice. "I–I'm not really sure, sir. But, if it's something you think I can do, I'd like to try."

The thin line of a smile formed on the man's sagging face. "My colleagues have agreed to meet with you tomorrow night and discuss any further questions you might have regarding your recent readings. We had already scheduled a meeting here to review Masonic business, but when I advised them of your presence, they suggested we devote some of our time to speaking with you."

Daniel shook his head. "Honestly, sir, I don't understand why busy men like you want to help somebody like me. Especially now since—you know. Since I'm not going to be part of your family."

Mr. Reed opened his mouth to reply, but Daniel held up a hand. "My pa always told me, 'When someone wants to do you a turn, don't be too proud to say yes.' I do have questions about things I've read, and I'd be honored to meet with your lawyer friends."

Virginia's father grinned and slapped the armrest. "Fine, fine. Mr. Lloyd and Mr. Wallace have been especially impressed with the questions you've sent back with Mr. Brown. They've looked forward to speaking with you face to face. Shall we say, eight o'clock tomorrow night?"

His mouth went dry. He recalled a time on the trail when his friend, John Breen, dared him to plunge off a twenty-foot cliff into the river below. He'd refused. Now, like then, common sense urged him to turn down Mr. Reed's offer. What made him think he could aspire to be a lawyer? To be a gentleman who wore fine clothes? And yet, his desire to move on with his life prodded him to say yes. He swallowed hard and nodded. "Yes, sir. That would be fine."

"Do you have any more questions I can relay to them before we meet?"

Daniel slid his jaw left. "No sir, but I've got one or two for you."

Mr. Reed's eyes widened. "Oh?"

"Would it be proper for me to meet up with Virginia before I leave? Do you think she'd agree to see me?"

Mr. Reed inhaled a deep breath then blew it out. "I don't know, son. I could get a message to her and ask. I suppose it is more a matter of whether her new husband, Mr. Murphy, will allow it."

Daniel and Long-Haired Brown spent the next day purchasing sacks of cornmeal and haggling with ranchers over the lowest price for three mules. They needed additional pack animals to transport all their goods back to the trading post.

Later that evening, Daniel met with Mr. Reed and his associates. They answered questions he'd submitted to them on Brown's last supply run, and he asked questions about the books he'd recently read. He returned all the books he'd borrowed, except for Mr. Lloyd's copy of *The Works of Daniel Webster*. He needed more time to digest its contents. In turn, each lawyer gave him another book to review.

Studying the faces of the men around the table, Daniel shook his head. "I'm not sure what you all see in me, but I'm mighty thankful." His eyes and nose tingled. Gratitude squeezed his throat. Afraid his voice would crack, he pushed out the next words. "If there's a way I can ever repay you, I will."

Mr. Wallace, sitting across from him, met his gaze. "You're a bright young man, Daniel, with a promising future. This is simply how we live out our Masonic code to value brotherly love, truth, and justice. As I'm sure you'd agree, those virtues are in short supply today."

Thumping his cane on the floor, Mr. Lloyd chimed in. "Hear, hear." The elderly man at the end of the table leaned in. "And Mr. Reed has witnessed those virtues in you, son. All of us have pledged ourselves to improving our budding community by fostering those qualities in others."

With a grunt of agreement, Mr. Reed nodded. "Always strive to reach your potential, Daniel. That is how you can repay us. Do not let any obstacle stand in your way. And, when you can, repay the kindness you've received from us by doing the same for others."

Sweat slicked the back of Daniel's shirt. He would do everything within his power to live up to their trust. "Thank you. All of you."

The next morning, after a breakfast of biscuits and beans, Daniel and Long-Haired Brown drove out to Mr. Campbell's mill to pick up their order of flour.

"Had a problem with some of our equipment yesterday," Mr. Campbell's foreman explained when they arrived. "I'm sorry, but your barrels won't be ready until tomorrow."

Daniel arrived back at the Reed's ranch at noon and found a note waiting for him.

Daniel,

Mr. Murphy has given his consent for you to meet with Virginia at three o'clock this afternoon. She and Mr. Murphy will be visiting Don Antonio Suñol at his home across from the State House on the Plaza.

James Reed

Daniel blinked to clear his vision. As if he'd eaten bear meat that wasn't fully cooked, his stomach churned. At least now he'd get some answers. But what if he didn't like what he heard? Scenes of a bear cub he'd seen fall into the Merced rapids flashed across his mind. The poor cub. Submerged beneath the cascades, it finally emerged for a gulp of air, only to be pulled under once again. He often wondered if the cub ever made it out of the treacherous river. Would he?

To see Virginia, but not hold her. To talk, but not kiss. To share future plans, but not a shared future. He nodded. Yes. He'd risk it.

Even if it made his already splintered heart shatter into irreparable pieces. Like it or not, at least he'd get some answers.

Too nervous to eat, he sat on a crate in front of his tent. To pass the time, he flipped through one of the law books he'd received last night, but the words merged into a mass of jumbled, meaningless letters. After an hour of trying to focus, he put the book down, washed, changed into clean clothes, and rode the mile-and-a-half into town.

On previous trips to San José, he'd purchased several items at Antonio Suñol's store, but had never met the Californio in person. Suñol's white-washed adobe brick home stood behind the man's store. He tied his horse to the post at the side of the house and surveyed the surrounding rancho of pear, peach, and fig trees. He only hoped his meeting with Virginia would prove as fruitful as the now-budding orchards.

"Welcome to my home." Don Antonio Suñol grasped Daniel's hand in both of his as he greeted him at the door. "I know you are not really here to see me, but rather to visit with my guests. However, perhaps you and I can get better acquainted at another time, yes?" The short, rosy-cheeked Californio patted him on the back and ushered him in.

He admired the man's beige morning coat with its velvet-trimmed lapels and cuffs. "Mr. Suñol, I apologize for intruding on your visit with the Murphys."

The smiling man tapped Daniel's shoulder. "Please, please, call me Antonio."

Daniel inhaled through his mouth in an effort to release the tension that gripped his muscles. Who was he to impose on Don Suñol's hospitality? What did he hope to accomplish? Even if Virginia told him why she chose Murphy over him, what difference would it make?

He followed Don Suñol down a short hallway and into a room on the left.

"We will all gather here in the drawing room, yes?" The plump man waved his open palm across his body, inviting him to enter.

The well-furnished salon caught Daniel by surprise. A round mahogany table nestled itself between several ribbon back chairs and a camelback cream-colored couch. A large floral-patterned rug covered the wood-planked floor. Thick red velvet curtains flanked large glass windows, allowing just the right amount of sunlight to enter the room. A young woman, her dark hair fastened atop her head with a jeweled comb, sat near a window panel that viewed the rear orchard. Her slender fingers embroidered a colorful pattern onto a skirt she had spread across the table in front of her.

"And this is my lovely wife, Doña Dolores Mesa Suñol." The middle-aged man, at least in his fifties, leaned over and kissed his young wife on the cheek.

Daniel stiffly nodded. "Good afternoon ma'am." *Lovely indeed. She looks half Don Antonio's age.*

The woman glanced up. A slight smile played on her lips. *"Buenas tardes,"* she said, and then returned to her embroidery.

"The Murphys are outside enjoying the perfumed blossoms of my fruit trees, but they should—" Suñol reached inside his coat, withdrew a gold pocket watch, and clicked it open. "Ah, yes. Just as I thought." Snapping it shut, he returned it to his pocket. "It is precisely three o'clock. They should be coming in momentarily."

An Indian servant arrived with a tea service and set it on the round table in front of the sofa. As he turned to leave, Virginia and John Murphy entered.

Daniel thought he'd prepared himself for this moment, but seeing her again anchored him to the floor. He couldn't move his feet. His arms. His mouth.

Murphy walked over and grasped Daniel's hand. Now clean-shaven and dressed in a gray frock coat and blue vest, the man barely resembled the rugged miner he'd met in the gold fields last year. "Good to see you again, Whitcomb." Murphy flashed him a wide grin.

Of course the man beamed. He'd stolen Virginia from him.

Murphy continued to grip his hand. "I know you and my wife have some catching up to do. I'll be in the study with Mr. Suñol discussing a new business venture."

Wife. The word stabbed his chest where his heart used to be.

"And, for the sake of propriety," Murphy's eyebrows rose, "Doña Dolores Suñol has agreed to remain in the parlor while you visit."

Virginia walked to the couch. Murphy and Suñol left.

And there he stood, still fixed to the floor.

Virginia poured a cup of tea and looked up. "Daniel, aren't you going to sit?"

That dimpled half-smile. That beautiful satin yellow dress. That intoxicating fragrance of lavender. Her graceful slender neck that had once worn his engagement gift of a turquoise- and diamond-studded cross.

Her smile faded. "Please, Daniel. Sit."

The room darkened. A cloud passed over the sun.

Over his soul.

"Well, if you're not going to sit," she said, reaching into her embroidery-trimmed reticule, I should at least give you this." She pulled out the turquoise cross and stood to give it to him.

He raised a hand. "Keep it." He sat on one of the ribbon back chairs. "I don't want it."

She curled her fingers around the cross and sat. Her face drained of color as she peered up at him with moist eyes. "I never meant to hurt you, Daniel."

"But you did." He folded his arms across his chest. His stomach twisted into knots.

She opened her hand and deposited the cross on the mahogany table next to the tea service. "Several times I tried to write a letter to explain why I eloped with John, but I just couldn't find the words."

"So, you said nothing." He growled under his breath, stood, and walked over to the window, then back to the sofa. When she had first entered the room, he couldn't move. Now, he couldn't hold still. "Did you marry him for the money?"

She hitched in a breath and fixed him with a gaze. Her eyes narrowed. "I can't believe you said that."

He ran a hand through his shoulder-length hair and clenched his teeth. "Why then? Why didn't you wait for me? Did the man force you to marry him?"

"Of course not." She lowered her head and bit her lower lip

Silence hung in the space between them.

Working his jaw, he paced back to the chair. "What then? I need to know."

Finally, she spoke. "John proposed to me in December, as soon as he returned from the gold fields. I told him I had promised myself to you. He didn't try to change my mind, but he also didn't withdraw his offer." She paused to sip her tea.

Daniel sat and crossed his arms again. Even though the spring sun had warmed the room, he shuddered. He waited for her to continue.

She rolled her lips inward. "Last December I met John's father, Martin Murphy Sr., and John's sister, Helen. She is so sweet. We met at a party Don Antonio hosted for San José citizens and the state legislators who had just arrived for their first legislative session."

The more she spoke, the faster her words spilled out. Her pitch raised with each sentence. This meeting probably wasn't easy for her either. He uncrossed his arms and let his hands fall to his lap.

"Around that time, John's brother, Martin Jr., and his wife, Mary, moved into the Hernandez house at the northern end of the plaza. Martin and Mary had owned a big ranch about twenty miles from Sutter's Fort, but recently decided to move to San José so they could be closer to family."

Her cheeks brightened as she talked about the Murphy clan.

"Actually, Martin and Mary bought 5,000 acres of land eighteen miles northwest of here where they plan to farm and raise cattle. They've ordered a twenty-room house, New England style, to be shipped from Maine and put on the land. It'll be pre-cut, piece by piece, to their specifications, labeled, crated, and shipped around the Horn, then transported here from San Francisco by wagon."

When she paused to take another sip of tea, a few drops sloshed out. She retrieved the cloth napkin from her lap and patted her chin.

He allowed his eyes to trace the curve of those delicate fingers. Fingers that once caressed his face. Fingers that now trembled.

Pulling his chair closer to the tea table, he lifted the teapot's cover. Steam rose. Still hot. He poured himself a cup.

"And you should see Martin and Mary's children." A faint smile traced her lips. "They have four rambunctious boys and three of the cutest little girls you could ever meet. Baby Nellie calls me Ah Na because she can't say Aunt Virginia yet."

He thought of the extended family she could have enjoyed if she had waited to marry him.

There wasn't any.

The only family she'd have, besides him, would be her parents, sister, and three brothers. He swallowed the hot tea and knew the burning in his throat wasn't from the drink. Why hadn't he thought of that before? He had no parents, no siblings. No aunts or uncles. He had nothing to offer. Now, she was part of a large, extended Catholic family.

But what about him? He ached to have a family. He adored Mrs. Reed, respected her husband and his accomplishments, and ever since the time spent with them on the wagon train, had considered Virginia's siblings as if they were his own. Now, once again, he had nothing.

He stood and returned his cup to the table. It clinked as it hit the saucer. A small ball of fire burned in his chest. She had promised to wait for him. She said she loved him. "Virginia, you made a commitment to me." He glared down at her.

Tears brimmed her eyes, then dribbled down her cheeks. She didn't bother to wipe them. "I know, Daniel. I'm so sorry. Please don't be angry. I couldn't bear it."

A muscle ticked in his jaw. He narrowed his gaze. "And how should I feel, Virginia? Happy?" He stepped closer. "I'll tell you how I feel." His voice rose. "I feel betrayed. I feel humiliated."

"*Por favor,*" Señora Suñol interrupted. "Let us speak with civil voices here."

Daniel raised tight eyes toward the ceiling. He squeezed them shut as fire raged behind them. It soon burned itself out, leaving only sadness in its wake. His anger melted into tears as he sank back into the chair. "I feel abandoned, Virginia." His voice came in a whisper. "I feel so alone."

A curtain of silence fell once again.

He fisted away his tears and sensed her eyes on him, but refused to return her gaze.

"I'm so sorry, Daniel. I understand you're angry. Ma and Pa were angry too. At first, I thought they'd never forgive me. But, after they met the Murphy clan, I knew they saw what had drawn me to John. Family has always been important to them, too."

Daniel held back the urge to pick up the necklace and throw it in her lap—or across the room. He also wanted to sit next to her. Comfort her. Kiss away those tears.

But he couldn't.

Not now.

Not ever.

He briefly let his gaze meet hers.

She stared at him through puffy, red eyes. "Do you think you'll ever be able to forgive me?"

He reached inside to find his heart, but found it wasn't there. All that remained were anger and sadness. "Someday. Maybe." He shook his head. "But not today."

He left, wondering if it would be the last time he ever saw her.

Daniel didn't talk much with Brown on the return trip to the gold fields. What could he say? He couldn't look back. But now, what could he look forward to?

In four months, he'd turn eighteen and receive Jim's promised inheritance. Should he move to San José where Mr. Reed's lawyer friends could help him study law? No. That would be too painful. Should he go back to San Francisco and rekindle his friendship with the Arnolds? Maybe. Should he just stay with Jim in the gold fields? Probably. Chief Juárez' words suddenly came to mind. His warning about an imminent Yosemite attack. When they got back to the gold fields, would there even be a trading post?

14

MERCED RIVER POST

April–August 1850
South Fork, Merced River Post

Daniel guided their wagonload of supplies up the rocky, rutted trail to the Merced River post. *One more mile.* He glanced over his shoulder. The three pack mules tied behind the wagon easily navigated the climb. The closer they got to the post, the more his stomach growled. Someone had a campfire burning. Hopefully they were near the post. Hopefully they had a large slab of beef roasting over it. And, hopefully, they'd be open to guests.

As they turned the next bend, smoky gray ash filled the air and invaded his lungs. The air now smelled more like smoldering wet wood. He glimpsed sideways at Long-Haired Brown.

Tight-jawed, the weathered mountain man narrowed his eyes. "The post. Yosemites."

With a nod of understanding, Daniel slapped his reins across the back of the lead horse.

Limik.

Jim's wives.

Jim.

Would they reach them in time?

Eight hundred feet from the post, Daniel jerked the horses to a halt, jumped down, and wrapped the reins around a low branch. The gray, smoke-filled sky made it appear more like night than midday. He coughed to clear his lungs, then fastened his red bandana over his mouth and nose. Brown did the same. Grabbing their rifles, they sprinted toward the post.

The post. The log structure they'd worked so hard to build last fall. Crackling flames shot through its roof and devoured the front wall. Every step brought Daniel closer to the intense heat. Heat that penetrated his jacket and simmered his skin. Heat that stung his eyes and strafed his face. A bucket-brigade of Yokuts made a human chain to ferry water from the nearby river to the burning building.

Where was Limik? He didn't recognize any of the Indians' soot-smeared faces.

"Brown! Whitcomb!"

Daniel turned at the muffled shouts of a familiar voice.

The shout came from Banyon who also had a bandana covering his mouth and nose. He was waving his arms at the front of a bucket brigade, giving instructions to the workers. Banyon appeared to turn the leadership of the bucket brigade over to one of the braves and then motioned to Daniel and Brown. "Follow me," he shouted as he waved them toward the riverbank. "I'll take you to Jim."

Daniel and Brown joined Banyon at the rushing water's edge, then followed him northeast as the man raced over rocks and boulders that traced the upward slope of the Merced River.

After about five minutes, Banyon stopped and dunked his bandana into the river to wash off the soot.

Daniel unknotted his neckerchief and choked out his burning question. "What happened?"

"Yosemites." Banyon doubled over, placed his hands on his knees, and panted. "They attacked the post. We battled 'em for two hours before they finally run off." He pointed upriver. "A few days ago, Yokuts women heard rumors of a Yosemite attack. Savage got friends from other mining camps to help, but not enough came."

The winded man finally straightened and slowed his breathing. "Savage and the others chased the renegades up the river. A few of us stayed behind to guard the post." Banyon paused to wipe his forehead. "Good thing we did. Some Injuns double backed, set fire to the post, then ran back into the mountains. Figured the best thing now is to meet up with Savage."

The trio continued to follow the riverbank deeper into the canyon. Again and again Daniel hauled his tired legs over huge boulders. As he clambered over yet another, his left foot slipped. He flung his arms out to keep his balance, but a second later, sharp stones stung his face and scraped his hands. Groaning, he pushed himself up and rushed to catch up with the others.

Around the next bend, Savage and the others stood talking. Rushing water roared in the background. He couldn't make sense of their huddled conversation. Once he reached the group, he recognized one of the men as Pasquale, a Yokuts chief who, with his 500-strong Yokuts tribe, had dug gold for Jim on the Tuolumne River.

The chief shook his head. "Do not think it wise to follow more." Pasquale held out his hands at shoulder width, then slowly brought them together. "Canyon too narrow."

Jim's face reddened. His eyes flashed. "I won't stop till I kill 'em all." His long blond hair whipped around his shoulders as he turned to address the other men. He raised his rifle and shouted, "We end this. We end it now," then waved everyone forward.

The river, sated with melted snow from the mountains' peaks, surged past Daniel. Its deafening roar drowned out any contrary opinion. The deeper Daniel trekked into the gorge, the more the canyon closed in on the group. Suddenly, arrows rained down from the granite cliffs above them. Screams rose from the men near the front. Those not hit scurried for cover. Daniel found refuge behind a large boulder.

The chief was right. The narrow canyon provided the perfect ambush.

"Retreat!" Jim's strained voice shouted from somewhere up ahead.

Daniel stayed at his position behind the boulder and picked off two Yosemites stationed on a nearby ledge. Other Yosemites managed to shoot down two Yokuts who raced past Daniel on his left. Two miners stumbled by him on his right, one shot in the arm, another in the shoulder, but the men continued to race back toward the post. Daniel covered the retreating clerks, miners, and Yokuts. Once everyone had safely passed, he trailed them back to the trading post.

Back at the post's remains, a headcount revealed six dead miners.

Two died during the Yosemite's initial raid on the post. Four died in the gorge. Jim's Yokuts lost five braves. The fire destroyed all of the post's merchandise. All except the iron safe that held Daniel's law books, the ledgers, and Jim's gold. At least they still had the supplies he and Long-Haired Brown had brought back from San José.

With the post and bunkhouses burned to the ground, and too tired to do anything else, Daniel camped outside with the rest of Jim's clerks, his wives, and Limik. The Yokuts braves went back to their tribe's village.

The next morning, Jim announced he'd establish a new post farther southwest. With their small wagonload of supplies, they traveled lower in the foothills. Jim found a place a week later about fifteen miles from the small town of Mariposa. Several miners had set up camp there at a spot where the Mariposa and Agua Fria Creeks met. Jim decided it would be a good place for a trading post.

Daniel breathed a sigh of relief. Although Jim had established his previous Merced River Post in friendly Yokuts territory, the Yosemites obviously believed it was too close to their territory. Daniel now realized first-hand why the other tribes called them the Yosemite, *Those Who Kill*, and not *Ahwahneechee*, as the tribe called themselves. Hopefully, establishing a new post lower in the foothills would avoid further troubles with the mountain Yosemite.

By early June, the Merced River Post seemed a distant memory. At their new Agua Fria Post, Limik, Homut, and Eekino continued to serve the men. The Miwoks and Yokuts continued to gather gold for Jim in exchange for supplies and trinkets. Daniel continued to keep his guardian's books for both the new Agua Fria Post as well as the Horseshoe Bend Post. Jim also explored the possibility of establishing another store about fifteen miles farther south near the Fresno River.

Thousands of miners flooded the gold fields during the warm summer months, multiplying Jim's profits. Despite his long, busy days, Daniel still made time in the evenings to tutor Limik and study his law books.

In July, after a long, hot day of reviewing financial records for both the Horseshoe Bend and the Agua Fria posts, Daniel retrieved one of his law books from the post's safe. He hoped a cool breeze would wend its way to the back of the store as he ate dinner and read. Finishing the last of his cornbread, beans, and fish the women had prepared, he realized he'd read the same page three times. Too many thoughts distracted him.

Next week he'd turn eighteen. Should he take Jim's inheritance and leave the gold fields? No. Before, he couldn't wait to get his inheritance so he could marry Virginia. Now, with her out of the picture, he saw how much the people here still needed him. What would Jim do without him?

And then there was Limik. She had taken great strides in her English-language learning, but wanted to learn more. Tonight, as she had done for the past several weeks, she sat across from him working on sentences he'd assigned her to practice.

Yes, he'd stay in the gold fields a little longer.

He pushed his empty plate aside and picked up his nib-tipped pen to jot down more notes from *The Works of Daniel Webster*. After reading a paragraph, his mind wandered once more. He thought about Mr. Lloyd, the lawyer who had loaned him the book. Everything about the large-framed, gray-haired man intimidated him. He recalled Mr. Lloyd's words from their meeting last March at the Reed's house.

"Son, Daniel Webster is one of the most highly regarded lawyers of our time, especially in the area of constitutional law." Mr. Lloyd, with cane in hand, tapped his walking stick on the floor as if to emphasize his point. "You would do well to study Webster's words. Perhaps it is an act of Providence that you both share the same first name. Are you aware that the name Daniel means, *God is my judge?*"

"Yes, sir." Daniel squirmed under Mr. Lloyd's scrutiny. Those eyes. Piercing gray orbs that penetrated his soul. "My pastor back in Illinois said that my name could be understood to mean *God is my judge*, as well as *God rules me*, or *Judge of God.*"

A slow thin smile spread over Mr. Lloyd's wrinkled face. "I dare say, son, you would be wise to embrace all three interpretations, using them, as it were, like a whetstone against which you sharpen and shape your character."

Daniel had thought long and hard about that statement. Last year, when he had blackmailed Banyon and Greeley into giving him a portion of the money they stole each month from the post's earnings, he had convinced himself it was the only way he could pay for the clues about his parents' deaths. Two wrongs made a right, he'd reasoned. Now, thinking about God as his judge, he wasn't so sure God would agree with that. He reread the page in *The Works of Daniel Webster* one more time.

Lastly, our ancestors established their system of government on morality and religious sentiment. Moral habits, they believed, cannot safely be trusted on any other foundation than religious principle, nor any government be secure which is not supported by moral habits.

If any practices exist contrary to the principles of justice and humanity within the reach of our laws or our influence, we are inexcusable if we do not exert ourselves to restrain and abolish them.

He brought the oil lamp closer and chewed on the words of the last paragraph. How could he hope to be a lawyer in search of justice if he didn't exert himself, even now, here in the gold fields, to restrain and abolish practices contrary to the principles of justice? Not doing so, according to Webster, would be inexcusable.

"Dan'l." Limik's small voice called out to him from across the wooden table in the dimly lit trading post. "Do you wish something more to eat?"

He glanced up. Lost in thought, he'd almost forgotten she was there. Yesterday he had made a list of vocabulary words and simple sentences for her, and she was now creating her own sentences.

He cocked his head. "No, I've finished my meal. I'm not hungry. Why do you ask?"

"You biting your—" She pressed her full lips together and started again. "You have been biting your pen all night. I think you will chew it off and swallow it."

He smiled at her self-correction. Recently, they'd worked on verb tenses. "Sometimes I bite my writing instrument when I'm thinking really hard about something."

"Oh, sorry I bother you." She ducked her head. "I mean, sorry to have bothered you." Light from the oil lamp shimmered off her long, raven-black hair.

"It's not a bother. I needed to take a break anyway." He noticed she had almost completely filled out the paper in front of her with sentences. "What are you working on tonight?"

As she looked up, a smile crinkled her oval-shaped face. "I write a—I am writing a story," she corrected herself. "It is one I often heard as a child."

He raised his eyebrows. "Can I see it?"

"It probably not make much sense." She covered the page with her hand.

Leaning forward, he lifted his chin. "You've never told me any stories you learned as a child. I'd love to read it."

She shook her head. "Not yet. I work on it more."

Sensing her discomfort, he didn't persist.

Soon after they established the Agua Fria Post, a town of sorts grew up around it—miners' tents, lean-tos, tarped saloons, and a few cabins. Next to his canvas-covered store, Jim built a house for himself and his wives. With the help of his workers, he also constructed a corral for his forty head of cattle, and canvas coverings for his sixteen mules. With Agua Fria as his base of operations, Jim also built a cabin near the Fresno River and set up two tents to sell merchandise to the nearby miners. He also erected a corral for his two riding mules, two horses, and twelve work-oxen that he housed there.

With so many miners swarming the gold fields during the summer months, they found it hard to keep both stores fully stocked. Jim's clerks constantly travelled to San José or Stockton to buy more supplies. Daniel, however, had more than enough to do maintaining the accounts for both posts. Jim didn't ask him to make any more supply runs, and he didn't volunteer.

One sweltering afternoon in August, Daniel sat at the back of the Agua Fria Post compiling the monthly records. He shifted in his wooden chair, hoping to bring fresh air to the sweat plastering his cotton shirt to his back. If only he could take a break and plunge himself in the cool waters of the Agua Fria Creek. Instead, he fanned himself with a handful of receipts and refocused. Leaning forward, he turned a page in the record book. To his surprise, he found a new entry.

Someone had slipped a new page into the journal. It listed the name of a new business partner, Benjamin S. Lippincott. He remembered Lippincott was a friend of Jim's from their journey to California. Last June, Lippincott had also attended Reed's dinner party. A rush of air filled his lungs. From reading the *Alta California* newspaper, he knew that last year Lippincott had also served as a member of the Monterey convention to draw up the proposed California State Constitution. He felt proud to know a man like Lippincott considered it worthwhile to invest in Jim's trading posts.

As he closed his journal and returned it to the shelf, Limik approached and tapped his arm.

"I must talk with you now."

Her soft, out-of-breath words gave him a foreboding chill. "What is it?"

She glanced around the busy post before answering. "I wash clothes in the creek this morning. Yokuts women speak of uprisings against whites."

"The Yosemites?"

She turned her head, as if studying those assembled in the store. "No. Not this time. Now, the Chowchilla, Chookchuney, and Pohonochee."

Daniel recognized the tribes' names. All local. All Yokuts. All faithful to Jim's Chowchilla friend, Chief José Juárez.

15

CONFRONTATION

September 1850
Agua Fria Trading Post

As summer gave way to autumn, temperatures in the gold fields cooled. Although the rumored Indian war never broke out, tensions between the miners and the local tribes continually flared.

On a Sunday afternoon in mid-September, when the sun had finally warmed the morning's chill, Daniel selected a tree stump outside his tent where he could sit and enjoy a well-deserved day off. He chuckled as two chattering squirrels chased each other on the ground then scurried up an oak. From his vantage point behind the canvas-covered post, he viewed several miners washing clothes at the creek.

He inhaled the scent of pine and opened his law book. After reading a few pages, his mind wandered. Several minutes later, he read the same paragraph again. With a thump, he closed the book, leaned back, and gazed at the treetops.

Would this valley remain peaceful much longer? A morning report told of prospectors near the Tuolumne River who burned down a Miwok village. That would surely enrage the neighboring tribes.

Miners said Miwoks near them stole their horses. But had they? And what right did the miners have to take the law into their own hands? It only brought them a step closer to an Indian war. If all the San Joaquin Valley Indians banded together to fight the whites, what would Homut, Eekino, and Limik do? Would they side with the whites? Would they go back to their tribes?

He absent-mindedly traced the gold lettering outlining his book's title. Last month, when Long-Haired Brown brought the book back from a supply run to San José, Daniel put it aside. What could he possibly learn from a book titled, *Commentaries on the Laws of England?* He wanted to be a lawyer in the United States, not England. That was before he'd found the note Mr. Lloyd tucked inside. He opened to the page where he'd placed the lawyer's note and reread the letter.

To our young Esquire in training, Daniel Whitcomb:

This book of commentaries, first published in 1765, is deemed one of the most essential books for young law students. All of our nation's formative documents such as our Declaration of Independence, the Constitution, and the Federalist Papers were drafted by men steeped in Sir William Blackstone's Commentaries on the Laws of England. As a young law student, it would behoove you to thoroughly review this volume. I daresay, to even memorize portions that are of particular interest.

Along with my Blackstone Commentaries, Mr. Wallace is gifting you the second edition of Noah Webster's Dictionary of the English Language. Both are books you do not need to return.

Finally, Mr. Reed is sending along a copy of Noah Webster's American Spelling Book. He hopes this book will help in tutoring the young Indian girl. We have recently read in the papers that some miners have indiscriminately murdered several of the natives there, and that these poor Indians have no recourse for justice. We commend you for your unbiased actions on their behalf.

We wish you well in your endeavors.

Sincerely,

E.M. Lloyd, Esq.

His benefactors' last load of books proved a treasure trove. Before receiving them, he found many of the terms in the law books hard to understand. Now, with the gift of Noah Webster's dictionary, he could look up any word he didn't understand.

And how thoughtful of Mr. Reed to also send a copy of Webster's *American Spelling Book.* His throat had tightened when he laid eyes on it. He had used this book when he was in school. Holding this new volume in his hands brought back memories of his one-room schoolhouse in Illinois. The sweet hickory fragrance that permeated their small learning space whenever they fired up the wood-burning stove. The whiff of lilac perfume worn by their schoolmarm after she and the town's banker began to court. The eye-watering smell of ammonia when it came his turn to clean Nat the Rat's cage.

How he revered what students dubbed the *blue backed speller*. Its lessons taught him how to spell and how to read. As a child, that ragged, hand-me-down speller helped him form not only words, but also thoughts about life, the world, and his place in it. To his great distress, his treasured blue backed speller perished in their house fire. Now, as Limik pored over the one Mr. Reed sent, it was as if his book had risen from the ashes to bring her new life. He recalled the night he'd given it to her. After explaining how to use it, she pressed it to her bosom, her eyes flooding with tears.

Daniel shoved aside thoughts about a possible Indian war and forced himself to focus on his studies. He re-opened *Blackstone's Commentaries*, determined to absorb its wisdom.

> *When the supreme being formed the universe and created matter, He impressed certain principles upon that matter, establishing certain laws of motion, to which all moveable bodies must conform. This is called the law of nature. So too, when God created man and gave him free will, He laid down certain immutable laws of human nature.*

Daniel paused, reached for the dictionary, and looked up the word immutable. *Immutable: unable to change.*

Was Jim's repeated phrase—*You can't possess what you can't protect*—one of those laws that couldn't be changed? Maybe. He jotted the question in the margin of his notes, then continued.

> *The Creator, as a being of infinite power, wisdom and goodness, has laid down laws for man: the eternal, immutable laws of good and evil. He has enabled human reason to discover these laws, and they are necessary for the conduct of human actions. Among others, these principles are that we should live honestly, should hurt no one, and should render everyone its due.*

As he leaned back and stretched his neck, two squirrels jumped from one tree limb to another. Once again, he considered the word *immutable.* Unchangeable laws of the natural world, and unchangeable laws of human nature. If God established laws of motion for nature, and laws of good and evil for humans, that must mean there were consequences when those laws were violated. Like gravity. The squirrels safely jumped from one branch to the next only because they landed before the law of gravity plunged them to the ground.

Scenes of his Illinois home, lying in ashes, flashed across his mind. Had his parents violated a law of human nature, resulting in their deaths? No. They were good people. For reasons known only to Flannery, the tavern owner chose to violate the laws of good when he and the Brody brothers burned down their house. His parents, trapped in the fire, suffered the consequences of those people's evil actions. Maybe that's why he was set on bringing Flannery to justice. The man deserved to suffer the consequences of his evil deeds, not his parents.

His mind shifted to the scene at the Merced River Post when the Ahwahneechee burned it to the ground. Like the miners who recently destroyed the Miwok village, it seemed both groups had violated the human-nature law of good. Those deeds didn't follow Blackstone's prescription to, "live honestly, hurt no one, and render everyone its due." His head hurt as he tried to apply Blackstone's words to his life in the gold fields. He jotted down his thoughts and questions, then went on to the next page.

The rule of right cannot be separated from the laws of eternal justice and the happiness of each individual. Each man has the right to pursue his own personal happiness. This law is binding over all the globe, in all countries, and at all times. However, because of an individual's need to live in a society, a person's happiness must be pursued without violating the laws of eternal justice. In order to secure the blessings of happiness, societies must form and administer just, and mutually agreed upon laws.

His mind swirled with words and ideas he wanted to understand but could barely grasp. One thing stood out, however.In his soon-to-be State of California, just laws needed to be established and enforced if all who lived here were to experience what Blackstone called their God-given right to happiness.

A week later, after everyone had gone to bed, Jim invited Daniel to a secret meeting inside the post. He glanced around the dimly lit room. Jim had also invited Banyon and a new clerk, Cunningham.

"I have a plan that might prevent an all-out Indian war," Jim said as they crowded around a back table.

Light from the oil lamp created larger-than-life shadows on the post's canvas walls as Banyon and Cunningham leaned forward.

"The four of us will travel with Chief Juárez to San Francisco. Eekino, Homut, and Limik will also join us."

A spasm of pain twisted beneath Daniel's ribs. San Francisco. He hadn't been there in over two years. Not since he'd abandoned the city and the Arnolds to run off with Jim to the gold fields.

"While in San Francisco, Banyon and Daniel will order needed supplies. Cunningham and I will dazzle the chief with the power and might of the whites. Once the chief sees the number of ships in the harbor, the wealth of the city, the power of our cannons and artillery—" Jim's voice slowed; softened. "Juárez will think twice about starting a war he's sure to lose."

Was there hesitance in Jim's voice? In the dim light, he couldn't read his guardian's face. If Juárez saw the futility of a war against the whites, it would save many lives. The plan seemed sound. But would it work? For Limik's sake, he hoped it would.

Four weeks later, Jim led their unkempt group of eight down the middle of Montgomery Street toward San Francisco's Portsmouth Square. Gentrified San Franciscans—women carrying parasols and men in top hats—strolled down wood-boarded sidewalks and stopped to stare and point at them.

Jim with his long blond hair, red shirt, and fringed buckskin pants. Chief Juárez dressed in his brightly colored sarape, pantaloons, and knee-high boots. He and the clerks in their worn-out wool trousers and red flannel shirts, their bedrolls and tents packed on their backs. The Indian women dressed in the white, loose-fitting tunics Jim provided all his female workers. To add to the spectacle, Banyon and Cunningham rolled a wooden barrel between them filled with gold dust.

When they reached the city's public square, Jim had them set up camp for the night. Daniel paused to read the names on the surrounding buildings. The Eldorado, Revere House, Parker House, a restaurant, print shop, and a post office, among others. Hundreds of masts from ships harbored in the city's eastern bay peeked over the rooftops of the buildings on Montgomery Street. He hoped the chief was as taken by the city's bustling commerce as he was. But, when Daniel glanced at the man, the chief's stone-chiseled face appeared as rigid as when they left the gold fields.

While erecting their tents on the plaza grounds, a middle-aged man dressed in a silk top hat and black frock coat approached them.

"Excuse me. Mr. Savage?"

"That's me." Jim crouched to pound a tent peg into the plaza's hard-packed dirt.

The stranger tipped his hat. "Ha-ware-ya sir?" The man, his speech peppered with an Irish brogue, reached out a hand.

Jim ignored the stranger and continued to pound.

Returning his extended hand to his side, the well-dressed gentleman rocked back on his heels. "Well now, I've been informed of your arrival, don't ya know, and bid you welcome ta our fine city." He pointed toward a two-storied structure on the east side of Portsmouth Square. "I'm ta owner of the S.F. House on Kearny Street. 'Tis my pleasure to be offering you and yours a meal and boarding for one night, to be sure."

Daniel stepped closer. Something about the man's syrupy-sweet voice sounded sickeningly familiar.

Jim straightened and stretched, as if to loosen a kink in his back. "Well, that's mighty neighborly of you. Seems like an offer we'd be fools to refuse. What do you think, boys?"

"A night in a real bed?" Banyon's eyes widened.

Cunningham took off his wide-brimmed hat and scratched his head. "You got real tubs? And hot water?"

"Aye. 'That we do, sir." The proprietor, now wearing an I've-got

-'em-hooked business smile, nodded and continued to rock back on his heels. "We have real beds, tubs, hot water and—" The man winked. "Aye, so much more."

Jim tilted his head. "Just one thing. I'm sure you're makin´ this offer in hopes of gettin' us to stay with you the whole time we're here. It'd be more to your advantage if you threw in two free nights." Jim gave the man his own winsome I've-got-'em-hooked business smile.

A corner of the man's mouth curved up. "Aye, sir. Now, ain't you the negotiator. Two free nights it is."

Was that admiration or contempt in the man's voice? Daniel couldn't tell.

"And, of course, two free meals. For all of us." Jim reached out a hand.

The man scratched the back of his head, slightly tipping his hat forward. "Aye, two free meals as well."

After they shook on the deal, Jim raised his chin. "Seein' as you know my name, mind tellin' us yours?"

"Aye. Where's me manners?" He waved again toward his building. "Most people think the hotel's name, S.F. House, means the San Francisco House. Actually, the name stands for me initials. Name's Sean Flannery."

Daniel's stomach spasmed. He tried to pull in a breath, but it caught in his throat. He reached for the pistol tucked into his waistband.

Flannery clicked his heels and gave Jim a slight bow. "Sean Flannery, sir. At your service."

16
FLANNERY

October 25, 1850
San Francisco

Daniel reached for his revolver. Before he pulled it out, Limik clenched her fingers around his arm. He allowed his gaze to meet hers. Those fierce, questioning eyes.

During their trek to San Francisco, he'd told Limik about the loss of his parents. The Brody brothers. Flannery. How he lived for the day when Flannery would stand trial for the part the man played in his parents' deaths. He even told her about Virginia.

Now, staring into her dark eyes, he nodded. She released his arm. He removed his hand from his pistol and swallowed the bile that rose to his mouth. Its sting still bit his throat, and rage still raked his heart. Somehow, some way, Flannery would pay.

Later that evening, having washed and changed into clean clothes, Daniel joined Limik, Jim, and the others for dinner. Flannery had reserved a table for them near a large window that looked out onto Kearney Street.

From his vantage point, Daniel observed the bustling activity around Portsmouth Square. To the left, small boys tossed a ball. On each corner, vendors sold sweetmeats and newspapers. A colorful array of passersby wove through it all—bearded men sporting bowler hats, women shouldering fringed parasols, and a few men with beige-colored skin and black braids down their backs that he'd heard others refer to as *Celestials*. Jim called them *China-men*.

Much had changed in the two years since he'd left the Arnolds and San Francisco for the gold fields. Back then, about 2,000 people claimed the bay city as their own. Now, according to an article he'd read in the *Alta California* newspaper just before dinner, San Francisco boasted over 25,000 residents, "including people from every corner of the universe and of every tongue."

And more changes were on the way. The week before they'd arrived in San Francisco, the SS *Oregon* had steamed in delivering long-awaited news. California had been admitted into the Union as America's 31st state. The paper outlined the activities planned for October 29 when the city would formally celebrate the event. California, a state. His state.

What if I stay in San Francisco and don't go back to the gold fields with Jim?

Limik tugged his sleeve. "What you thinking, Dan'l? You so quiet."

She put on a bold face, but he sensed that the unfamiliar sights and sounds of the city frightened her. She'd gone back to her old ways of speaking, dropping what her blue backed speller called *helping verbs*. She'd almost mastered those before they left Agua Fria.

Instead of revealing his thoughts, he explained the bustling activity around them. "See those men carrying armloads of silver trays from the kitchen to the tables? They're called *waiters*. Hopefully they'll bring out our food soon. I'm starved."

He followed Limik's gaze as she stared at the men delivering food to the dinner guests and the bus boys carrying dirty plates and glasses back to the kitchen.

"This so hard to believe." Her thin fingers touched her lips. "Why men do these things? Why not women?"

She turned in her chair and studied the activity on the far side of the room. Daniel frowned. A mutton-chopped, middle-aged man stood behind the bar and served elbowing customers pints of ale and shots of whiskey. Eager gamblers crowded around tables as they waited for a seat at various games of chance. Only a few women roamed the room, but each disappeared up the staircase when a man wrapped his arm around her. Fumes of cigar smoke and brandy wafted over to their dining area, along with the hum of voices and the clink of coins.

Limik turned back to their table and lowered her head. "I only hope Chief Juárez not do those things."

He strained to hear her soft voice.

"I see him drink firewater of whites only once. He get mean and hurt others when he do that. He love playing games, too. When he play, he think he know more than everyone else. He try to trick them. If he lose, he get mad and hurt them."

Daniel hoped their food would come soon. The brightness of the room made him nauseous. Light from the chandeliers' flaming globes reflected off the room's glass pillars and mirrored walls. So much light in such a dark place.

After taking in the overly lavish sight, Daniel determined he would at least enjoy his meal—in spite of the fact it came from the hands of a murderer. Just as he turned back to the table, Flannery strode over and stationed himself behind Jim. Two waiters followed in his wake balancing trays of food atop their shoulders and palms.

With a flourish of his hand, the proud proprietor announced the name of each dish as the white-gloved, black-coated waiters set them on the table.

Partridge.

Quail.

Duck.

Beef.

They placed a platter of seared brown steak directly in front of Daniel. Its seasoned scent tantalized his taste buds. He hoped Flannery would stop talking so they could eat.

After announcing the final main dish of wild goose, Flannery grasped the edges of his tailored black coat and rocked back on his heels while the servers stood at attention.

"I trust you will find this meal to your satisfaction." Flannery raised his chin and continued to rock. "To be sure, I've hired the best chefs in the city." As if playing keys on a piano, Flannery tapped Jim's shoulder. "And I encourage you and your guests to try your luck at our gambling tables." With a final gesture, the man swept his hand across his chest, drawing attention to the selection of beverages placed on the table. "My establishment also serves the finest draughts, wines, and champagnes. Aye, lads. You won't be disappointed."

Banyon curled his fists around his fork and knife. "Enough yabberin' already. Let's eat!"

Guffaws rang out around the table.

Flannery dipped his chin. With a side-glance at his waiters and a tilt of his head toward the kitchen, he dismissed them. He, however, remained.

Daniel speared a slab of beef from the platter in front of him. The others spooned or stabbed samples of food from smoking hot plates, stirring up a clang of silverware and grunts as elbows bumped and beverages burbled into crystal goblets.

Slowly chewing a savory bite, Daniel kept a watchful eye on Flannery. The proprietor strutted around the table and lightly tapped each person's shoulder as if flaunting an inflated sense of superiority. When he reached Daniel and Limik, he paused.

"And who might this beautiful creature be?" Flannery's spindly fingers stroked Limik's long, black hair. "Aye. A most beautiful specimen of the aborigines, to be sure."

Aborigines? Daniel balled his hands and shoved back his chair, its wooden legs screeching across the polished planked flooring. Before he could stand, Limik caught one of his wrists beneath the table.

Limik raised her head toward Flannery. "I come from the tribe of Miwoks. I am Limik, cousin to Eekino, wife of Mr. Savage."

Pride swelled Daniel's chest. Limik knew how to hold her own.

Flannery stroked his beardless chin. "Well, I am confused, to be sure. Are you a cousin of Mr. Savage's wife, or are you married to Mr. Savage?"

Limik's long dark lashes waved in a slow blink. "Eekino is a wife of Mr. Savage." Her measured words spoke with fierce intensity. "I am not his wife. I am a cousin of Eekino."

"Well, now." Flannery shot her a flirtatious half-smile. "'Tis certainly good news." He stroked Limik's hair again.

Unable to bridle his rage, Daniel shot out of his chair. "Sir, you take liberties that—"

Before another word escaped his lips, a young man rushed up.

"Mr. Flannery." The messenger paused to catch his breath as he held up a note. "Mr. Tyndale sent over a runner. Says you need to meet him right away at the Exchange Office. Says it's urgent."

Flannery, seemingly unfazed by Daniel's outburst, clucked his tongue. "Always an interruption." He surveyed the group. "To be sure, I am sorry, but I must rush off." His final gaze rested on Limik. "I do hope to get better acquainted with each of you very soon."

Daniel shuddered with disgust.

After Flannery left and Daniel sat, the young man addressed the travelers. "I apologize for Mr. Flannery's sudden departure. Business matters, you know."

Jim eyed the young man for a moment, then stood. "Why, Hamilton. Chester Hamilton." He clapped the young man on the back. "Well I'll be. Haven't seen you since I bought goods here back in '46." Jim pointed to Daniel. "Hamilton, meet my accountant, Daniel Whitcomb."

Hamilton shook Daniel's hand. "Glad to meet you, sir."

Hamilton's limp handshake and tone didn't match the self-confidence suggested by the young man's apparel—white shirt, a two-inch-wide horizontal silk tie, and a gray frock coat.

"Yes sir," Jim glanced around the table. "I would have been dead in the water if Hamilton hadn't advised me to find someone to keep my books once I set up my trading posts. He's the most honest money-handlin' gent I ever met. Tried my darndest to get him to join me in the gold fields, but even the lure of diggin' up free gold couldn't drag him from his dandy job at the Exchange."

Jim's focus returned to Hamilton. "Now you work for Flannery, 'eh?"

"Yes, sir." Hamilton nodded as Jim sat.

Jim pointed to Daniel. "Well, Whitcomb here has worked out just fine. He learned to keep his pa's books back in Illinois where his family owned a blacksmith shop. Like you, Hamilton, he's as honest as they come."

Daniel's insides blazed. He shot Jim a narrow gaze. *So that's all I am to Jim? A bookkeeper who happened to work out just fine?*

"Glad to hear it." Hamilton pressed his lips together, pausing to study Daniel for a moment. "Ah, Mr. Whitcomb, if you don't mind, might I speak with you for a moment?"

A corner of Daniel's mouth tugged up, unaccustomed to having someone refer to him as *Mr. Whitcomb.* "Sure." He stood. "And it's just Daniel. Or Whitcomb, if you'd like."

He followed Hamilton to a more private corner of the dining room.

"If Mr. Savage says you're as honest as they come, then I wonder if I could trust you with a confidence regarding my employer." Hamilton spoke in a low tone.

"Your employer—Flannery?"

"Yes. Mr. Flannery. As his bookkeeper, I've run into a little problem. Since Mr. Savage has vouched for you, I'd like to appeal to your sense of decency. If you could just take a look at my accounting journal—"

Daniel held up a hand and shook his head. He didn't want to get involved with anything related to the man responsible for his parents' deaths. "I'm sorry, but Mr. Savage's businesses are small compared to Flannery's. I don't think I can help."

The man's pleading gaze bored into Daniel. "Please. Just take a look. I'd be forever in your debt. Perhaps after dinner? Mr. Flannery has a meeting at the Exchange. Sometimes these meetings take all night. We could be in and out of his office before he returns."

Daniel ran a hand over his journey-fatigued face. A chance to get into Flannery's office? He didn't want Flannery to find out who he was, at least not yet. But if he could find proof of a link between Flannery and the Brody brothers, maybe he'd find it in the man's office. It was a long shot, but worth investigating. "Sure. I'll see what I can do."

"Fine, fine." Hamilton's words rushed out. "Meet me at the bottom of the staircase at eight o'clock. And, if I can ever return the favor, please let me know."

Daniel shook Hamilton's outstretched hand. "Eight o'clock. I'll be there. And assuming I can be of some help, I think I know a way you can return the favor."

At eight o'clock, Daniel met Hamilton at the bottom of the hotel's staircase and followed him to the second floor. After traipsing down several hallways, Hamilton stopped in front of a door labeled *Office.*

Hamilton, holding up a lighted oil lamp, handed it to Daniel as he unlocked the door. Following him inside, Daniel surveyed the rose-papered sitting room. Everything in the chamber spoke of Flannery's inflated sense of importance. He brushed a hand over an ornately carved wing-backed chair, noting how it matched the blue satin brocade sofa. Passing by the fireplace, he whistled at the white marble mantelpiece and its relief sculptures of roses and winding grapevines.

"Mr. Flannery entertains his guests here," the accountant said as he followed Daniel's gaze. Hamilton led Daniel to the far-left back corner of the hotel suite and unlocked another door. It squeaked open. "This is his actual office."

Before entering, Hamilton pointed to a room behind them on the far right of the suite. "Mr. Flannery's bedroom is over there. He prefers to have his living quarters and workspace in the same place since he often works late."

Trailing Hamilton into the office, Daniel eyed tall bookcases filled with journals and ledgers. As the accountant reached for a ledger labeled *1850*, Daniel glanced at the spines of the other journals filling the bookcase. Each was dated with a year and span of months going back to 1842. Daniel quickly scanned their labels until he found one dated *1846 January-February*. Flannery and the Brody brothers had burned down his family's home in February of 1846. What secrets did that ledger hold? He raised trembling fingers along the ledger's spine.

"This way, sir."

Reluctantly, Daniel strode over.

"Until four months ago," Hamilton said, "I worked at the Exchange down the street." Hamilton stood and flipped through the ledger's pages. "Then Mr. Flannery offered me more money to work for him. A good deal more than I made at the Exchange. But Flannery warned that the increased pay came with an occasional *need for discretion*. I wasn't exactly sure what he meant by that."

Stopping at a page titled *1850 September Expenses*, Hamilton continued. "To be honest, I guess I had an idea what that meant, but there has never been a problem. Until now." The accountant pointed to two columns labeled *Outside Contractors—San Francisco*. Below the columns were a list of names and dollar amounts.

Hamilton cleared his throat. "I oversee this ledger, and it contains all transactions dealing with hotel purchases, shipping bills, and staff salaries. Last week, however, Mr. Flannery entered these names and figures himself." He shook his head. "I don't know what to make of it. None of the names listed here are vendors we've used before. And there's no note in the ledger as to the services these people performed. If we were ever audited, it would look as though I wasn't doing my job properly."

Hamilton waved a hand at the dated journals and ledgers that overflowed the bookcases. "Believe me, Mr. Flannery is meticulous when it comes to keeping records. These books date back to business ventures he had before moving to California."

Daniel's heart drilled through his chest. What if Flannery had a record of payments he made to the Brodys? Of course, he didn't expect the ledger to say, *Payments made to Matthew and Josiah Brody for burning down the Whitcomb's home,* but if the dates coincided with the fire, what if he had a record of paying them? That, along with the brothers' written confession could make a solid case against the man.

Fingering the account sheet in front of him, Daniel read off the names listed in the contractors' column. "Mooney, Scannell, Mulligan, Dutch Charley." Daniel glanced back at Hamilton. "Flannery's only listed last names, initials, or nicknames." He ticked a muscle in his jaw. "Sorry to say, but I think this is a list of men Flannery pays to carry out his dirty work."

"What do you mean?" Hamilton took a step back, his voice quivering. "D–dirty work?"

Closing the journal with a thud, Daniel stepped to the office window. He stared at the pinpoints of light flickering inside tents, shanties, and businesses—shelters that stretched out toward the darkened waters of the bay.

This morning when Daniel and the others had arrived by ship from Stockton, he had marveled at the deserted vessels choking the port's entryway. Their ship captain explained that crews of those abandoned ships had deserted their posts as soon as they reached port, many not even waiting for their ships to anchor. Without unloading their ship's cargo, the sailors ran off for the gold fields to seek their fortunes. *But not Flannery*, Daniel mused. Men like him would reap greater profits by remaining behind in a city like San Francisco.

Daniel turned back to Hamilton. "How much do you know about Flannery?"

Hamilton shrugged. "Personally, I know nothing about the man. I know Mr. Tyndale actually owns this hotel and hired Flannery to manage it. I hear he pays Flannery a handsome sum, as well as a percentage of the profits. But I don't keep Flannery's private books. I only record and balance the hotel's income and expenses." Deep lines formed between Hamilton's brows. "If you think Flannery is involved in illegal activities, I—" He ran a hand through his russet brown hair. "I don't know what to do. Can you help me?"

Fatigue and frustration washed over Daniel. He knew first-hand what Flannery was capable of. "Men like Flannery will do anything to make a profit, that much I know." He sized up the accountant. You're asking me what you should do?" Reaching across the desk, Daniel picked up the ledger and handed to Hamilton. "If you value your life, don't do anything. Don't ask any questions. Just keep on balancing the books."

The young man stiffened. "I don't know if I can do that."

A flicker of an idea worked its way through Daniel's tired brain. "On the other hand, if you think you—"

"Aye. Working late, Hamilton?"

Daniel's blood froze. Flannery had gotten back early. How much had he overheard?

"Y–yes, Mr. Flannery." Hamilton let out a nervous chuckle. "Working late. You know me. Work, work, work." Hamilton cleared his throat. "I was asking Mr. Savage's bookkeeper for his thoughts on some billing transactions. He showed me a way we can save money."

"Good, good." Mr. Flannery set a yellow-ribboned cardboard box on the table. "That's why I stole you away from the Exchange Office, Hamilton. I was told you had a way with numbers. Always looking for ways to make more money. To be sure, that's what I like most about you, son."

Flannery reached out to shake Daniel's hand. "And thanks for your help, Mr. ah, well, that's embarrassing. Guess we haven't been officially introduced."

Daniel returned the handshake and quickly swallowed a gulp of the pulverized steak that now rose to his throat. How could he keep Flannery from finding out who he was? "No, Mr. Flannery, we haven't been introduced yet. You can call me Cipher. It's my nickname in the gold fields. Short for cipherin' since that's what I do for Mr. Savage."

"Cipher, then." Flannery's grip tightened. "I must say, any tips you can give Hamilton here are surely welcome. God knows you've got your work cut out for you, keepin' track of Savage's expenses and all that gold a-flowin' his way."

Daniel's head buzzed. He inhaled a gulp of air, hoping to cut their conversation short. "I really need to go now, sir. Mr. Savage still wants to meet up with me tonight."

"Of course, of course." Flannery nodded and released Daniel's hand. "Before you go, however, I have a favor to ask."

A favor? All he wanted to do was wrap his hands around the man's neck. He hoped his forced smile hid his rage. "What's that?"

"I noticed you sat next to that young aborigine at dinner earlier and—"

Daniel clenched his fists. "Her name is Limik."

"Fine, fine. Limik." Flannery waved a dismissive hand. "I'd like to give her this gift." He picked up the cardboard box and handed it to Daniel. "I couldn't help but notice the awful rags that girl wore. Surely, she would enjoy something more, ah, feminine. And I would like to dine with her here in me suite if she would be so kind as to receive me gift and wear it. Would you please pass this on, and invite her to sup with me at, say, seven o'clock tomorrow evening?"

Like the boiling waters of a steam engine, pressure built behind Daniel's eyes. "I'll pass on the invitation, Mr. Flannery. But I have to warn you. If she agrees, Mr. Savage will insist that a chaperone accompany her." He doubted Jim would really care, but *he* surely wouldn't allow Limik to visit this despicable man by herself.

Flannery scratched his head. "A chaperone, eh? Most disappointing. Well, if you'd at least pass along the invitation, I'd appreciate it. Write me a note and slip it under me door before three o'clock tomorrow. Either yes or no. I must give me chefs enough time to prepare the meal." He reached into his vest and pulled out a silver dollar. "Something for your troubles, to be sure."

Daniel narrowed his eyes. "As a matter of fact, Mr. Flannery, Limik's capable of writing her own response. But I'll deliver the message." He pushed Flannery's hand away and strode from the room.

17
FLANNERY'S LEDGERS

Daniel. Banyon. Wake up!"

It was too early for a knock on his hotel room door. Too early to even read the face of his pocket watch. Daniel stumbled out of bed and lit the oil lamp on the nightstand. He then glanced at Banyon who snored away on the other side of the room. That man could sleep through a thunderstorm.

With the oil lamp in his hand, Daniel slowly cracked open the door and recognized Jim in the hallway. He opened the door wider and stared at the man's puffy, purple-ringed left eye.

"What happened to your face?" Daniel asked.

Jim fingered his swollen lid. "Nothin'." He shook his head. "This morning, I need you and Banyon to git down to the wharf, pronto. Need you to see a cooper 'bout some barrels. Corner of Dupont and Filbert. Made an early appointment for you to buy barrels to ship our merchandise with us back to Stockton. Need you to also shop for supplies. While you do that, Cunningham and I'll give Juárez a tour of the city."

Daniel knew that, once they bought their needed supplies, they'd take the goods by steamship from San Francisco to Stockton where hired hands would meet them with wagons, horses, and mules. They'd then transport the goods from Stockton to their trading posts. But he hadn't thought about needing to buy barrels to contain the shipments.

Rubbing sleep from his eyes, Daniel moaned. "But why so early? The sun's not even up."

A smile tugged at the corners of Jim's mouth. "Last night I won six newly-made barrels in a poker game from a cooper named Schmidt. Since we still need about another ten barrels for all the goods we want to buy, he promised me first pick of the rest if I get there by seven this morning with the order and the money. Seems barrels are in short supply in San Francisco."

Jim slid a leather bag off his shoulder and handed it to Daniel. "Make the best deal you can for ten more barrels. Afterwards, you and Banyon purchase the supplies on our list. Meet us back here for lunch at one o'clock." Jim turned and left.

Banyon sat up in bed. "Who was that?"

"Jim. Wants us to get down to the wharf right away to order barrels."

Not an early riser, Banyon laid back down and yanked the covers over his head. "What time is it? Seems like it's the middle of the night."

Daniel grabbed his pocket watch from the nightstand and opened it. "Six o'clock. Our appointment's at seven." He snapped the watch cover shut, then lit two more oil lamps to brighten the room.

After he washed and shaved, he realized Banyon still hadn't gotten up. He playfully tossed a pillow at the large man's head. "No time to waste."

"Can't we at least get breakfast?" Banyon groaned.

"Nope. Best get movin'."

As Daniel dressed, his mind churned with thoughts of Limik like water on a steamboat's paddle wheel. No time to tell her about his meeting with Hamilton or Flannery's dinner invitation. He yanked up his socks harder than usual. He didn't want Limik to have dinner with that deplorable dog. On the other hand, he needed to find a way to get into Flannery's office without the man's knowledge.

After their appointment with the cooper, he and Banyon walked two blocks north to a shop Jim recommended as a good place to order canned goods.

While crossing another muddy street, Banyon bumped Daniel's arm. "Sure glad you and me got saddled with orderin' supplies instead of takin' Juárez around San Francisco." The large man stopped for a second, took off his broad-brimmed felt hat, and wiped his forehead with a red handkerchief.

Daniel glanced up at the sound of approaching hoofbeats just in time to see a speeding carriage lumbering toward them.

"Watch out!" he shouted. He grabbed Banyon's arm and dragged him out of the way.

"Daggone city folk!" Banyon raised a fist at the driver. "In too much of a danged hurry. Everyone of 'em."

When they reached the safety of the wood-planked sidewalk, Daniel sized up the large man and then squeezed his lips tight to stifle a laugh. Mud splattered Banyon's woolen trousers, his long-sleeved white shirt, his red suspenders, his face, and his scraggly beard.

As Banyon wiped off his clothes, Daniel snickered. "You can't just stop in the middle of a city street to have a conversation. And why would you rather be out buying supplies instead of taking Juárez around San Francisco?"

Banyon stuffed his muddy handkerchief into his pocket. "Didn't ya hear 'bout the fight Juárez had with Savage last night?"

"No. What happened?"

They continued down the wooden sidewalk, their boots thunking with each step.

"Well, ya know how we brought that barrel of gold to San Francisco? And how Savage says one-third of it belongs to his Indian workers? And one-third's his, and one-third's for our expenses?"

"Yeah." Shifting the weight of the leather bag he'd thrown over his shoulder, Daniel tightened his grip on its strap. "Jim says he plans to deposit his gold and the Indians' gold in a bank here for safe-keeping. What about it?"

Banyon turned at the sound of another carriage rushing down the street. "Last night Juárez claimed he had a right to spend some of the Indjuns' gold 'fore Savage locks it up in a bank, him bein' their chief and all. Juárez wanted to go out drinkin' and gamblin'."

"Let me guess," Daniel said. "Jim said no."

Banyon nodded. "That's when their fists went a-flyin'."

"That explains the black eye Jim had this morning." Daniel stopped to check his pocket watch. Ten o'clock. Hopefully they could buy most of their supplies before one o'clock. Then he'd tell Limik about Flannery's gift. Although she wouldn't like the idea, he would ask her to meet with the man. If she agreed, he'd find a way to keep her safe that would also give him time to gather evidence against the man.

Three hours later, they returned to the S.F. House's dining room.

"So, where's Savage and Juárez?" Banyon removed his hat and wiped his forehead with his soiled bandana. "I'm starved."

"You're always hungry." Daniel gave him a spirited backslap and studied the seated guests. No Jim, no Cunningham, no chief, and no Miwok or Yokuts women. He checked his pocket watch. Ten past one. "They'll be here soon." He was trying to convince himself more than Banyon. What if something had happened to them?

When no one showed up by half past one, Banyon threw up his hands. "Jim said he'd pay for our meals, but I'm done waitin'. Maybe they'll let me charge the meal to his account."

"Let's just wait a little—"

Banyon strode over to a table.

Daniel figured that Jim, Cunningham, and the chief could take care of themselves, but he worried about the women. Maybe they were in their room, or out for a walk, or in someone else's room. He mounted the stairsteps two at a time to the second floor.

When he knocked on the women's door, Eekino hesitantly cracked it open. Seeing Daniel, she flung it wide.

"So glad it you. We not see El Rey all day."

Daniel stood in the hallway and cocked his head to the side. "Didn't you eat with Mr. Savage and the chief this morning?"

Eekino frowned. "They never come for us. We not know how to get food. We stay in room."

Daniel worked his jaw as heat rose from his chest. *Typical Jim.* The man hadn't given a thought as to how the women would care for themselves. Daniel escorted them downstairs. Using some of the supply money, he ordered lunch.

The waiters brought out a tasty meal of curried sausages, peas, squash, and Irish potatoes. The women said they didn't want much, so he ordered them bowls of clam chowder, cooked carrots, and bread.

After downing several bites of sausage, Daniel turned to Limik. "Last night in Flannery's ledgers I think I found evidence of illegal activity. But I need to do more investigation. His clerk is willing to help."

Limik held her spoon in midair. "Ledgers? Like books you keep for El Rey?"

Daniel nodded. "Flannery records date back to before my parents' deaths. I want to get into his office when he's not there. I could look at the '46 ledger to see if he made any payments to the Brody brothers around the time of our house fire."

Putting down her spoon, Limik leaned closer. "It sounds like big trouble. I do not want you in danger, Dan'l."

He ran a hand across his face. "If I can't find a legal way to link Flannery to my parents' deaths, I don't know if I can keep myself from taking matters into my own hands."

"Dan'l. You would not. You could not—"

"I could. And I would." He clenched his hands until his fingernails bit into his palms. He imagined himself squeezing Flannery's throat.

"No." She shook her head. "Stop. You must not say such things." She brushed her fingers against his. "How can I help?"

Sweet Limik. How could he think of involving her? He clenched his teeth and turned back to his plate. Stabbing another bite of sausage, he popped it into his mouth and chewed, but found it hard to swallow.

Limik scooped up another spoonful of soup.

Suddenly, he wasn't hungry anymore.

"There is a way you might be able to help." He turned to her again.

She met his gaze. "What? Anything."

He sensed something in her large, glistening eyes. Something he'd never noticed before. More than concern. More than fear. Maybe even more than friendship.

Filling his lungs with air, he slowly pushed it out. "Flannery's invited you to dine with him tonight in his hotel suite. You are to slip an answer under his door before three o'clock. He also asked me to give you this." He pulled out the large, yellow-ribboned box he'd hidden beneath the table and placed it in front of her.

"Dinner in that man's room?" She slid the box to the side. "I not go anywhere near him. He frighten me."

Daniel noted Limik had slipped into her broken English. Obviously, she feared Flannery. So did he. Spreading a hand flat on the table, he held her gaze with a stare. "I would never put you in danger. And I wouldn't ask you to do this if I could think of another way."

Her gaze shifted to the box.

He lightly touched her arm, and she turned back toward him. "What if you wrote Flannery a note and agreed to have dinner with him here in the dining room? I'll get Hamilton to loan me an office key. If you keep Flannery down here for a while, it'll give me time to go through his ledgers."

Limik's forehead furrowed.

With his heart thumping in his chest, his words tumbled out. "I'll ask Banyon to keep an eye on you the whole time. He'll eat dinner down here too, and if Flannery tries anything, he'll jump in and rescue you."

She sat silent for a moment. "If that help you, Dan'l, then, yes. I do it. But only if Flannery meet me here."

Daniel rubbed his hands together. "I think this'll work. But if Flannery happens to mention me, he thinks my name is Cipher. Don't let him know my name's really Daniel Whitcomb."

At seven o'clock, Daniel met Limik in the hotel lobby. Appearing radiant in Flannery's gift of a yellow satin dress, she seemed to float down the staircase. He recalled how long it took his seamstress stepmother to make such an elegant gown for the wealthy women in Springfield. He admired the delicate beauty of its design. Its three-layered flounced skirt. Its circular neckline. Its triangular-shaped bodice panel. A bodice that accentuated Limik's youthful figure. The yellow taffeta silk provided a stunning contrast to her dark long hair and eyelashes.

When Limik reached the bottom step, she offered him a hint of a smile—a quiet smile that tugged at his heart. "It is beautiful, is it not?" She let her hands brush the smooth sides of her full skirt.

Before Daniel could translate his emotions into words, Flannery arrived.

"Oh my, oh my." Flannery let out a low whistle. "Ain't you a lovely gem? To be sure, the first night I laid me eyes on ya, I purchased that gown." Taking Limik's hand, the short man kissed it and didn't let go. "I paid a seamstress to watch ya from a distance and make any alterations she thought necessary. I hope you didn't mind her helpin' ya to dress this evening."

"Thank you. No." Limik pulled back her hand. "I not know how to put on all these fancy clothes. She help very much."

Flannery led Limik into the dining room. Daniel trailed two steps behind as the Irishman wrapped an arm around Limik's waist.

When Limik stiffened, Daniel resisted the urge to yank the man's arm out of its socket.

"To be sure," Flannery crooned, "I'm glad you agreed ta meet with me. Aye. Even if 'tis only here in the dining room. After we eat, perhaps I will show you a view of the city from me suite. Like you, the city 'tis a most stunning sight at night."

Once again, Daniel envisioned his hands around the man's throat. He quickened his pace and hurried to the other side of Limik. "Mr. Flannery. Since you and Limik are dining here this evening, Mr. Savage felt there was no need for a chaperone. Meeting with Limik alone in your room, however, is out of the question. Propriety. I'm sure you understand."

"Well, yes, yes. I suppose." After pulling out a chair for Limik, Flannery circled to the other side of the table and waved a dismissive hand. "Then, I suppose there is no need for you to stay, eh, Cipher? Off with ya now."

Daniel clenched his jaw, nodded at Flannery, and flashed Limik what he hoped was a calming, but conspiratorial grin. A quick check of the area assured him Banyon was in place to keep watch. Gripping the office key in his pocket, he hurried to the staircase and sprinted up the steps.

A nearby church tolled eight bells, pulling Daniel's nose from the journal. He'd been at Flannery's desk studying the '46 ledger for an hour. He'd found nothing.

A scratching noise rose from the back corner. Daniel froze. Careful not to make a sound, he turned, only to see a mouse nibbling a crumb. He released a breath he didn't know he was holding.

He scanned the January pages once more. Then he saw it. On the fourth accounting sheet for the month of January, the expense column listed a payout of $300 to both Josiah and Matthew Brody.

The office door squeaked open.

"Almost finished?" Hamilton's lanky figure stood in the doorway.

Daniel slapped a hand over his heart as if to keep it in his chest. "You just shaved ten years off my life. What are you doing here?"

Hamilton strode over to the desk. "Came to see if I could help."

With a trembling finger, Daniel pointed to the description of work the brothers did for Flannery.

Hamilton's brows crunched together as he read it out loud. "Removal of approximately 350 lbs. of harmful rubbish. What does that mean?"

"It means—" Daniel swallowed to steady his voice. "It means Flannery thought my parents were a pile of rubbish that needed to be tossed out." Daniel's stomach soured. What had his parents ever done to that evil man? Their paths had only crossed when Flannery came to the blacksmith shop to purchase new horseshoes, get a bridle repaired, or have Pa or Morgan Savage make new hinges for his tavern doors or cabinets.

Daniel pointed to Matthew and Josiah's names in the ledger. "Last year I found written confessions by these Brody brothers."

Hamilton leaned closer.

"The brothers said Flannery paid each of them $300 to smoke my parents out of our home. It also said Flannery added fuel to the fire, and when the boys tried to stop him, the fire got out of control and burned our house to the ground. My stepsister and I weren't home at the time."

Deep lines formed between Hamilton's brows. "And your parents died?"

Bile rose in Daniel's throat. "Yep. My pa was a blacksmith. Pa was a large, well-muscled man. Between him and my stepmother, I guess together they probably weighed about 350 pounds."

"So this"—Hamilton tapped his finger on the entry"—along with the Brody brothers' confession, could prove Flannery killed your parents?"

Daniel wiped sweat from his forehead and nodded.

Pushing Daniel aside, Hamilton pulled out a blank journal sheet from a desk drawer. "I'll copy down these figures and sign an affidavit stating it is a true copy of this journal page. Then I'll find a safe place to hide it until it's needed."

His insides trembling, Daniel stood. "I can't thank you enough, Hamilton. You've got more sand than I gave you credit for."

Hamilton's bespeckled face tightened. "Sand?"

"A phrase I picked up in the gold fields." Daniel slapped him on the back. "I've got to check on Limik. "Copy these fast. Don't want Flannery catching you."

Nodding, Hamilton sat, pulled out a quill and ink, and began to write.

Daniel returned to the dining room around half-past eight as Limik and Flannery were finishing their meal.

"I not feel well," he heard Limik say as he approached their table. She stood and thanked Flannery for the dress and the dinner. When Flannery rose and offered to escort her to her room, Daniel stepped between them.

"Mr. Flannery," Daniel said. "I just passed Mr. Hamilton in the lobby. He says there's a man at the bar who needs to speak with you. Says the man's name is Dutch Charley."

Flannery let out a low growl. "I told that brute never to meet me here." The short man then pasted a smile on his face and kissed Limik's hand. "So sorry to cut our time short, my dear. 'Twas so sweet to dine with you. To be sure, I hope we can do this again sometime."

Daniel breathed a sigh of relief. *Over my dead body.*

After Flannery left, Limik fell back into her chair.

From across the room, Daniel's gaze met Banyon's. His companion nodded. Daniel hadn't shared any details with Banyon about the evening's events. He only said he feared for Limik while she dined with Flannery, and that he couldn't be there himself. Banyon agreed without question.

As Daniel escorted Limik to her room, he told her what he'd found in Flannery's ledger. Every muscle in his body ached from the evening's ordeal. Limik's eyes betrayed the same exhaustion. When they reached her room's door, he squeezed her hand and left.

Later that night, Daniel woke trembling. His nightshirt, wet with sweat, clung to his chest. He dreamed he confronted Flannery with the ledger's evidence. He challenged the man to a duel. Limik stepped between them and got shot in the crossfire. Had the bullet come from his gun, or Flannery's? He replayed the nightmare. His hand shaking as he raised it and fired two shots. Flannery falling in a heap. Limik between them, a gush of scarlet flowing from her side. Two dead bodies at his feet. He'd finally gotten justice, but at what cost?

In the morning, already late for breakfast, Daniel forced the images from his mind. While dressing, he reviewed the evidence against Flannery. The man had killed his parents. No doubt about that. But were the ledger entries and the Brody brothers' confessions enough to convince a jury? Probably not.

When he arrived in the dining room for breakfast, everyone was almost finished.

Jim greeted him with an upraised cup. "Glad you could join us Daniel. You just missed my announcement. Since it's Sunday, I've given everyone the day off. Most likely me, Banyon, and Cunningham'll spend the day gamblin'. No law against that in San Francisco."

Banyon and Cunningham gave each other approving nods and punches.

Jim sipped from his cup. "Later this evening," he continued, "the women and I are seeing a play at the Jenny Lind Theatre."

Daniel studied those around the table. In his rush to join them, he hadn't noticed the women wearing new outfits—Homut and Eekino in green day dresses gathered at the waist; Limik in a blue one with ruffled sleeves—maybe Jim's way of apologizing for yesterday when he'd abandoned them.

A scene from Daniel's nightmare invaded his thoughts. Limik lying in a pool of blood. He shook his head to cast out the image and noted the others around the table. Juárez was missing.

"Where's the chief?" he asked. Although Daniel hadn't yet ordered, a waiter placed a dish of bacon and eggs in front of him. He gratefully shoveled a forkful into his mouth.

"Got himself arrested last night." Jim took another sip of coffee.

"What?" Daniel looked from Jim, to Banyon, to Cunningham, and back again to Jim. His voice rose. "Why? 'cause he's an Injun?"

Cunningham leaned back. "No. Savage gave the chief some gold after touring the city yesterday. The fool got drunk while gamblin', then fought with the tavern keeper when he lost and didn't pay up. The police finally arrived and carted him off to jail."

"But we'll get him out, right?" Daniel stared across at Jim.

Jim's eyebrows rose. "Eventually. I'll let him stew for a while. Maybe bail him tonight. At least he can't cause more trouble while he's there."

As he ate his eggs and bacon, Daniel sensed Limik watching him. He wanted to talk more about the ledger and ask her details about her dinner with Flannery, but he'd have to wait until they were alone.

Limik lightly touched his sleeve. "Dan'l, what will you do today?"

Before he could answer, Jim raised a hand. "Don't think you should make plans for today, son. Not till you hear the surprise I've got for you." Jim looked over at the hotel's entrance and smiled. "In fact, my surprise is walkin' in right now."

Daniel turned just as Dr. Arnold entered the hotel lobby. His old friend from the wagon train. His old friend who had taken him in when he first arrived in California. His old friend whom he had abandoned to run off with Jim to the gold fields.

18
THE ARNOLDS

Daniel rushed to Dr. Arnold's side and grasped the man's warm hand.

The elderly doctor locked his arms around Daniel. "I thought I'd never see you again, son."

The doctor's bear-like hug and thick gravelly voice conveyed soul-watering sentiments Daniel longed to hear.

Acceptance.

Love.

Forgiveness.

Daniel led Dr. Arnold to the table and made introductions. "I'd like you all to meet Dr. George Arnold. As a few of you know, Dr. Arnold and his wife took me in when I first arrived in California."

Standing, Banyon shook the doctor's hand. "Pleased to meet ya, sir. Daniel's told me a bit about you. Can't believe you let this rogue live with you for two years."

Head tilted to the side, Cunningham's brows drew together.

Dr. Arnold and Daniel sat while a waiter poured everyone more coffee.

"When our wagon train reached Sutter's Fort in '46," Daniel explained to Cunningham, "I had no place to go, so the Arnolds invited me to live with them in San Francisco. Me being only fourteen and all."

Daniel glanced sideways at Jim, anticipating at least a hint of remorse.

His guardian's face remained blank.

Only once had Jim apologized for abandoning him on the wagon train before they reached California. They never spoke of it again.

Cunningham still looked confused.

Working to keep the edge out of his voice, Daniel explained. "I lived with the Arnolds for two years before Jim, my legal guardian, reappeared and convinced me to join him in the gold fields."

Dr. Arnold shook hands with Cunningham and Jim, then nodded to the women. "Indeed. I am delighted to make your acquaintances. I am ever so grateful to Mr. Savage for sending an emissary to my home last evening, suggesting I meet you here this morning."

The past two years had taken a toll on Dr. Arnold. While the former Englishman looked as distinguished as ever in his charcoal gray frock coat, high-collared white shirt, and black silk cravat, Daniel couldn't help but notice the bags under the elderly man's eyes. The additional wrinkles on his face and hands. The tired blue eyes beneath those bushy gray eyebrows.

"Mrs. Arnold also wanted to accompany me this morning, but she is a tad under the weather." Dr. Arnold sat and sipped his coffee.

Fear shot through Daniel, as if a rope had lassoed his soul. "Nothing serious, I hope."

"No, no." Dr. Arnold shook his head as his cup clinked on its saucer. "It is merely a head cold, but I didn't want her to catch a draft."

"I'd love to see her. Think she's up for a visit today?"

"I am sure she would relish it, but I assumed you had important business to finish in town. Mr. Savage noted you will only be here another two days."

Jim drained his cup. "Gave all the boys the day off, sir. It bein' Sunday and all."

Daniel drew in a quick breath. "Maybe I could go back with you now to visit with her?"

Dr. Arnold's eyes glistened. "That would be wonderful, my boy."

Limik tugged Daniel's sleeve. "May I come too?" She spoke so softly he had to lean down to catch her words.

"Dr. Arnold, if Jim doesn't mind, could Limik also join us?"

A smile spread across the doctor's face. "Indeed. I am sure Mrs. Arnold would enjoy her company as well."

Daniel shifted his gaze to Jim.

His guardian waved him off. "Sure, sure."

After breakfast, Daniel followed Dr. Arnold and Limik outside. Waiting for them at the curb stood a large, enclosed carriage coupled to a pair of magnificent black horses. The animals' silver harnesses jangled as their tails brushed off circling flies. Daniel helped Limik into the black-polished hackney cab. When he entered, he brushed his hand across the silk-lined interior. Life on the gold fields paled in comparison to the grandeur of city life. *Why did I ever leave?*

Fifteen minutes later, they pulled up in front of the Arnolds' house.

Home. As he gazed at the familiar, two-story dwelling, emotions washed over him. He missed not having a place to call home. People to call a family. Parents to call Ma and Pa.

As they sipped tea in the Arnolds' sparse but elegantly furnished parlor, Limik leaned forward in her gold, wingback chair.

"Dr. Arnold?" Her voice came soft as she twisted her locked fingers in her lap. "Why your words sound different than Dan'l?"

The doctor's eyes twinkled. "I was born in a country far across the ocean. It is a place called England."

Limik's eyebrows floated. "Like ocean at end of San Francisco city?"

"Something like that. But it's another ocean on the other side of this great land."

"Then why you come all the way here?"

Daniel picked up the teapot from the low marble-topped table in front of him and refilled his cup. He hadn't told Limik how much the doctor loved to tell stories. And he'd forgotten how much he loved hearing them.

The elderly man set his cup on the mahogany table next to his burgundy armchair and edged to the front of his seat, obviously eager to begin.

"You see, my dear, years ago my father and my older brother John moved from England to Canada to work for the Hudson Bay Company to help in the management of their offices in Montreal. I never went into the family business because of my interest in medicine. When they, along with my mother, crossed the ocean to live in eastern Canada, I stayed in England to work at the world's first ophthalmic hospital."

Mrs. Arnold laid her knitting aside and cleared her throat. "That's just a fancy word for an eye hospital, my dear Limik. Sometimes Dr. Arnold likes to throw around big-sounding words." She glanced at her husband over the bridge of her wire-rimmed glasses.

The man nodded in his wife's direction. Daniel caught the unspoken message that passed between them. *You're right my dear, thank you for catching me on that.*

Daniel had seen them share that silent love language on many occasions. A silent love language he hoped to learn if he ever fell in love again.

"Then one evening at a dinner party," Dr. Arnold continued, "I was introduced to two American physicians who spoke of opening an eye clinic for the poor of New York City. Mrs. Arnold and I believed the Lord wanted us to help in that work, so we moved to America."

Daniel swallowed a sip of tea. "Was that when your father disinherited you, Dr. Arnold?"

The elderly man nodded. "Indeed. My father thought I was throwing away my education by serving the poor. We had built up a significant savings from my practice in England, so we were able to live a comfortable life in New York. Indeed, I never heard from my father again."

Dr. Arnold's chair creaked as he leaned back. "In '43 my brother John wrote to say Mum had died of tuberculosis. By that time, due to their company's expansion, he and father had moved to the Pacific Northwest Territory. Father died shortly thereafter. A few months later, the Hudson Bay Company decided to open a business in Yerba Buena."

Mrs. Arnold picked up her knitting needles once again and pointed the tips toward Limik. "Yerba Buena is what they used to call San Francisco when Mexico still controlled California."

"Yes." Dr. Arnold nodded and gave his wife a thank-you-dear smile. "Since my parents had died, leaving my brother all alone, he volunteered to pioneer the company's expansion in Yerba Buena, now known as San Francisco. Shortly after that, we received a letter from John inviting us to join him here."

Dr. Arnold drew a hand across his chin. "We had no children. God had not seen fit to bless us in that way. John hoped we would join him out West so that we could have, as he put it, a new relationship with each other in a new country. He purchased two lots near the company's office here and wrote that he was reserving the second one for us, should we wish to join him."

"And that is how you met Dan'l?" Limik asked. "On the wagon train to California?"

Mrs. Arnold nodded and chuckled. "Looking back on it now, I suppose it was a foolhardy thing to do, us being in our late fifties and all. But I had never met Dr. Arnold's brother, so we joined the next wagon train and headed West. That is how we came to be friends with Daniel, his stepsister Hannah, and the Savage family."

At the mention of Hannah, Daniel's heart lurched. He hadn't thought about his stepsister since his reunion with the Reeds a year and a half ago.

"My practice here in Yerba Buena was slow at first," Dr. Arnold said. "Now, however, with the swell of people coming to San Francisco, I can barely accommodate all who need my services."

He turned to Daniel. "In fact, although they are not common eye ailments, right now I am treating several patients who suffer from the same eye disease your stepsister had. Amblyopia. I have also treated a few with strabismus."

Limik's face pinched.

Clearing her throat once more, Mrs. Arnold glanced at her husband.

"I am sorry, dear." Dr. Arnold chuckled. "As you may have noticed, Mrs. Arnold has to remind me not to throw around my fancy medical terms. On the wagon train, I treated Daniel's stepsister for what is commonly called a lazy eye, or as it is known in my profession, amblyopia. She made great improvement until—"

Daniel stopped listening. His grief over Hannah's death was still raw. Instead, while the good doctor continued his story, he turned his attention to Mrs. Arnold.

Earlier in their visit he'd learned that, in his absence, she'd taken on many of the chores he'd previously done—buying groceries, feeding the horses, cleaning the stable, weeding the garden. Now she looked too frail to keep it up. He knew Dr. Arnold earned enough money as an eye doctor to hire out the work, but Mrs. Arnold was a proud and stubborn woman.

He studied the soft lines on her pallid, bespectacled face. An icy coldness pricked the nape of his neck. He inhaled a shaky breath as an odd mix of sadness and anger washed over him. *I never should have left them to join Jim in the gold fields.*

When Dr. Arnold paused to refill everyone's teacup, Daniel ventured a thought. "Mrs. Arnold, why don't you hire someone to take on the extra chores around here?"

"We have tried, Daniel." Her aging voice wavered, but her tone emerged vibrant as ever. "I have gone through several housekeepers and stable boys, but in a city where money and greed reign supreme, diligent and honest workers are hard to come by." She clucked her tongue. "But, enough about us, dear. What about you?"

Daniel shared about Virginia, the Brody brothers' confessions, his law studies, tutoring Limik, and the possibility of an Indian uprising in the gold fields.

While he briefly chronicled the highlights of the past two years, he caught a glimpse of Limik surveying the Arnold's parlor from her seat across from him. Her gaze finally settled on the shelves lining the far wall that overflowed with books. When he told the Arnolds he was teaching her to read, her focus shifted to him. A soft smile traced her full lips. She lifted her head slightly as he shared her desire to write an account of her people's oral legends.

When he finally described what he'd found in Flannery's accounting books, Mrs. Arnold leaned forward, removed her spectacles, and pulled her thin black-and-gray-peppered brows together. "Did you say one of the names in Flannery's ledger was *Dutch Charley*?"

"Yes ma'am." Daniel nodded.

"Peculiar. I believe I have heard that name before, but I cannot recall where."

Daniel sipped his now tepid tea.

With a shrug, Mrs. Arnold returned her spectacles to her nose and resumed her knitting.

Dr. Arnold picked up a dark cherrywood pipe from the table next to him and packed it with tobacco.

When Daniel caught a whiff of the pipe's smokey sweet aroma, it ignited a flood of treasured memories. Evenings on the wagon trail around their campfire as the Arnolds, Savages, and Reeds swapped stories. Relaxing nights in the Arnolds' San Francisco home while he and the doctor read books and Mrs. Arnold worked on her sewing, knitting, or quilting. How had life become so complicated?

Daniel leaned back as Dr. Arnold exhaled a curl of smoke. Thoughts swirled in Daniel's head. Illinois. The wagon trail. San Francisco. The gold fields. What did he really want out of life?

"Dr. Arnold?" Daniel finally broke the silence. "I think I'll leave Jim and the gold fields. I can come back here and live with you, help out around the house, and take up blacksmithing again."

A gasp escaped Limik's lips. She quickly pressed a hand to her mouth.

"I see." Dr. Arnold sucked his pipe then blew out another puff. "But, is that what you *really* want, son?"

Daniel thought for a moment, then hung his head. "No sir."

Gesturing with his pipe, Dr. Arnold leaned forward and held Daniel with a stare. "Son, I do say, you have a passion for justice. God has blessed you with a sharp mind. Our growing territory has far too many dishonest lawyers and politicians." The doctor shook his head. "But you? I do not think there is a dishonest bone in your body." He paused to puff again.

Ha! If he only knew about me bribing Greeley and Banyon, and stealing money from Jim. He swallowed hard, trying to remove the rock lodged in his throat.

Dr. Arnold continued. "As a lawyer, I think you would make a real difference, my boy. Why, maybe one day you could even run for a political office."

"Oh," Mrs. Arnold gasped as she raised one of her needles and waved it in the air. "Do not even get me started regarding corrupt politicians. Our city is chock-full of them. Take, for example,

Councilman Sam Brannon. I hear he hires thugs to deal with people who do not vote the way he wants. Those ruffians also beat up citizens who do not bother to vote. The whole council is a wasp's nest of criminals who care nothing for the wellbeing of their—"

Mrs. Arnold's needles froze in midair. She tilted her head. "Dutch Charley. Yes. That is where I have heard that name. I read about him in the *Alta California*. He's a volunteer fireman. Several months back, a newspaper article accused State Senator Broderick of hiring Dutch Charley and others to crack a few heads in order to get people to vote the way he wanted. But no one has been able to bring a charge against Senator Broderick or his ruffians that would hold up in court."

The fiery woman laid her needles in her lap and charged on. "The article said that, once Senator Broderick gets his chosen people into office, he commandeers half their wages. It's because of him that the Vigilante Committee formed last year."

"Now, dear." Dr. Arnold gave her a look Daniel had often seen on his own father's face whenever Daniel spoke off the top of his head.

"Don't you *dear* me." Mrs. Arnold dropped her needlework to her lap and turned toward her husband, her hands on her hips. "It is not just what I hear. I read those things in the newspaper. I sure do wish that editor—what was his name?"

"Edward Gilbert." Dr. Arnold gave her an I'll-just-let-you-finish-dear smile.

She nodded. "I sure do wish Mr. Gilbert was here and not off in Washington. It seems there is no one left in our city who will print the truth. I would not be surprised if Senator Broderick procured Mr. Gilbert's election as one of our U.S. representatives to get him out of the way."

Daniel pulled back his shoulders. "I could continue my law studies here in San Francisco while helping out around the place. Jim promised that, when I turned eighteen, he'd give me five percent of the profits from his prospecting and trading post businesses. We're three months past that date, and he has yet to offer me the money. Maybe I can ask him for it now."

Glancing at Limik, Daniel noticed her eyes widen, but she quickly turned away.

Dr. Arnold laid his pipe next to the open book on his table. "You cannot run from your responsibilities, Daniel."

You mean like I ran away from you and Mrs. Arnold? Daniel glanced at the floor, avoiding the doctor's gaze.

Dr. Arnold inhaled deeply, then slowly exhaled. "From what you have told me about Chief Juárez and the tensions in the gold fields, I think, right now, you are needed there more than here. You must use your influence with Mr. Savage and the other miners to seek justice for the Indians as well as the prospectors."

Daniel thought of the Texan miner who had murdered Chief Latario, and how a few of the chief's braves killed the Texan responsible for the deed. He also recalled how a group of miners then retaliated by slaughtering most of the Indians in Chief Latario's village. If Jim hadn't stepped in, the situation would have turned into an all-out Indian war. He also remembered how a group of Miwoks brutally murdered Jim's friends, Benjamin Wood and his partners, while they mined near the Tuolumne River.

Not that he didn't want to help, but how could he make a difference? "I don't think it'll matter much if I go back with Jim or not." Daniel shrugged. "I have no influence there."

Dr. Arnold shifted his gaze from Daniel to Limik. "Indeed. I think you have already had more of an influence than you realize."

Confused, Daniel shook his head.

A tongue-clucking sound rose from Mrs. Arnold's corner of the room. "Daniel, I do not know why you cannot see it. It is as plain as day. Miss Limik likes you. And you like her."

Limik giggled and pressed a hand to her lips.

Stunned, Daniel blinked several times. It was true, he didn't *dislike* Limik.

Mrs. Arnold leaned toward Daniel. "You must help Mr. Savage get through these skirmishes between the Indians and the whites. See what comes of it. As for this Mr. Flannery fellow, if you have gained the confidences of his clerk—" She paused and squinted. "What is his name?"

"Hamilton."

"Hamilton. You must get Mr. Hamilton to sign something that

says he has seen the record of payments to those Brody brothers. Give that statement to Dr. Arnold. He will keep it safe until a case can be made against Mr. Flannery. Now that California is a state, I trust the lawless nature of our city will soon change for the better." She leaned back and gave a heavy sigh. "I pray it does."

Daniel stood and strode over to Mrs. Arnold. Kneeling in front of her, he planted a kiss on her soft, white cheek, then grasped her hands. "I've missed you so much. You don't mince words. And you're usually right."

She fixed him with a mock glare over the top of her spectacles. "Usually?"

He shrugged and returned a teasing grin. "Well, almost always." Growing serious, he shared a sudden thought. "I can't bear to leave you two here without help. What if Limik stays with you until I come back?" He glanced at his Indian friend. "That is, of course, if she wants to."

Limik bit her lower lip. "Leave Homut and Eekino? Leave El Rey and the clerks at the trading post?"

Her gaze pulled him in, and he saw another, silent question in her doe-like eyes. *Leave you?*

Daniel stood. "It was just a thought."

He studied Limik as she eyed the knitting in Mrs. Arnold's lap. Dr. Arnold's reading material on the table beside him. The volume of books lining two of the room's walls.

She finally met his gaze, and her eyes brightened. Turning to Mrs. Arnold, she sat tall in her chair. "I am a good cook. Dan'l can tell you." Her voice came soft and steady. "I am also a hard worker." Her focus shifted to Dr. Arnold. "I know I can learn much from the two of you. I would very much like to stay with you until Dan'l returns, if you will have me."

A curtain over Daniel's heart rent in two. He'd always thought of Limik as a sister. Now, suddenly, he realized she meant more to him than just a sister. Could he really return to the gold fields without her?

19
GOODBYES

October 28, 1850
San Francisco

The following evening, Daniel took Limik for a stroll to the wharf. He leaned on a wooden rail and breathed in the salty air as the fog rolled in. Across the bay, the sun slipped behind the mountains.

Limik stared out over the churning waters. "I will miss you, Dan'l."

I'll miss you too.

His mind framed the words, but his mouth couldn't say them. He cared for Limik. He cared about her happiness. He cared about her future. But not like he'd cared about Virginia. "I'm glad you agreed to stay with the Arnolds. It means a lot to me."

A cool breeze blew in, and Limik shivered. Should he drape his arm around her shoulders? Pull her in close? Something inside said *yes*. Ignoring the voice, he handed her his buckskin jacket. "We should get back. I have more to pack before we leave tomorrow."

Tugging the jacket over her shoulders, she gazed up at him. Pain flashed in her eyes. She glanced away.

His breath caught in his throat. She wouldn't be part of the *we* that boarded the steamer tomorrow.

They walked back to the hotel in silence. When they turned the corner, a large man staggered into their path and bumped into Limik.

Daniel steadied her as she tumbled toward him.

"Oh, 'scuse me," the man slurred. He righted himself, attempted a few steps, then fell against Daniel.

The smell of alcohol on the man's breath seemed strong enough to fuel a blaze. Daniel set him upright.

Had the drunk really lost his balance, or was this a ruse to rob them? As the man fought to regain his balance, Daniel stepped in front of Limik and whipped his gun from his waistband.

The unshaved, disheveled man raised his hands. "Ah, no need of that. Ol' Charley don't mean no harm. No sir. Just a bit too much drinkn'. Out celebratin' with my pals."

Two other men approached, but between the fog and fading light, Daniel couldn't make out their features.

"Charley. Be off with ya now. Don't be a-botherin' people."

Daniel immediately recognized the first man's Irish brogue. Flannery. Still clutching his revolver, Daniel wrapped Limik beneath his other arm.

Flannery stepped out of the fog.

When Limik flinched, Daniel drew her closer.

"Well, well." The second man's southern drawl rolled off his tongue, syrupy and thick. "My dear Flannery. You didn't mention Daniel Whitcomb was in town."

Wide-eyed, Flannery stared at Daniel. "B–but, I thought your name was Cipher."

The second man patted Flannery's shoulder. "My dear, dull-witted friend. Don't you recognize the son of that abolitionist, Nathan Whitcomb from your hometown?"

Daniel raised his revolver. Flannery's companion looked familiar. He noted the stranger's large frame and dark hooded eyes. Tyndale. The plantation owner from Missouri. He'd met Tyndale that night at Mr. Reed's dinner party.

Daniel released Limik, grasped his gun in both hands, and aimed it at Flannery's chest.

I could end this here and now. Get justice for Ma and Pa.

"I know you killed my parents." Daniel's voice, tight with rage, came out high and thin. He willed his trembling hands to steady.

Flannery's self-assured smile slid into place. "Son, I had nothin' to do with your parents' deaths. But I must say, 'twas a pity you weren't there to save them."

Raw anger flashed through Daniel's body. He lunged closer.

Tyndale held up a hand. "My dear boy. Surely you wouldn't gun down a man in cold blood. Now, however, if you've a mind to challenge Flannery to a duel—well, that's another matter. I'd be more than happy to serve as witness."

"Wh–what?" Flannery stepped back. "Wait just a minute. No one said anything about a duel."

Hoping to drown out the thrum that pounded in his ears, Daniel shouted. "It's time my parents got justice!" His breath quickened. He wrapped a finger around the trigger.

This chance may never come again.

Limik placed her hand on top of the gun's barrel. "No, Dan'l. This not justice. This revenge."

His mind swirled with snippets from last night's dream. He and Flannery with pistols drawn. Limik stepping between them. Limik lying in a pool of blood.

His body froze.

Slowly, Limik pried the revolver from his hands.

Flannery, Tyndale, and Charley faded into the fog.

Daniel stared into the darkening night until his head began to clear. Finally, he turned and gazed at the revolver at Limik's side.

What was he thinking? He'd almost murdered a man. Every muscle in his body quivered.

Daniel didn't recall walking back, but moments later he and Limik stood in the hotel lobby. He fingered the butt of his gun beneath his shirt. He didn't remember sliding it back into his waistband.

Shaking, Daniel grasped Limik's hands. "Thank you for stopping me. If you hadn't been there—" His throat tightened, and he couldn't squeeze out another word.

Limik's large eyes held him with a stare. "I afraid you angry if I take gun. I had to stop you. If you kill that man—" She shook her head. "If you had killed that man, then you not be same Dan'l I now know. It make you a different Dan'l. I not want a different Dan'l. I think you not want either."

He studied her soft eyes, set jaw, full lips, and even the indent above her chin. They all spoke of a strength and wisdom he hadn't seen before—her strong character tinged with a precious innocence. He would have sullied that if he shot Flannery.

After tomorrow he had no idea when he'd see her next. After tomorrow he might lose her forever. The way he'd lost Virginia. He closed his eyes and leaned in for a kiss.

"Daniel!" A man shouted from down the hallway.

Daniel blinked and looked up. He released Limik's hands as Banyon ran toward him.

"Help me get Jim outta the gamblin' parlor." The clerk approached, lines of worry creasing his forehead. "Jim's lost nearly all the gold!"

As if still enveloped in a fogbank, Daniel shook his head to clear his mind. "What are you talking about?"

Banyon drew up in front of him. "Been keepin' an eye on the chief all day. He's dreadful drunk in a saloon across the street. Thought the Injun might start a fight, so me and Cunningham tried to rustle him out, but he won't come. I came here to get Jim, but he won't leave 'cause he says his luck's about to turn."

Daniel turned to Limik. "Please wait here while I see what's going on."

She nodded and touched his sleeve. "Please be careful."

Trailing Banyon, Daniel entered the gambling parlor. He spotted Jim playing cards at a table near the bar.

Jim threw back his head and clapped the shoulder of the man next to him. "Bet I can call out the name of the next card you draw from that deck."

The well-dressed man pulled a watch from his vest, glanced at it, then returned it to his inside pocket. "Why not. It's about time I let you earn back some of your gold. Tell you what." The man's eyebrows rose. "I'll draw four cards, face down. You pick one and name it."

Before the man could lay out the cards, Jim jumped onto the table.

Daniel shuddered. From the way Jim swayed, he guessed his guardian was drunk.

The clinking of coins, tinkling of piano keys, and din of voices quieted as all eyes turned towards Jim.

Raising his arms, Jim flashed a wide grin. "Bet my weight in gold I can rightly name the card I pick."

The man snapped down four cards.

Daniel cringed. He doubted this would end well.

Jim stomped his boot on a card. "Ace of spades."

The man turned over the card. "King of diamonds." A corner of the gambler's mouth turned up. He raised an eyebrow. "How much do you weigh?"

Jim dragged a bag of gold to the bartender's scale and weighed out 160 ounces of gold.

After Jim paid his debt, he agreed to go with Daniel and Banyon to rescue Juárez. They met Cunningham across the street and wrestled the drunken chief out of the saloon and into his hotel room.

Minutes later, Daniel joined the others in Jim's suite where they weighed the remaining gold they'd brought from the foothills. Thirty-two ounces.

Daniel rubbed the back of his neck. He hoped thirty-two ounces would get them back to Agua Fria. They had arrived in San Francisco with six hundred pounds. That was only five days ago.

The next morning, as Daniel packed his things, he couldn't get Limik out of his mind. If Banyon hadn't interrupted him last night, he would have kissed her. He would have held her close. He would have told her how much she meant to him. But he hadn't done any of that. Maybe he never would.

Somewhere nearby, a cannon boomed. Daniel flinched. Two more shots thundered. His muscles stiffened with each explosion. In addition to his lost opportunity with Limik, last night's encounter with Flannery had shaken him to the core.

A fourth cannon blasted.

"Guess the party's begun." Banyon wound a rope around his small bundle of clothing and his blanket roll.

Today San Franciscans would celebrate California's entry into the Union. Daniel wished he could stay and enjoy the festivities, but Jim booked their departure before they knew about the event.

"I hope hearing those cannons puts the fear of God into Juárez." Banyon picked up his hotel pillow, squeezed it, then added it to his belongings. He gave Daniel a mischievous grin. "I doubt Flannery will miss this much."

"Here. You can take mine too." Daniel tossed his pillow at Banyon's head, but the man caught it midair and stuffed it into his bundle along with his other gear.

"Chief Juárez can be a real old scratch," Banyon said, "but he's got clout with most Injuns in the gold country. If that old devil comes back tellin' stories 'bout all the mighty ships he's seen in the harbor, all our cannons, and all the soldiers garrisoned at the Presidio, the Injuns are bound to think twice about goin' to war with us."

A possible war in the gold fields. At least Limik would be safe with the Arnolds in San Francisco.

And what of *his* future? Now, more than ever, Daniel wanted justice for his parents' deaths. The evidence he'd uncovered made Flannery his primary suspect. The Brody brothers' confession said Flannery paid them each $300 to torch his parents' home. Flannery's ledger confirmed it. The brothers also accused Flannery of participating in the deed. Those confessions were safely tucked away in Mr. Reed's safe.

Hamilton had signed an affidavit stating he'd seen Flannery's accounting books listing the payments to the Brody brothers. That affidavit, along with Hamilton's copy of the ledger page was now safely stowed in Dr. Arnold's safe.

But had they missed something? Who concocted the plot? Flannery? What possible motive did the man have for killing his parents? Those questions remained unanswered.

He'd have to find answers to those questions later. For now, Daniel collected his things and turned his thoughts to today's events. The *Alta California* said a grand parade would wind through the streets of San Francisco at midday, concluding in Portsmouth Square. One of California's supreme court justices, Nathaniel Bennett, would then deliver a speech. He wished he could attend. Tonight, there'd be a grand ball. The guest list included esteemed citizens from all over the state. He imagined Virginia and John Murphy would attend. By then, however, he and the others would be on a steamship headed for the gold fields. All of them except Limik.

At one-thirty, Dr. and Mrs. Arnold, along with Limik, joined Daniel and the others at the docks to say goodbye.

He hated goodbyes. He'd said too many in his short life of eighteen years. After quick hugs for everyone, he boarded the ship.

As they steamed out of the bay and up the Sacramento River, Daniel questioned his resolve to return to the gold fields. Legally, he could ask Jim for his promised inheritance. Why didn't he?

Dr. Arnold's parting words came to mind. *Right now, I think you're needed in the gold fields more than here. Use your influence with Mr. Savage and the other miners to seek justice for the Indians as well as the prospectors.*

Daniel mulled over his name's meaning. Pastor Lovejoy said it meant *God is my Judge*, as well as *God rules me*, or *Judge of God*. Would he be able to live up to any of those ideals?

Before leaving Illinois, Pastor Lovejoy told him to always serve the cause of justice. If he did, Daniel now wondered where that path would lead. Had their trip convinced Chief Juárez that an Indian uprising would be madness? What if the Indians did start a war? How many would die before it was over? Would he survive? At least Limik was safe.

Limik.

He fingered the place on his arm where, just a year and a half ago, she'd slashed him with a knife. Still tender, it now showed a scar.

He tested the remnants of another scar. The one Virginia had carved onto his heart. Still there. Still painfully tender.

Would he ever truly love again?

20
PEACE PIPE

November 22, 1850
Burns Creek, California

"Woah," Jim shouted to his team of horses.

"Why we stoppin' here?" Banyon shouted from the second wagon as Jim slowed his. "We still got four hours of daylight."

Daniel, saddle-sore from their long journey, didn't care why they stopped. Only that they stopped. They'd spent the last three weeks on the trail—ever since their steamer reached the port of Stockton. Jim had ordered two wagons, six horses, and five mules to be ready for them when they arrived. Transferring all their supplies from the ship to the wagons and donkeys, they'd been riding hard ever since. Jim, in a hurry to get back, gave them few breaks except to stop for meals and sleep. Daniel couldn't remember when he'd been so bone-tired.

"Woah," Jim shouted again as he brought his two-horsed wagon to a halt. "We're stopping here," he told Banyon, "'cause we're gettin' closer to Injun trouble."

Banyon pulled his wagon up alongside Jim's. "And exactly where are we?"

Daniel had the same question but was too tired to ask.

"Burns Creek." Jim extended his leg, and with a creak, set the wagon's brake. He climbed down and stretched. "We're just a stone's throw from a mining camp. I figure there's safety in numbers."

Daniel dropped from his saddle. With reins in hand, he walked to coax life into his legs and seat. As he limbered up, he ambled over to Jim's wagon where Jim, Homut, and Eekino had begun to unload supplies for camp.

Fastening his reins to a nearby branch, Daniel helped unload. "Like Banyon said, it's only midday," Daniel shot Jim a puzzled look as his guardian handed him a bundle of supplies. "You said we stopped early 'cause of Injun trouble? If trouble's coming, shouldn't we push on? Not that I mind, of course." Daniel set the gear on the ground and rubbed his still partially numb rear.

"Got friends at a nearby ranch." Jim handed Daniel another bundle. "John and Robert Burns. The Burns came out from New England in '47. Started ranchin' here. Two years later, they discovered gold." Jim pointed towards the creek behind them and the grove of miners' tents that lined it. "After word got out about the Burns finding gold, a mining camp sprung up. Locals call it Burns Creek. Most of these miners have bought goods from us at the Agua Fria Post." Jim lowered his voice. "Aim to find out what's been happenin' around here before we walk into the thick of it. The Burns'll probably know."

Daniel set the pack of supplies near the women and shrugged. "I don't understand."

Jim glanced at Banyon and Cunningham who were unhitching the other wagon's horses. He then shifted his gaze to Homut and Eekino as they unpacked the cooking gear. "Remember how, when we reached Stockton, Juárez took off without a word?" Jim lowered his voice even more. "I had hoped our trip to San Francisco would've convinced the chief that the whites were here to stay. I had hoped he'd use his influence to urge the Injuns to make peace. But my hopes—well, I'm not sure they're gonna pan out."

Having unloaded the supplies they needed to make camp, Daniel unsaddled his horse and brushed him down. The women started a fire and prepared a late afternoon snack of canned fruit, beans, and fresh tortillas.

After a brief rest, Jim asked Daniel to resaddle his horse. Daniel moaned. He didn't think he could spend another minute in the saddle.

A corner of Jim's mouth turned up. "It's not for you. It's for me. I'm gonna ride over to Burns' ranch. I'll be back by sundown."

As they saddled the gelding, Jim continued to speak so only Daniel could hear. "Not a word 'bout what I've said to the others, son. Best not to worry 'em. First we'll see if the Burns brothers have heard anything about Injun trouble."

As Jim rode off, Daniel twisted his felt hat between his hands. His dinner of beans churned in his stomach. Jim never confided in him. This was a first. He had a feeling it might not be the last.

By the time Jim returned, Daniel and the others had finished their evening meal. Stars began to poke out between the thick November clouds. Cunningham and Banyon, bundled up in their wool coats, sat near their tents playing cards as moths swirled around their lanterns. Homut and Eekino ground acorns near the campfire.

Taking up a seat on a rock near the women, Jim called Daniel over.

Daniel picked up a piece of kindling and poked at the fire before he sat. "What'd you find out from the Burns brothers?"

"Nothin' I didn't already guess." Jim shoveled a spoonful of beans into his mouth and chewed. "Said there's been some trouble up and down the valley. A few days ago Injuns near Agua Fria killed a white."

Daniel sucked in a breath. "Anyone we know?"

Jim wagged his head. "Also said natives down by the Kaweah River been demandin' tobacco, blankets, or beads from whites comin' into the territory. A few weeks ago a feller named John Wood came in and built a cabin. He and a group of friends started cuttin' down trees and mining gold. The Kaweahs gave 'em ten days to clear out."

"Before what?"

"Before they skinned 'em alive."

Daniel shuddered. He'd heard stories of Indians peeling the skin off people's bodies while still alive. But wasn't that just back East? He hadn't heard of Indians doing that out West. His nerves went on high alert. Chills, like ants, ran up and down his spine. He reached for a nearby blanket, threw it over his shoulders, and tugged it tightly around his shoulders.

Jim set down his pan of half-eaten beans. "Before goin' back to Agua Fria, we'll warn the clerks at the Fresno Post. It's more vulnerable to attack. Then we'll return to Agua Fria."

The next day Daniel rode out in front of the supply wagons and was first to reach the Fresno Post. A group of Indians had gathered near the front. He assumed they had come, as usual, to trade gold for supplies. He recognized two of them as Jim's friends—Chief Ponwatchee, a Yokuts Nootchu, and Chief Bautista, a Miwok. Homut and Eekino were from their tribes. Two years ago, at their chiefs' urgings, the women had become Jim's wives.

While Jim pulled up behind Daniel and greeted the chiefs, Homut and Eekino clambered out of the wagon and ran over to greet their Miwok and Yokuts kin.

Daniel understood some of the Miwok and Yokuts languages. He overheard the women tell their relatives about the thousands of people in San Francisco, their large ships, the booming cannons, and seemingly endless supply of food.

Jim secured the horses, entered the post, and motioned for Daniel to follow. Before going in, Daniel noticed Chief Juárez joining the group of Indians. He couldn't make out what the chief said, but after Juárez pounded his hand with his fist, several other Indians grunted and nodded. Daniel's insides twisted.

Inside the post, Greeley pulled out Jim's ledger for inspection. Daniel shook his head. Greeley still hadn't caught on that Jim couldn't read.

"As you can see," Greeley told Jim, "the store made a good profit while you were gone."

Daniel peered over Jim's shoulder. It had.

Greeley tugged his beard. "Although, this past week, the Yokuts and Miwoks workin' for you ain't brought in much gold."

Jim ran a hand across his face. "Bring out the pipe."

Greeley reached behind the counter and withdrew a long-stemmed wooden pipe. Two feathers hung from the middle, attached by a short leather tie. It was the ceremonial pipe Chief Bautista had given Jim when he married Eekino.

Jim filled the pipe with tobacco and strode outside. Daniel followed. Everyone else stayed inside.

More Indians joined the group, including several from Chief Juárez' Chowchilla tribe.

Jim held up the pipe and invited his friends to sit with him. He motioned for Daniel to sit on his right.

Surprised by the offer, Daniel's shoulders stiffened. *What if this doesn't go well?*

Jim sat cross-legged on the packed dirt, his usual look of self-confidence replaced by tired eyes and a long face.

Chiefs Ponwatchee and Bautista joined the circle on Jim's left. The remaining Indians arranged themselves to complete the ring—all except Chief Juárez, who stood alone outside the group.

Jim lit the pipe, puffed on it, then passed it in silence.

His guardian's gaze followed the pipe's path as it passed from one man to another. When it reached the midway point, Jim spoke. "I consider you all friends." He spoke in the Miwok language, understood by both the Chowchilla and Yokuts. "And yet, I know some here do not wish to be friends with the white man. They hope to unite the tribes for war. I tell you, if the Indians make war on the whites, every tribe will be wiped out. None will be left."

Daniel's muscles tensed. A pain shot across his back.

Jim glanced at Juárez. "I have just returned from where the whites are more numerous than wasps and ants. If war comes, every Indian will be killed. This I do not want. I know you do not want it either."

The pipe had almost completed the circle. Many nodded in agreement and mumbled their support for peace.

Pulling in a deep breath, Jim continued. "Chief José Juárez has just come back with me from the place where the whites are very numerous. He can tell you what I say is true."

Juárez stepped forward but remained outside the circle. The chief drew back his shoulders and raised his chin. "Our brother has told his Indian relatives much that is true. We have seen many people. The whites are very numerous."

Daniel expelled a breath. This seemed to be going better than expected.

Juárez stepped closer and narrowed his gaze. "But I also tell you the white men are of many tribes. The far-off ones I saw with my eyes are not like the tribe of whites that dig gold in the mountains. The tribes I saw are more pale than the gold diggers. They wear tall hats and fine jackets. The whites in the big village we visited will not help the gold diggers in the mountains if the Indians make war against them."

Jim let out a low growl.

"These other white tribes only thirst for gold so they can continue their games and pay for their strong water." Juárez's voice picked up speed. "When gold diggers visit them and run out of gold to pay for those things, these other tribes drive the gold diggers back to the mountains with clubs to find more gold." He pointed at Jim. "They strike them down, just as your white relative struck me while I was with him."

Several Indians within the circle grumbled.

Juárez grew more animated. "The white tribes in the big village will not war with the Indians in the mountains. They cannot bring their big ships and guns here to us. We must unite before the gold diggers increase. If we wait, they will grow too great for us to bring war upon them."

Daniel shifted his position on the ground. His legs felt as if they had been poked by pins and needles.

Several of the Indians in the circle looked up at Juárez and nodded their approval.

Jim stood, fisted his hands on his hips, and studied the faces of those around him. "I speak to you now not as a white man, but as your beloved El Rey Güero." Unlike Juárez, Jim spoke in a calm, quiet voice. "Chief Juárez, as my friend, went with me to the whites' big village. I have listened attentively to what he told you. He has told you some truth. But he has also spoken of many things which he knows nothing about."

Jim tapped his own forehead. "He told you things he saw in his dreams while strong water made him sleep. Strong water I told him not to drink. The white men in the big village and the gold diggers in the mountains all come from the same tribe. They will come and fight against the Indians. Their numbers will be so great that every tribe who joins in war will be destroyed."

Chief Ponwatchee, still sitting, glanced at Jim, then at those seated in the circle. "I believe what my relative says. He would not wish to bring harm upon us or his wives. I do not think it wise to war against the gold diggers."

Chief Bautista nodded in agreement. "El Rey keep our relatives,

Homut and Eekino, his wives, safe. He protect friendly tribes. I believe what he say."

At this, Juárez leaped into the circle and pointed at Jim. "He tells lies to his Indian relatives." Juárez' face twisted in anger as his voice rose. "He is no longer our friend or brother. He will help white gold diggers drive us from our country."

Several in the group nodded in agreement. Their murmurs grew louder.

Daniel spotted another chief, José Rey, standing outside the circle with two of his Chowchilla braves.

Chief Rey now entered the circle and stood next to Juárez. "My people are ready to join Chief Juárez in a war against white gold diggers." Rey raised his fist. "If all the tribes join us, we will drive the whites from our mountains. The whites will run and leave their property behind. Those who join with us will be the first to obtain the gold diggers' property."

At the promise of plunder, several around the circle raised their fists.

The peace pipe had returned to Jim. He grasped it, shook his head, and trudged into the post.

Daniel stood and waited for the tingling in his legs to stop. The Indians slowly dispersed. Soon, only Homut and Eekino remained.

Entering the post, Daniel joined Jim as he reviewed the post's supplies with Greeley and Long-Haired Brown. After taking stock of the merchandise on hand, Jim instructed two of his other clerks, Kennedy and Stiffner, to help Banyon and Daniel bring in four barrels of flour from the wagons, and the packs of supplies from two of the mules. After Daniel updated the post's accounting ledgers to reflect the deposit of the new supplies, Jim ordered Banyon, Cunningham, and Daniel to mount up for the ride back to Agua Fria.

"But we've been ridin' hard for three weeks." Banyon had just taken a seat on one of the post's wooden chairs and removed his boots. "Why not spend the night here and ride out in the morning?"

Jim shook his head. "Best to get back to Agua Fria soon as possible. It's only a few hours. Gotta warn the miners along the way and the settlers in Mariposa 'bout a possible Injun uprisin'."

As they prepared to leave, Jim turned to Brown, Greeley, Stiffner, and Kennedy. "You four abandon this post at the first sign of danger, ya hear? I can replace supplies. I can't replace you."

The men nodded.

Beneath his woolen shirt and oilskin duster coat, Daniel's heart raced. Jim always put business before personnel. The man's sudden show of sentiment could only mean one thing. War would come.

And it would come soon.

21
FRESNO POST

December 13–22, 1850
Agua Fria Trading Post

To help ward off the December chill, Daniel tugged his woolen blanket tighter around his shoulders. He opened a law book on the table in front of him and read. Plagued with thoughts of an Indian war, he couldn't focus. Nothing made sense. He slammed the book shut with a thud. If only the infernal rains would stop.

He gazed at his mud-covered boots. Following several weeks of this deluge, mud had now splashed everywhere—from his felt hat to his food. In the past few weeks, only a trickle of miners had come to buy goods, and even fewer Indians brought gold to trade for needed provisions. The incessant downpour had put him, as well as everyone else at the post, in a foul mood.

"You pulled that card from your sleeve," Banyon yelled at Cunningham.

Daniel turned to gaze at the two clerks seated around an empty barrel near the Agua Fria's pot-belly stove.

Cunningham threw down his cards. "You callin' me a cheater?"

"Does a skunk have stripes?" Banyon glared at his friend. "You're a cheat'n liar. I should'a won that round, but you pulled a queen outta your sleeve. What else ya got stashed up there?" Banyon grabbed Cunningham's wrist.

Both men stood. Cunningham wrenched his friend's arm, but Banyon refused to release him. The two twisted and turned, knocking over the barrel. Cunningham pulled back his free arm and punched Banyon in the face. Howling, Banyon covered his left eye with both hands. Reeling back, the clerk tripped over his chair and tumbled to the floor.

Two cards fell from Cunningham's sleeve.

Sauntering over, Daniel collected the cards. "You dropped these." He handed them to Cunningham. "You owe Banyon an apology."

Cunningham shrugged.

Daniel scowled. "Either you tell him, or I will."

The morning of December 15 the rain finally stopped, and the sun poked out between a break in the clouds. Since it was Sunday, Jim volunteered to watch the store so the clerks could take the day off. It seemed his guardian had mellowed some since his failure to make peace with chiefs Juárez and Rey. Cunningham and Banyon didn't stop to question Jim's motives. They simply announced they'd spend their free time in Mariposa and invited Daniel to join them.

Daniel waved them off. "No thanks." He dragged the post's table closer to the stove and pointed to the law books stacked on top of it. "Got plenty to do. Besides, you know I don't drink. There's not much else to do in town besides that."

Banyon winked at Cunningham. "Of course there's more to do than that. Why, you can meet a pretty woman and impress her with all your book-learnin'."

Cunningham punched Banyon's shoulder. "That's right. Then you can buy her a nice meal. And who knows? You might even strike up an interestin' conversation with her before we head back."

The men laughed.

"Ha, very funny." Daniel threw his notebook at them. "Bye, fellas. Have fun."

Shortly after the clerks left, a well-dressed man walked into the post. Someone Daniel didn't recognize.

"Well, Colonel Johnston." Jim came out from behind their make-shift counter and shook the tall, lanky man's hand. "Good to see you."

Daniel studied Johnston. Did he know him? Anyone dressed in a ruffled white shirt, neckstock, and black frock coat in the gold country made a memorable impression. No. He'd never met the man before.

"Haven't seen the likes of you since last spring," Jim said. "Wasn't it up at Belt's store on the Merced River? What brings you 'round these parts?"

Johnston nodded. "It's good to see you too, Savage. I'm here in my capacity as an Indian agent. I'm following up on rumors that you know something about a possible Indian raid."

Daniel had never met an Indian agent. He knew President Polk had appointed quite a few after the Mexican War. He also knew Polk had tasked them with visiting the new territories. But he didn't know one had come to the gold fields. Hoping to join their conversation, Daniel offered Johnston his chair. "If you two would like to sit, I can put on a pot of coffee."

Agent Johnston removed his silk top hat and placed it on the table. "I would appreciate that very much."

Johnston and Jim sat.

When Daniel brought over the coffee pot and a tin of biscuits, Jim raised his eyebrows. "Not goin' domestic on me now, are ya son?"

Heat rose from Daniel's chest to his face. He set the coffee and biscuits on the table. "No, sir. But Homut and Eekino are washing clothes at the creek. I just brought over what I thought they might serve you."

Jim threw back his head and chuckled. "Just teasin' ya, boy. Sure do 'preciate how you've picked up the slack 'round here. Especially since Limik's gone."

At the mention of Limik, Daniel's throat burned.

"When you fetch our cups," Jim added, "Bring three. Maybe your thoughts on the natives can give Johnston here more insight than just hearin' from me."

Daniel returned with the cups, poured the coffee, and sat.

Johnston ran a hand across his tired, beardless face. "I've traveled throughout the area since spring and have spoken with many tribal leaders. I sympathize with their position. As I understand it, leaders under Spanish and Mexican rule gave the natives rights to as much land as they needed for habitation."

Daniel scanned Jim's face, then Johnston's. Before Jim could respond, Daniel jumped in. "Agent Johnston, Jim has a saying I've come to appreciate. He says, 'You can't possess what you can't protect.' Not many Spaniards or Mexicans came to these foothills back then. The Indians had little trouble protecting their traditional hunting grounds. But since gold's been found, everything's changed. More prospectors arrive each day, overrunning the Indians' hunting grounds. There's no way the natives can continue to live off the land."

Jim nodded. "And the natives don't view property like us. They don't understand how a person can say he owns a piece of land. To them, the land is for the benefit of everyone, as long as they respect each tribe's traditional areas."

Johnston swallowed a sip of coffee. "Well said. And now that these two, very different cultures have come into conflict, a few skirmishes are bound to arise."

Jim arched a brow "Oh, believe me, there'll be more than just a few skirmishes. Several chiefs 'round here have boasted they plan to make war on the whites. Even promised plunder to any tribe that joins them."

Johnston shook his head. "I've recommended that the government establish depots throughout the area to help distribute needed goods to the natives. Items such as beef, flour, and blankets. Hopefully, if their basic needs are met, it will make up for the loss of their traditional hunting grounds. And, hopefully, they'll be less likely to make war. However, just in case, I've also suggested we set up military outposts throughout the area."

"Sounds fair." Daniel swirled the coffee in his tin cup. "That way, if either side gets out of line, the situation can be dealt with quickly before things escalate."

"Have you heard the news?" A voice came from the post's canvas entrance.

Daniel turned to see who had arrived. It was Nate Filmore, a local miner. His long brown beard looked more unkempt than usual.

The prospector waved his arms and ran over to their table. "It's John Wood and his friends. All but two's been slaughtered by Kaweahs."

Johnston's face paled. "I heard Wood had been warned to leave, but I didn't think the Kaweahs would carry out their threat."

Filmore's eyes grew wide. "Oh, they carried it out, all right. Right down to skinnin' Wood alive, just like the Injuns threatened. Wood and thirteen others. Only two men survived. One of 'em, Boden, got his arm shattered by arrows when he fled. He's over at Cassiday's right now. Looks like they'll have to amputate the arm to save his life."

Johnston stood, his chair legs scraping across the packed dirt floor. "I'll investigate and rush off a report to Governor Burnett and the Commissioner of Indian Affairs." He turned to Jim. "If it's all right with you, I'd like to bed down here for the night."

"Fine by me," Jim said. "We can talk more when you get back."

Johnston rode out with Filmore to Cassiday's place. Shortly after he returned, a runner came in from Four Creeks. Indians there had attacked a man named Pedro Lopez and twenty-five of his vaqueros. Lopez and his men had driven a thousand head of cattle from Los Angeles to the gold fields when they stopped to rest. Witnesses said about 300 Indians burst out from the nearby oak grove, slaughtered the men, then drove the cattle into the hills.

Fear spread throughout the mining camps. Without provocation, several of Jim's Yokuts workers were shot on sight. Jim warned Eekino and Homut to stay near the post. Fewer Indians came in to trade gold.

Several days later, as Daniel chopped wood out behind the post, he observed Yokuts women packing up their woven baskets and cooking utensils. Braves gathered their weapons and meager clothing from their cone-shaped bark tepees. One by one, the Indians marched away from their camp. Daniel rushed inside to inform Jim.

"Round up as many miners as possible," Jim ordered Daniel. "We've got to stop our Injuns from fallin' in with Chief Juárez or Chief Rey. If our Yokuts join up with those bands, there's no way we can protect 'em from what's to come."

Daniel convinced fourteen of the nearby prospectors to ride out with Jim in search of the missing Indians. Johnston also joined them.

After two days and thirty miles of rough riding through the foothills, Jim and Daniel were the first to find what was left of their Yokuts' most recent encampment.

Jim dismounted and kicked at the smoldering remains of a

campfire. "They probably left early this morning. Most likely, they've joined up with Chief Juárez and his Chowchillas."

A twig snapped on Daniel's left. He whipped out his pistol and twisted in his saddle. Two small boys, no older than three, appeared from behind an oak. Their tear-stained, dirt-smudged faces told their own story. They shared one ratty blanket between them and pointed to the tree. With a tap of his heels and pistol still in hand, Daniel slowly urged his horse forward.

Behind the tree, an old woman rested against the oak's trunk. Her head lolled to the side.

More twigs snapped. Daniel twisted to the right. Jim, now on foot, approached with his Colt in one hand and his horse's reins in the other. His guardian approached the woman and touched her shoulder. Lifeless, she fell over.

"Must've been too hard for her and the little ones to keep up." Jim's voice remained flat. "Guess they got left behind." Jim holstered his gun and swung back into the saddle. He pointed to a nearby hill. "Should be able to catch up with 'em before they reach that rise."

Daniel's jaw went limp. He thought about Limik being abandoned at the age of five when everyone in her village died. "We can't just leave these boys here to fend for themselves."

Jim tugged his reins left, prompting his horse to face Daniel. "Why not? Their own people abandoned 'em."

With his pulse pounding in his ears, Daniel jumped off his horse. "That's right. I forgot. You don't have a problem abandoning people." He pressed his hat tighter on his head. "Just go. I'll catch up."

Daniel handed the boys his canteen. They gulped down the water. He then withdrew several pieces of beef jerky from his saddle bag and passed a handful to them.

To Daniel's surprise, Jim swung down from his horse. He untied a blanket from his bedroll and tossed it to him.

Daniel caught it in midair and gave it to the boys.

"Son, your kindness'll be the death of us." Jim's voice, quiet, yet firm, held no tone of reproach. "Now, get back on your horse. We'll return for these young'uns after we meet up with their kin and convince 'em of their folly."

By midafternoon the miners reached the next rise. Jim pointed to the Indians encamped on the nearby hill.

Chief Juárez, standing among his warriors, cupped his hands and turned to face them. "El Rey," Juárez shouted at Jim across the gap. "Do not approach us. It will not go well with you, my old friend."

"Yes, we have been friends." Jim shouted back from atop his horse. "And now, as your friend, I ask that you encourage my Yokuts and Miwok kin to return with me. I wish no harm to come to them." Jim motioned toward the fifteen armed men beside him. "And I wish no harm to come to you."

Juárez waved clenched fists above his head, then lowered his arms. "It too late for that. Harm already come. Not to me, but to you."

Jim's face went taut. He massaged a spot above his right eye.

What did the chief mean? Daniel's skin prickled. What harm had come to Jim? Had something happened they didn't know about? Daniel tapped his horse's flanks with his heels and sidled up next to Jim.

His guardian waved him back. Jim stood tall in his stirrups and glanced over again at Juárez. "For very little labor your tribes and my Yokuts and Miwok kin can obtain enough gold to purchase clothing and food for many seasons. The whites are not going away. We must learn to live in peace."

Juárez let out a devilish cackle that carried from his hill to theirs. "This a hard way to make a living, Jim Savage. We will now supply our wants by stealing from whites."

A few of the weathered miners grumbled. Ned Filmore, cradling his rifle in one arm, guided his horse closer to Jim's. "Let's just take 'em now and be done with it."

Agent Johnston maneuvered his horse between Filmore and Jim. "Gentlemen, let's not start something we cannot undo."

"Jim Savage!" Once again, the chief's screech filled the space between the two hills as he waved his clenched fists. "You must stop deceiving the whites by telling lies. We no longer friendly Indians. We deadly enemies. As long one white remain in our country we promise to plunder and kill."

"Jim." Daniel tugged his guardian's bridle and pointed to a hill off to the left. "Looks like more Indians are coming to join Juárez. Maybe 200 or more."

Jim squinted against the sun's glare. "Could be Chief Rey's group. Or, worse, those renegade Yosemites. Can't tell from here." Jim pulled in a ragged breath. "Either way, we're outnumbered." Jim turned his horse around the way they'd come. The others followed.

As promised, Jim stopped back at the Yokuts' previous camp to pick up the small boys. "Homut and Eekino might enjoy having two little ones running around the post."

Daniel dismounted and hoisted the boys up to Jim.

A corner of Jim's mouth turned up as he settled the boys in front of him. Daniel hadn't seen his guardian soften at anything since that day on the wagon train. That day when his wife gave birth. That was almost five years ago.

The return trip to Agua Fria took a day and a half. When they dismounted, Eekino ran up to meet them, her long black braid bouncing across her back.

"Come quick." She grabbed Jim's arm as soon as he finished tying up his horse. "Bad news. Big, bad news."

Daniel trailed Eekino, Jim, and the two boys into the post. Near the back sat Long-Haired Brown slouched in a chair. Homut dabbed a gash on his head with a damp cloth.

Daniel hadn't seen Brown since last month when they visited the Fresno post after their trip to San Francisco. As he approached the injured clerk, a ball of fear formed in his chest. *Is this what Juárez meant about harm coming to Jim?*

"What happened? Was the Fresno post attacked?" Jim's high-pitched tone frightened Daniel more than Brown's bleeding head and limp arm.

The clerk studied Jim with bloodshot eyes. "Day before yesterday. Injuns raided the post. Stole all the goods. Spirited away all the cattle... horses... mules."

Daniel glanced around the otherwise empty post. The ball of fear rose to his throat. "What about Greeley? Kennedy? Stiffner?"

He'd never seen the big trapper cry, but Long-Haired Brown didn't even try to stop his flow of tears. "Chowchillas, I think it was. Maybe some Chookchances and Yosemites too. Came in with hatchets, crowbars, rocks, arrows. Smashed everything in sight they didn't wanna take. Shot arrows or threw rocks at anything that moved. When Greeley tried to stop 'em, they beat him over the head with rocks till he fell at their feet. Kennedy, Stiffner, and me—"

Brown wiped his face with the back of his good hand, then continued. "The three of us ran out. Fast as we could. Maybe 200 Injuns shootin' arrows, plunderin', screamin'."

The man's breath hitched. More tears fell. He pressed his trembling lips together as if willing himself to finish. "Didn't have a chance. Kennedy and Stiffner collapsed. Knew I was next. While some Injuns ran into the store to steal more goods, Polonio—remember him? He was always one of the more friendly Chowchillas. He jumped between me and some renegades fixin' to fall on me. One Injun got hold of my arm and twisted it. Broke my wrist. I threw him off with my good hand and ran to the river. Jumped in and swum fast as I could. Cracked my head on a rock. Ran all the way to Quartzburg 'fore I stopped."

Brown mopped his damp face with his bandana and paused to catch his breath. "Don't know what kinda scene I left behind. Don't even wanna guess. All's I know is, while swimmin' 'cross the river, there was a powerful smell of smoke."

While Homut and Eekino tended to Brown, Daniel helped Jim round up thirty-three Agua Fria prospectors to ride out to the Fresno Post the next morning. Agent Johnston insisted on joining them.

Every muscle in Daniel's body quivered as he prepared to leave. What would they find at the post? Grim images of mangled bodies flashed across his mind. He didn't want to go. But word of the attack on the Fresno Post spread like wildfire. The crisp December air grew thick with revenge. He had to go. Maybe he'd find a way to keep things from getting out of hand.

It was past midday before they neared the post. Daniel groaned as stubs of the corral's burned-out fence posts came into view. He and the clerks had worked long and hard to make those fence posts. The stench of smoldering wood made him gag.

Urging his horse closer, the charred store came into view. His chest burned as if someone had scraped his insides with a dull knife. Even from here, he could see that the goods they'd brought back from San Francisco had either been stolen or were part of the scorched remains. The only thing standing was the empty iron safe, its door hanging by one hinge.

Daniel dismounted and, with reins in hand, stepped closer. Taking in the sight, he froze in his tracks. Beneath the flapping of buzzards' wings lay the bloodied bodies of Greeley, Stiffner, and Kennedy. All were stripped naked. He assumed the man with the bashed-in skull was Greeley, but after a day in the sun with buzzards pecking at them, it was hard to tell one man from another. As the scent of rotting flesh filled his nostrils, Daniel retched.

"Grisly business," came Jim's voice behind him.

Covering his nose with his bandana, Daniel turned as Jim and Johnston approached.

Jim glanced at Johnston and pointed to the remains of Stiffner and Greeley. "See those six or seven arrows in two of my clerks? And the twenty or so in Greeley?"

Johnston nodded.

"The Injuns hated Greeley more." Jim crunched his eyebrows together. "I heard he cheated 'em on a regular basis. Didn't give 'em a fair trade for the gold they brought in. I told him to stop, but he didn't listen. That's why he's got more arrows."

Daniel swallowed hard, the taste of bile still in his mouth.

Pulling a handkerchief from his pocket, Johnston held it to his nose and talked around it. "So, they stripped their dead bodies, laid 'em out here next to each other, then shot their bodies with arrows?"

Jim nodded. "Their way of showin' disrespect."

The buzzards didn't seem to mind how many arrows pierced the naked bodies. They simply hopped between the shafts as they pecked at the exposed flesh.

A muscle in Jim's jaw twitched as he clenched his teeth. "Once word of this gets out, gonna be near impossible to prevent an all-out Injun war."

22
CHASING RENEGADES

December 22, 1850–January 8, 1851
Fresno Post, Agua Fria Post, and Gold Country Hills

The December wind whipped across Daniel's face as he and the others who'd ridden with them shoveled a final load of dirt onto Greeley's grave. They had buried the three clerks' remains, but Daniel couldn't bury images of their buzzard-pecked bodies. His stomach clenched as he viewed the mounds.

One of those graves could have been mine.

He removed his broad-brimmed felt hat and studied the faces of the men around him. "Seems like there's more we should do. Maybe say a prayer."

Nate Filmore tugged on his long beard and tossed one more shovelful of dirt onto Greeley's grave. "I ain't no prayin' man, but I know'd Greeley. He was a cheatin' son-of-a-gun, but he sure didn't deserve this. S'pose a little prayer couldn't hurt."

Everyone removed their hats, but no one prayed.

Daniel laid down his shovel and shrugged. "Guess I'll do it." He glanced at Jim and Agent Johnston who stood in front of what used to be the Fresno Post.

The post that now lay in ashes.

Just like his home in Illinois.

He squeezed his eyes against the memory. A memory that pressed so hard against his breastbone he couldn't breathe. Forcing his eyes open, he willed air into his lungs. He cupped his hands around his mouth, about to call Johnston and Jim over, then remembered Jim wasn't a praying man either. He dropped his hands to his sides.

Twisting his hat between his hands, Daniel bowed his head and cleared his throat. "Lord, we've put to rest the earthly remains here of Greeley, Stiffner, and Kennedy. We ask You to also put their souls to rest." He paused and lifted his head to glance once more at the post's ashes, the graves, and the men surrounding them. "And bring peace to this land. Help us not be vengeful. Help us be just and fair. Amen."

For a few seconds, no one moved. Then Nate pressed his tattered hat onto his head and spit. "Well, can't say as I won't be vengeful. Them Injuns deserve whatever's comin' to 'em." He picked up his shovel and left. The others followed.

As Daniel glanced once more at Jim and Agent Johnston, Jim waved him over.

"Takin' a few of the miners here with me to Horseshoe Bend," Jim said as Daniel approached. "Figure we can round up a group of men to help us hunt down the Injuns responsible for this." Jim gazed at the still smoldering remains of the post, his face as gray as the ash. "Johnston wants to head back to Agua Fria and get a report off to Governor Burnett."

"I'll ride with you, Jim," Daniel offered.

"No." Jim shook his head. "I want you to ride along with Johnston to Agua Fria. Spread word 'bout what you saw here. Gather as many as you can. I'll come back with volunteers from Horseshoe Bend and join you at Agua Fria. Once we've got a crew, we'll ride out together and track down those who did this."

Daniel, Johnston, and a few others rode back to Agua Fria. When Daniel rounded the bend leading to the post, shredded pieces of the post's canvas-covered tent came into view. *Not here too!* Daniel's heart wrenched. Smashed sluice boxes, pieces of broken barrels, and crushed canned goods poked out through flailing bits of fabric that flapped in the wind.

With his pulse racing, Daniel dug his heels into his horse's sides and galloped forward. As he neared the post he recognized the wiry, mustached figure of Sheriff Burney standing next to the structure's gutted remains.

Blood pounded in his ears as Daniel jumped off his horse. "What happened?"

"Just got here myself, son." The sheriff spit out a wad of tobacco. "Seems the post was attacked by Injuns while you were gone."

"Where's Banyon? Cunningham? Brown?" Daniel's throat constricted. As he scanned the area, his vision blurred. "Any sign of Homut and Eekino?" His pitch rose. "The two boys?"

Sheriff Burney grasped the lapels of his long duster coat and tugged. "A few prospectors witnessed the attack. Said Injuns took hatchets and knives to the tent, carted off what they could, and ruined the rest. Forced the squaws and the boys to go back with 'em to the hills. As for Banyon, Cunningham, and Brown, well—" The sheriff rubbed one end of his mustache between his thumb and forefinger. "I'm afraid they're gone."

"Gone? You mean dead?" As if someone had thrust a knife into his gut, Daniel doubled over in pain. He grabbed his horse's bridle to steady himself.

Seconds later, Agent Johnston and the others rode up. "Looks like we're too late," Johnston said as he dismounted.

A familiar shout rang out in the distance. Daniel looked up. A large man dressed in torn woolen pants and a red flannel shirt emerged from a gully several yards behind the flattened post. A blood-stained cloth encircled his head. Long-Haired Brown.

"Glad you're back." Brown huffed as he approached. "Where's Savage?"

Relief flooded Daniel's chest. He rushed forward and wrapped his arms around the big man. He knew Brown wouldn't like it, but he did it anyway.

Brown patted Daniel's back as if testing the temperature of a hot pan. "Now, now. No need to get all sentimental."

"I thought you were dead." Daniel released his friend and stepped back. "Jim'll be here in a few days. He rode to Horseshoe Bend for reinforcements." He peered around Brown. "Where's Banyon and Cunningham?"

Dark shadows ringed Brown's bloodshot eyes. "Since business has been a little slow, Cunningham went to Burns Diggings for a few weeks to help a friend build a cabin."

Daniel let a corner of his mouth turn up. It sounded like the other clerks were safe after all.

Brown shook his head. "But I found Banyon's body down there this mornin'." The man pointed his thumb over his shoulder toward the gully from which he had come. "Just finished diggin' his grave."

Daniel's stomach dropped. Grisly images from the Fresno Post, like a stampede of horses, raced across his mind.

With a trembling hand, Brown rubbed his bandaged head. "I went out early this morning to do some huntin' and trappin'. When I got back—if only I'd been here."

Daniel swallowed hard. He grabbed Brown's shoulder and shook it. "No. If you'd been here, you'd be dead too."

For Daniel, the days between Christmas and New Year's passed without celebration. But not without a parade of memories. An uninvited parade.

Rising at dawn on Christmas day, Daniel pushed aside his blankets. He also tried to push aside the recollections. Illinois recollections. Christmas recollections that leaked in through cracks of loneliness.

Ma's flakey-crust mincemeat pie. Hannah's giddy laugh as she opened her Christmas presents. Simple presents made by loving hands. Like the doll Pa made from scraps of wood and sawdust. Like the hand-me-down dress from the pastor's wife Ma had altered to fit Hannah's smaller frame. Like the pain of cutting his hand while carving Hannah a whistle, and the pain's disappearance when his stepsister excitedly unwrapped her whistle Christmas morning.

The only tangible memory he still had of his family was his father's old boots. The boots he'd tried to repair as a surprise birthday present for Pa the night of the fire.

The night he'd lost everything.

His stomach twisted as he pulled on his father's boots and rubbed his fingers over their worn leather sides. Although still a little large, he'd been wearing them since he returned from San Francisco.

Why did I come back here? I should be in San Francisco. With Limik and the Arnolds.

His insides still twisting, he shut the door on his Illinois memories and tromped over to the remains of the post.

Fortunately, not all of his belongings had burned up in the Agua Fria raid. He'd lost his old canvas bag that contained extra shirts and pants, but he still had his prized leather satchel, a parting gift from Dr. Arnold. As usual, he'd stored the satchel inside the store's safe, one of the few items the Indians couldn't carry off. Unlocking the safe and opening its creaking iron door, he pulled out his leather pouch. It contained all the books he'd recently received from his lawyer friends. It also had his notes, letters from Pastor Lovejoy, and a recent letter from Dr. Arnold.

Moving to his tent, Daniel sat on the ground and withdrew Dr. Arnold's letter.

Dear Daniel,

I trust you are safe, and hope you are able to exert a positive influence there in the gold fields. Every day, newspapers report new atrocities committed either at the hands of the natives or by the whites.

Mrs. Arnold and Limik send their love. The young girl continues to thrive under Mrs. Arnold's tutelage, and my dear wife's health seems to improve with the endeavor.

Looking forward to your return once a semblance of peace has been restored.

Daniel folded the letter, returned it to the satchel, and pulled out one he'd written to Dr. Arnold the previous night. Reading it over, he sighed as he reviewed his account of recent attacks. Although careful not to reveal the grisly details, he knew they'd all be sick with worry if he didn't mention them. He needed to let them know he was okay. He reaffirmed his commitment to stay in the gold fields until a truce could be found between the miners and the Indians.

But, he wondered, *how long will that take?*

In spite of his growling stomach, Daniel shrugged on his wool coat and rode over to the Mariposa Post Office. While there, maybe he could find out why Jim hadn't returned yet with reinforcements.

"Can't say as I know more than you," Sheriff Burney said when Daniel stopped by his office. "Savage is probably havin' a hard time gettin' men to join him on the hunt. He'd get a lot more volunteers if they knew they was gettin' paid to track down the Injuns."

Daniel nodded his agreement and continued to the post office. He didn't expect any new letters, but that didn't stop him from checking.

"Nothin' today, son." The clerk behind the counter pushed up his spectacles. "Might try again tomorrow. Heavy rains in the valley have slowed deliveries."

Turning to leave, Daniel spotted Agent Johnston outside with Sheriff Burney. The sheriff tugged on his mustache as he talked with Johnston. "So the volunteers might get paid after all? Well, that's good news."

The agent nodded and shook Daniel's hand when he approached. "I was just telling Sheriff Burney that I am on my way to San José for a meeting with Governor Burnett." The Indian Agent tapped the saddle bag slung over his shoulder. "I will hand-deliver my report to the governor concerning the last two months of Indian uprisings and request immediate state and federal aid. It is my recommendation that we fund a battalion to track down the offending renegades. The sooner we round up their leaders, the sooner we can begin peace talks."

Two days after Johnston left for San José, Jim returned from Horseshoe Bend with a force of forty men. His guardian looked as though he hadn't slept since he'd left the Fresno post. Usually clean-shaven, the man's face was now whiskered with more than a week's worth of growth. Jim's short temper, along with the stench from his unwashed clothes, kept everyone at bay.

When Jim discovered the Indians had also plundered his Agua Fria post and taken his wives as well as the two boys, Daniel saw murder in the man's blood-shot eyes. He saw the same look in the eyes of the men who returned with Jim. Many of them were friends of the Fresno clerks. Daniel's hope of a peaceful solution to the Indian War fluttered away like the slashed pieces of canvas that had once covered the post.

Sheriff Burney, encouraged to hear that Agent Johnston was requesting government funds to bring in the Indians responsible for the attacks, recruited another thirty men. After a meeting at the saloon with those willing to go after the Indians responsible for the raids, the group elected Sheriff Burney as their captain.

When Jim heard the sheriff would lead the group, his brows pulled together, but he held his tongue. Undoubtedly, the man thought he should have been chosen to lead the expedition. After all, it was his posts that had been attacked.

Burney thanked the men for their confidence and turned to a tall, thin man on his left. "As captain, I appoint Skeane here, a veteran of the Mexican War, as my lieutenant."

Jim, standing next to Burney, clenched his fists. His face turned red. Daniel knew Jim had also fought in the Mexican War. In fact, he'd been a member of Colonel Frémont's battalion. There was no one more qualified to serve as lieutenant than his guardian.

To Daniel's surprise, however, Jim again kept his mouth shut.

"And Savage," Burney laid a hand on Jim's shoulder, "I want you and Whitcomb to ride up front as scouts. You know this country better than anyone."

Jim grunted his assent, turned, and strode away.

Although he sensed it hurt Jim's pride, Daniel breathed a sigh of relief when the volunteers voted to put the sheriff in charge. He'd seen the look of revenge in Jim's eyes. With a lawman as captain instead of Jim, perhaps the results would be more in line with the rule of law than the rule of vigilantes. He could only hope.

23

THE RENEGADES' TRAIL

January 6, 1851
California Gold Country Hills

Riding as a scout next to Jim, just behind Burney, Daniel did his best to keep up as the sheriff led the volunteers southeast toward the foothills. Jim picked up the Indians' trail several times, only to lose it again in the thick undergrowth.

As dusk approached, the western clouds took on a crimson tinge. Burney ordered Jim to ride ahead and locate a good place to camp for the night. Jim dug his heels into his horse and Daniel followed.

Twenty minutes later, Jim pulled up and dismounted. "This is a good flat area, and there's a creek nearby." Jim pointed to the pines on his left.

Daniel hadn't noticed the gurgling stream. He nodded, glad Burney had chosen Jim as their scout.

After unloading gear from their horses, Daniel collected wood as Jim prepared a campfire. Burney and the others would appreciate its warmth once they rode in.

As the sun moved closer to the horizon, a group of about twenty saddle-weary men straggled in from the southwest. The group wasn't Sheriff Burney's.

The lead man dismounted. "Name's Howard," the man introduced himself to Jim. "Been ridin' hard all day from my ranch near Burns Creek. These here are my ranch hands." He pointed to the mounted men behind him. "Been trackin' Injuns that raided my ranch night before last. Dang renegades stole all my horses and mules."

Jim shook Howard's outstretched hand. "We're chasin' after Injuns that burned down two of my trading posts."

As the two talked, Burney and the others rode in. Without dismounting, the sheriff maneuvered his horse next to Jim to meet the newcomers.

Howard, standing next to Jim, didn't bother to introduce himself to the sheriff. "Aim to get my horses back," Howard told Jim. "Figured your group could help. We followed the Injuns' trail into the hill country, then realized we might need a bigger force. Heard you was out huntin' Injuns too, so we decided to find you instead."

Jim turned to the sheriff. "Mostly likely, Howard's horse thieves plan to meet up with the same Injuns we've been trackin'."

Burney nodded. His leather saddle creaked as swung down from the saddle. "Savage, why don't you and Whitcomb ride out with Howard while there's still some light. See if you can pick up the thieves' trail before dark. Meanwhile, the rest of us will finish setting up camp. If you find the trail, we'll pick it up in the morning."

Every muscle in Daniel's body ached. The last thing he wanted was to ride out again. But when Jim mounted his house, so did he. With Jim in the lead, they rode out with Howard and a few of his ranch hands. It didn't take long for Jim to pick up the trail of Howard's horse thieves. As the sun slipped behind the foothills, Jim led them back to camp.

With the expedition now numbering ninety-two, the two groups rode out before daybreak. Jim led the way as he and other trackers followed the thieves' trail into the mountains. Nightfall forced them to stop before they could locate the Indians' site.

As Daniel finished his meal of beans and biscuits, several of the men near his campfire boasted about the number of Indians they'd killed since coming to the gold fields.

A young man leaned back on a rock and scraped mud from his boots. "Last week, after pannin' for gold all day, me and my partner came back to our tents and found two Injuns rummagin' through our stuff. Shot 'em both through the head 'fore they even saw us comin'."

An older man with a gray-streaked beard spit in the dirt. "Lost two of my partners last month when a party of braves came up behind us and stole our mules. Before we could draw our guns, my partners had knives stickin' 'tween their ribs. I escaped with just an arrow in my arm. They was both good men. And we'd worked long and hard to buy them mules."

The young man leaning against the rock sat up straight. "I say, we find one of their villages, take 'em by surprise, and pay 'em back in spades."

A miner near the campfire rotated his makeshift spit as he roasted a rabbit he'd caught that afternoon. "Yeah. And after we kill all the braves, we'll take the women as our squaws. I wouldn't mind bringin' home two or three of 'em to keep me warm at night."

Daniel's stomach soured. He couldn't swallow another bite of beans. He let his spoon clatter to his plate. What would some of these men do if they came upon Limik in the woods? He shuddered. At least she was safe in San Francisco.

A young prospector sitting next to Daniel nudged him with the toe of his boot. Daniel recognized him as one of the miners from Horseshoe Bend.

"You're Whitcomb, right? Daniel Whitcomb?"

Daniel nodded.

"And you've know'd Savage for a good spell now, right?"

Daniel sipped his lukewarm coffee and nodded again.

"I heered tell Savage can run all day and all night. Run a hundred miles through the mountains, then sit and laugh 'round a campfire, still fresh and lively-like. That true?"

Splashing the rest of his coffee into the fire, Daniel mused. Maybe the Indians no longer thought of Jim as a god or a king, but it seemed he now had new admirers. He narrowed his eyes and scowled at the young, beardless prospector. "What do *you* think?"

Early the next morning the group rode deeper into the mountains. Once again, Burney sent Jim and Daniel out to scout ahead. This time, however, the sheriff proposed they give Daniel and Jim about an hour of lead time, rather than follow fifteen to twenty minutes behind.

Daniel was familiar with the tactic. They'd used it many times on their trip out West from Illinois. Whenever they came upon Indian tracks or travelled past Indian burial grounds, one or two scouts rode farther ahead to make sure the path was safe. If all was clear, the rest would follow about an hour later.

An hour into the ride, Daniel's muscles tensed. What would happen when he and Jim found the Indians that burned down their posts and stole Howard's horses? Would he and the men suffer the same fate as Greeley and Banyon? In spite of the cold January wind that whipped across his nose and stung his cheeks, sweat gathered beneath his armpits and trickled down his spine. His gloved fingers went numb. He forced himself to loosen his deathlike grip on the reins.

After twenty more minutes, Jim slowed his horse and came to a stop. "Daniel," he whispered. "Look." He pointed to an incline. "Up there. What do you see?"

About 500 yards away, smoke rose from the top of a steep hill. Daniel squinted. "Is that—"

Jim rubbed his gloved hands together. "I think we've got 'em."

After tying up their horses, Jim motioned for Daniel to follow.

Crawling behind Jim up the slope, prickly green weeds bit at the exposed flesh between his coat sleeves and gloves. By the time they neared the hill's crest, Daniel's neck ached from lifting it to keep his face from scraping the ground.

Jim slunk behind a large oak and motioned Daniel over. From there, they observed the Indians' activity in their makeshift village.

About 400 braves moved about the encampment. Carcasses of horsemeat hung from nearby trees. A rudimentary corral near the edge of the village contained about forty horses and a smattering of mules. Daniel saw a few blanketed braves toting rifles—blankets and rifles Jim had formerly stocked in the Agua Fria post.

Daniel followed Jim back down the hill. They mounted their horses and rode back to the group. Sheriff Burney listened to their report then ordered the men to make camp for the night.

After an early dinner, Burney gathered the men, and drawing in the dirt with a stick, explained their plan of attack. "Later tonight, we'll leave about twenty men here with the horses while the rest of us approach the base of the hill on foot."

Twirling the end of his mustache, Burney's voice picked up speed. "Be sure to keep out of sight. We'll wait at the bottom of the hill until well past midnight. Savage and Whitcomb'll scout ahead to make sure the Injuns are asleep. They're bound to post sentries, but, even if we can't pick 'em off before they alert the others, we'll still catch the bulk of 'em by surprise."

Around three in the morning, with only the moon and stars to guide them, Daniel and Jim crawled back up the hill. When it looked clear, Jim gave the prearranged owl hoot to signal the others forward. As they neared the summit, Daniel heard what sounded like a dog's bark. He stopped. An Indian sprang from the woods. Jim whirled his knife at the native.

He missed.

A dog hadn't barked. The hidden sentry had signaled a warning.

Burney immediately rose up. "Charge!"

The smell of adrenaline was almost palpable as the men behind Daniel sprinted toward the top. Burney, Howard, and Skeane took the lead. Fortunately, they had military training. Unfortunately, apart from Jim, the men behind them didn't.

As Daniel and Jim joined the rush up the hill, the greenhorns in the rear hurried past, firing their rifles.

"Darn fools!" Jim shouted. "Don't shoot till ya actually see an Injun!"

Too late. By the time they reached the Indian's camp, Lieutenant Skeane and two other volunteers had been shot by friendly gunfire. As the battle ensued, arrows whizzed through the air and rifles fired from every direction.

By the time a faint light rose in the east, twenty-six braves lay dead. Daniel recognized one of them as Chief José Rey. The rest of the Indians had fled into the chaparral. The horses and mules Daniel had seen in the corral were gone. Baskets of flour, probably stolen from the post, along with Indians' storehouses of pine nuts and acorns, lay strewn about the village. In the middle, near several campfires, stood two bark-covered wigwams.

Daniel approached one of them. Next to it sat an old squaw who'd been shot in the thigh, her wrinkled face contorted in pain.

Not far from her lay a young, wounded prospector. Daniel recognized him from the Agua Fria mining camp. The poor man had been shot in the neck, but his low moans still evidenced life.

Before Daniel could assist either of them, the old woman rolled onto her good side, picked up a nearby bow, and notched an arrow. She raised the bow and pointed the arrow at the wounded man.

Daniel moved to draw his gun but froze.

Blam!

The old woman fell. Her bow and arrow clattered to the ground.

Jim, with pistol in hand, stood a few feet away. His guardian had done what he couldn't.

Ignoring a wave of nausea, Daniel rushed over to the wounded man. He whipped off his bandana, knelt, and pressed his kerchief to the prospector's neck, hoping to stop the flow of blood. He recognized him. Charlie Houston. An amiable young fellow from Tennessee.

Charlie looked up and tried to talk, but no words escaped his lips.

"Need help here!" Daniel shouted. Continuing to press down, he glanced up at Jim.

But Jim wasn't looking at him.

Daniel followed the man's gaze to see what had captured his attention. A few feet over lay the twisted, bleeding bodies of two Indian boys. The boys Jim had placed under Homut and Eekino's care.

24

YOU CAN'T POSSESS WHAT YOU CAN'T PROTECT

January 8, 1851
California Gold Country Hills

Jim stood atop the oak-studded mountaintop with slumped shoulders. Staring at the boys, his face twisted with pain.

"You can't possess what you can't protect." Jim mumbled the phrase again.

And again.

And again.

Daniel had seen that hopeless look on his guardian's face only once before—when he lost his wife and baby daughter.

A long wail from the wounded prospector brought Daniel's attention back to Charlie.

Daniel glanced down and readjusted his pressure on the young man's neck.

Once again, Charlie tried to speak, but only managed a gurgle. Charlie's panicked eyes grew wide. He thrashed for a moment, then lay still.

Daniel closed the young man's eyelids. Tossing the bloodied bandana aside, Daniel viewed the surrounding carnage. The natives tried to protect their homeland by plundering Jim's posts, stealing Howard's horses, and murdering prospectors and store clerks. When the whites tried to protect themselves, they ended up killing both friendly as well as hostile Indians. There had to be more to life than just trying to protect your possessions. Daniel tried to make sense of it.

He couldn't.

As if moving in a fog, Daniel obeyed Sheriff Burney's order to pursue the fleeing Indians into the chaparral. Two and a half hours later, seven more Indians lay dead. The rest of the renegades escaped into the mountains, including Chief Juárez. At least, to Howard's satisfaction, the Indians had left the stolen horses and mules behind.

"Burn the whole encampment," Burney ordered before he allowed the volunteers to return home. "We don't want 'em comin' back to retrieve their food supplies."

Two days after they returned to Agua Fria, Sheriff Burney asked Jim and Daniel to join him at his Mariposa office. He wanted their help drafting a letter to the governor detailing the latest skirmishes.

"Make the letter stronger," Jim urged Burney as he sat across from him in the sheriff's office. "We don't rightly know how many we killed. Say forty or fifty."

Daniel knew they'd killed thirty-three Indians. He and Jim had counted the bodies in their search for Homut and Eekino. They never found the women. Why did Jim want the sheriff to say they killed more than they did?

Burney dipped his quill into the inkwell and read aloud what he'd written so far.

> *We reached the village just before sunrise. However, before there was enough light to ensure our bullets hit their mark, their sentinel discovered us. Since the natives had seen us, I ordered a charge and yelled for the Indians to surrender. Some ran off, some seemed disposed to surrender, but others fired on us. They numbered about 400. We killed from forty to fifty, including one of the renegade chiefs, José Rey.*

Forty to fifty? Daniel wanted to confront the lie but figured it wasn't his place.

Jim leaned toward Burney. "And don't forget to ask for permission to keep pursuin' them renegades. I hear tell that Indian Commissioners from Washington arrived in San José earlier this month. Asked the military to escort 'em to the gold fields so as to keep the peace 'round these parts. Seems they don't want us chasin' those maraudin' Injuns on our own."

Burney tugged on his mustache. "Been told the commissioners hope to make peace treaties with the Injuns. I say, first we give the rebels a good drubbin'. Once they've come to respect our power, it's more likely they'll keep their part of the bargain."

Jim grunted his agreement.

Again, Daniel shook his head. He doubted Jim just wanted to give the marauders a healthy respect for the whites' power. No. He'd seen it in the man's eyes. He wanted revenge. But Jim couldn't do it alone.

His guardian picked up Burney's report and pretended to read it. Giving the impression he'd finished, Jim laid it back on the table. "Along with askin' for authority to keep chasin' the renegades, make sure you ask for funds." Jim's pitch rose. "We need to pay the volunteers, and we need more weapons. The men won't keep fightin' for free. After all, they got claims to work."

The sheriff dipped his quill into the inkwell.

Daniel shot Jim a cold, hard stare. "What about Homut and Eekino?"

Lowering his head, Jim remained quiet for a moment. Blinking several times, he pushed back from the table. "Now, don't get me wrong, sheriff." The edge had disappeared from Jim's voice. "I'm all for makin' treaties with Injuns who really want peace. Heck, I think the idea of settin' aside parcels of land for the natives, something Agent Johnston suggested, just might work. Lord knows, they deserve it."

Daniel followed Jim's gaze as the man paused to glance out the sheriff's window. Several miners dressed in red flannel shirts and corduroy trousers passed by. "We've overrun the natives' huntin' grounds by the thousands." Jim spoke in a faraway voice. "Tryin' to stop the flow of prospectors is like tryin' to hold back an ocean wave with a teaspoon. But, it's gonna be darn near impossible for the Injuns to keep livin' like they used to."

Jim rubbed his stubbled chin and turned toward the sheriff. "The way I see it, if the friendly Injuns agree to live on reservations, we'll need to clothe and feed 'em. Just till they learn to fend for themselves. Of course, Uncle Sam needs to pay for it."

Burney leaned back and slid his jaw left. "I see where you're goin' with this. If the digger Indians who gave you gold in exchange for goods at your trading post move to reservations, you're out to lose money. But if the government gives the natives free food and clothing to pacify 'em, you'll still make a profit by supplyin' the Injuns the needed goods at the government's expense."

A slow smile spread across Jim's face. "I'm thinkin', when the commissioners get here, I'll suggest they contract us traders to purchase and supply the Injuns with what they need."

Daniel balled his fists, craned his neck, and studied the ceiling. Jim. Always the businessman. Revenge and profit. That pretty much summed him up.

By mid-January, the Agua Fria post had a new canvas cover and they'd begun to restock its shelves. On the morning of the fifteenth, Agent Johnston rode up to the post while Jim, Daniel, and Long-Haired Brown struggled to fasten a gate onto the opening of the new corral.

"I have news from San José." The agent dismounted, tied his horse's reins to a fencepost, and stomped his feet as if to warm them. "Got coffee inside?"

"Always." Jim nodded. "Help yourself."

Brown glanced up. "Yeah. But give us the news first."

A cool wind whirled dead leaves around Daniel's feet.

Johnston, dressed in a black woolen overcoat, hugged his arms to his chest. "The governor authorized the formation of a battalion to deal with Indian uprisings. I suppose, between my reports and the sheriff's letters, he's seen the wisdom of it."

Jim paused in his effort to fasten the leather-braided hinges to the end of the gate. He shot Johnston a pinched look. "But what about the commissioners from Washington? When they get here, aren't they gonna tell us to stop chasin' the hostiles?"

"True," Johnston nodded and stomped his feet again. "When I met with the governor, he said the commissioners asked for a military escort to accompany them to the gold fields. I estimate they'll arrive in a few weeks with a force of a hundred men under the command of a Captain Keyes. He's a good man—a graduate of West Point. But Keyes goes by the book. When the Washington men arrive, you'll have to follow their lead."

Straining to hold the wooden gate in place until Jim secured the leather strips on the other end, Daniel adjusted his grip and glanced up at Johnston. "Is that a bad thing, goin' by the book?"

Johnston pressed his lips together. "It's just that both Keyes and the commissioners consider this a federal, not a state issue. Once they arrive, they have the authority to order the battalion to stand down."

Jim shook his head. "A treaty won't mean much to Injuns like Juárez. To them, it's just a piece of paper. Paper they've never seen with words they can't read. The renegades gotta know we aim to back our words with the lead in our rifles."

"And that brings me to my last piece of news." Johnston glanced at the weak morning sun that tried to break through the clouds. "When I told Sheriff Burney the governor had authorized the formation of a state militia, the sheriff said you should reassemble the Agua Fria volunteers. He wants to meet with everyone today at three in front of the Whittier Hotel. People are demanding a response to the attack on Cassaday's camp last week."

"It wasn't just an attack!" Brown raised a clenched fist as he continued to support the middle of the gate with his other hand. "It was a butcherin' nightmare! What them Injuns did to Cassaday and the other men was worse'n what happened at the Fresno Post. Didn't the sheriff give you the details?"

Before Johnston could answer, Brown stuck out his tongue and made a slicing motion. "They cut out Cassaday's tongue and pinned it with an arrow over his heart. And who knows if that was before or after they cut off his legs."

Stinging bile rose in Daniel's throat, just as it had the first time Brown told him the story. He turned his head in case he had to retch.

"Yes, the sheriff gave me the details." Johnston's voice took on a gravelly tone. "Since you now have authority to form a battalion in response to these depredations, the sheriff has called a meeting so you can elect a commander and mount a response."

"I see." Brown scowled as he once again clutched the bulk of the gate's weight with both hands. "We gear up and make plans to go after the Injuns just until the commissioners arrive and tell us to stand down. Good idea."

Daniel winced, noting the sarcasm in Brown's voice. Jim finished fastening the gate's hinges, then motioned for Daniel and Brown to release the gate's weight. The leather hinges held firm.

Jim pushed the gate, and it swung open. He then pulled it shut and fastened it with a wire loop attached to the fence post. Glancing back at Johnston, Jim added, "You say Sheriff Burney wants me to call a meeting so we can elect a commander and mount a response? Isn't Burney going to lead the militia like he did the others?"

"I don't know." Johnston shrugged. "He just asked me to deliver the message."

By three o'clock, Jim had volunteers assembled in front of Agua Fria's Whittier Hotel. As Sheriff Burney appeared on the hotel's second-story outdoor balcony to address the group, Daniel clenched his jaw. *Will more bloodshed really accomplish anything?*

"As you may have heard," the sheriff began, "the governor has authorized us to form a militia to quell the Indian uprisings. The state legislature is creating a war fund. Those joining our militia will earn $5 a day."

Cheers rose from the crowd. Burney held out his hands to quiet them. "I had the honor of leading you in the last two expeditions, but my duties as sheriff weigh heavily upon me. I cannot do both jobs and expect to do them well. As sheriff, I will support the battalion in any way I can, but you need to choose a new leader. Whomever you choose will assume the rank of battalion major, with commensurate pay."

Several men nominated John Kuykendall, a man from Tennessee with some military experience. Others called for another former military man, John Boling.

"I say we make Savage head of the battalion," someone else shouted.

"He knows more about these Injuns than any of us," came a voice behind Daniel. Daniel turned and saw the vote of confidence came from Nate Filmore.

"If he can't bring 'em in, no one can," yelled another.

"Nah, I say Major Harvey's more suited to the job," a man near the front shouted.

"Yeah. Major Harvey went to West Point. I say he should lead us to go after the renegades."

Sheriff Burney finally called for a vote. When it was over, the sheriff commissioned Jim as Major James Savage of the Mariposa Battalion.

Glancing at his guardian, Daniel saw the trace of a smile on his lips.

Later that evening, Brown headed off to a saloon to celebrate. Jim invited Daniel to eat with him inside the refurbished post. "I bought two steaks from a rancher today and thought I'd share one with you," Jim said.

Tired of the beans and beef jerky he usually ate with Brown outside their tents, Daniel agreed.

Halfway through their quiet meal, Jim paused and leaned back. "Sure wish we'd caught Juárez on our last Injun raid. With Chief Rey dead, I think the tribes that followed him will come in and make treaties. But those who follow Juárez? They'll probably keep on plunderin' and killin' until we catch up with 'em."

"So that's the plan? To find and kill Juárez?" Daniel jammed a fork into his steak and sawed off another piece.

Jim shook his head. "Maybe there's a chance we can convince Juárez and those following him to make treaties without more killin', but I'm not sure about the Yosemites." Jim studied one of the biscuits he'd bought yesterday in Mariposa, then finally bit into it.

Heat rose in Daniel's chest. He pressed his hands against the table and leaned back. "I don't think you really intend to bring in Juárez or the Yosemites. I think you're out for revenge. Revenge or profit. That's all that matters to you."

Jim stiffened. His brows shot up.

Had he said too much? Daniel's heart pounded against his breastbone. Jim had been good to the Indians. He'd protected them from vengeful miners. At least, at first. Before the Indians burned down his posts and butchered his clerks. Daniel lowered his eyes. "I'm sorry. I had no right."

Silence.

Why didn't Jim say anything?

Daniel's pulse thrummed in his ears as he continued to stare at his half-eaten steak.

"No." Jim's fork and knife clattered to his tin plate. "I'm glad you spoke your mind. Maybe you're right. Maybe that is all that matters to me." Jim stood and with slouched shoulders shuffled out.

Over the next two days, Daniel helped Jim build a smokehouse. The man only said what needed to be said to get the work done. Daniel wanted to resume their last conversation but didn't know how to begin. Finally, while hammering nails into a board, Jim broke the silence.

"Since I'm no longer the Indian's El Rey Güero, I suppose being the major of a battalion could be considered a close second."

Daniel paused midway through his hammer's swing, surprised at what he figured was Jim's attempt at humor. He turned to size up his mentor's expression, expecting to see Jim's usual self-assured smirk. Instead, he only saw glazed eyes and sagging cheeks.

With a thud, Jim tossed his hammer to the ground and squatted on a nearby boulder. "Daniel, I have a question."

Daniel stepped back. Jim never asked him questions.

"You've read the Good Book, right?"

Almost dropping his hammer, Daniel shot his guardian a dazed look. "Umm," Daniel hesitated. "Yeah. My folks read the Bible to Hannah and me every night before bed. But I haven't read it much since."

Jim stared at his half-nailed board. "You brought one out with you from Illinois, right?"

"A Bible?" Daniel's face grew hot. Where was Jim going with this? "No," he finally answered. "Our family Bible got burned up in the house fire. But Dr. Arnold gave me one on the wagon trail." Daniel kicked a nearby stone. "I brought it with me when I left the Arnolds to join you out here in the gold fields." Daniel swallowed. "Why do you ask?"

"I've been thinking." Jim paused and glanced at his hammer on the grass. "I've been thinking a lot since I saw those dead little Indian boys."

Another pause.

Jim's haunted eyes met Daniel's gaze. "And I've been thinking a lot since you accused me of only wanting revenge. Revenge, or profit."

More silence.

Daniel shifted his feet. Jim always sounded confident. Always spoke his mind. Not today. Today, he sounded hesitant. Vulnerable.

The man finally spoke again, his focus somewhere in the distance. "Seems I heard somewhere that the Good Book says, *life does not consist of possessions.* Something like that. You heard that one before?"

Daniel set his hammer on a three-legged stool and reached for his canteen. He pressed the cold metal to his lips and drew a long gulp. He needed a moment to think. Yes, he'd heard that passage before. He felt as though something had lodged in his throat. He took another sip before he answered. "I do recall our pastor back in Illinois giving a sermon on that verse. I only remember 'cause Ma made us memorize it. The whole thing says, *Not even when one has an abundance, does his life consist of his possessions.*"

More awkward silence.

Daniel's chest tightened. What else could he say? He thought about Dr. Arnold's advice when he told the good doctor he'd rather stay in San Francisco than return to the gold fields. *You must use your influence with Mr. Savage and the other miners to seek justice for the Indians as well as the prospectors.* He glanced back at Jim. Maybe this was where it started.

Pulling in a deep breath, Daniel worked to talk around his constricted throat. "Seems to me, that's pretty much what you've been doing. Making your life consist of your possessions. And up until now, you've protected those possessions pretty well. But," he paused, "the Indian raids put a stop to that." Daniel kicked another stone. "Seems like you might need to rethink your little phrase about only possessing what you can protect. Rethink what really matters in life."

Jim ran a hand through his long blond hair, now greased with dirt and sweat. He shrugged. "It's a fact of life, Daniel. You can't possess what you can't protect. The Injuns can't protect their land, but they're scramblin' to hold on to it. I did my best to protect the people and the things I cared about, but obviously I didn't do enough. If life isn't about what you can hold on to, then what's the point?"

Daniel's breath hitched. He'd gone this far. He couldn't act lily-livered now. "Maybe you're looking at it all wrong. Instead of looking at what you possess, maybe you should look at what possesses you."

More silence.

Jim finally lifted his hammer and pounded another nail into the board he'd abandoned. "Enough yappin´. This smokehouse won't build itself."

25

THE SOUTHERN GENTLEMAN

February 10, 1851
Agua Fria, California

Several days later Daniel rode over to the Mariposa Post Office. To his surprise, he had received a letter from Pastor Lovejoy in Illinois and one from Limik in San Francisco. He'd wait until he returned to Agua Fria to read Limik's letter but tore into the one from Pastor Lovejoy.

December 3, 1850
Princeton Township, Illinois
Dear Daniel,

I am sorry I haven't written since your last letter, informing me of your encounter with Mr. Flannery in San Francisco. I conveyed your findings to the sheriff. He said that the journal entry stating Flannery paid the Brody brothers for the "removal of trash" and the Brody brothers' confessions might be enough to warrant the man's arrest, if Flannery still lived in Illinois. Arresting Mr. Flannery on suspicion of murder while he resides in San Francisco, however, might be difficult, short of the man's written confession.

I have not written sooner because someone burned down our house near the end of October. Fortunately, no one was hurt because we had taken the family to Springfield where I was invited to give a series of messages. Before the fire, I had received anonymous notes demanding that I stop helping runaway slaves. If I didn't, I was warned I would experience severe consequences.

Soon after our house burned down, the sheriff apprehended the man who started the fire. He was a drifter making his way from Pennsylvania to California. The perpetrator confessed he had been hired by a southern gentleman, but claimed he didn't know the man's name. He did, however, provide a description of this "southern gentleman" and his last known whereabouts. This "southern gentleman" was soon caught, and admitted that a large plantation owner from Missouri had hired him to find someone to either scare me into stopping my so-called underground railroad activities, or to kill me. The southern gentleman refused to provide his contact's name or his own real name because if he did, he claimed his family would be at risk. A trial date of November 19 was set for both the drifter and the southern gentleman, but on November 11, both men were found dead in their cells. The doctor said it looked as though they had been poisoned.

Perhaps this unidentified southern gentleman who hired the drifter is the same person who hired Mr. Flannery to orchestrate the fire at your home. I don't know what else I can do from here to help you in your quest for justice, but I thought you would like to learn of this possible connection. I look forward to hearing from you in the near future. In the meantime, I continue to pray for your safety and for peace regarding your parents' deaths.

Your friend,

Pastor Lovejoy

As Daniel rode back to Agua Fria, he turned the details of Pastor Lovejoy's letter over in his mind. If there was a connection between Flannery and the southerner who hired someone to burn down Pastor Lovejoy's house, how could he investigate it here in the gold fields? Hopefully, with the arrival of the Indian Commissioners from Washington, peace would return to the area, and he could get back to San Francisco.

Since they were low on supplies, business at the Agua Fria trading post slowed. Jim sent Long-Haired Brown and Cunningham to San Francisco to purchase more goods, but until they returned, there wasn't much for Daniel to do.

When he got back to the post, he poured a cup of coffee, pulled out a tin of biscuits he'd purchased in Mariposa, and sat down to read Limik's letter.

January 2, 1851

San Francisco, California

Dearest Daniel,

I learn much from Dr. Arnold and wife. They very kind. I work every day at spelling and reading. Mrs. Arnold teach me knitting. I happy to do housework and cook. They also teach me things about their God. He very different from ours. He talk to people more than ours do. At night Dr. Arnold read to us from a book he call Bible.

Dr. Arnold read newspaper stories about Indian wars in the gold fields. I fearful often. I fear for cousin Eekino. I fear for you.

Yesterday Mrs. Arnold take me to city for, as she say, a shopping trip. We eat lunch in café near Portsmith Square. Dr. Arnold say it spelled Portsmouth. Why it spelled like word for mouth if it sound like moth?

You remember Mr. Hamilton? He still work for Mr. Flannery. He see me and Mrs. Arnold at lunch in Portsmouth Square and sit at table next to us. He pretend he not talking to me. He say people watch him. He turn his back to me but say man who work on Mr. Tyndale's money books was killed walking home one night. Mr. Tyndale now ask Mr. Hamilton to work his books as well as Mr. Flannery's money books. Mr. Hamilton say he find out something about Mr. Flannery in Mr. Tyndale's books. Mr. Hamilton want to bring you information, but he afraid to write in letter. Afraid people kill him too. He leaving to find you in Agua Fria.

Please write soon. I enjoy my life here but miss cousin Eekino. Miss you also.

Limik

Daniel reviewed the letter's date. Even though it was written a month ago, his mind raced at the thought of a possible connection between Tyndale and Flannery. Wasn't Tyndale from the south? Wasn't he from Missouri? Or was that Mr. Gwin? It seemed so long ago when he met those southerners at Mr. Reed's dinner party. His chest burned as he reread Limik's closing words. *I enjoy my life here but miss cousin Eekino. Miss you also.* The ache in his chest told him he also missed her. More than he'd been willing to admit.

A few days later, just before sunup, Jim entered Daniel's tent. "Get dressed. Pack a bag and bedroll. We're ridin' out to meet the Washington D.C. commissioners."

About ten minutes later, Daniel, still bleary-eyed, hefted his saddle bags over his shoulder and met Jim at the corral. To his surprise, Chief Bautista and four braves rode up.

Daniel drew his pistol.

"No, Daniel!" Jim pushed Daniel's arm down. "Bautista's on our side now. Put that thing away."

"You could have warned me," Daniel mumbled as he shoved his pistol back into his waistband. "How was I supposed to know?"

Chief Bautista nodded to Daniel in a sign of peace. "Chief Rey force us follow him," he addressed Daniel in his broken English. "Say if we not help destroy El Rey's posts, all my tribe suffer same fate as whites. My braves help in attack, but we keep Jim's wives safe."

Daniel shook his head at the confusing Indian politics. He saddled his horse and mounted. In the growing light, he searched the faces of Bautista and his followers. Behind the four braves, he spotted two others. "Is that—"

"Yes." Chief Bautista nodded. "Homut and Eekino. We bring back El Rey's wives. We all ride to meet men sent by Great White Father."

Daniel assumed the chief meant the Indian Commissioners. How did Jim contact Bautista and convince him to come along?

Never one to show affection, Jim didn't lift Homut or Eekino down from their horses to embrace them. He didn't grasp their hands or pat their arms. Instead, he approached Bautista's horse, nodded to the chief, and then to Homut and Eekino. He stroked the women's horses then swung up into his own saddle and waved his hand forward. "Let's move out."

Daniel occasionally glanced over at Jim as they headed northwest to Belt's Ferry & Trading Post where the commissioners had set up camp. Even though Jim hadn't shown his Indian wives any physical affection at the post, it seemed something about the man had changed. His guardian often turned in his saddle to catch a glimpse of the women. His taut lines of revenge now gave way to deep folds to concern.

When the sun rose to the middle of the sky, they stopped for a brief lunch. As they remounted to continue their trek, a wagon approached.

Daniel squinted at the driver in the distance and made out the familiar bulky frame of Long-Haired Brown. Probably returning from his trip to San Francisco. As the wagon drew closer, he saw what looked like Limik sitting next to Brown. Could it be? His breath caught in his throat.

Two pack mules loaded with supplies clomped behind the wagon. Two men on horses trailed the mules. He recognized one rider as Cunningham who'd gone with Brown to San Francisco for supplies. He then made out the second rider—Flannery's clerk, Chester Hamilton.

26
LIMIK

February 12, 1851
Belt's Ferry and Store, North Bank of the Merced River

Daniel's pulse raced. He swung off his horse before Brown stopped the wagon. *What is Limik doing here?* She'd traded in the dresses she wore in San Francisco for the simple white, loose-fitting tunic Jim had given her in the gold fields. When Daniel helped her off the wagon's bench seat, she laid her hands on his shoulders. His throat tightened. She didn't let go after he set her on the ground.

Daniel pulled his brows together. "What—"

She pressed a finger to his lips. "Dan'l, please do not be angry. I could not stay with the Arnolds knowing my cousin and my people in danger. Knowing you in danger."

A knot formed in his stomach. "But now *you're* in danger." A thumping in his chest tamped down his anger. He pulled her in for a hug.

Jim rode over and called down from atop his horse. "Well, Miss Limik. This is a surprise. After you finish greeting Daniel, I'm sure Homut and Eekino will be glad to welcome you as well."

Miss Limik? Jim had always referred to Eekino's cousin as Limik. Yes. Something about the man had changed.

Jim sidled his horse closer to Brown's wagon. "Seems you picked up a stray." He pointed at Hamilton who sat on his horse near the mules behind the wagon.

Brown tugged his beard. "Name's Hamilton. Seems he's got

somethin' for Daniel. Appears to know Limik too. I said he could tag along."

Daniel grasped Limik's hand and led her over to Homut and Eekino.

After a moment, Jim, still in the saddle, addressed Brown and Cunningham. "You two continue on to Agua Fria with the supplies. "Hamilton, you ride in the wagon with Brown. We'll have Miss Limik ride your horse so she can join us on our trip to Belt's Ferry. We're meetin' with federal commissioners there to discuss the renegade tribes. Need to reach the ferry by nightfall."

Daniel's muscles tensed as he scanned Jim's face. "Why do you need Limik? Why not let her return to the post with Brown and Cunningham?"

Furrows formed between Jim's brows. "The chief and I have had our differences. When we meet with the commissioners, Chief Bautista will probably trust Miss Limik to be his interpreter more than he'll trust me."

"I go with you," Limik said as Hamilton dismounted.

Eager to know why Hamilton had come to the gold fields, Daniel stared up at Jim. "Can Hamilton and I have a brief word before we go?"

"No." Jim nudged his horse with his heels and tugged the reins left. His horse let out a snort as Jim turned back toward the trail. "Gotta reach Belt's Ferry before dark."

Hamilton climbed aboard the wagon and shouted to Daniel. "I'll explain everything when you get back to Agua Fria."

When they arrived at Belt's Ferry later that evening, the men set up camp while the women prepared a quick meal. After eating, Chief Bautista, his braves, and Limik followed Daniel and Jim up the wooden steps into Belt's trading post. Homut and Eekino remained at the campsite.

Agent Johnston introduced Jim to the three Indian commissioners—McKee, Barbour, and Wozencraft. Jim shook their hands.

Daniel studied the commissioners' clothing. They looked out of place. *Why do government people insist on wearing dark frock coats and ruffled white shirts with neckstocks out here in the gold fields?*

Agent Johnston introduced Jim to Captain Keyes. The captain, probably in his early forties, stood erect as he shook Jim's hand.

"I've heard good things about you," Keyes said.

"Thank you, sir." Jim replied. He then introduced Daniel. "And this is my assistant, Daniel Whitcomb."

Daniel worked hard not to let his jaw drop as he returned Keyes' hearty grip. Jim had never referred to him as his assistant.

Jim introduced Chief Bautista and his braves, then pointed to Limik. "And this is Miss Limik, cousin of my wife, Eekino. She will translate for the chief."

With a raised brow, Captain Keyes studied Limik's petite frame.

"Perhaps you think I am not able?" Limik's voice, usually soft and reserved, came out steady and firm. She had also changed.

"I speak and write English. Also fluent in Miwok and Yokuts tongues, and some of Yosemite language."

Fluent? She must have learned that word from Dr. or Mrs. Arnold. A sense of pride shot through Daniel as he observed her newfound confidence.

Daniel, Jim, and Keyes' assistant arranged chairs around a rectangular oak table. When finished, everyone sat.

As the commissioners spread out papers in front of them, Keyes peered at Jim from across the table. "I hear the Mariposa Battalion has chosen you as their leader. Is that correct, Mr. Savage?"

"Yes, sir." Jim sat tall, leaned forward, and returned the captain's direct gaze.

Keyes nodded in Chief Bautista's direction. "And I see you have already made efforts toward peace with the natives."

"Yes, we have." The corners of Jim's eyes pinched as he glanced over at the chief. "At first, Chief Bautista followed the renegade, Chief Rey, one of the main rebels. The Injuns that followed chiefs Rey and Juárez were the ones who plundered my two trading posts, along with some Yosemite bands."

The captain shuffled through his papers. "Yes. Terrible business. Especially what they did to your clerks. I read the reports."

Jim's Adam's-apple bobbed. "The first time we tried to bring in the hostiles, both Chief Juárez and Chief Rey escaped. The second time we led chase, Rey was killed. If we hadn't carried out our expeditions,

I doubt Bautista would've come in. I'm now askin' to continue our raids until all the renegade tribes agree to make peace."

The captain's lips pressed into a firm line. "That may not be necessary, Major Savage. A few days ago, Juárez met with us here. He agreed to stop plundering and signed a treaty."

Jim's eyes flickered. His mouth went taut. "He's a wily one, Captain. I wouldn't take him at his word. Did he say he'd also get the tribes followin' him to come in?"

"No. He wouldn't go that far." Keyes shifted in his chair. "Only his main band of Chowchillas have agreed to stop fighting. But that's a start."

"So where's that Injun-lovin' government agent, eh?" A loud voice boomed near the store's entrance.

Daniel twisted in his chair. A medium-built, short-bearded man in a black overcoat strode into the post. Four companions dressed in long, canvas duster coats trailed behind him. The intruder stared at Agent Johnston who stood next to the potbellied stove refilling his coffee cup.

"If you are referringto me," Johnston raised his brows, "I am Agent Adam Johnston, Indian sub-agent for the San Joaquin Valley. And who might you be?"

One of the men behind the intruder stepped forward. "Why, this here's Major Walter Harvey, a man from West Point, and now a minin' engineer. We're all part of his Holmes County Minin' Company. He led us out here by way of Texas in '49."

Harvey shot the man an I-can-speak-for-myself stare.

His companion's shoulders slumped as he lowered his head.

From where he sat, Daniel had a good view of Harvey's face. He didn't like what he saw. The man's deep-set eyes, bushy brows, and dark mustache that flowed into a trimmed beard gave the appearance of a strong-willed man used to getting his own way.

Harvey stepped closer to Johnston and raised his chin. "Well, sir, I'm originally from Georgia, but a solid Californian now." The man's southern accent slipped into the conversation the more he spoke. He gestured to the men behind him. "And, well sir, we're all here to let you know our minin' group in Bear Valley won't put up with these infernal

Injun attacks. Like Governor Burnett said, push all them natives east to the other side of the Sierras, and be done with 'em."

"Well sir," Johnston drawled in a mock southern accent. "Perhaps you are not aware that Governor Burnett resigned his position last month. John McDougal now serves as governor."

Harvey ran a hand across his bearded face. "Of course I know that, sir." The man's pitch rose. "I am quotin' our previous gov'ner." Shorter than Johnston, Harvey stiffened as if to improve his stature. "We heard you were gonna meet with federal Injun commissioners about this matter, and we wanted to make our opinions known."

Agent Johnston pointed to the men around the table. "The commissioners, Major Savage of the Mariposa Battalion, and a group of natives are here now discussing that very issue. Take it up with them if you'd like."

Harvey drew his brows together as he gazed at the group. He pulled in a sharp breath, held it for a moment, then released it. "Well sir, I believe I've made my stance clear." His voice bellowed like a hungry cow. "Let's go, men. We're done here. For now."

Once Harvey left, Keyes broke the silence. "Major Harvey, eh? I once knew a Walter Harvey from West Point. I imagine he's one and the same."

"Sounds about right, Captain." George Belt, the store's owner, spoke up from behind the counter. "He comes here occasionally to buy goods. Always has a group of men with him. Likes to brag about his exploits crossin' the deserts between Texas and California. Occasionally mentions his time at West Point."

Captain Keyes' blue eyes glinted. "Well, the Harvey I knew entered West Point when he was fifteen. I was his artillery instructor. The boy accrued so many demerits his first few months they soon dismissed him. He had an inflated ego. Found it hard to follow the rules. Can't imagine how he could have gained the title of major."

Jim cleared his throat. "Returning to matters at hand, Captain Keyes, I'm here askin' permission for my men to continue chasin' natives that plunder and kill. If we don't counter their attacks with equal force, they'll have no reason to stop."

Daniel glanced at Limik. Her dark eyes flashed. He guessed she didn't agree. But she hadn't witnessed the massacre perpetrated by the chiefs' braves at the Fresno post. He doubted she knew how the Kaweahs had mutilated Cassaday's body.

Her face taut, Limik leaned closer to Bautista as she translated the conversation. The chief shook his head but said nothing.

Captain Keyes drew back his shoulders. The brass buttons on his dark blue, double-breasted military coat appeared brighter. "Major Savage, my official capacity here is to protect the commissioners. You, as Major of the Mariposa Battalion, are free to appoint company captains and other ranking officers since yours is a state militia, not a U.S. government battalion. While it is true you are tasked with quelling the Indian uprisings here in the San Joaquin Valley, I must remind you that you fall under the authority of the U.S. Indian Commissioners, not the state government."

Jim glanced at the three men to the captain's right. Like a defensive cat, Jim's back arched as he pressed his hands to his knees and opened his mouth to speak.

The first commissioner held up a hand before Jim could speak. "Mr. Savage." The commissioner's set jaw made him look like someone who wasn't afraid to speak his mind. "We appreciate the work you have done in convincing a few tribal leaders to come in and make peace treaties." The commissioner rested his arms on the table and steepled his fingers. "We believe Californians should take a defensive rather than an offensive stance regarding the natives until we have had time to investigate matters for ourselves."

Limik sat straighter. Her face brightened. She translated the commissioner's words for Chief Bautista.

The chief and his braves grunted in apparent approval.

Jim's hands, resting on the table, balled into fists. "So, that's a no? We shouldn't pursue Indians who plunder our livelihood and kill our friends?"

Limik continued to translate.

The lines etched into the chief's weathered face deepened. His mouth drooped into a frown.

The first commissioner turned toward the man on his right. "How would you put it, Mr. Barbour?"

The man gave no immediate answer. Instead, he packed his

cherrywood pipe, took a few draws, then held it aloft as he spoke. "My colleague, Dr. Wozencraft, is not exactly saying that you cannot, under any circumstance, pursue the natives."

Daniel squinted. That's exactly what it sounded like. He took an instant dislike to Mr. Barbour. For one thing, the second commissioner's nose seemed too large for his small eyes and lips.

Mr. Barbour lit his pipe, puffed smoke, then waved it in the air as he continued. "What Dr. Wozencraft is trying to say is that we acknowledge the Indians here in California were once numerous and powerful. And while it is true that the previous governor of California stated a war of extermination would continue to be waged until the Indian race should become extinct, that is not exactly what he meant."

Daniel scratched his head. *Doesn't anyone in the government say what they really mean?*

After Limik interpreted, Chief Bautista clenched his jaw. The braves leaned toward the chief and murmured, but Daniel couldn't understand what they said.

Mr. Barbour squeezed the bridge of his long nose. "The governor was speaking in hyperbole. What he meant was, maintaining our current course, the natives' extermination is inevitable. Men like Mr. Harvey might wish to pursue such a course, but it is not our desired direction as a nation."

Jim rubbed his forehead. "So." He glanced at Mr. Barbour. "You don't want us to go after the renegades if they attack us?"

"Mr. Savage." Dr. Wozencraft's large fist thudded on the table. His beefy jaw slid forward. "Our primary task is to make treaties with the tribes that are so inclined. We authorize you to subdue only those bands that refuse to make treaties."

In the end, the commissioners promised to provide the Indians with goods such as blankets, flour, beef, farming tools, and seeds to help them farm the land the government would set aside for them. The Indians had to agree to settle on the reservations and to stop attacking whites. Dr. Wozencraft handed Bautista a written draft of the treaty.

Limik reviewed the document, occasionally asking Daniel for

help. After translating the information for Bautista and his braves, the chief crossed his arms, leaned back and closed his eyes.

A moment later, Bautista uncrossed his arms. "Hee-e," he nodded. Daniel recognized the word—Miwok for yes.

Bautista continued to confer with Limik. After their exchange, she translated for the commissioners. "Chief Bautista say he discuss the treaty with elders of his Miwok band. If all agree, then, yes, he come in to sign treaty. He promise to speak with leaders of other Miwok bands. He tell them to also make treaties with the whites."

The following evening, Daniel and the others returned to Agua Fria. Limik settled in with Eekino while Daniel searched for Hamilton.

"He's gone to Mariposa to stay at a hotel and look for a job." A corner of Brown's mouth drew up. "He ain't much for sleepin' on the ground. Said he'd check in tomorrow afternoon to see if you was back yet."

The next morning, Daniel and Jim walked over to Agua Fria's Whittier Hotel. Jim had passed word for the 200 volunteers of the Mariposa Battalion to meet him there at ten o'clock. Once assembled, he explained they were now under the authority of the commissioners, not the governor. They could no longer pursue the renegades unless the commissioners gave them permission.

"If we can't go after them maraudin' natives," one miner complained, "what are we s'pposed to do while we're waitin'? They gonna pay us to just sit around?"

Jim rubbed his jaw. "We'll conduct drills on an open plain five miles south near the foothills where there's plenty of grass and water. I expect all of you to meet me there in two days. The commissioners agreed to pay us from the first day we mustered in. Whether we fight or not, we'll keep gettin' paid till the day we muster out."

Grunts of approval rose up among the men. Within the last two years, thousands had rushed to the gold fields. Finding gold in creeks or streams wasn't as easy as it had once been for these men. At least fighting with the battalion promised a steady income.

Once the meeting ended, Daniel returned to the post and continued to inventory the merchandise Brown and Cunningham had brought in from San Francisco.

Jim arrived an hour later and invited Daniel, Brown, and Cunningham to sit with him at a table near the potbellied stove. Daniel sat close to the stove as it crackled out its warmth. He rubbed his hands together. Although the weather had warmed some since last month, a February chill still filled the air.

Homut and Eekino strode over with coffee, beans, and tortillas, and set them on the table.

Jim nodded his thanks. After sipping his coffee he glanced at his clerks. "Brown and Cunningham, I'm gonna put you in charge of the post here while I serve as major of the battalion." He took another sip. "Daniel, tomorrow when we ride out to the plain near the foothills, you'll assume the rank of lieutenant and serve as my aide."

Stiffening his shoulders, Daniel struggled to push out his next words. "I'm grateful for the honor, sir. But I'm not sure I want to fight in the battalion."

Jim pulled in a quick breath and set his tin cup on the table with a clunk. "I guess I assumed you'd want to join me." He leaned back and ran a hand through his hair. "But, you turned eighteen last July, right? Officially, I'm not your guardian anymore."

Daniel almost toppled his coffee. Jim actually remembered his birthday?

Pulling his brows together, Jim continued. "If you don't join up with the battalion, will you go back to San Francisco?"

A weight pressed down on Daniel as if he carried a bag of rocks on his back. "I'm not sure yet." He shifted his gaze from Jim to the still half-empty shelves of the post. "I'll give you an answer by tonight."

Daniel finished the inventory by late afternoon. He shrugged on his coat and stepped out in search of Limik. As the sun struggled to find its way through the gray clouds, he found Limik pounding acorns with Homut and Eekino near the corral. He invited her to join him on a short walk to the creek.

"Do you know what Hamilton wants to tell me?" he asked as

they followed a dirt path that wound past several miners' tents and lean-tos.

"It important. That all I know." As the breeze picked up, Limik pushed strands of her long black hair from her eyes. "It something about Mr. Tyndale in San Francisco."

Daniel kicked aside an oak branch that lay across their path. "Must be really important for him to ride all the way out here."

Limik stopped and faced him. "Dan'l, I have something I must tell you." She rolled her lips inward. "I decide not to stay here with Homut and Eekino. I go back to my people. I want help Yokuts and Miwok understand that fighting the whites no good. I want help stop more killing."

As if someone had dumped a bucket of melted snow over his head, Daniel fought to catch his breath. His insides shook. "No. I won't let you. It's too dangerous." He grabbed her hands and met her gaze. "I think we should both go back to San Francisco. You can continue to stay with the Arnolds, and I'll rent a room somewhere and find a blacksmithing job."

Limik squeezed his hands, her dark eyes moistening. "No, Dan'l. I have something else important to tell you." She inhaled a quick breath. "Dr. Arnold tell me he get much comfort and direction from a book he call Bible. One evening, he read something from it he say very important. He ask me to remember words and tell you." Her eyes pinched. "I do my best, but not sure if it perfect. It say, 'If you wish to save your life, you lose it. If you wish to lose your life for my sake, you find it.'" Her face relaxed. "You know why Dr. Arnold have me say these words to you?"

His throat constricting, Daniel recalled Dr. Arnold's parting words. *Son, I believe there's something important God wants to do through you in the gold fields.* He released Limik's hands and shook his head. He wasn't sure he believed Dr. Arnold's words. He had to start thinking about himself. Let Agent Johnston and the commissioners worry about getting justice for the Indians. This wasn't his fight.

Limik grasped his hands again. "Dr. Arnold tell me about someone named Jesus. He the one who say these words." Her eyes brightened. "I never hear of this Jesus before, so Dr. Arnold explain him. Say he come as a human to tell us about God. That he one with the Great Father. That he die for all the bad things people do. Then, he rise from the dead. I think it wise to follow such a person and do what he say. I believe he want me to go to Yokuts and Miwok to help stop fighting."

Daniel's mind whirled. He knew the Indians had their own spiritual beliefs. He never thought of telling Limik about his. But then, the Arnolds were more religious than he was. *Does she really think God's telling her to go back to her people?*

He had to talk her out of it.

"How do you know God's telling you to go back to the Yokuts and Miwok? Maybe God wanted you to come back here so I could see how much I've missed you."

Tugging her hands, he stepped closer. "To tell you—I love you."

He kissed her forehead and released a puff of air. A wisp of vapor arose. He'd forgotten about the February chill. He forged ahead. "To tell you I never want to lose you again." *Do I dare? Yes.*

He kissed her lips. Those full, warm, soft, lips.

She kissed him back.

He lifted his arms to embrace her. He ached to hold her and not let go.

She stiffened and pulled away.

He reached for her hands, but she pulled them behind her back.

Air whooshed from his lungs. "I'm sorry. I had no right to kiss you. Will you forgive me?"

She stared at the ground. "It not the kiss, Dan'l. When I in San Francisco, I miss you, too." She met his gaze. "I love you, too. I come here to find you, but it not enough. I need find self, too."

Now he felt the cold. A cold that slashed through the lining of his wool jacket.

A cold that slashed through his chest and heart.

He'd opened himself to the possibility of loving again, only to get thrown over a cliff.

"I understand," he mumbled.

He and Limik returned the post in silence. As she returned to pounding acorns with Homut and Eekino, he stumbled into the post. Numb from Limik's decision to return to her people, he barely noticed Hamilton waiting for him at the back table.

27

HAMILTON

February 15, 1851
Agua Fria Post

Daniel licked his lips as he plodded to the back of the post, hoping to savor the sweet taste of Limik's kiss. No use. Its tang had faded.

Trembling, Daniel paused at the post's stove to warm himself. Not able to shake the evening's chill, he sat across from Hamilton without removing his coat. "So, what brings you here?" he asked.

Still dressed in his city clothes of a white shirt, a horizontal black silk tie, and a gray frock coat, Hamilton set a leather satchel on the table and unfastened its clasps. He withdrew a sheet of paper and slid it towards Daniel. "I came for two reasons," he said. "One, to find a job. Two, to show you this." He tapped the paper.

Daniel glanced at the page—a columned list of figures. Not sure what to make of it, and still nursing the sting of Limik's rejection, his eyes glazed over. He looked up at Hamilton. "Why come here to find a job? Did something happen with Flannery? And any luck finding a job in Mariposa?"

Nodding, Hamilton pressed his wire-rimmed glasses closer to his face. "The Mariposa Mining Company needs another accountant. As of tomorrow, I'll be on their payroll. Part of my salary will include room and board. I'll be working at the Frémont Building on Charles Street."

"Good for you." Daniel squeezed his eyes shut, hoping to shake off thoughts of Limik. "So, why'd you leave Flannery?"

"That's the second reason I came. To show you this." Hamilton tapped the paper again. "I copied these dates and figures from pages in Mr. Tyndale's accounting ledgers."

"Tyndale?" Daniel crunched his brows together. The name sounded familiar, but he couldn't remember why.

The thin accountant blew out a heavy sigh. "Let me start at the beginning. As you may recall, before Mr. Flannery hired me, I worked at the Exchange Office in San Francisco. When I left the Exchange, a man named Watkins took my place. Watkins and I kept in touch, and we occasionally lunched together. Two months ago, Watkins left his position at the Exchange to work as Mr. Tyndale's accountant. Tyndale owns the S.F. House managed by Mr. Flannery."

Daniel scratched his head. He vaguely remembered a Mr. Tyndale owning the place where Flannery worked.

"Five weeks ago," Hamilton continued, "Tyndale asked me to work a few extra hours each week as his accountant until he could hire a new one."

Daniel cocked his head. "You just said your friend Watkins started working for Tyndale two months ago. Why did Tyndale need to hire a new accountant five weeks ago?"

"Tyndale had to find a new accountant because—" Hamilton hunched forward and lowered his voice. "Because Watkins was murdered five weeks ago on his way home from work. An eyewitness identified the thug as Dutch Charley."

Dutch Charley. Foggy images formed in Daniel's mind. The night he walked Limik to the wharf in San Francisco. The night before he went back to the gold fields. Yes. That was the night a drunk named Charley bumped into him and Limik on their way back to the S.F. House. Flannery and a man named Tyndale had appeared out of the fog. Daniel's stomach clenched at the memory. He would've shot Flannery on the spot if Limik hadn't stopped him.

"I started getting suspicious about a week after Watkins' murder." Hamilton's shaky voice drew Daniel back to the present. "I heard some of Tyndale's men talking about Watkins. How he'd asked too many questions and knew too much for his own good. They said they didn't want to end up like him."

"And you think Tyndale had him killed?"

Hamilton slowly nodded. "Remember, Tyndale owns the S.F. House. Flannery only manages it. I figured Tyndale must have had Watkins killed because of something he found in Tyndale's accounting ledgers. That's when I remembered what you told me about Flannery. That, if I valued my life, I should ignore any inconsistencies in Flannery's ledgers. It occurred to me that Watkins may have also found discrepancies in Tyndale's ledgers and started asking too many questions. I believe that's what got him killed."

His blood pumping faster, Daniel studied the sheet in front of him and dragged his finger across the numbered rows. "You say there's evidence here of Tyndale's misdeeds?"

"I believe so." Hamilton's voice picked up speed. "Remember when we found Flannery's September 1850 journal entry? The one that read, *Outside Contractors, San Francisco*? And next to that entry were names like Mooney, Scannell, and—"

"And Dutch Charley." Daniel's stomach lurched. I remember now."

"Then," Hamilton's voice lowered, "I helped you find Flannery's journal entries showing a connection between Flannery and the Brody brothers."

Daniel raked a hand through his shoulder-length hair. "Your affidavit about Flannery's payment to the Brody brothers—their payment for *taking out the trash*. That's still stashed in Dr. Arnold's safe, right?"

"Right." Hamilton pulled in a breath and pointed to the last column. "In Tyndale's ledgers I found a payment to D. Charley on the same night as Watkins' murder."

Reviewing the journal record, Daniel recognized puzzle pieces sliding into place. The last item showed a payment of $350 to D. Charley. "So Tyndale hired Dutch Charley to get rid of Watkins last December, just like Flannery used Dutch Charley and a few others to carry out his dirty work in San Francisco last September. Did the eyewitness convict Dutch Charley of Watkins' death? Did Charley confess that Tyndale put him up to it?"

Hamilton wagged his head. "When it came time for the trial, the witness recanted his testimony. The case was thrown out."

Daniel sighed. "And that's when you decided to leave town?"

"No." Hamilton tapped the columned paper once more. "That's when I took an even closer look at Tyndale's ledgers. Knowing that Flannery and Tyndale were business partners and knowing they employed some of the same shady people for questionable purposes *and* knowing there was a connection between Flannery and your parents' deaths, I reviewed not only Tyndale's current accounting books, but also his entries dating back to 1846."

Daniel's face flushed hot. He pressed his palms to the table. "And?"

Wide-eyed, Hamilton removed his glasses and wiped the lenses with a handkerchief. "Considering what happened to Watkins, I didn't think it wise to write you a letter explaining what I'd found. Tyndale has friends in high places." The young man's voice thinned. "If Tyndale had suspicions about me, I figured he'd find a way to read any mail I sent out. That's when I decided to come here in person."

"So, what did you find?" Blood pounded in Daniel's ears.

"I've copied all the questionable expenditures here." Affixing his spectacles to the bridge of his nose, Hamilton pointed to the first item in the columned list. "Tyndale's account book shows a payout to someone or something dated January 20, 1846. See here? It reflects a draft was made out to Southern G. in the amount of $500. It's listed as payment for *business services rendered in Illinois.*"

Hamilton pointed to the second item. "This one shows a $500 payout to S. Flannery dated February 10, 1846. That was the night of your parents' murders, right?"

Daniel clenched his jaw and nodded.

"Again, this expense is listed as a payout for *business services rendered in Illinois.*"

As Daniel studied the sheet in front of him, a pattern began to unfold.

"So," Daniel tapped the sheet, "it's possible Tyndale paid Flannery $500 in January to make my parents stop helping runaway slaves. From Flannery's February '46 ledger, we know Flannery paid the Brody brothers $300 to start our house fire."

"And look at the third item on the page." Hamilton's pointed. "There's another reference here to Southern G. dated October 20,

1850. It shows an additional payment of $500 to this Southern G. for *business services rendered in Illinois.*"

Daniel pulled in a slow breath, then blew it out. "October 20, 1850. My pastor in Illinois said someone burned down his house at the end of October. Maybe Tyndale hired this Southern G. to arrange both my pastor's fire and my family's fire."

Eying the fourth entry on the list, Daniel read it out loud. "Campaign contribution to William Gwin for $5,000 dated October 26, 1850. What do you make of that?"

Hamilton shook his head. "I'm not sure. I don't think it's connected to the other payouts I listed, but I thought I'd include it. Gwin is a personal friend of Tyndale. Both are southern slaveholders. Gwin has a plantation in Mississippi. Tyndale's is in Missouri. I'm sure Tyndale's $5,000 contribution helped grease palms that led to Gwin's senatorial seat."

Daniel tapped the sheet again. "Mrs. Arnold wrote to me about Gwin. She said Senator Gwin supported every federal bill that would strengthen the Fugitive Slave Act. On the other hand, she said the newspaper man, Gilbert, a U.S. representative from California, opposed each of those bills."

"Knowing that," Hamilton said, "I wouldn't be surprised if Tyndale's other questionable payouts are also linked to the cause of slavery."

Daniel's mouth went dry. Another puzzle piece fell into place. When he first met Tyndale and Gwin, Mr. Reed had introduced them as the two southern gentlemen he had invited to his dinner party. Tyndale and Gwin had exchanged smiles when they talked about the possibility of California entering the Union as a slave state. His parents, along with Pastor Lovejoy, had worked to smuggle runaway slaves across Illinois into Canada.

"I think you're right." Daniel leaned back. "My parents and our pastor were links in the underground railroad. Getting rid of them would have made it harder for slaves to find freedom. That would have meant greater profits for men like Gwin and Tyndale. But who's the actual mastermind behind it all?"

"We'll need more evidence to figure that out." Hamilton pointed to the bottom of the page. "As you can see, I've signed my name here, stating these are true and accurate records found in Flannery and Tyndale's accounting ledgers. I think this evidence can help us build a case against Flannery, and maybe even against Tyndale for the death of your parents, as well as for Watkins' murder."

Daniel quirked a brow. "Did you say *us*?"

Hamilton's gaze bored into Daniel's. "If Flannery and Tyndale find out I copied these figures from their ledgers, they'll kill me. Watkins was my friend. I want justice for his murder, just like you want justice for your parents. I'll keep this evidence safe until the time is right."

Finally, the post had warmed up. The smell of wood smoke blanketed the room. Daniel shrugged off his coat. "If everything we've figured out so far is true, you might end up having to guard this paper with your life."

Daniel's stomach growled, but he wanted more than tortillas and beans. "How about we ride over to Mariposa for supper. My treat. We can talk more there."

Before Hamilton could answer, Jim entered the post. "Daniel. I need to see you, Brown, and Cunningham tonight." He strode over to their table. "We'll all meet up here in an hour for dinner. I've got important business to discuss."

"Guess I'll take a rain check on supper," Hamilton said as he rose to leave.

Daniel nodded. After Hamilton left, he retrieved a law book from the safe to read while he waited.

An hour later, Jim thumped a bottle of whiskey and three glasses on Daniel's table, pulled out a chair, and sat.

"None for me," Daniel said, pushing the glasses away from him.

A smile flicked across Jim's face. "I know. These are for me, Brown, and Cunningham."

Moments later, the two clerks joined Daniel and Jim at the table in the rear.

Jim poured himself a shot of whiskey, then passed the bottle to his two clerks. "Brown and Cunningham," he said after taking a sip, "I need you two here to manage the Agua Fria Post while I'm out routing the Ahwahneechee."

Daniel glanced at the two men. A haunted look filled their eyes, but they both nodded. No doubt, images from the Indian raids at the Fresno Post and Cassaday's Crossing flashed across their minds. With Jim taking many of the miners out to search for renegade Indians, there'd be fewer men left behind to protect the clerks.

Jim turned toward Daniel, a muscle twitching in his jaw. "What about you, son? Made up your mind yet? You gonna join up with me, or go back to San Francisco?"

Daniel leaned toward Jim, his stomach tighter than the knots on a hangman's noose. "I had planned to return to San Francisco with Limik." He swallowed hard. "But she's going back to live with her people." He glanced up as Eekino and Homut brought over tins of tortillas and beans. "When you ride out to the battalion's training ground, I'll ride out with you."

28
TREATIES AND RENEGADES

February 15–March 23, 1851
Agua Fria to Wawona, California

Three days later, Jim stood on the back of a wagon to address 200 battalion volunteers camped on the plain near the Mariposa foothills. "I've appointed three company captains to help lead the campaign," Jim yelled out across the open ground. He pointed to three men standing next to the wagon. "The companies will be led by captains Kuykendall, Dill, and Boling. We've assigned each volunteer to serve under one of them. Daniel Whitcomb, holding the rank of lieutenant, will act as my aide. The captains will now read off your names and company assignments."

Daniel thrust out his chest and pulled back his shoulders. *Hopefully, this is how a lieutenant should look.*

The captains read the names of those assigned to their companies. When finished, Jim gave further instructions. "Company A, led by Captain Kuykendall, will move farther south to train near Fine Gold Gulch. That way, if Injuns near the Fresno or the San Joaquin Rivers give us trouble, we'll have men there to deal with it. Since most of the skirmishes have been between the Merced and Chowchilla Rivers, Companies B and C will continue training here."

"How long till we see some action?" a young miner yelled out.

"Yeah. I signed up to fight Injuns, not play soldier," another shouted.

More murmurs arose.

Jim pulled out his pistol and fired into the air.

Recoiling at the explosion, Daniel covered his ears.

The men quieted down.

"Like I said before," Jim's face reddened as he shouted, "we wait for word from the commissioners. It'll happen soon enough. Get yourselves ready. Until then, we drill to sharpen our shootin' and survival skills." He turned to Kuykendall. "Have your company head out to Fine Gold Gulch within the hour."

Although officially Jim's aide, Daniel trained alongside the other men who served under Captain Boling. He joined Jim for meetings with the captains and read Jim their reports.

As they trained on the Mariposa plain throughout the next week, men from nearby mining camps and ranches rode in almost daily with updates of Indian attacks throughout the area, including Ridley's Ferry, Red Banks, and Solomon's Gulch. Daniel marked each skirmish on a map.

Showing the map to Jim, he pleaded with him to send fighters north to Solomon's Gulch. Limik's Miwok tribe, under the leadership of Chief Bautista, had settled there.

Jim laid a hand on Daniel's shoulder. "I wish I could, son. I'll send word to the commissioners, but we can't move without first gettin' permission."

On the morning of March 15, a rider galloped into the training camp, jumped off his horse, and paused only a moment to catch his breath before handing Daniel a message from the commissioners. Reading it, Daniel rushed over to Jim's tent.

"Seems 200 Indians plan to meet with the commissioners at Camp Frémont." Daniel read Jim the note as the man shaved. "The Washington men want you to come and help them negotiate the treaties."

"We'll head over immediately," Jim said, patting his face with a towel. "You'll ride with me. I'll need you to read whatever treaty the commissioners come up with. I want to make sure my Injuns get a fair deal."

Daniel's heart smiled. The man who had once tricked the Indians into believing he'd been sent here on a moonbeam was now fighting to make sure the natives received fair treatment. Limik would be pleased.

Riding the fifteen miles south as fast as their horses would allow, Daniel and Jim arrived at Camp Frémont by late afternoon.

By the end of the negotiations, Daniel was proud of the deals Jim helped negotiate. The commissioners promised the Indians a reservation on the Merced River where they could farm and raise livestock. Also, thanks to the translation efforts of Chief Cipriano, the chiefs promised their bands would stop raiding white encampments.

Dr. Wozencraft invited Jim and Daniel to join the commissioners in their tent in a celebratory glass of brandy.

After pouring a glass for Jim, Dr. Wozencraft attempted to pour one for Daniel. Painfully recalling his first encounter with alcohol, Daniel placed a hand over his goblet. "No thanks, sir."

"Suit yourself, son." Dr. Wozencraft filled the remaining glasses.

After Jim took a sip, he gazed at the commissioners across the table. "I believe we've peacefully resolved tensions between the whites and the natives north of us." He sipped again. "But I doubt the Chowchilla to the south and the Yosemite in the east will negotiate so easily."

Dr. Wozencraft lifted his glass in a salute. "Well, let's hope you're wrong, Major Savage. Let's hope you're wrong."

As Jim predicted, the Chowchilla and the Yosemite, along with the Nootchu and Kaweah continued to raid white encampments. The commissioners finally granted the battalion permission to ride after them.

Jim ordered Daniel to dispatch a rider to Captain Kuykendall. "Write up orders for Company A to ride south and bring in the Chowchilla and Kaweah."

It had begun. A chill in Daniel's spine needled his neck. "And what will the other companies do?"

"We're ridin' east with Boling and Dill to rout out the Nootchu and Yosemite."

Daniel shuddered as he recalled the meaning of the name, Yosemite. *Those who kill.*

At sunrise the next morning, Daniel prepared to ride out with

Companies B and C. Every muscle in his body quivered. His leather saddle creaked as he forced himself to sit tall. He had to look the part of a lieutenant. Jim raised a gloved hand and motioned the battalion forward. With a quick glance at the Mariposa plain, he wondered if he'd ever lay eyes on it again. Nudging his horse forward, Daniel trotted along behind Jim and a young Nootchu Indian guide named Injun Bob.

"I can't wait to whup those Injuns," one miner hollered as they rode off.

"You and me both," another shouted back. "They done killed my partner when he tried to stop 'em from snatchin' our mules. Can't wait to finally avenge his murder—and maybe get our mules back."

Jim turned in the saddle and told Daniel to pass an order down the line for the men to ride in silence. "They gotta learn to be still as Injuns," Jim said, "if they ever hope to catch any."

Daniel considered the odds of their success. Some men, like Jim, had gained military experience during the Mexican War. Others had fought their way against Indians while crossing the plains. Most, however, knew nothing about fighting the natives. They'd only come West to strike it rich. As he passed down the order to maintain silence, he considered that most of the volunteers had lost a friend or relative since coming to the gold fields. Had these men only joined the battalion to get revenge?

As they rode east into the foothills, images flashed across his mind of the clerks killed at the Fresno Post—Stiffner, Kennedy, and Greeley—their bodies filled with arrows as buzzards pecked at their naked corpses. He shuddered. Would he see more grizzly scenes like that before this all ended?

Recalling how he'd once blackmailed Banyon and Greeley into giving him money to buy clues about his parents' murderers, he cringed. Then his heart warmed as he remembered how he, Banyon, and Greeley later became friends. He buried Greeley at the Fresno Post. Long-Haired Brown buried Banyon at the Agua Fria Post. Daniel clenched his jaw and tightened the grip on his reins until the leather bit into his hands. He prayed Jim and the company captains could keep the men's emotions in check, including his, as they went up against the marauders. This was supposed to be a mission of peace, not revenge.

A light rain fell as they ascended the foothills. Jim ordered them to stop for the night.

On the second day out, the rain continued, but Jim pressed on. By early afternoon the deluge turned into a raging storm. Daniel shivered in his saddle. Even with his oilskin coat, the rain soaked through. He could barely make out the outline of Jim's horse through the downpour as he rode behind him. When Jim finally ordered the battalion to stop at the base of a spur in the Sierra Nevadas known as Black Ridge, Daniel breathed a sigh of relief. He couldn't wait to dry off and warm himself at a fire.

After Daniel helped the others set up camp, Jim waved him over to his command tent where he sat sipping coffee with captains Boling and Dill.

Daniel poured himself a cup of coffee from a pot hanging over a firepit. A lean-to of sorts had been erected over the fire to keep it going. Joining Jim inside the command tent, he pulled up a stool.

"There's one good thing about havin' the cold rains come now." Jim clutched the corners of his blanket tighter around his shoulders. "It's certain the Injun rancherias higher up'll be under a pile of snow."

Captain Boling puffed on his pipe. "That'll make it harder for the natives to run off when we meet up with 'em."

Jim nodded. "Just over the next ridge, our scouts say there's a Nootchu village on a fork of the Merced. Let's try to reach their village before they even know we're here. Catch 'em by surprise."

"I talked with Injun Bob earlier," Daniel said, warming his hands around his tin cup. "He says his young wife lives in that village. They call the area *Wawona*. Says they named it after the spirit guardians who supposedly make their homes in the big trees around these parts."

Captain Dill stood and splashed the rest of his coffee in the dirt outside the tent. "Well, guardian spirits or not, I'm hopin' the Nootchus will surrender once they see us. I doubt they'll want to put their women and children in danger. Like you said, Major, it'll be pretty hard for 'em to escape through the snow."

The next morning, guided by Injun Bob, Jim ordered most of the men to trudge their horses and provisions up the steep mountain, leaving only a squad of men at the base camp. Daniel was glad his father's boots finally fit. The snow, now four feet deep in places, would've easily soaked through his socks if he'd worn his old ones.

By the time they reached the ridge's thickly forested summit, the sun began to set.

Injun Bob pointed to campfires dotting the floor below.

"A Nootchu village," Jim whispered.

"*Wawona.*" Injun Bob uttered the word in a hushed, almost reverent tone. Daniel didn't believe the tall redwoods had guardian spirits, but the way Injun Bob's said the name still made him shudder.

Jim ordered the men to make camp. "No fires, and no talking. You'll have to survive on a supper of dried jerky. I want to take the village by surprise."

After Daniel untied his bedroll, he glanced at the stars. Few were in sight. The snow had stopped, but clouds still obscured the sky. The tall pines, cedars, and firs surrounding them also blocked his view. Flopping onto his blankets, Daniel couldn't remember a time when he'd felt so bone-tired. From his blistered hands to his aching calves, his entire body vibrated with pain. He didn't bother to set up his small tent. Instead, he buried himself beneath his blankets. Inhaling a deep breath, he hoped to at least find solace in the fragrant scent of the pines. Instead, his skin prickled at the thought of what might lie ahead.

At first light, Daniel crept off with Jim and eighty others to descend the ridge. The rest remained at the summit to guard the horses and provisions.

Jim ordered the men to move under the cover of trees and bushes as they inched forward. Creeping toward the village, Daniel caught glimpses of women draped in deerskin and rabbit fur as they scurried in and out of their snow-covered bark teepees. Some carried baskets and rocks to various fire pits where they worked to prepare a meal.

Several older men sat near the campfires. A few young braves brought over wood to keep the flames going.

How many of those braves took part in the attack on our Fresno River and Agua Fria posts? Daniel aimed his rifle, ready to fire. Then, seeing a small group of children chase two dogs around the huts and camp-fires, he lowered the barrel.

When they reached the edge of the village, Jim raised a gloved hand and shouted. "Advance!"

With loud shrieks and raised rifles, the men scrambled out of the woods and surrounded the camp.

The Indians immediately lifted their hands. "*Paz! Paz!*"

Daniel knew the word—*peace* in Spanish. Before the miners, the only non-Indians the natives had met were Spaniards, and later, the Mexicans. Having traded with both groups over the past sixty years, most Indians had gained a basic understanding of Spanish. It made sense that they now used this language to address their intruders.

Moments later, a deep voice rang out. "El Rey Güero!" An Indian wrapped in a bearskin and touting a tall headdress approached Jim from the center of the village. The Nootchu Indian bowed, then excitedly spoke with Jim in the Yokuts language.

Captain Boling, standing next to Jim, shot the major a confused gaze.

Jim lowered his rifle. "This is Chief Ponwatchee, chief of the Nootchu," Jim explained. "I didn't realize this was his village. He says his people won't put up a fight. Ponwatchee, his brother, and their two tribes used to work for me finding gold in order to buy supplies from our trading post. My wife, Homut, is from his brother's tribe."

Daniel breathed a sigh of relief. At the sound of a barking dog, he turned to see several young boys chase the animal around the teepees.

Jim and Chief Ponwatchee continued to speak. Daniel did his best to translate for Captain Boling. "The chief says he still has feelings of friendship for El Rey Güero. They don't want to fight the whites anymore. They want to live with us in peace."

Boling kept his rifle trained on the chief. "You think we should believe him?"

Daniel nodded. "Jim does."

After Jim explained their mission to the chief, Ponwatchee agreed to go to the Fresno reservation.

Jim called both captains over. "Order the men to lower their weap-ons, but stay on alert. The Nootchu have promised to come in peace."

Jim allowed the Indian women to retrieve their blankets, furs, and any utensils they wanted to take with them from their shelters. He then ordered his men to search the Indians' huts for weapons. To Daniel's surprise, before they could begin their search, the Indians torched their bark homes as well as their remaining stores of food.

The chief crossed his arms and nodded at Jim. "This prove I speak truth. We follow you to our new home."

As they escorted the Nootchu to the battalion's campground at the top of the ridge, Daniel heard the chief tell Jim about a small band of Pohonochee living on a nearby branch of the Merced River. Jim sent Injun Bob to the tribe to explain that the battalion would attack if they didn't immediately join Chief Ponwatchee and his band on their journey to the Fresno reservation.

For dinner, Daniel cooked a small rabbit he'd shot in the woods. Landon, one of the newest battalion members, came over and begged a bite. "All I've got is jerky. Didn't know we was supposed to find our own meals out here."

As Daniel cut off one of the rabbit's legs to share with Landon, a group of Pohonochee Indians approached the camp. Landon saw them too. The youth jumped up and pointed his rifle at them, finger ready at the trigger.

Daniel pushed Landon's rifle barrel down. "Can't you see they want to surrender?"

The Pohonochee had stopped in their tracks and raised their hands. Then, one of them shouted out.

Landon nudged Daniel. "What's that brave saying?"

"He's telling the others not to be afraid. He says the whites won't hurt them."

Jim greeted the Pohonochee and ushered them into the camp. They immediately settled themselves next to the Nootchu. More Pohonochee continued to wander in. Eventually, the groups numbered almost 200.

Things had gone better than Daniel imagined. At least, for now.

Since Injun Bob spoke the Yosemite's language, Jim sent him out with another Nootchu to explain the battalion's mission. "Let the Yosemite know that, if they come in on their own, as the Nootchu and Pohonochee have done, it will save much bloodshed."

Daniel hoped it would work.

The next morning, after an early breakfast, Daniel and ten others from Company C took their turn guarding the camp's perimeter. Inhaling the crisp cool air, Daniel took in the fresh pine scent. He noted the nearby roar of the rushing Merced. The pounding of pestles as Nootchu and Pohonochee women ground acorns. The squeals of children as little ones chased each other. The clink of pots and pans as soldiers prepared breakfast.

Near the end of Daniel's shift, an Indian wrapped in a bearskin advanced toward his position at the edge of camp. Daniel's blood froze. He raised his gun as the man continued to approach. A crown of what appeared to be the down of bird feathers encircled the man's head. In the middle of the Indian's crown stood a single feather.

"Indians approaching!" Daniel shouted. He scanned the area for more renegades. He saw none.

The man stopped in the snow about twenty feet from Daniel.

Several armed soldiers ran to Daniel's side, along with Jim and Chief Ponwatchee.

Ponwatchee pointed to the Indian. "El Rey, this Chief Tenaya. Leader of the Yosemite."

29
YOSEMITES ON THE TRAIL

March 23–25, 1851
Wawona to Yosemite Valley, California

With his rifle still pointed at Chief Tenaya, Daniel studied the frail bronze figure in front of him. He forced his trembling hands to still. The chief's stiff stance, set jaw, and deeply wrinkled face portrayed the image of a proud man who'd lived a long, difficult life.

"I speak the Yosemite language," Ponwatchee told Jim. "I translate for you, El Rey."

Jim raised his chin. "Ask the chief if his braves have also come, or if he has come alone."

Nodding, Ponwatchee complied. Tenaya spoke a few words and shook his head no.

"He says he comes alone," Ponwatchee translated from Ahwahneechee to Miwok.

Keeping his rifle raised, Daniel scouted the woods, searching for any movement. Recalling the banshee war cries of the Yosemites who burned down their Merced River Post last year, he expected a group of warriors to bear down on them any moment.

Jim crossed his arms. "Invite Chief Tenaya to sit by the campfire so we can talk."

Ponwatchee wagged his head no. "El Rey, the chief fears you might harm him. Allow my people to give him food and drink. This will calm his fears. After that, I will translate whatever you wish."

Daniel stiffened at Ponwatchee's suggestion. Would the two chiefs conspire against them in private?

Jim agreed, but to Daniel's relief, he ordered several men to watch from a short distance. Jim also doubled the guard protecting the perimeter.

An hour later, Daniel joined Jim, Tenaya, Ponwatchee, and the two captains as they sat around one of the battalion's campfires. Daniel tried to focus on what was being said but found himself constantly on the lookout for more Yosemites.

Ponwatchee translated Jim's words for Tenaya. "The Great White Father desires peace between the Indians and the whites. He has sent men to make treaties. If you bring in your tribe as the other chiefs have done, there will be no war."

Glancing at the Yosemite chief, Daniel tried to read his expression.

The old Yosemite, sitting cross-legged on a blanket provided by Ponwatchee, narrowed his eyes. "And where will you take us?"

Jim, also sitting cross-legged, pointed south. "To a plain near the Fresno River. A place has been prepared there for you to live. All your needs will be met until you are able to provide for yourselves."

Arching his back, Chief Tenaya raised his head. "No. You do this for the purpose of avenging your personal wrongs. My people do not want anything from this Great White Father you speak of. Our Great Spirit is our father, and he has always supplied us with what we need. We want nothing from the white men. Our women are able to do our work."

Tenaya pointed north. "Let us remain in the mountains where we were born—where the ashes of our fathers have been given to the winds. I have said enough." Tenaya crossed his arms.

Clenching his jaw, Jim pointed an accusing finger at the chief. "If you and your people have all you desire, why do you steal our horses and mules?" He shouted at the chief in the Miwok language, not pausing for Ponwatchee to translate into the chief's language. "Why do you rob the miners' camps? Why do you murder the whites, plunder and burn their houses, and stir up other tribes to do the same?"

Ponwatchee attempted to translate Jim's Miwok into Ahwahneechee, but Tenaya raised his hands. "I understand these words." He crossed his arms once again.

Daniel let his jaw drop. The chief had answered Ponwatchee in Miwok. *I bet that old man understood every word Jim said.*

Captain Boling rested his hands on his knees and leaned forward. "What's going on, Major? Care to translate for the rest of us?"

While Jim explained what had transpired so far, Tenaya, arms still folded across his chest, gazed out beyond the ridge.

Finally, holding his head high, Tenaya spoke again in Miwok. "It is true. My young men have sometimes taken horses and mules from the whites. It was wrong for them to do so." The old Indian continued to stare into the distance. "But it is not wrong to take the property of enemies who have wronged my people. My young men believed the white gold-diggers were our enemies. Now we know they are not. We will be glad to live in peace with them. We will stay here in our home and be friends."

The chief fixed his gaze on Jim. "My people do not want to go to the plains. Some of those tribes are very bad. They will make war on my people. We cannot live with them on the plains. Here, we can defend ourselves against them."

Daniel shook his head and wanted to shout. *You're the ones the Yokuts and Miwoks call "those who kill." You're the ones who stirred up all the other tribes to fight the miners.* Daniel's stomach clenched as he recalled his first encounter with the Yosemites at Big Oak Flat. The day Limik warned him not to let Totuya, the chief's granddaughter, escape. Perhaps he should have listened back then. He was listening now.

A muscle in Jim's jaw twitched as he leaned toward Ponwatchee. "I want to make sure Chief Tenaya clearly understands me. Please translate my Miwok words into the Yosemite language for him."

Ponwatchee nodded.

"Your people must go to the commissioners and make peace with them." Jim's voice came deep and firm. "If they do not, your young men will again steal our horses. Your people will again kill and plunder the whites. If you do not make a treaty with the Great White Father, your tribe will be destroyed. None will be left alive."

Tenaya jutted his chin forward. "It is useless to talk about who destroyed your property." He spoke again in the Miwok language. "If the Chowchillas do not boast about it, then they are cowards. They are the ones who led us on. I am old. You can kill me if you like. But why would I lie to you? You who knows more than all the Indians? I promise that, if you allow me to return to my people, I will bring them in."

Jim stroked his rough, blond-bearded chin. "I will speak with my captains about this." Taking leave of Tenaya, Jim led Boling and Dill into the command tent. Daniel rose as if to follow, but Jim held out a hand. "You stay and watch the chief with the others."

As if punched in the gut, Daniel's stomach lurched. Wasn't he Jim's lieutenant? Shouldn't he be present during this meeting? Apparently not.

Jim and the captains decided to let Tenaya return to his people. "We will give you one day, and one day only," Jim said. Take this as a sign of good faith. But do not take it as a sign of weakness. If you are not back after one day, we will come and hunt you down."

The next day, the old chief came back, still alone. "My people will soon come to your camp," he told Jim. "I told them of your Great White Father who, as you tell us, is so good and rich. I told my people they would be safe. They agreed to come and make a treaty."

Daniel choked down his swig of coffee. The chief's sarcasm cut through, even in the Miwok language. He doubted every word that came out of the old man's mouth.

The next day, Tenaya stayed with them at the camp. Just as Daniel thought, no Yosemites appeared.

Jim asked Tenaya why they hadn't arrived as promised.

"The snow is deep and they cannot travel fast." Tenaya motioned with his hands. "Our village is far down in a valley. It will take my people time to climb out and meet you here."

"A storm blew in overnight," Jim admitted to Ponwatchee. "Tell Tenaya I'll give 'em one more day. If they aren't here by tomorrow, we'll ride out and drag 'em in."

The Yosemites still failed to arrive the next day. Jim had Daniel call the captains over to his tent. Under Jim's orders, Captains Boling and

Dill selected several men from their companies to remain at camp in order to guard their provisions and watch over the 200 Indians who had already surrendered. The rest of the battalion would ride out in search of the Yosemites.

Daniel's pulse raced. Had Jim left enough men at camp to guard the remaining Indians? Did they have enough men to take on the whole Yosemite tribe?

Once the men packed their animals, Jim gave the order. "Mount up!"

With Tenaya as his guide, Jim led the battalion in a single column over the snow-packed mountains.

Daniel shivered in his saddle as he followed along behind Jim, Tenaya, Injun Bob, and Captain Boling. It wasn't just the deep snow that chilled him to the bone. *I bet Tenaya's leading us into a trap.*

As the snow deepened, Daniel stiffened. His horse, along with several of those in front of him, struggled to keep their footing.

Captain Boling kicked his heels into his horse's sides and urged his mount to move up alongside Jim's. He conferred with the major as they bumped along in their saddles. The captain eventually dropped back next to Daniel. "Tell the man behind you to move up and ride in front of Major Savage."

"Why's that, Captain?" Daniel leaned in his saddle, straining to see what danger might lie ahead.

"It's hard work for a horse to forge a trail through the snow, son," the captain said. "The major and Tenaya will guide the front rider along until that man's horse tires. The lead man will then fall out of line and have the next soldier behind you take his place. We'll maintain this rotation until we reach the Yosemite's rancheria."

The plan worked well. Since Tenaya had walked from his village to their camp in one day, Daniel figured that, by horse, it would take half that time to reach the Yosemite's village.

After riding about three hours, a group of Yosemites approached. With one hand gripping his reins, Daniel reached for his rifle, but the ragged Indians simply trudged past the battalion's column.

"See." Tenaya pointed to his people from atop the horse Jim had loaned him. "It is as I have said. My people are willing to make peace and go with you to the plain."

Jim raised his hand to halt the battalion. Daniel counted the number of blanketed and fur-draped Indians that passed by.

After tallying the first twenty, a young woman about his age stopped and craned her neck to glance up at Jim. Tugging her bearskin fur more tightly around her shoulders, she squeezed her brows together. Her eyes then widened, as if recognizing Jim. Pulling her head back even more, she launched a ball of phlegm.

The spittle landed on Jim's pantleg. He glanced at it, then met the young woman's gaze.

Daniel winced. He remembered where he'd seen the Yosemite girl before. Totuya. Tenaya's granddaughter.

Jim turned to the chief. "Where's the rest of your band?"

"This is all who are willing to go with me to the plain," Tenaya said. "Many in my village come from other tribes, either from Tuolumne or from Mono tribes in the east. They have all returned with their wives and children to their other homes."

Jim's eyes flashed with anger as he pointed east toward the high Sierras. "They wouldn't be able to cross those mountains in the deep snow. You do not speak truth. They are still at your village or hiding near it."

Daniel's gaze followed Jim's hand that still pointed toward the Sierras. Those high snows had once trapped Virginia and her family. He realized the truth of Jim's words. Even Indians wouldn't dare cross those mountains now. Once again, Tenaya had played them for fools.

A ruckus rose from the rear of the column. Daniel sucked in a fast breath and glanced down the row of mounted horses. In the rear, Indian children danced in circles as the women clapped their hands and laughed.

Daniel tilted his head. Had the Yosemite families also played a trick on them? Continuing to watch, the women and children began to move down the path toward the battalion's camp, stepping into the snow-trail the horses had left behind.

Daniel chuckled to himself. He was growing as cynical as Jim. The Indian families were just happy to see that the horses had left a well-packed trail in the snow leading to the battalion's camp on the ridge. The rest of their journey would prove less difficult than the one they'd had so far.

Daniel turned back to Jim and Tenaya.

"I've been told that you have over 200 in your tribe." Jim pointed to the rear of the column. "You may now walk with those families back to our camp on the ridge. One of your young braves will ride with us as a guide. I will go to your village and find those who did not come with the others. They *will* come with me if I find them."

Tenaya protested, but Jim ordered him off his horse. Jim grabbed the horse's reins and galloped with it to the end of the column. When he returned, a young brave sat on the animal. "Go now with your people to our camp," he ordered Tenaya.

Jim then raised his hand. "Forward!"

30
YOSEMITE VALLEY DISCOVERED

March 25, 1851
Yosemite Valley

The battalion followed the Yosemites' tracks for another hour. Less snow appeared on the ground as they descended to lower elevations. The dense forest gradually thinned, opened, and eventually gave way to a wide plateau. Jim raised a hand to halt the men. A large snow-dusted valley spread out before them.

The Yosemite guide pointed to the face of an immense cliff on their left, shadowed by the declining sun. "*Tu-tock-ah-nu-lah*," the Indian murmured, as if uttering a prayer. He then shifted in his saddle and pointed to a stupendous rock wall flanking the opposite side. "*Lo-ya*," he named the other granite guardian of the valley. He pointed to a distant rockface. "*Tis-sa-ack*." The native then lifted an outstretched arm and pointed to a waterfall that seemed to leap into the valley from the edge of its lofty cliff. "*Po-ho-no*."

Jim motioned the men forward.

Daniel gazed in wonder at the jaw-dropping sight. A light haze hung over the valley. Clouds shrouded the higher cliffs and mountains. An exalted sensation swept through his body—a tingling that flowed from his head to his toes. He'd never seen such a sight. It brought tears to his eyes. Tears he didn't bother to wipe away.

Having paused to take in the view, Daniel hadn't realized he'd gotten out of line until Jim rode up beside him.

"Better keep up with us, son," Jim warned. "Unless you fancy losin' your fine mop of hair. I don't believe old Tenaya for one minute when he says there's no more Yosemites out here. Why, they might even be lurkin' along this trail, just waitin' to pick off stragglers."

Several of the men laughed as Daniel rejoined the column. He didn't mind. But he also didn't want to risk losing his scalp.

After the battalion safely descended into the valley, Daniel helped build a blazing fire. The tired horses grazed on the abundant grass found in the meadow, and the captains posted guards. Meals were cooked and bedrolls laid out. A few men pulled out pipes and exchanged stories while others swapped jokes. The men's voices faded, however, when Daniel eyed the mysterious grandeur of the now darkened cliffs encompassing the valley. No wonder the Yosem-ites refused to leave the area without a fight.

"We should give this valley an appropriate name," one of the men said during a lull in the conversation.

Daniel gazed across the campfire. The idea had come from Dr. Bunnell, a physician from Michigan.

The men suggested several names for the valley, some romantic, some foreign, and some Daniel recognized as places in the Bible.

"I think we should give it an American name," Bunnell finally proposed. "No need to go to a foreign country to name an Ameri-can scenery. The grandest, I must say, that has ever yet been looked upon. The name of the tribe that occupied this valley seems more appropriate than anything offered so far. I propose we name the valley Yosemite."

"Devil take the Injuns and their names," shouted a short man known as Tunnehill. "Why in blazes should we honor those vagabond murderers?"

"Let's call it Paradise Valley," a miner nicknamed Mad Anthony recommended.

After several other ideas were put forward, O'Neal, a large, rol-licking Texan, stood. "Hear ye! Hear ye! A vote will now be taken to name this valley." He shouted the suggestions and called for a vote. The men, almost unanimously, adopted Yosemite.

The next morning, after an early breakfast, Daniel helped spread Jim's order to fall in. The men mounted their horses or mules and followed behind Jim as he tracked the Yosemites' trail to the banks of the Merced River.

Jim had Injun Bob ask the Yosemite brave where they should cross the river in order to pick up the Yosemite's trail on the other side. The guide shook his head and let loose a volley of words even Injun Bob couldn't understand.

The Yosemite finally calmed down and explained. "Not here. Must cross farther on to find trail. If you want cross here, must wait until later. If cross now, river sweep you into canyon."

When Injun Bob finished translating, Jim shook his head. "Now I *know* this Yosemite's lying. If we wait until later, the melting snow'll make the river even deeper. He's protectin' Yosemites he knows are nearby. We cross here."

Every muscle in Daniel's body tensed as he urged his horse into the icy river. What if his mount lost his footing on the slippery rocks? Slowly navigating through the rushing waters, Daniel heard a loud splash as he reached the other side. He turned in his saddle and saw the large Texan, O'Neal, thrashing in the Merced.

O'Neal uttered a string of colorful words as he and his horse scrambled out.

Mad Anthony laughed and tossed the Texan a blanket. "Maybe at least now ya won't smell so bad!"

Jim soon picked up the Yosemites' trail. He led the battalion to the base of the large granite formation that the Yosemite guide had called *Tu-tock-ah-nu-lah*.

Daniel pointed out a collection of Indian bark huts near a creek that flowed into the river. Jim ordered Daniel, O'Neal, and Tunnehill to check it out.

They trotted over but found no Yosemites.

As the battalion continued to follow the natives' trail east, Injun Bob pointed to smoke rising in the distance. Jim sent Lieutenant Chandler and four of his men to investigate.

When they returned, the lieutenant shook his head. "Can't get through that way. The trail's too narrow and it's blocked by huge boulders."

Jim ordered the men to cross the river again. Hopefully, they'd be able to pick up the trail on the other side.

Throughout the day, the battalion crossed and re-crossed the frigid waters several times. As the sun journeyed across the sky, melting snow from the granite peaks swelled the river's flow, making each crossing more difficult. Despite the challenge, the battalion rode farther east into the valley following Indian trails and periodic columns of smoke. Near the base of the large granite formation the guide had called *Tis-sa-ack*, another group of huts came into view. Jim ordered Captain Boling and a few of his men to dismount and investigate.

"Looks like the Injuns recently deserted those huts, Major," Boling reported when he returned. "We didn't spot any Injuns 'round there now."

Jim ordered the captains to organize scouting parties and examine each branch of the valley. "Explore as far as you can before dark, then meet back at the grove of oaks near the mouth of the canyon. The area someone named Indian Canyon last night."

Jim hadn't participated in naming prominent places in the valley, but he didn't seem to mind the men's initiative.

While detachments spread out in all directions, Daniel joined Jim, Captain Boling, Dr. Bunnell, and five others and as they clambered up a large outcropping of fallen rocks. They stayed below the snowline near the southwest base of *Tis-sa-ack*.

Two hours later, a peculiar formation of rocks attracted Daniel's attention. As he approached, he saw the structure consisted of one large rock resting on several smaller ones. He crouched to glance inside. Something moved. He aimed his rifle and stepped closer. Loose stones crunched beneath his boots.

As his eyes adjusted to the dim light, the form of an old woman took shape in front of him. Sitting on the ground, she hovered over the remnants of an almost exhausted fire. Her frail figure and heavily wrinkled face reminded him of pictures he'd once seen of Egyptian mummies. She didn't appear alarmed or surprised to see him. She simply sat and stared at the fire.

"I found one," Daniel called out. "Over here." Not seeing any other Indians, he gathered more fuel for the woman's fire while he waited for others to arrive. Jim and Dr. Bunnell soon joined him inside the alcove.

"Where are your companions?" Jim asked the old woman. She appeared to ignore him. His guardian tried using words from several languages in order to communicate, but the old woman simply sat stone-faced. Jim finally tried a few words Daniel recognized as part Pohonochee, part Nootchu.

The old Yosemite suddenly met Jim's gaze. Her eyes narrowed as she spit out several words Daniel didn't understand.

Jim turned to face Daniel and Dr. Bunnell. "She says we have to hunt for them if we want to find them," Jim translated.

Jim turned back to the woman. "Why were you left here alone?"

With her eyes still pinched, she replied, "I too old to climb rocks."

Jim allowed Daniel to give her some jerky he'd brought for the afternoon's expedition. Jim then pointed to the gathering clouds. "Looks like a storm's comin'. Best we meet up with the others at the rendezvous sight."

Back at the grove, a group of men under Lieutenant Gilbert's command reported following a steep trail up a southeastern slope that led to the granite spires the guide had referred to as *Poo-see-na-chu-ka*.

"We found a good-sized village of huts there," one of the men reported, "but no Injuns."

A squad under Lieutenant Chandler's company described climbing the heights at the northeastern end of the valley. "We followed Injun trails leading to the top of a canyon that overlooked a small, reflective lake," the lieutenant said, "but never saw any natives."

"We hiked farther up above that lake," another man added. "We struck a fresh trail where a good deal of Yosemites must've passed. A few of us proceeded on foot and followed the tracks but lost 'em near the cliff. We searched carefully, picked up the trail again, then lost it once more."

Others reported finding large stores of acorns, and baskets of chinquapin nuts, pine nuts, and grass seeds. Others found caches of wild rye, dried worms, and scorched grasshoppers. Nothing the men in the battalion would eat. As directed, the men burned all the food stores in hopes of forcing the marauders to come in and make a treaty.

One squad discovered an encampment of abandoned robes and

blankets made from rabbit and squirrel skins. In another, they found drums, wooden flutes, and ornaments made of bones, bear claws, bird bills, and feathers. In many camps, they discovered the bones of horses and mules—the only remains of animals stolen from the ranchers and miners.

When all the men finally gathered at the camp near Indian Canyon, a soldier from Captain Dill's company shouted out. "Look what I found in one of them villages." The man held up a bridle and part of a rope. "These here were stolen from me whilst I was deliverin' a message to Company A at Fine Gold Gulch. You know, 'fore the commissioners done give us permission to ride out after them renegades. Guess the Injuns must've ate the horse that was attached to 'em."

Daniel was grateful for the plentiful supply of dry wood gathered by the guards who'd remained at the grove to watch over their provisions. While some men started campfires, Daniel and the others raised crude shelters comprised of poles and brush.

After Daniel set his up structure, he stood back and examined it. "Well, it's not pretty, but it'll do." He shivered as a cold wind blew in from the snowy Sierras. It numbed his nose and bit his cheeks. He covered his face with his gloved hands and blew warm air into them.

"Our food stores are gettin' low," Jim announced to the captains after dinner. "And looks like a storm's headin' our way. Come daylight, have the men ready to ride to our camp on the ridge. We'll take the Injuns we've left there back to the commissioners' camp on the Fresno so the chiefs can sign treaties. The next time we come back to this valley, the Yosemites' trails should be clear of snow. We'll have more time then to rout out the rest of 'em."

April 1, 1851
Commissioners' Headquarters
"I see you made it back safely, Major Savage," Dr. Wozencraft greeted Jim as the bulk of the battalion arrived at the commissioners' headquarters. "But where are the Indians you were to bring in?"

Daniel and Jim dismounted before Jim answered. Stomping his

feet, Jim handed Daniel his horse's reins. "The Nootchu, Pohonochee, and Yosemite chiefs all agreed to come in and make treaties, but they've got women and children with 'em," Jim said. "That slowed us down. They'll be comin' along soon with Captain Boling and some of his men."

The rest of the battalion rode in behind Jim, dismounted, and led their horses toward the corral. Daniel trailed along with Jim, his horse in tow, but walked slowly enough to overhear Jim's quick report to the commissioner.

"Our food stores ran low, so I ordered most of the battalion to ride on ahead with me. I left a small force with Captain Boling to bring in the Injuns. The renegades are all tired and hungry, so they won't be a problem. Should arrive by tomorrow afternoon."

The commissioner raised his bushy brows. "We are most eager to hear your full report, Major. Please join us in our tent for some food and drink. You can give us the details then."

Tired from the long ride, Daniel led the horses into the corral and thanked the men who were assigned to water, feed, and groom them. He then joined Jim at the commissioners' tent to take notes of their discussion. At least it beat having to stable the horses.

An orderly from Captain Keyes' regiment brought in cups of coffee while Jim detailed the battalion's encounter with the various tribes. By the time Jim had described the trails, huts, and food stores they found in Yosemite Valley, the orderly had served everyone plates of steak, potatoes, carrots, and biscuits.

Daniel sighed. *Finally. Meat that's not jerky.*

As they ate, Jim told the commissioners he believed many more Yosemites still remained in the valley. "So, you can see why I'm anxious to go back as soon as possible."

By the next afternoon, Captain Boling and his squad still hadn't shown up with their Indians. Jim sent out a small detachment, along with saddlebags of food, to bring them in. When that detachment didn't return, he sent out a larger group, fearing treachery on the part of the Indians. Just before dark, Captain Boling's squad straggled into camp, along with the two detachments sent out to find them. No Indians accompanied them.

Jim's eyes widened as if he'd seen a ghost. "Where's all the Injuns?"

Captain Boling, his head low, dismounted. "I'm sorry, Major. Last night the Injuns snuck off without a sound. Didn't discover they were gone till dawn. Tried trackin' 'em, but the trail just scattered every which way."

Daniel swallowed. The battalion had worked hard to bring in the renegades.

Captain Boling pointed toward the foothills. "Their trails mostly went along brush-filled ravines on the rocky side of a mountain. Couldn't follow 'em with our animals, so we tracked 'em best we could on foot. Eventually, we gave up."

Jim threw his arms up. "Ya lost all 350 of 'em? They just disappeared?"

Boling's shoulders sagged. "Yes, sir." He finally paused and let his gaze reach Jim's. "I take full responsibility. I was derelict in my duty."

Daniel stomach dropped to his boots. The battalion had ridden through the pouring rain to reach the Nootchu. They'd tromped through drifts of snow to reach Yosemite Valley. After suffering bone-numbing cold, gut-wrenching hunger, and cross-eyed fatigue, they now had nothing to show for it?

"At least I have one captain capable of accomplishing a mission." Jim clenched his jaw. "Kuykendall's company came in yesterday with one hundred Kaweahs."

"What about the Chowchillas, Major?" Captain Boling asked.

Daniel felt sorry for the man as Boling conferred with Jim. The captain looked as if he hadn't slept in days.

"The renegade Chowchillas refused to make peace." Jim shook his head. "We'll have to send out another party to bring 'em in. Go get some grub and shut-eye. We'll talk more in the morning."

Jim turned to Daniel. "I need you to ride to the Fresno Reservation. The commissioners informed me that Chief Bautista and his tribe arrived there from Solomon's Gulch about an hour ago. Ask Bautista to ride back with you and meet me in my tent. Maybe there's still a way to get the renegades to come in without a fight."

Biting down a smile, Daniel nodded. "Yes, sir. Right away."

It had been a month since Limik had decided to live with her Miwok tribe under Chief Bautista's leadership. Daniel hadn't seen her since the day he'd kissed her. Now tasked with asking Bautista to meet with Jim, maybe he'd also have a chance to speak with Limik.

Maybe now she'd be ready to go back with him to San Francisco.

31

A PROPOSAL

April 1–12, 1851
Fresno River Reservation to King's River

A Miwok brave helped Daniel locate Chief Bautista. When Daniel found him, the chief stood nose to nose with another Miwok leader. The two gestured as they spoke in what looked like a heated conversation.

The loud argument sounded like the chief would be busy for a while. Daniel turned to the brave. "Can you take me to Limik, cousin of Eekino?"

"I know her," the brave said. "I take you there now."

Limik sat near a fire pounding acorns with Eekino. Her raised brow and wide smile indicated she was surprised but glad to see him. When he asked her to join him for a walk, she agreed.

Daniel reached out his hand, and she took it, entwining her fingers around his. His heart smiled. "I'm glad Eekino agreed to go with you to live with the Miwok."

"And what of Homut?" Limik asked as they walked along the riverbank. "She still at trading post?"

He released her hand, picked up a few stones, and tossed one into the river. "No. When Jim and I rode out with the battalion, Homut went to live with her Yokuts relatives."

Limik turned to glance back at Eekino. "I hear you find hidden valley of Yosemites."

"We did." Daniel flung another stone into the Fresno River. "But

I suppose you also heard the Yosemites didn't come in to make a treaty. Jim plans to go back for them once the snow melts."

"Will you return with him to fight Yosemites?"

Daniel nodded. "We gotta go. If we don't, they'll keep plunderin' the miners, and the miners'll keep killin' the Indians." He dropped the remaining pebbles and placed his hands on her shoulders. "The battalion should have things wrapped up in about a month. After that, I'll be ready to go back to San Francisco."

Her shoulders tightened beneath his touch.

"Will you go back with me once I muster out?"

Limik grasped his fingers, lightly kissed them, then turned to watch the women working.

He followed her gaze. Two women and a young girl sat together wrapping redbud fibers around willow coils to finish their new watertight baskets. Another woman removed hot stones from the fire and placed them in a coiled basket filled with water.

Still holding his hands, Limik finally turned back to him. "I meet every day with elders' wives. Teach many how to speak English. Show how to cook food we receive on reservation. How to sew clothes like Mrs. Arnold. It take me many, many more months to do all this."

"At least tell me you'll think about it." Daniel watched the river as it rushed over boulders and dislodged broken branches. His heart churned with it.

He heard her pull in a deep breath and blow it out, but she remained silent.

A chill shook Daniel's body as he shifted his gaze from the river to Limik. "You really don't want to return with me, do you?" His words tumbled out sharper than he intended.

"No, it not that, Dan'l. It just that I—" She hesitated. "I afraid whites not want me live in city. Maybe think I only belong on reservation."

His chest burned at the thought of people judging her because she was an Indian. His heart ached even more at the thought of living without her. He dropped to one knee and grasped her hands. "I love you, Limik. I want to marry you. It doesn't matter what others think." The words raced past his lips before he could stop them.

The corners of Limik's eyes crinkled. Her lips quivered. She took a step back. "I not ready yet, Dan'l. I need stay here and help Miwok and Yokuts understand treaties. Understand whites. Please tell me *you* understand."

He clenched his jaw and stood. "I understand you're saying *no* to marrying me." He shook his head. "I gotta go."

She clutched his arm. "I not say *no*, Dan'l. I just not yet say *yes*."

His heart hammered as he pulled away.

Perhaps, like Virginia, he'd lost Limik forever.

By the time he returned to Chief Bautista, it seemed the hammering in his heart had drilled a hole clean through it. The two Miwok leaders, having completed their conversation, departed with grunts of disapproval. Obviously, the chief's discussion with the other leader hadn't fared any better than his encounter with Limik.

Bautista agreed to ride with Daniel to see Jim. Neither said anything on the ride to the commissioners' headquarters.

Once they dismounted and entered Jim's tent, the major explained his reason for inviting Bautista. "Do you know why the Indians who said they'd come in to make treaties decided to flee?"

Chief Bautista stood erect and crossed his arms. "Yes. I know why they flee," Bautista said. "Two nights ago, Chowchilla runners come to our reservation. Spread lies about whites. Say all who come to reservation will be slaughtered by whites like deer trapped in valley."

Jim ran a hand through his greasy hair. "Do you think, after meeting with you, those Chowchillas went to Black Ridge to talk with the Indians we had gathered there?"

The chief nodded. "Yes. They say they would go to warn them also. Chowchillas tell all Indians of vision their medicine men see. They tell all Indians they see a cloud of white men gather in foothills and plains. Say whites not forgive Indians for killing friends and relatives. For taking whites' property. Say whites will swoop down like hawks on Indians at reservation after all tribes sign treaties. This scare Indians you gather. This why they escape during night without your soldiers knowing where they go."

Jim rubbed his chin. "Think you can spread word to all those Nootchus, Pohonochees, as well as the Yosemites and Chowchilla, that they were scared off by lies? Let them know we promise to protect 'em if they come in and make treaties."

"We will do this, El Rey. We Miwok know you speak truth."

Jim blew out a breath. "Thank you, Chief Bautista. I have great respect for you. Be sure to tell 'em they gotta come in now. Those sent by the Great White Father will soon move south to make treaties with tribes in lower California. Once they're gone, there'll be no protection for the Indians in the north who haven't yet made peace. They'll be punished and destroyed."

A few days later, Bautista and his braves came back with 100 runaway Indians. More natives soon followed until all returned. All except the Yosemites.

32

A MASSACRE

April 13–May 25, 1851
Fresno River to the Tule River, Central California

The commissioners called for a force of men to remain at the Fresno Reservation and watch over the tribes that had already made peace. Jim chose several from Company A to remain. He then ordered Captain Kuykendall to take the rest of his company south to the San Joaquin and Tule Rivers in pursuit of the Kaweah and other renegades who had refused to make treaties. He ordered Captain Boling to make another expedition into the Yosemite Valley to bring in Chief Tenaya and his tribe. Daniel accompanied Jim and ninety men from both Companies B and C to pursue the Chowchilla south of the Fresno River.

Every night, Daniel wrestled with his decision to return to San Francisco. Yes, once he mustered out of the Mariposa Battalion, with or without Limik, he'd go back to the Arnolds. The friendships he'd forged with the men around the campfire were no substitute for the bonds of a family. And the Arnolds were the closest thing he had to a family.

Every day, like blossoms torn off by the spring wind, memories of his life in Illinois were rent away. Maybe he could convince Hamilton to return with him to San Francisco. Together they could confront Flannery with the evidence they'd gathered. Ever since his parents' deaths, his well of despair had grown deeper and darker. Once he brought Flannery to justice, he hoped that despondency would disappear.

After a few weeks on the trail of the Chowchilla, a courier rode into camp with a message for Jim from the commissioners.

Daniel read it to his guardian. "We request that you and your aide immediately return to the Fresno Reservation. Captain Kuykendall brought in a delegation of Kaweah, and the Yosemite have surrendered to Captain Boling. We need your help in negotiating the treaties."

As Daniel and Jim rode to the reservation, Daniel's heart grew lighter. Two more troublesome tribes had agreed to make peace. Maybe now Limik would be ready to go back with him to San Francisco.

When he arrived at the reservation he searched for Limik but couldn't find her. Eventually, he met up with Eekino.

"She help white leaders make treaty with Yokuts near Kings River," Homut told him. "Chief Watoka want his Chonemne Yokuts make peace, but elders afraid. Limik go to help."

Daniel spent the next several days assisting Jim with the Kaweah negotiations. On May 25, the commissioners summoned Jim and Daniel to their tent.

Dr. Wozencraft waved a letter in his hand and shifted his beefy jaw from side to side. "I'm afraid we've got bad news, Major." He handed the letter to Jim.

Jim pretended to read it, then offered it to Daniel.

"Why, Major Savage." Daniel widened his eyes, feigning shock over the news Jim had supposedly read. "How can Washington do this? How can they expect the commissioners to stop making treaty negotiations after they finish spending their second $25,000 allocation? Do you think we'll be able to convince the remaining tribes to make peace before those funds run out?"

Lines formed on Jim's forehead. His face darkened. Then, as if remembering to appear as if he'd already digested the news, he raised his chin. "We'll have to, son. If we don't wrap this up soon, the miners and Injuns are gonna keep killin' each other."

Dr. Wozencraft nodded. "My sentiments exactly, Major. The

darned fools in Washington have no idea how things work out here. There is no way we can stretch our remaining funds far enough to satisfy the needs of the Indians who have yet to make treaties. We must try, however. We must do the best we can with what we have left."

June 28–July 3, 1851

To Daniel's relief, the Yosemites and all the warring tribes in the San Joaquin Valley made treaties by the end of June. Jim sent word for the battalion members to rendezvous at his Fresno Trading Post on July 1.

Once the battalion had assembled, Jim made an announcement. "Men, as of today, you are officially mustered out of the Mariposa Battalion. It's been a privilege to serve as your leader."

Whoops and hollers rose as men tossed their hats into the air.

Daniel thought he'd feel more relieved, but the announcement only left a gnawing, empty pit in his stomach. Would he follow through with his decision to return to San Francisco? Limik hadn't finished her work with Chief Watoka's tribe near the Kings River. And the last time he spoke with Hamilton, the accountant still had no desire to return to San Francisco.

Jim slapped Daniel on the back. "Son, I sure do hope you'll stick it out with me for a few more months. Now that this business with the battalion's over, I need to get my tradin' affairs up and runnin' again."

Daniel agreed to stay with Jim. For how long, he wasn't sure.

Over the next month, Daniel helped Jim file the requisite papers and $1,200 fee granting him the right to work as an Indian trader. That gave Jim authority to trade with all the reservation Indians between the Chowchilla and Kaweah Rivers. Based on the number of Indians Jim registered under his jurisdiction, the government promised to reimburse Jim for the costs of beef, blankets, clothing, seeds, and agricultural equipment he would purchase for the tribes. And of course, the price tag for those goods would include an acceptable profit margin. That income, along with Jim's continued business with gold miners, would rake in a great deal of money.

"And don't forget, once you do decide to leave," Jim told Daniel after all the paperwork had gone through, "I've promised you five percent of all my earnings." Jim gave Daniel a half-smile. "I do hope you'll stay as long as you like. After all, the longer you stay, the more profit you'll earn, wherever you go. And, one more thing. I need you to write the government a letter explaining what we lost at the Fresno River Post last December. I reckon that Injun raid cost us about $25,000."

Daniel grimaced. He doubted Jim's losses amounted to that much, but, yes, he'd stay until Jim received his reimbursement for the Fresno River Post losses. Besides, like Jim said, the longer he stayed, the more money he'd take with him—wherever he decided to go.

In the spring of '52, Walter Harvey and John Marvin approached Jim with a business venture. They planned to establish a ferry downriver at Cassaday's old crossing. They needed Jim's help on the deal.

"I've got enough cash saved up to join their partnership," Jim told Daniel. "I think it'll turn a good profit."

Daniel didn't like the idea of Jim going into business with the likes of Walter Harvey. It was rumored that Harvey still held a grudge against Jim because the men in the Mariposa Battalion had chosen Jim instead of Harvey as the Mariposa Battalion leader. Daniel reminded Jim of their first meeting with Harvey when the braggadocios man interrupted their negotiations with Chief Bautista and the commissioners back at Belt's Ferry. How Captain Keyes said the man had been kicked out of West Point. How Harvey said all the Indians should be pushed east of the Sierras.

Jim finally agreed with Daniel and pulled out of the deal. Instead, Daniel helped Jim form a partnership with John Marvin, the battalion's former quartermaster, to purchase a license for a ferry crossing on the Kings River.

It seemed there was always one more problem to fix, one more letter to write, one more account to balance. Maybe Daniel would leave by summer.

When the warmer of weather of spring melted the snow, miners discovered that panning for gold in rivers and creeks wasn't as profitable as it used to be. Easy gold was hard to find for a lone prospector, or even for a partnership of two or three. Daniel feared Jim's profits from trading with miners had come to an end. He made plans to leave by June.

But then, to Daniel's surprise, many in the gold fields began to form small companies.

He marveled at the miners' ingenuity. Men banded together to set up lines of wooden sluice boxes, sometimes a thousand feet long. They'd place the boxes in moving water and shovel dirt into them, causing any gold to fall to the bottom of the box once the water washed out the dirt. Other miners formed companies to dig shafts and tunnels in order to reach gold that could no longer be found on the surface.

With the development of these new techniques, more prospectors once again flooded the gold fields. Skirmishes between the miners and the Indians flared to greater heights. Californians began to complain about reservation lands the commissioners had granted the Indians. Some miners flagrantly squatted on the Indians' promised properties. California legislators talked of cancelling the Indian treaties. But Daniel knew that, legally they couldn't. The treaties had been created by the federal government, not the state. Daniel pored over local newspapers to keep up with the latest news.

In May, he read about resolutions the state legislature had recently passed. He could barely contain his rage when he learned that state politicians had urged California's U.S. senators and representatives to vote against the treaties the battalion and the commissioners had worked so hard to obtain. The Indians had agreed to give up their lands. Surely the United States government *had* to keep its promises. Didn't they?

On the morning of July 3, Daniel considered returning to San Francisco. A year had passed since he mustered out of the Mariposa Battalion. Maybe he could do more there to help the Indians. Jim had hired two new clerks, and Daniel had trained one of them to take over as Jim's accountant.

Daniel had just opened the safe to put away the post's ledger when the sound of pounding hooves approached. His muscles tensed. No one rode that fast on a hot July morning. Not unless it was an emergency. He locked the journal in the safe and rushed outside. A large man dismounted and tied his horse to the post's rail. He recognized the man as O'Neal, the Texan he'd met while in the Mariposa Battalion.

"There's trouble down at Kings River." O'Neal paused to slap his felt hat against his knee. "Came to tell the major. We might not be a battalion no more, but that don't mean we can't help uphold the law."

Daniel's pulsed raced. As far as he knew, Limik was still near the Kings River. "What kind of trouble?"

"Been told Chief Watoka and about sixty of his braves walked into Campbell and Poole's store near Poole's Ferry." O'Neal shoved his felt hat back onto to his head. "The Injuns complained they hadn't gotten the clothing and blankets they'd been promised. Gotta respect the sand of that chief. The store manager, a feller named Edmunds, told 'em to leave. The chief, by way of some woman interpreter, reminded 'em Poole had built his store on reservation land, and that Poole owed 'em the clothes and blankets. Then, this English-speakin' Injun woman handed the store owner a note signed by Major Savage hisself. Been told the note said somethin' like—"

"Let me guess," Daniel interrupted. "It said:

The holder of this note, Chief Watoka, has made treaties with Federal Commissioners for the lands you now occupy. As promised, no molestation or hindrance will be given to whites traveling through his area. However, Chief Watoka can and will prevent all illegal encroachments on his peoples' land."

Signed,
Major James Savage
Mariposa Battalion

O'Neal blinked at Daniel, his mouth hanging open.

Before the Texan could ask how he knew the note's contents, a corner of Daniel's mouth drew up. "I know what it said because I wrote it. Major Savage had me hammer out every word of it in the presence of the commissioners before they left. The chief has every right to tell those whites to leave if they're not providin' the Indians their promised goods. The government's already paid those traders to provide the tribes on that reservation with their needed supplies."

The big Texan shook his head.

Daniel's wry smile quickly disappeared.

"That ain't the worst of it," O'Neal said. "Campbell and Poole made like the Injuns threatened 'em for no reason. Got everybody riled up. Them and Harvey gathered 'bout twenty-five men, left a few at the store for protection, then crossed the river with the rest. When they reached Watoka's rancheria, all hell broke loose. It was a massacre. Heard Harvey and the others killed at least eleven braves and one squaw. Ten other Injuns was badly wounded."

An Indian woman was killed? Daniel's mind whirred. His stomach twisted. "Was the woman they killed the one who interpreted for the chief?" Daniel couldn't keep the quiver out of his voice.

"Yup. Believe it was."

Daniel doubled over in pain. *There's only one Indian woman I know who speaks English. Limik.*

33

SHOWDOWN

July 3–August 15, 1852
Fresno River Reservation to Campbell's Store

W*hy didn't I do more to take her away from all of this?* Daniel moved as if in a fog. He couldn't imagine life without Limik. A world without Limik. He couldn't eat. Couldn't sleep. He couldn't even cry.

Jim told O'Neal the battalion no longer had authority to act, either on behalf of the miners or the Indians. Over the next week, Daniel tried to find out more about the massacre, but little information was available. Some claimed as many as thirty Indians were killed. He wanted to ride out to Watoka's rancheria, but Jim urged him to wait.

"Too dangerous right now for a lone rider. I can't go with you right now, or spare any of my clerks. Best to wait it out."

Two weeks later, the newspaper said Dr. Wozencraft, currently in San Francisco, had drawn up warrants for Walter Harvey as well as the others involved in the attack on Watoka's tribe. The paper also said a detachment of dragoons would soon arrive from Benicia to arrest Harvey and those responsible for the murders.

Daniel balled up the newspaper and threw it in the trash. *Not if I get to him first.* When Daniel told Jim the news at breakfast, Daniel let it slip that he wanted to hunt down Harvey on his own. Jim advised against it. "Harvey's got powerful friends. Best we do things the legal way."

Over the next week, tribes fearing for their safety attacked any whites crossing their reservation. When a messenger arrived from

Dr. Wozencraft authorizing Jim to call for an Indian council at Four Creeks to help settle the trouble, Jim asked Daniel to ride with him.

"Of course," Daniel said. "But I can't promise what I'll do if I meet up with Harvey." His mouth went dry. "Do you know I asked Limik to marry me?" Just saying the words out loud shattered what little remained of his heart.

Jim tucked his pistol into his waistband and reached for his M1819 Hall rifle. He stopped and laid a hand on Daniel's shoulder. "I'm sorry Daniel. No. I didn't know you'd proposed to her. But you can't dwell on her death. It'll eat you alive. Trust me. I know."

Daniel studied the man's haunted eyes. Yes. Jim knew what it meant to lose a loved one. He also knew the man had never fully recovered. *Will I?*

They rode hard toward Four Creeks from morning until nightfall. They finally pulled off the trail and made camp about five miles south of Charlie Converse's ferry.

The next morning, Jim roused Daniel before daybreak. "Let's move out."

Daniel yawned and rubbed sleep from his eyes. "No breakfast first?"

"We'll chew some jerky while we ride. No time to make a fire."

On their way to Four Creeks, they met up with John Marvin.

"Had breakfast yet, Savage?" Marvin called out as he sidled his horse next to Jim's.

Daniel remained on his gelding a few steps back as the two friends paused on the trail.

"Nah. On our way to Four Creeks. Gonna call an Injun council to discuss what happened over there. See if we can calm things down." Jim took off his hat and scratched his head. "What was that scamp Harvey thinkin', anyway?"

Marvin shrugged. "You know how hot-headed he is."

Jim replaced his hat. "And you know how hard the battalion worked to make them treaties. Now that fool's unravelin' it all. Why, Harvey never even signed up to join the battalion once the men picked me 'stead of him as their leader. That man's just nothin' but a loudmouthed glory hound."

"And a murderer," Daniel mumbled.

"Can't say as I don't agree." Marvin shrugged again as he glanced at Daniel and Jim. "But, seein' as it's Sunday, why don't you two join me for quick breakfast? I'm headed over to Campbell's store, just up the road a piece. It won't take long"

Daniel's stomach growled.

Jim rubbed his chin, as if contemplating the idea.

Marvin tilted his head south and shot Jim a half-smile. "They serve some good grub there, and a man's gotta eat. Maybe we can hammer out a few more details regarding our ferry on the Kings River."

"We need to get to Four Creeks as fast as possible, but we could use some breakfast." Jim nodded and tapped his heels into his horse's sides.

As they rode towards Campbell's store, Marvin asked Jim about his work as a government trader. "I hear it pays well."

Jim gave the man a sideways glance. "You hintin' at rumors I'm part of that so-called California Ring?" His voice rose. "Those scalawag government traders who lie about the number of Injuns they're feedin', then sell off the extra supplies?"

"Course not." Marvin readjusted his hat. "Just askin' if it's profitable, that's all."

"You know it is, or I wouldn't be doin' it." Jim growled. "But I'm not about to cheat the Injuns. I've been friends with some of 'em since I set foot in California. Why, some have proved better friends than most whites."

Twenty minutes later, they pulled up in front of Campbell's store. After securing their horses, they ambled inside. There, at one of the tables, sat Walter Harvey.

Daniel clenched his teeth.

"Sorry," Marvin whispered. "Didn't know *he'd* be here."

"Mornin' gents," Campbell greeted them from behind the counter. "What can I do for ya?"

Harvey's gaze rested on Jim. "Not all of 'em is gents, Campbell."

"How about breakfast, Campbell?" Marvin said. "My treat. And, I think we'll eat outside."

Daniel pressed a hand to his waist to check his pistol. It wasn't there. Sweat formed on his forehead. Then he remembered.

He'd stowed his Colt in his saddlebag before they broke camp this morning.

Before he or Jim could protest, Marvin ushered them outdoors. Marvin invited them to sit with him on wooden benches in front of the post.

"I'd like to give Harvey a piece of my mind." Jim snarled as he sat.

"Well, if you do, then you won't have much left." Marvin tried to lighten the mood. "Of your mind, that is."

Jim scowled.

A few minutes later, Campbell brought out tin plates filled with ham and eggs. "And I'll bring out some coffee too."

While Campbell went back inside, Daniel retrieved his Colt from his saddlebag. Just in case he needed it.

Marvin glanced up as Daniel shoved the pistol into his waistband. "What 'cha ya gonna need that for, son?"

"In case a snake crosses my path." Daniel returned to the bench and sat.

Jim stabbed at his eggs and ham, stuffing chunks into his mouth. He occasionally glanced back at the store.

After several bites, Daniel lost his appetite.

Marvin studied Daniel's half-eaten meal. "You gonna finish that?"

Daniel scraped the rest of his food onto Marvin's plate. "Nah. You can have it." Daniel stood and drained his coffee cup. "Think I'll take my plate and cup inside."

Jim grabbed Daniel's arm. "I'll go with you."

As Daniel and Jim entered the store, Campbell glanced up from behind the counter. "All finished, gents?"

"Now, Campbell." Harvey pushed his unfinished bowl of mush to the side and crossed his arms. "Why'dya keep callin' that government trader a gentleman? Savage ain't nothin' but a liar and a thief."

Jim's face reddened. He clenched his fists and strode over to the man.

Harvey stood, his chair scraping across the wooden floorboards.

"Think you'd better take that back." Jim raised his chin and stood eye to eye with the man.

Harvey's jaw jutted forward. "Why, I never take back things I know to be true."

Marvin entered the post. "Gentlemen, let's not start somethin' we can't finish."

Jim glanced over his shoulder. "Oh, I aim to finish this." He pulled back his arm and smashed his fist into Harvey's jaw.

Harvey fell back and crashed into his chair. He growled like a bear, rose, and charged Jim. The two grappled and exchanged blows.

Harvey fell to the floor.

Jim kicked him in the side. "That's for all the Injuns you murdered on Watoka's rancheria." Two more hard blows to the ribs. "And those are for Limik."

Harvey groaned, rolled onto his side, then grabbed Jim's leg and wrestled him to the ground.

In the struggle, Jim's pistol fell from his waistband. Both men stood. Harvey landed a punch to Jim's midsection.

Jim reeled back.

Marvin scooped up Jim's pistol from the floor.

Harvey glanced over at Marvin. "Is that my pistol, Marvin?"

"Nah, it's Jim's," Marvin said.

As Jim regained his balance, Harvey eyed his own pistol lying on the table, grabbed it, and aimed it at Jim.

Before Daniel could pull out his Colt, Harvey fired four bullets into Jim's chest.

Jim fell to the floor.

"No!" Daniel screamed, yanking out his gun.

Marvin grabbed Daniel's arm before he could raise his pistol.

"Don't make things worse, boy," Marvin warned. He pried the cold steel from Daniel's hand.

Daniel raced to Jim's side. "Get me towels! Blankets!" he shouted. "Anything to stop the bleeding!" Tears streamed down Daniel's face as he lifted Jim's head. Blood flowed from the holes in his mentor's chest. "Jim," he cried. "Open your eyes. Don't you die on me too."

Campbell scurried over with an armful of towels and pressed them against Jim's wounds.

Jim's eyelids flickered open. "Gotta tell you somethin', boy," he whispered. His breath came in short gasps. "Got gold buried out behind the smokehouse at the Fresno River Post. Should be more'n enough for your five percent."

"Don't talk now." Daniel leaned over Jim. "Wait till after we get you patched up." He turned his head to the side and wiped his nose on his sleeve.

"Gotta say it now." Jim coughed. "Come closer."

Daniel bent lower.

"There's more gold in that bank in San Francisco. You know. Portsmouth Square. Ask for Henry Naglee." Jim coughed again. "I put it in both our names. Half belongs to the Injuns." Another cough. "See my friends get it. The rest—" Jim spit out blood. "The rest is yours. I—"

Jim trailed off in midsentence.

The man stopped breathing.

His eyes, unblinking, stared at the tarped ceiling.

Daniel glanced up, then back at Jim. "No." He whimpered, cradling Jim's head.

"It was a fair fight." Harvey whined. "You all saw it."

Daniel's heart thumped against his chest. His pulse pounded in his ears.

First Limik. Now Jim.

He rested his former guardian's head on the floor and reached for his gun. It wasn't there. Marvin had wrenched it from him. He didn't need it. Like a raging bull, he lunged at Harvey and tackled him to the floor.

Campbell and Marvin scrambled to pull them apart. Marvin wrestled Harvey's pistol from his hand. Campbell drew Daniel aside while Marvin pinned Harvey's arms behind his back.

Two men raced in. "Heard shots," one said. "Came to find out—" He stopped short when he saw Jim's lifeless form sprawled out on the floor.

"Better ride over to Ft. Miller and tell Major Patten what's happened," Marvin said, still restraining Harvey.

The man ran out.

Campbell, having pulled Daniel's arms behind his back, leaned his head over Daniel's shoulder. "Can I let you go now?"

Daniel nodded.

Campbell released Daniel. Marvin let go of Harvey.

"Like I said," Harvey rubbed his ribs, "it was a fair fight. I'll be over at my ranch if Major Patten wants to talk to me."

Marvin, still holding Harvey's pistol, raised it to block the man's path. "Think you'd best stay here till Major Patten arrives."

Daniel asked Campbell for a blanket to cover Jim's body.

Before Daniel could drape the covering over his guardian's corpse, several Indians entered the post, two of them women. Daniel recognized one of the men as Chief Pasquale, Jim's friend since they'd mined gold on the Tuolumne River.

The women wailed at the sight of Jim's bloodied body. Running to his side, each buried her hands and face in his blood. Chief Pasquale knelt and moaned. "My White Father, El Rey Güero," he cried. "Who has done this evil deed?"

For the next few days, Daniel walked around as if in a fog. The man he'd lived with through snowstorms, Indian raids, hunger, and feasts now lay dead.

Chief Pasquale spread the news of El Rey's death among the tribes.

The evening before Jim's burial, hundreds of Indians and whites gathered at the site of Jim's Fresno River Post near Coarse Gold. They would bury him there the next morning.

Braves from both Miwok and Yokuts tribes built large fires and danced around them. Their mournful death chants echoed off the nearby hills. Indian women rocked their bodies as they intoned haunting dirges. Their ghostly laments made Daniel's blood curdle.

Daniel glanced through the smoky haze. At the edge of the crowd he spotted Major Patten talking with two of Jim's Fresno clerks.

Daniel strode over, hoping to have a word with the major.

"I don't think I'll be able to charge Harvey with Savage's murder," Patten told the clerks as Daniel approached.

His chest heaving with anger, Daniel broke into their conversation. "What do ya mean, ya can't charge him?" Daniel threw up his hands in disbelief. "That snake shot an unarmed man. I saw it."

Patten laid a hand on Daniel's shoulder.

Daniel shrugged it off.

Patten stepped back. "Son, Harvey's got friends in high places. Besides, the army doesn't have jurisdiction to arrest civilians. All I'm sayin' is, short of a U.S. attorney filing charges, I'll have to turn Harvey over to the civil authorities."

Daniel's eyes grew hot. "Harvey is friends with all the judges 'round here." His voice rose. "Helped get most of 'em elected. He'll get off scot-free." His throat stung, as if someone had rubbed it with sandpaper. His vision blurred and his body shook.

Chief Pasquale joined the group and grasped Daniel's arm.

"Dan'l. Please speak my words to the major."

Daniel nodded.

"Major Patten," the chief began. "What shall we do now?"

Daniel translated for Pasquale.

"To whom shall we go?" the chief continued. "In the mountains, the whites hunt us like wild beasts. Here on the reservation we are shot down like cattle. And now, our great friend, El Rey Güero, is dead. What shall we do?"

Patten slid his jaw left. "I'll personally investigate the attack on Watoka's band. And I'll see that your Indian treaties with the government are protected." The major narrowed his eyes. "But your leaders must promise me something in return."

After Daniel translated, the chief nodded. "What must we do?"

"Get the tribes who have left the reservations to promise they won't retaliate for Harvey's attack on Chief Watoka's reservation rancheria. All valley Indians must stop stealing cattle. They must return to their villages or reservations."

Pasquale nodded. "I do as you say."

Tired and hungry, Daniel turned to leave. He would bunk down at the Agua Fria Post tonight. His limbs moved as if weighted with sandbags. He hadn't slept well since Jim's murder. He glanced up and thought he saw the faint outline of Limik in the distance. *Great. Now I'm seeing ghosts.*

As he shuffled over to his gelding, the figure he'd seen in the distance drew closer. The ghost now ran towards him.

It wasn't a ghost. Limik ran the rest of the way and fell into his arms. He held her as if he'd never let go.

34

September 15, 1852
San Francisco, Californio

It was almost midnight by the time Daniel rode Limik back to the Agua Fria post, but finding her had renewed his spirit. They sat at a back table in the post and ate a few cold biscuits as Limik unfolded her story. She hadn't been at Chief Watoka's rancheria when Walter Harvey raided it. She had gone farther south to the San Joaquin River to help out Chief Tom-Kit's Pitcachee band.

After sipping water from a tin cup, Limik leaned her head back and closed her eyes. "I finished now with my work here." Her voice came soft and tired. "Only a few elders agree their people need a new way of life. Most want to keep old ways."

A muscle in Daniel's jaw twitched as he clenched his teeth. His heart squeezed, hearing the sad finality in her voice. "I'm sorry, Limik. I know how hard you've worked to help the tribes."

Opening her eyes, she leveled her gaze. "Our old ways of hunting and gathering no good now." Her voice rose as she leaned toward him. "The tribes just take what White Father offer—beef, clothing, tools, seeds." She shook her head. "But how long White Father offer these things? I afraid. What happen here in valley if my people not learn to live in new ways in new land? If El Rey, I mean, Major Savage, still alive, he help. But now? Now, he gone forever."

"So, what are you saying?" Daniel worked to keep his tone steady. How would she answer? His heart still shuddered from Jim's death and the Indians' pre-burial wails and chants. *Does she still want to stay here with her tribe?*

Limik slowly blinked and reached across the table. "I say I ready go now to San Francisco. I say yes, I want to marry you. I no longer afraid what others think."

As if jolted by the battery Jim once used to make the Indians think he'd appeared here on a moonbeam, Daniel's heart sparked to life. He reached out and grasped her hands.

"But, Dan'l," she said, squeezing his fingers, "I want wait until back in San Francisco to marry. I want Arnolds to come to ceremony." She put a hand to her mouth and giggled. "I never see a white marriage, but, I think they must have some ceremony, yes?"

The next day Limik and Daniel, along with the two clerks Jim had hired to work at the Agua Fria post, rode out to Jim's burial ground. There, with both Indians and whites, Daniel watched as they laid the enigmatic man to rest.

"You know," Daniel said, as he and Limik strode back to their horses, "despite some bad things Jim did during his life, in the end, he gave his life to protect his friends."

Enveloping her hand in his, Limik nodded.

Daniel warmed to her touch. "Jim always used to say you have to protect what you want to possess. But in the end he possessed what was most important—his friendship with the Indians."

He told Limik about the gold he'd dug up near the smokehouse. "Jim said it amounted to five percent of the profits he promised me when I turned eighteen. I'd say it's a lot more than five percent. It's definitely more than enough to get us started on our new life together."

Limik reached up and held his face between her hands. "And perhaps it also pay for your studies to be a lawyer?" Hope danced in her eyes. "I think you would like this, yes?"

He gently pulled her close for a kiss. A kiss to say how proud he was of her. A kiss to say thanks for her love, understanding, and support. A kiss to say it would take him a lifetime to learn how to return that kind of love—and that he wanted to take a lifetime to return it.

The following day, Daniel rode with Limik to Mariposa in hopes of convincing Hamilton to return with them to San Francisco.

"I've got a good job here at the Mariposa Mining Company," Hamilton told Daniel when he and Limik explained their plans. "But perhaps it's time to stand up to bullies like Flannery and Tyndale." The thin accountant pushed his glasses more firmly onto his nose and grinned. "Besides, if you two aren't getting married until you get back to San Francisco, I suppose I'd better ride along as chaperone."

Before heading to San Francisco, Limik's cousin, Eekino, insisted on a wedding celebration at the reservation. After the traditional gift giving, food, and dance, Chief Bautista pulled Daniel aside.

"You and El Rey Güero good to Indians, young Dan'l. I sad to see you go, but give you my blessing in marriage to Limik. May you both return to us again someday."

Daniel rested a hand on the elderly man's shoulder. "We will, I promise. Jim had money set aside for you and his other Indian friends. It's in a bank in San Francisco. Once we're settled, we'll return and order whatever your tribes need on the reservation."

The next morning, Limik sat next to Daniel on the supply wagon's bench seat as he urged the team of horses forward. "We'll make a brief stop in San José to pick up the Brody brothers' confessions from Mr. Reed," Daniel told Limik. "Then, it's on to San Francisco."

Hamilton followed close behind in a second supply wagon.

Once they arrived at the Reed's home, Daniel introduced his old friends to Limik and Hamilton. After explaining their plans to confront Flannery, Mr. Reed retrieved the Brody brothers' confessions from his safe.

"Please promise you won't take any chances," Mr. Reed said as he handed the whiskey labels to Daniel. "Men like Flannery and Tyndale will do whatever it takes to retain their power and their money. I'm afraid you're like David going up against Goliath."

Daniel shook Mr. Reed's extended hand. "Thank you, sir." A small smile tugged at the corner of his mouth. "As I recall, David did pretty well in that battle. Besides, I've got the law on my side." Daniel patted his leather pouch where he'd placed the incriminating labels. "And we have a plan."

Daniel and Hamilton camped out on the Reed's property that night, but Mrs. Reed insisted Limik sleep in the bedroom Virginia once shared with Patty.

The next morning, the trio pushed on to San Francisco.

Once they reached the city, Daniel stopped at the Arnolds. Mrs. Arnold, ecstatic about their wedding news, couldn't stop hugging Limik. She and Limik withdrew to the kitchen to discuss ideas for a dress and wedding activities, while Daniel met with Hamilton and Dr. Arnold in the parlor to finalize a strategy to trap Flannery.

Two days later, Daniel drove with Hamilton and Limik to the S.F. House where he had Limik leave a note for Flannery at the hotel's front desk.

Dear Mr. Flannery,

I in San Francisco and want to say yes to your offer for dinner. It almost two year since we see each other, but I like to meet again. I still have yellow dress you give me for first dinner. Please leave note at front desk if you want to meet. I come any day this week.

Sincerely,

Limik

Daniel returned with Limik the next day to see if Flannery had responded. For their plan to work, Flannery needed to think Limik was here on her own, so Daniel watched from a safe distance.

Daniel held his breath as the desk clerk handed Flannery's response to Limik. Without opening the envelope, she scurried across the street to Portsmouth Square. He followed a few minutes later and met her on the far side of the plaza near Clay Street.

With trembling hands, she handed Daniel the note. "You read, Dan'l. I too nervous."

Dearest Limik,

I was so pleased to receive your note. I would relish the opportunity to see you again. Would you do me the pleasure of joining me for dinner in my suite, either Thursday or Friday evening? Shall we say around seven o'clock? I look forward to hearing your response.

Daniel helped Limik write a return note choosing Friday evening, and stating she would feel more comfortable meeting Flannery in the hotel's dining room. That gave them four days to get their plan in motion.

On Friday evening, Limik entered the S.F. House. She arrived fifteen minutes early. As planned, she sat at a four-chaired round dining table in the middle of the hotel's dining room. Daniel and Hamilton took up a spot close enough to hear, but far enough to remain out of sight.

Daniel watched from behind several potted plants as Flannery arrived. "Ah, still so beautiful in your yellow gown," Flannery said. "It still takes me breath away."

Halfway through the meal, Flannery ordered a second decanter of wine. As Daniel had suggested, Limik kept the man's glass full, but refused any for herself. Daniel, too excited to eat, kept his head down as he picked at his dinner of ham, peas, and Irish potatoes.

Twenty minutes later, Hamilton raised his chin and nodded toward the room's entrance.

Hamilton's two expected acquaintances had arrived. The men glanced in Hamilton's direction then sat at a table directly behind Limik and Flannery.

Hamilton nodded to Daniel. "It's time."

After grabbing his leather satchel, Daniel strode over to Flannery and Limik. He and Hamilton pulled out the extra chairs and sat.

Flannery, with a slightly inebriated grin, waved them off. "'Scuse me, gentlemen. Can't you see, me lady friend and I are enjoying a private dinner?"

"Not anymore." Daniel shoved Flannery's plate aside. The man's silverware clattered against his dish. "Miss Limik is my fiancée," Daniel said. "She only agreed to meet with you so we could show you evidence that proves you killed my parents." Daniel pulled out the Brody brothers' confessions and slapped the wrinkled paper labels on the table.

Flannery shifted his gaze from Limik to Hamilton, then to Daniel. "I remember you." The man's nostrils flared. "You're that Whitcomb boy, ain't cha? Aye. You almost shot me the last time you was here."

Daniel nodded at Limik, their prearranged signal for her to leave.

As Limik slipped out of the dining room, Flannery scanned the scrawled confessions in front of him.

"This proves nothin', don't cha know." The Irishman slid the whiskey bottle labels back to Daniel. "I insist ya leave 'fore I throw ya out."

With a trembling hand, Flannery sipped his wine.

"Not before you look at what else we found." Daniel pulled out two more papers and laid them on the table. "Hamilton here copied these figures from accounting journals. One shows transactions from your 1846 ledger, and the other shows figures from Tyndale's books."

Flannery's eyes widened as he glanced at Hamilton, then studied the columned pages.

Daniel tapped the paper on the left. "Looks like we could make a mighty strong case for your part in my parents' deaths. Your own records show you paid each of the Brody brothers $300 in January of '46 for *taking out the trash*. That's the exact amount the brothers' whiskey-label confessions said you paid them to help burn down my parents' home in '46."

The Irishman's jaw went slack. He inhaled several shaky breaths, then pulled the papers closer. After examining them, he pushed them aside, picked up his wine glass, and downed several more gulps. He shot Daniel an icy stare. "Even if them boys' confessions hold up in court, which I doubt they will, your parents' deaths were in Illinois, not California. They can't try me in this state for that crime, don't cha know." The man's face twisted into a malicious grin. "And, if authorities in Illinois try to cart me back there, why, me friends here will make sure that never happens."

Daniel leaned forward, his heart pounding against his breastbone. "I'm sure you're right." He wagged his head as if defeated. "I just wanted to hear you say that you did it. You're the one responsible for my parents' deaths."

Flannery's face flushed. An evil grin spread across his face as if he'd won a high-stakes poker game. "Yes, I did it. I certainly hired those boys to help me kill your parents. And I was paid handsomely for it." He raised an upturned hand as he glanced around the room. "How d'ya think I came to own all of this?"

"But you don't own it." Hamilton leaned in. "Mr. Tyndale owns it. He just pays you to manage it."

"True, true." Flannery pursued his lips. "But, to be sure, 'tis me who reaps all the benefits."

Daniel's insides shook. He wanted to yank out his pistol and shoot the man right where he sat. Or, at least pistol-whip that grin off his face. "So why'd you do it, Flannery? For the money?"

Flannery drained his wine glass, then slowly filled it again. "A southern gentleman approached me, don't cha know. He offered me a handsome sum to cleanse our area of abolitionists. To be sure, those poor Brody boys thought they was just playin' a wee prank. They had no idea what I had in mind when they helped me burn down your parents' home."

Pieces of the puzzle fell into place. Flames flared inside Daniel's chest. "You say a southern gentleman approached you?" Daniel's voice rose as he pointed once more to the sheet with Tyndale's ledger entries. "This unnamed Southern Gentleman must be the one who received these payouts from Tyndale. The ones made out to *Southern G.* dated January 20, 1846 and the one dated October 20, 1850." He shoved the paper under Flannery's nose. "This first date was just before my parents' home burned down in '46. The second was shortly before the fire at Pastor Lovejoy's home last December." Daniel ran his finger beneath the lines referring to the Southern G.

Tyndale's Journal

January 20, 1846 Southern G. $500 Business services rendered in Illinois

February 10, 1846 S. Flannery $500 Business services rendered in Illinois

October 20, 1850 Southern G. $500 Business services rendered in Illinois

October 12, 1850 William Gwin $5000 Campaign contribution

December 21, 1850 D. Charley $350 Services rendered in San Francisco

Daniel fought to keep his voice from cracking. "Do you know the name of this *Southern G* person? Or were you merely a tiny cog in Tyndale's wheel?"

Flannery pinned Daniel with a stare. "I was not just a cog in a wheel," Flannery spat out. "And I never said Tyndale was behind it all. I'm just sayin' I played a vital role." He sat back and raised his chin. "My benefactor thought I was so important, don't ya know, he paid to move me here to keep me safe."

Daniel's eyes burned with rage. He pointed again to the copy of Tyndale's transactions. "Well, several months back, the person behind all of this had someone poison the *southern gentleman*. He was found dead in his cell while awaiting trial in Illinois. The authorities had proof that this *southern gentleman* was the one who hired the arsonist who burned down Pastor Lovejoy's house."

Daniel glanced at Hamilton and raised his eyebrows, hoping the accountant would catch on to the ruse he was about to pull. "Before this *southern gentleman* was poisoned, he named *you* as the person he hired to burn down my parents' house."

Flannery's eyes widened. His upper lip trembled.

Hamilton nodded. "That's right. The authorities in Illinois assume this *southern gentleman* was poisoned in his cell by the person who hired him to arrange those murders."

Daniel leaned closer to Flannery. "Was it Tyndale or Gwin who actually hired the *southern gentleman* to find people in Illinois to burn down their neighbors' homes? If you come clean now, the authorities might just drop the murder charges against you for my parents' deaths."

Daniel's heart rent in two as he let his last words fall from his lips. He wanted Flannery to pay for murdering his parents. The vile man had already confessed to the crime. But, in order to force Flannery to reveal who was behind it all, he realized he might have to allow this despicable man to escape those murder charges.

Flannery buried his face in his hands. "It was Tyndale who put us up to it." He moaned. "He paid the *southern gentleman* to hire people in Illinois to frighten or kill the abolitionists. Tyndale just wanted to stop people from helpin' slaves get across the border into Canada. Many of them runaway slaves was from his Missouri plantation." The man let his hands drop to the table. "Aye, it weren't personal, don't cha know. Just business."

Daniel turned to the men seated at the table behind Flannery. "Gentlemen, I assume you heard all of that?"

"Sure did, son." A stout, bearded man wearing a fringed, buckskin jacket stood. "You're comin' with us, Flannery."

The color drained from Flannery's face. "Sheriff Hays. I–I didn't know you was a-sittin' there."

The second man, dressed in a black waistcoat, white shirt, and black vest also stood. "That was the plan, Sean," the well-dressed man said. "I daresay, after hearing your confession, the sheriff can now place you under arrest."

Sheriff Hays took Flannery into custody as the second man shook Daniel's hand. "Name's Henry Byrne, District Attorney. I've heard good things about you, Mr. Whitcomb. Mr. Reed and his lawyer friends speak very highly of you."

Wide-eyed, Daniel glanced at Hamilton as he shook Byrne's hand. He knew Hamilton had arranged for the sheriff to listen in on their conversation, but he had no idea he'd also invited San Francisco's district attorney.

As the group exited the dining room, Limik approached and grasped Daniel's arm. "You now at peace, Dan'l?" Her large brown eyes locked onto his. "You now get justice for parents' murders?"

He nodded and watched as the sheriff escorted Flannery out of the hotel. "I always thought once I found out who killed my parents, the emptiness of losing them would go away. Now I see that, even if Flannery is prosecuted for their deaths, it won't bring them back. My family's gone. But, all along, God's been providing me with a new family. I just didn't see it till now."

Limik's forehead furrowed. "What you mean?"

Daniel stroked her cheek. "He gave me the Arnolds, my friendship with the clerks at the post, the men in my battalion, and he gave me Jim." He brushed back a strand of Limik's long, dark hair and smiled. "And, most of all, he gave me you."

Three weeks after receiving Chief Bautista's blessing in the gold fields, Daniel stood at the altar of the First Presbyterian Church of San

Francisco. He fiddled with his borrowed neckstock as he waited for Dr. Arnold to escort Limik down the aisle. He tugged at his new waistcoat and shirt. Everything felt too tight. But, for the first time, his father's boots, all polished and shined, fit perfectly.

Flannery had agreed to testify against Tyndale as long as the authorities dropped the charges against him for the murder of Daniel's parents. Although it still pierced Daniel's heart that Flannery had escaped prosecution for their murders, he knew the man would one day stand before God for his evil deeds.

As news of Tyndale's trial spread, people came forward to testify against Dutch Charley for the murder of Hamilton's friend, Watkins. And, thanks to the proof Hamilton found in Flannery's ledgers, the district attorney promised to prosecute Flannery as an accomplice in Watkins' murder.

Daniel heaved a sigh. At least the man who killed his parents would be put away for a long time.

He gazed at the friends who'd gathered to witness his marriage to Limik. He wished Jim was among them. Despite the man's faults, Jim had given life for his friends. Now, in committing his life to Limik, Daniel vowed to do the same for her—and all the others God would bring into his life. His adventures in the gold fields might be ending, but, gazing at Limik as she walked down the aisle, he knew another was about to begin.

Sutter's
Fort
Sacramento
American River
Cosumnes River
Sacramento River
San Joaquin River
Calaver
Stockton
Stanis
Merced
San Francisco
Bay Area
Pacific
Ocean
San Jose

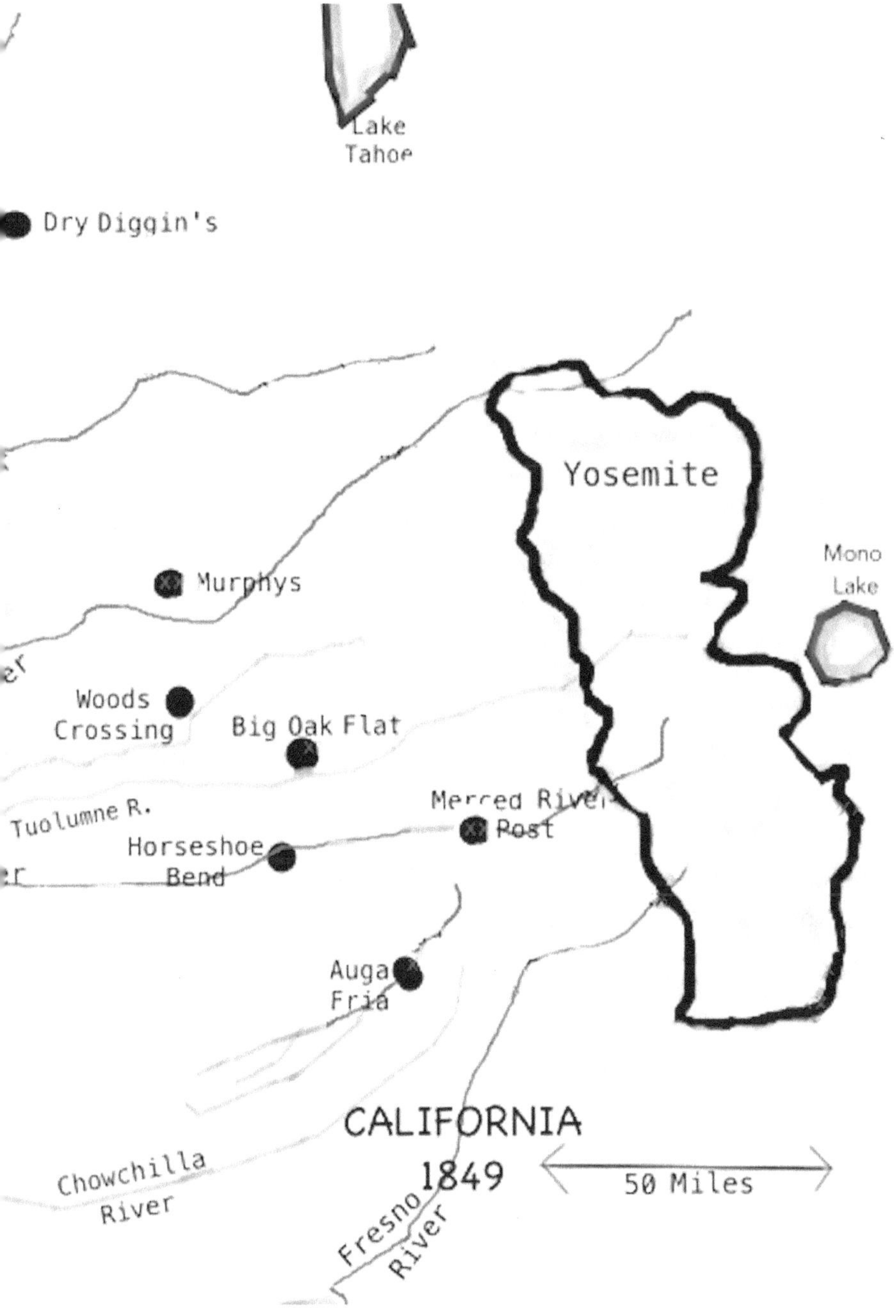

Lake Tahoe
Dry Diggin's
Yosemite
Mono Lake
Murphys
Woods Crossing
Big Oak Flat
Tuolumne R.
Merced River
Post
Horseshoe Bend
Auga Fria
CALIFORNIA
1849
50 Miles
Chowchilla River
Fresno River

HISTORICAL AND FICTIONAL CHARACTERS

In Alphabetical Order
Chapter Number in Parentheses

1. Arnold, Dr. George - fictional character (18)
2. Arnold, Mrs. Caroline - fictional character (18)
3. Arnold, John - fictional character (18)
4. Banyon - fictional character (6)
5. Barbour, George W. - historical character (25)
6. Bautista, Chief, also known as Kee-chee and Vow-ches-ter - historical character (20)
7. Belt, George - historical character (25)
8. Bennett, California Chief Justice Nathaniel - historical character (19)
9. Bob, Nootchu Indian Guide (Possibly Pokotucket) - historical character (27)
10. Boden, Frank - historical character (21)
11. Boling, John - historical character (23)
12. Branham, Isaac - historical character (2)
13. Brannon, Sam - historical character (18)
14. Breen, John - historical character (3)
15. Broderick, State Senator David C. - historical character (18)
16. Brody, Josiah - fictional character (2)
17. Brody, Matthew - fictional character (2)
18. Brody, Mr. - fictional character (2)
19. Brown, Long-Haired (Anthony) - historical character (2)
20. Bunnell, Dr. Lafayette - historical character (29)
21. Burnett, Governor Peter - historical character (21)

22. Burney, Sheriff James - historical character (22)
23. Burns, John and Robert - historical characters (20)
24. Byrne, Henry - historical character (32)
25. Campbell, William - historical character (2, 30)
26. Cassaday - historical character (21)
27. Colton, Alcalde Walter - historical character (4)
28. Cunningham, Stephen Mandeville - historical character (15)
29. Dill, Captain William - historical character (27)
30. Dutch Charley, Charles Patrick Duane - historical character (18)
31. Eekino - historical character (10)
32. Filmore, Ned - fictional character (21)
33. Flannery, Sean - fictional character (4)
34. Frémont, John C. - historical character (12)
35. Gilbert, Edward - historical character (4)
36. Greeley, John (also Greely) - historical character (6)
37. Gwin, William McKendree - historical character (4)
38. Hamilton, Chester - fictional character (16)
39. Harvey, Walter - historical character (23)
40. Hays, Sheriff John Coffee - historical character (32)
41. Johnston, Adam (Colonel and Indian Agent) - historical character (21)
42. Jones, Zachariah - historical character (2)
43. Juárez, aka Chief José - historical character (11)
44. Kennedy, James - historical character (20)
45. Keyes, Captain Erasmus D. - historical character (23)
46. Kuykendall, John J. - historical character (23)
47. Limik - fictional character (1)
48. Lippincott, Benjamin - historical character (4)
49. Lloyd, E.M. - fictional character (13)
50. Lopez, Pedro - historical character (21)
51. Lotario, Chief - historical character
52. Lovejoy, Pastor Owen - historical character (8)
53. Lugo, Don Antonio - historical character (9)
54. Marvin, John G. - historical character (30)
55. McDougal, John - historical character (11, 25)
56. McKee, Redick - historical character (25)
57. Mooney, Cornelius (Con) - historical character (16)

58. Mulligan, Billy - historical character (16)
59. Murphy, John - historical character (2)
60. Naglee, Henry - historical character (31)
61. Pasquale, Chief - historical character (6)
62. Patten, Brevet Major George W. - historical character (31)
63. Ponwatchee, Chief - historical character (20)
64. Poole, John - historical character (30)
65. Reed, James - historical character (2)
66. Reed, James Jr. - historical character (8)
67. Reed, Mrs. Margaret - historical character (2)
68. Reed, Patty (Martha) - historical character (2)
69. Reed, Thomas - historical character (8)
70. Reed, Virginia - historical character (2)
71. Rey, Chief José - historical character (20)
72. Savage, Jim - historical character (1) and burial memorial (32)
73. Scannell, David - historical character (16)
74. Skeane, Lieutenant E. - historical character (22)
75. Southern gentleman - fictional character (24)
76. Stiffner, John - historical character (20)
77. Suñol, Doña Dolores Mesa - historical character (13)
78. Suñol, Don Antonio - historical character (5, 13)
79. Taylor - fictional character (11)
80. Tenaya, Chief - historical character (1)
81. Totuya (Maria Lebrado) - historical character (1)
82. Tyndale, John - fictional character (4)
83. Wallace - fictional character (13)
84. Watkins - fictional character (26)
85. Watoka, Chief - historical character (30)
86. Whitcomb, Daniel - fictional character (1)
87. Whitcomb, Hannah - fictional character (3)
88. Wood, Benjamin - historical character (6)
89. Wood, John - historical character (20)
90. Wozencraft, Oliver Meredith - historical character (25)

AUTHOR'S NOTE

Yosemite Trail Discovered is dedicated to my writing friends who have encouraged me on this journey, especially those in my J.A.M. and SCBWI-NT critique groups. You know who you are! It is also dedicated to my teacher friends who work endless hours in the classroom helping students gain a love for learning. May you be doubly-blessed for your above-and-beyond service to the next generation.

Thank you, dear reader, for joining me in Daniel's adventures. If you haven't already read the first volume of *The Whitman Discoveries*, I want to personally invite you to read about Daniel's adventures along the Oregon Trail in *California Trail Discovered*.

Can I ask you for a favor? If you enjoyed the story, please tell a friend and consider leaving a review of *Yosemite Trail Discovered* on your favorite social media platform or bookseller's website. Word-of-mouth is the best way to introduce stories to new readers.

I'd love to hear from you. You can email me me at mariesontag@mariesontag.com or stop by my Facebook page, facebook.com/AuthorMarieSontag and drop me a note. Also, be sure to check out https://www.mariesontag.com/resources/ for activities and discussion questions regarding *Yosemite Trail Discovered*.

Until our next adventure!

Marie Sontag

ABOUT THE AUTHOR

Marie Sontag enjoys transporting middle grade and young adult readers to various time periods and locations by creating stories that bring the past to life. Her fifteen years of teaching middle school and high school have given her insight into what students find entertaining, and her B.A. in social science and M.A. and Ph.D. in education provide her with a solid background for writing historical fiction.

Born in Wisconsin, she spent most of her life in California, but now lives with her husband in Texas. When not writing, she enjoys romping with her grandkids, playing clarinet and saxophone in a community band, and nibbling red licorice or Tootsie Pops while devouring a good book.

Visit Marie online at:
> http://www.mariesontag.com/